Murgatroyd's Christmas Club

BY

Stephen Bailey

Fishcake Publications

MURGATROYD'S CHRISTMAS CLUB.

Murgatroyd's Christmas Club

Published by Fishcakes Publications

71 Royds Avenue, Linthwaite, Huddersfield, HD7 5SA

www.fishcakepublications.com

ISBN 978-1-909015-17-3

Paperback Edition

This book is for my wife, family and friends
and all those marvellous people who worked,
and still do work,
in the Yorkshire textile industry.

CHAPTER 1

MURGATROYD'S CHRISTMAS CLUB.

'What's for dinner?' This question was asked every day by Willie Arkenthwaite. If he didn't ask it in the mill canteen every weekday at noon, he asked it at home on Saturdays and Sundays at half past twelve. It wasn't that he needed to ask the question, it was just that he did, because more than anything else Willie liked his food. He asked, 'what's for tea?' every day as well, much to the annoyance of his wife Thelma, but she had, over the years, become used to it and for the most part, ignored it.

Willie was a smallish, plumpish, valley man with a good sense of humour. He was in his early forties, (although he looked much older,) sporting a fast receding hair line, a usually overfilled beer belly and most of the time a pair of iron soled leather clogs. There were those in the village who swore he went to bed in them.

He lived in the large village cum small town of Grolsby. Which, as everyone knows, nestles in the fold between two steep hills to the west of the heavy woollen district of the West Riding of Yorkshire and certainly to the east of the customs post on the Lancashire/Yorkshire border.

Willie lived in a small cottage in a row of similar dwellings, aptly named Cutside Cottages, on a strip of land close to the centre of the village, with the canal in front, almost near enough to jump into from his front doorstep and separated from it only by the towpath. At the bottom of his back garden was the river, if you could call it that, for it was nothing more than a large meandering stream.

The only way to approach Cutside Cottages was along the canal towpath, where at weekends in Spring, Summer and Autumn, a few pleasure craft could be observed chugging along the canal from lock to lock, the occupants trying to see as much as possible of the pleasant countryside, interspersed by dark satanic mills. During the week the canal was a much busier place, with working barges plying back and forth carrying their loads of coal and other commodities.

1

Cutside Cottages were very old, having been constructed at the time the canal was built some one hundred and fifty years earlier. They were built in locally quarried Yorkshire sandstone and a header stone in the middle of the row had the date 1803 carved in it. They had at the time of the canal construction housed the canal staff, the lock-keepers, the maintenance staff and the people who worked on the wharf, loading and unloading the endless queues of barges that were in those days the only means of transporting goods up and down the valleys. They were neat little houses with a good size front living room and a kitchen with small pantry at the back. Two good bedrooms and a small bathroom were upstairs. There had been three bedrooms and a stone privy in the garden when they were built, but they had all been modernised after the war when they had been bought from the canal company by Murgatroyd's Woollen Mill, a quarter of a mile further up the valley, to be used as employee housing.

To say that number six Cutside Cottages was overcrowded would be an understatement of the truth. There resided within its portals, Willie, his wife Thelma, his wife's mother, three children with ages ranging from five to fifteen, two cats and a dog. Not to mention a collection of rabbits in cages, and hens in a run that inhabited a part of the back garden. Also located there were Willie's favourites, his pigeons, which lived in the garden in a beautiful white and black painted cote.

Thelma was most of the time somewhat fraught, what with her half invalided, nagging mother who interfered in absolutely everything and the three children, especially during the school holiday periods. The overcrowded state of the house, the animals both inside and out, her part time job as a cleaner for Mrs Margaret Murgatroyd up at the big mill house, all the washing, ironing, cooking and general housework, and the thousand and one other things that had to be done, got on top of her with frequent regularity.

The old lady being a martyr to her bad back and always enjoying ill health, had forced herself into being chair bound soon after she had arrived to live with Willie and Thelma following the death of Thelma's father several years previously. She had entrenched herself in the most comfortable chair in the house, at the side of the cottage range, and demanded a large roaring fire from first thing in the morning until last thing at night, Winter and Summer alike, as she was 'starved through to the very marrow' at all times. From her very well selected position she could see into the kitchen and out of the front window, so that she could nosy in all directions at one and the same time. She knew everybody and everything that passed by the cottage, and much to everyone's dismay she kept up a constant running commentary on the goings on outside the house. To add to the annoyance of the constant monotonous drone, she would wave to acquaintances that passed by and beckon them in for a chat. She moved from her chair only to eat or sleep, and to perform the little necessities of life, and only then with much exaggerated difficulty. In her free time between noseying, she would moan on at Thelma about Willie, the children, her various complaints and illnesses and was gradually wearing Thelma to a state of nervous exhaustion.

Willie escaped most of these problems, although he was fed up to the back teeth with her. He was normally a placid man, but in fits of anguish from time to time he could raise a mental picture of the old lady swinging from a gibbet, or being tortured during the Crusades, or even just simply being helped to fall into the canal. He once ventured to enquire of the Rag and Bone man if he would take her away in exchange for a couple of balloons for the children, but the rag and bone man took a good look at the lady and declined the offer on the grounds that two balloons was too high a price to pay for an old lady, and particularly that old lady.

Willie got around the problems of the household because of his daily routine, which read: Rise on the first blast of the mill hooter, get dressed, go downstairs, pack up breakfast to be eaten at the mill, clean out the range and fill the coal buckets to keep the old lady warm, go outside to talk to the pigeons, check the hens and the garden, and then off to the mill. Later it was dinner in the mill canteen, home for tea, straight out into the garden in Summer or the potting shed in Winter, back inside about eight o'clock, wash, shave, and off to the club or pub until closing time. With this routine he carefully avoided the majority of domestic conflict. He was happy with his lot, for he was too thick not to be. He hadn't any spare money, it was almost always spent each week, but he was content with life and lived the same daily routine year in and year out.

*

One bitterly cold day in January 1951, Willie was sitting in his usual place in the mill canteen at Murgatroyd's mill, having enjoyed yet another of Greasy Martha's dinners, for so the canteen lady was affectionately named after the copious quantities of fat in various forms that she served up on a daily basis. He always sat on the same table in the corner of the dining area, with his three mates from the dyehouse, where they were dyer's labourers. They all wore the same iron soled clogs and thick leather aprons that almost touched the floor, even through their dinner break. They were playing cards, a type of cribbage with local variations, for a halfpenny a corner a game. They had played this particular brand of cribbage for as long as anyone could remember, and they played every dinner break as soon as they had finished eating. A stranger watching them could be forgiven for not understanding the game, as it was rumoured in the mill that over the years they had introduced so many local variations that they could no longer understand it properly themselves. They always talked whilst they played, usually something and nothing about pubs, clubs, football, dogs, horses or some other topic of local interest. But today the conversation was of a more serious note, namely, the state of their personal finances following Christmas and New Year.

'I've got nowt left until I get paid on Friday,' said Arthur Baxter looking very glum.

Dick Jordan looked up. 'I think I'm worse than that because I owe the coal man for ten bags as well as having nowt.'

'What have you gone and got ten bags for all at once?' enquired Arthur.

'Nay it were the wife. I don't know what on earth she were thinking about. I says to her we're running a bit low on coal, see if you can catch the coal man and get him to drop a few bags into the cellar, cos they'd have tided us over till the cheap coal comes in Spring, and beggar me if she hasn't gone and had ten bags put in when I get home from my work and it's week before Christmas and all my money's spoken for. I could happen have found the brass for three bags, but

4

not ten all at once. I shall be bound to get some overtime in or stop drinking or summat to pay for that lot.'

Dick took a deep breath and sat back. He wasn't given to making speeches of that length, it had overtaxed him both mentally and physically and he certainly wasn't prepared for the next sarcastic comment that came from Willie.

'You must have a right big fire if three bags will last you until Spring. We burn a bag a week at our house.'

'Aye it's alright for you,' responded Dick, 'you've got your mother in law to pay for yours.'

'Aye you're right,' he replied, lying through his teeth. Willie never let onto anyone just how the family finances were standing and as usual he made full use of his audience to expound the virtues of having an over generous mother-in-law living in, knowing full well that she never spent a penny on them or contributed to the household budget, and also knowing that his lying would catch up with him one day. Building his mother-in-law up to being a saint in front of his pals had become quite an art with Willie, to the point where some of them almost believed him.

Lewis Armitage being the fourth member of the card school, the philosopher of the group, and the one who said the least but made the most sense when he did, said, 'you know Willie it must be grand to have a kind and generous mother in law who buys your coal. What else does she buy for you?'

Willie huffed and puffed a little then said 'Err. Err. Err groceries, yes err groceries.'

'Does she hell as like,' retorted Arthur Baxter.

'She does. She does,' Willie shouted.

'You're a liar.'

'I'm not a liar. It's true.'

Lewis decided it was time to cool things down. 'Willie I think it's your turn to play.'

'Aye Lewis, so it is. Sorry.'

Play recommenced and they made a couple of rounds of the table in silence until Arthur claimed victory. Being two pence to the better, he shuffled the cards and dealt another hand.

Whilst the dealing was taking place, Willie started talking yet again. 'A bit of a big problem this shortage of money after Christmas you know. These women spend all the money they can lay their hands on.'

'Doesn't affect you though does it?' asked Dick Jordan.

'Why?'

'Well with your over generous mother in law, all you need to do is to hold your hand out and she contributes.'

'It's not just exactly like that,' he replied hesitantly

'Just exactly what is it like then? It sounds like it to me.'

'What does that mean?'

'Well I can't see why you're complaining. She buys your coal, she buys your groceries. Do you ask her for money every time you're getting a bit short?'

Willie was getting worried. They were cornering him and he really didn't have a way out, so he continued in silence playing cards seeing that it was his turn to drop.

'Come on Willie,' said Arthur, 'you haven't answered Dick's question yet.'

'Err, err, what was the question Dick?'

'You know full well what the question was, without pretending. Trouble is you either can't or won't answer it.'

'Come on,' said Lewis, 'it'll have gone bedtime and we'll still be here arguing all that time; there's nobbut another ten minutes left and it's back to work. So let's get on and finish the game.'

'Have you got a winning hand Lewis?' asked Willie, being very glad of having the opportunity to change the subject.

'Never bother about the winning hand, what about answering my question?' Dick persisted.

But Lewis countered him with a sharp, 'shut up and let's finish the game.'

They played quietly for a while without any further interruption when, having just played and not having a particularly good hand, Arthur said, 'It's a problem is Christmas. You make sure that Father Christmas comes to the kids, you give the wife as good a time as you can afford, you buy a turkey, the in-laws come and eat you out of house and home, you go back there and do the same to them on

Boxing Day, you go out and have a drink or two, the kids break their presents, the in-laws moan and groan, the wife's tired out and you've nowt left. It's a right horrible mess.'

'Come on,' said Lewis. 'We've not had as bad a dinner time as this for weeks and anyway, I've got a winning hand.'

'You must have, you're making enough noise over it,' said Willie as play recommenced and Lewis won easily.

Being the winner it was Lewis' turn to shuffle and deal. A job he hated. 'Err, err, don't think we've time for another hand today.'

'Course we have,' said Arthur. 'Come on, get on with the dealing. But you know this shortage of money after the so called festive season is a bit of a beggar; it happens every year and I can't see how we can do owt about it. It doesn't matter how you scrimp and scrape, you can never get enough money together ready for it.'

Willie belched loudly, without apology.

'Ready for what?' interrupted Dick.

'For Christmas you daft devil.'

Dick, being a man of few words, stared in admiration at Arthur whom he admired for his talent of being able to speak at great length on almost any subject.

'Come on lads, just this last quick game to finish with. I've dealt myself a rotten hand, so you've all got a chance of winning.'

The four of them picked up their cards and examined them.

'Terrible.'

'Awful.'

'Bloody rotten.'

Were three of the comments that were heard, to be rounded off with, 'A shocking state of affairs is this. You aren't fit to have charge of a pack of cards-don't know why we left you to deal.'

'I don't have to deal again ever if you don't want me to,' said Lewis gleefully. 'Anyway it's your lead-off and get a move on, we've no time left.'

They had almost finished when the mill hooter sounded twenty to one and they rushed to finish the game. Greasy Martha was watching them. 'Come on you lot, hooter's gone and I've to clear up yet.' She finished the sentence with an indiscreet cough, making the dead ash from the remains of her cigarette, which was stuck to her bottom lip, fall onto the serving counter, making her sweep it off onto the kitchen floor with the back of her hand.

'There's nothing but cleanliness and hygiene in this establishment,' said Arthur. 'Nothing like a bit of Martha's fag ash mixed with your dinner.'

'Sod off out of it,' shouted Martha, being at her usual uncouth best, 'and don't bloody well come back again if you don't bloody well like it.'

"Bye Martha.'

'Bysie wysie, Martha dearest.'

'Adieu, adieu, until the morrow.'

'See you later alligator.'

They didn't turn around to see the gesture that followed them, nor to hear the cursing that accompanied it.

'Remarkably fine woman, our Martha.' Said Lewis as they descended the stairs to the mill bottom where they worked.

'They don't build them like her anymore.'

'No, thank goodness.'

They arrived back at the dyehouse, laughing and joking, all thoughts of money forgotten.

*

Work to Willie was a monstrous drudge. Not that, in comparison to many other more automated jobs, dyehouse labouring could be described as monotonous, or as a drudge, but to Willie's simple mind it was. He worked fairly hard and always did his job well provided that he always kept to the well tried routine. But if the routine was altered for any for any reason, he had difficulty in tuning his mind into anything new. The pigeons didn't help. His mind was usually more on them that on his paid job, for they were the number one love of his life.

Five o'clock could never come soon enough for Willie. As soon as the mill hooter sounded, he would take off his thick leather apron and hang it on the cold water valve handle at the side of the number seven dye winch, then very quickly wash his hands, put on his heavy, old, tweed coat and cap and make his way home as fast as he could.

This particular day was no exception. He rushed along the canal bank towards Cutside Cottages, accompanied by Arthur Baxter who lived nearer the village, his iron soled clogs making a clanking sound on the concrete path, accentuated by the severe frost that had lain there for many days. Occasionally the noise would reach a crescendo as he broke the ice on the top of a frozen puddle lying in a hole in what had at some time been a good concrete road. His breath hurried out of him as if he were on fire, making a smoke haze in the bright early evening moonlight.

As he opened the door of number six, Willie was already repeating under his breath. 'Your Willie's home, our Thelma. Get your coat off Willie, your tea will be on the table in a minute.'

And sure enough, as he opened the door which led directly into the living room and the tremendous heat of the huge blazing coal fire hit him, his mother in law started, 'Your Willie's home our Thelma. Get you coat off Willie, your tea will be on the table in a minute.'

Willie was inclined to tell the old lady to shut her cake hole, he felt like this every day when he arrived home, but as usual he kept quiet, took off his coat, washed his hands again and sat at the table ready for tea.

Thelma appeared out of the back kitchen with their tea, being helped by Josie their daughter.

'We've got your favourite for tea today, Dad.'

"Tripe and onions?'

'Yes, that's right.'

'Goody goody gumdrops come on Grandma and you kids. Come and sit down and let's get on with it before it goes cold.'

Josie carried in a huge steaming pan of stewed tripe and onions which she put on the table. Thelma followed with a giant teapot in one hand and a plate containing a mountain of bread and butter in the other.

'By gum this looks right good,' said Willie. 'Come on Grandma, you're last again.'

'It's me back, it ain't half giving me some gip today, it must be the cold. I'm starved through to the very marrow; this weather'll be the death of me.'

Willie prayed silently for more and harder frosts.

Josie served out generous helpings of the piping hot stew. There were large lumps of tripe, rings of onion and a delicious creamy white sauce with yellow blobs of melted butter in it.

As was the privilege of the family bread winner, Willie was served the first helping and immediately grabbed a full slice of bread, folded it in half, and dipped it into the creamy sauce in his dish.

'Willie! We haven't got ours yet.'

Willie immediately stopped eating and stared at his mother-in-law. If looks could have killed, they would have been sending for the undertaker a few minutes later.

'Yes, my mother's right,' said Thelma trying her best to calm what could have developed into a very tense situation.

Willie turned his gaze to Thelma, who met his eyes directly and Willie, knowing when he was beaten, sat back until everyone else was served.

'But it was so good. Come on, get on with finishing serving and let's get to it.'

'Come on Dad, have some patience. It will be all the better for waiting.'

Willie smiled at Josie who was the apple of his eye.

When everyone was served she said in a rich American southern drawl, 'Okay you guys. Let battle commence.'

Willie dived in again with his folded bread, slurped noisily and sucked the sauce from it, dunked the bread again, greedily wolfed the soggy mess and grabbed another piece. With the bread being dunked by his right hand and a fork in his left hand deftly picking out lumps of tripe and rings of onion, it wasn't long before his dish was empty.

'Is there any more?' he enquired.

'Aye but you'll have to wait until we've all finished before we start dishing out any more,' replied Thelma without looking up from her eating.

'Nay. Come on let's get on with it. Its fair right good and I could eat another half a dozen platefuls right now.'

Grandma looked up from her half empty dish. 'Well I'm not rushing for anyone, especially you. It's bad enough having to eat this sort of thing in the first place without being rushed.'

'Well in that case you'd best go out and buy us all some fillet steak tomorrow, and then we can all eat in the manner like what you are accustomed to.'

'You know very well that my back won't let me.'

'Thelma can get it for us then, all you need to do is to give-'

'Willie,' interrupted Thelma. 'That's quite enough of that.'

'Give us some more tripe then.'

'Oh, all right, pass your dish over here.'

Willie passed the dish over to Josie, who, having filled it to the brim passed it back to Willie, who then greedily slurped, slopped and sucked his way rapidly through the delicious second helping. Having emptied the dish, he once again enquired. 'Any more?'

'Sorry Daddy, you've had the last of it. There's none left.

Upon this information Willie picked up his dish, raised it to his lips and drank down the last few drops of the sauce. Then, looking to see if anyone was watching, and discovering that no one in particular was, he raised the dish to his face once more. This time it was to lick the dish as clean as a new pin, only to find that someone was now watching him.

'Willie!' came the screech from Thelma. 'How dare you?'

'Ee it's so good I can't bide to waste a drop.'

'I told you, when you were insisting on marrying him, that he would be no good for you, our Thelma. But would you take my advice? No you would not. Your dear late father would turn in his grave if he could see the carry on.'

'For heaven's sake shut up mother.'

'Aye, put a sock in it why don't you. Pour the tea or something,' said Willie who sat back, opened his mouth and belched out loud saying, 'That's a lot better.'

'See what I said. He hasn't even got the manners of a pig. You might silence me again, but you'll see that I was right. This marrying below your station has got you nowhere.'

'Marrying below her station! By gum you've some room to talk, you a skivvy and your husband a cesspit emptier for the council. If marrying me wasn't above her station, I'd like to know what was. Don't forget we've got an inside toilet here, no going outside freezing to death. You nobbut had a brick privy down the bottom of the garden. You live in the lap of luxury at me and Thelma's expense, we have to have a roaring fire from morning until night, Winter and Summer alike, all for your benefit, and you accuse Thelma of marrying below her station. Absolute rubbish, poppycock, and I'll thank-you to mind your own manners in future, or else.'

Willie in one and the same breath pointed to the door, sat back and sighed. He was more than well pleased, even astonished at his performance as he wasn't given to making clever speeches. He observed that his mother-in-law was shedding a tear or two and Thelma had her arm around her mother's shoulder.

'There, there now, mother. Willie didn't mean it.'

'Oh yes, Willie did mean it,' he said. Willie was trying to maintain his masterly control of the situation. 'Unless she keeps her interfering gob tight shut where I am concerned, she can pack her bags and get out.'

More than a tear or two was flooding from the old lady now and Josie looked reproachfully at her dad.

'Dad, look what you've done now.'

'Josie. Don't interfere in matters that you know nowt about. Now Grandma! Stop blubbering and listen to me.'

For the first time ever, Willie was beginning to have visions of being the master in his own home. Although he didn't quite know how to continue and a little ball of phlegm in his throat was just beginning to annoy him. But he threw caution to the wind and breezed in.

'Starting with the next lot of coal what we have delivered, you can pay for it and all that what we buy after, you can pay for that and all. Or you can starve. So suit yourself.'

He snooked up the phlegm, rolled it around his mouth and swallowed it again, dreading what the outburst to his reply might be. He didn't have to wait long to find out.

'Nay lad,' she wailed, 'ah can't afford to pay for t' coal and ah need a big fire, else ah shall be starved through to the very marrow. Ah don't know what ah shall have to do.'

'Well suit yourself. I'm not paying for no more coal. Now is anyone going to pour me another pot of tea or not?'

Thelma poured Willie his pint pot of strong tea and the others got a cup each. The young children were beginning to get restless and Thelma sent them off to play in the back kitchen.

Willie drank some of the tea with his teaspoon, 'Cos it's hot.' And then when it had cooled a little he noisily drained it and put it rather harder than usual onto the table.

'Right! I'm off to look at my pigeons,' he announced.

He got up from the table and marched as uprightly, smartly and masterfully as he possibly could away into the back kitchen to find his hurricane lamp. He filled it with paraffin from a can, lit it, pumped up the pressure and made ready for off to the pigeon cote.

CHAPTER 2

Arthur Baxter knocked on the door of number six Cutside cottages and, without waiting for a reply, walked straight in as he did most weekday nights.

'Evening all. Willie out in the back?'

'Hello Arthur,' said Thelma. 'Yes, he's out in the back with the pigeons. Getting rid of some tonight aren't you?'

'Yes, we're setting them off on their long journey tonight; it'll take them two days to get there. Not every day we send them as far as Lands End. No, it's a hell of a long way, but they'll look after them well on the railway. Anyway I'd best go and give him a hand with them.'

Arthur lifted the latch on the back door and went out into the cold, black night, observing Willie at the bottom of the garden in the pigeon cote, from which shafts of bright light pierced the frosty night air.

'That you Arthur?' came the muffled voice from within the pigeon cote.

'Aye. Have you got the baskets out yet?'

'Nay, I was waiting for you coming. Come on give us a hand, they are at the back of the hen run.'

Arthur followed Willie round and in the light of the hurricane lamp they pulled away the dirty old tarpaulin to reveal two large wicker panniers used solely for transporting pigeons. They picked them both up together, taking one side each, and carried them back to the cote.

'Which of them are we sending Willie?'

'Well I don't rightly know. We could send them all. Tha knows that if we put them six to a basket they're all right so there'll be no problem.'

'Well why not. It won't cost us any more to send the other two and then at least they can pick out which they want and send the others back in the baskets.'

So the two friends slowly collected the birds one by one and put them into one of the baskets. Willie had a few words of encouragement for each of them.

'Now Henrietta, you go and be a good girl for your new daddy. Claudine, you will have to pull your socks up if your last race as anything to go by, else you might end up in an oven with a crust over you.'

As he spoke the birds looked at him as if he was demented, each bird turning its head in small jerky movements from side to side, but he went on giving each one a fond stroke or two. Finally they were all in and the panniers were locked, labelled and placed on top of one another again.

'What train they going on?'

'Oh not until half past ten tonight because they're not leaving Leeds until ten o'clock tomorrow morning,' replied Arthur.

Willie and Arthur were partners in the pigeons. Willie was the works manager and Arthur the company secretary. Willie did the feeding, nursing, talking to and mucking out, whilst Arthur made the arrangements with the local pigeon society secretary, did the necessary paperwork, and collected the prize money. Not that the latter part of his job had needed much effort recently. The pigeons had to live in Willie's back garden because Arthur lived in a house with no garden, so at the year-end it was usually Arthur who had to pay a substantial sum of money as his share of the running expenses. Prize money was divided equally as it arrived.

They picked up the two panniers. Willie was at the front with his hands meeting behind him on the large, wide handle of the bottom basket and Arthur bringing up the rear holding the opposite handle. The only access to the back garden was through the cottage and so in they trooped into the coolish atmosphere of the back kitchen and then the hot temperature of the living room.

Arthur looked firstly at the huge fire burning in the black leaded cottage range and secondly at the old lady sitting very comfortably in her corner near the roaring fire.

'Willie's been telling us how generous you are, buying all this coal to keep this big roaring fire going Mrs Woofenden. It's very good of you; it is, to keep it so warm. I wish somebody'd buy coal to keep our house as warm as this.'

The old lady was momentarily dumbfounded. Thelma looked uncomfortable and kept quiet. Willie would have kicked Arthur, or bitten his own tongue out for his earlier stupidity in lying about the coal, but he could do neither from the position he was in and the latter was only a thought anyway.

The old lady found her tongue again after a short but very pregnant silence. 'Oh he has, has he?'

'Aye, he has. I wish my mother-in-law would buy us some coal. You're a very lucky lass Thelma.'

Willie, even though he was not so bright, decided it was time to change the subject. 'Come on Arthur, or we shall miss yond train and there's not another tonight.' And with that he began to pull the two panniers and Arthur towards the front door.

'Don't forget which day you set off,' said Thelma.

'Aye, don't come back in the early hours disturbing us all,' growled the old lady.

'No, we'll just take the birds up to the station and have a quick one on the way back.'

'Goodnight all,' shouted Arthur as he was pulled through the front door and into the cold, frosty night once more.

They turned left out of the house and along the canal towpath, the few, distantly positioned bright gas lamps casting long shadows on the two friends and their load. They passed the village wharf and turning circle where there were two barges tied up for the night. One, the local boat, was empty, the other, displaying St Helens as its home town, was loaded with coal from South Yorkshire on its way back to Lancashire. The few dirty windows in the cabin at the stern showed a weak glow from the poor oil lamps. As they looked in through the windows, the bargee and his wife were having a meal. Both were the colour of their cargo, neither having washed since Christmas.

'It would be grand to live on one of them barges, never need to wash, no mother-in-law, nowt to bother about all day but to see the scenery and be out in the fresh air and sun,' Willie said thoughtfully.

'You've nowt to bother about anyway. With a generous woman like Mrs Woofenden living with you, life must be five star all the way.'

'You should come live there and try it. You'd soon change your tune.'

'Nay I've enough with what I've got!'

'You most certainly have.'

The two figures walking smartly in time with each other, made their way slowly from the canal tow path, along the village, past the by now darkened shops and the well illuminated pubs and up the steep hill to the railway station. Entering the dimly lit entrance hall they put the panniers down on the floor by the booking office window, which was closed as expected, and inspected the silent edifice for signs of life. Finding nothing and nobody, they opened the door marked Station Master and walked in to be met by a huge blazing fire in an old cast iron fireplace. There was a deathly silence over the room except for the crackling of the fire and the hiss of the gas lamp, until Arthur broke the silence.

'Good heavens! It's Evans.'

'What is?'

'That is,' said Arthur pointing to a half smartly attired British Railways employee sitting in a rickety armchair next to them in front of the fire.

'It's not!'

'It is. You know.'

'I thought it was a corpse waiting for the next train to Boot Hill.'

At this last exchange, Willie bent over the figure reclining in the chair, and stared intently into this third face. The never emotive visage of Owen Evans, stationmaster, ticket salesman, ticket collector, porter, cleaner, gardener and general factotum of Grolsby station, remained unmoved. Willie passed his hand slowly up and down in front of the impassive face.

'No sign of life. Told you it was a corpse.'

Suddenly Owen Evans moved, and then opened his mouth, 'Nos dahr.' He didn't move again.

'What were that?' Arthur enquired.

17

'Nay, search me. It sounded as if it was Chinese or a pig in labour or something.'

'Happen it's a Russian Spy.'

'What would a Russian spy be doing in a dump like this?'

Owen Evans moved again and spoke, 'Look you Willie Arkenthwaite, what is it you was wanting?'

'Hey look Arthur, its Owen the Horrible and we've awakened him from his beautiful dreams.'

'I wasn't asleep.'

'You could have fooled us,' said Arthur. 'We were just going to run away with the days takings.'

'It wouldn't have been worth your while; you can't get far on three shillings and four pence.'

'You've taken three shillings and four pence already today and it's only half past eight at night? British Railways won't half be paying a big dividend this year.'

'Now look here you two. What is it that you was wanting? I'm very busy and I haven't got the time to waste on the likes of you.'

Willie looked at Arthur. 'Never, boyo, have I heard the Yorkshire mother tongue spoken with such a stupid accent.'

'Suit yourself. If you don't tell me what it is you was wanting, I shall shut up shop for the night and that will be that.'

'We've brought two baskets of pigeons.'

'Very kind of you, I'm sure, but I've had my tea already.'

"We've brought two baskets of pigeons to go to Lands end.'

'So why didn't you say so in the first place?'

'We did.'

'Well you didn't. So, anyway, what are you two reprobates coming all the way on here with a basket of pigeons each to send them all the way to Lands end for?'

'Cos we've sold them to a racing man down there.'

'How come an intelligent man from Lands End, which incidentally is nearly part of Wales, has bought two baskets of pigeons from two loonies like you? Mind you now, thinking about it, his intelligence I suppose could be brought into doubt. However, I being but a humble Stationmaster, whose sole purpose in life is to despatch all human life and its effects to its chosen destination, have no right at all to question your purpose in sending these pigeons all the way to Lands end on a cold, cold night.'

He finished his speech and smiled at them in eager anticipation of a suitable retort.

Willie and Arthur stared at one another and then at Evans.

Arthur was the first to speak. 'The reason we are sending them to lands End is to keep you in a job for a while longer, to find something to do on a cold Tuesday night and of course for the money.'

Owen Evans smiled again. 'You don't need the money William Arkenthwaite. From what I hear, you're living very comfortably off your wife's mother and saving your wages every week. And as for you Arthur Baxter, it's a well known fact in the valleys that you're the richest working man around here for miles. Now, so let us get on with the all important job of paperwork for the pigeons, we wouldn't want them running all around the railway system in ever decreasing circles without paperwork, now would we? By the way, can they read?'

Evans stood up and walked over to a very old desk in front of the ticket window. Willie, having been dumbfounded for a few seconds, found his voice again. 'How do you know about my mother-in-law?'

'It's all over the village. It's a well known fact that she gives you twenty pounds every week.'

'By gum I wish she did.'

'You mean she doesn't?'

'Does she hell as like.' Then thinking of the claim he had made in the canteen at dinner time. 'Well not quite anyway.'

'What about the coal?' asked Arthur.

'What about the coal?'

'What about what coal?' asked Evans.

'Come on Willie, Evans wants to hear about how your mother-in-law buys all your coal.'

'Coal and twenty pounds a week? Bach, there's a nice situation. Gosh you must be rolling in it.'

'In What?'

'Money you daft head. Wish I was a couple of hundreds behind you.'

Willie felt a slight discomfort at the back of his throat, so he had a good snook up, rolled a ball of phlegm around his mouth, walked over to the fire and spat out into the flames, before saying. 'It's not true. I'm skint.'

'You don't need to sell the pigeons, isn't it?'

'We bloody do need to sell the pigeons.' Willie began to raise his voice, just a little bit.

'Ah well, never mind. Do you have the address almost in Wales where the pigeons are going?'

Arthur produced a dirty, scruffy, crumpled piece of paper from his coat pocket and Evans filled in the paperwork, forms for the pigeons despatching thereof, and at the same time singing Land of My Fathers in a rich baritone voice. Meanwhile, he smiled to himself whilst stealing a few quick glances at Willie.

'Is the entertainment free, or will you be paying us to listen?' asked Willie.

'Free to a friend like you any time, boyo. Will you be paying with money or is it account?'

'Eh?'

'Two pounds six and three pence in money. Now!'

Just as Arthur produced the money, the bell rang to let Evans know that the Leeds train had left the neighbouring station and would arrive in four minutes.

'Best get these baskets onto the platform,' said Evans reaching for his hat and coat that were hanging on a nail behind the office door. 'Come on you two, when this one's gone its locking up time.'

They carried the two baskets on to the platform, waited for the train, loaded the baskets into the guards van and the with a collection of nos dahrs, bora dahrs and good neets, the two pals took their leave of Owen Evans and set out back downhill towards the village.

They hadn't gone more than two strides when Evans shouted at them, 'Don't forget to remind me to charge you for the platform tickets when I see you again.'

CHAPTER 3

The streets were deserted in the cold, midwinter evening and there was an air of calmness and serenity all around, broken only by the occasional loud belch from Willie.

'Crown and Anchor or t' club?' asked Arthur.

'Oh, let's go to t' club. Ale'll be cheaper there.'

They turned into Albert Street, the main thoroughfare of the village, and slowly caught up with a solitary figure heading in the same direction. Arthur nudged Willie, who observed Arthur put his finger onto his lips to motion strict silence and speed up to a cat burglar type quick creep towards the back of the figure. Willie followed the action and, as they arrived at the sauntering figure, their paths diverged and the came alongside him, one on each side.

Arthur shouted, 'Now,' upon which they picked up the man by his arms and propelled him forward as fast as they could and until they tired and put him down.

The man was too shocked to protest, too weary to bother and too slow to know what it was about anyway.

Willie and Arthur stood before him beaming.

'Evening Eustace,' said Arthur.

'Evening Useless,' said Willie

Eustace had by now forgotten about the acute state of shock in which he just had been. 'Hello Willie, hello Arthur. Are you going to the club?'

'Yes are you?'

'Yes. Where have you been?'

'With the pigeons, to the station.'

'Have you? With the pigeons, to the station? What for?'

'To send them to Lands End.'

'To lands end? The pigeons? Have you? What for?'

'Cos we've sold them to somebody.'

'Have you? Sold 'em? To somebody in Lands End? What for?'

'Come on Arthur, it's too cold to stand out here listening to him. Let's get off to the club.'

'Why have you sold your pigeons to somebody in Lands End, Willie?'

'Are you actually going to the club Eustace?'

'To the club, er, er, yes, to the club.'

'Come on then.'

'Yes, yes, with you now Willie.'

'Yes now come on, it's bloody cold,' roared Arthur.

They walked along, encouraging Eustace to keep up with them, and hadn't gone far when Arthur stopped and looked in the brightly lit shop window of Harry Howard, of whom the notice over the door pronounced Licensed to sell Intoxicating Liquor.

'Join our Christmas club,' he read aloud. 'Bit late isn't it? Still, it's not a bad idea for next year, put a bit away with him each week until next Christmas, then at least we shall be able to afford some booze for the festive occasion, not like this year when we had a right dry do.'

Eustace came to life again. 'Would you? Join his Christmas club? Save some money with him? Not a bad idea.'

'Come on,' shouted Willie. 'Let's get to the club before we freeze to death.'

Another two hundred yards along the road and they entered the portals of the Grolsby Amalgamated Working Men's Club Affiliated. Inside, the bright lights momentarily dazzled them, and the heat took their breath for a moment.

They hung their flat caps, overcoats and scarves on the row of hooks that lined the cream walls of the mid-brown, lino-floored entrance hall and made their way through the dark stained door at the end into the main bar. The room was filled with men, some playing snooker, there were two tables, some playing darts, some dominoes, some cards and others just sitting or standing, drinking, smoking and talking. The room as sparsely but comfortably furnished, very warm and a thick blue to yellowish-grey pall of smoke looked down from above onto the proceedings.

There was a chorus of 'Evening all.' Or 'Willie.' Or 'Arthur.' Or 'Eustace.' And the three friends exchanged greetings with everyone in return as they picked their way through the throng, to the bar.

Arthur took great care not to loose Eustace and as they got to the bar, he said in a loud voice to no one in particular, 'What was it Dr Snodbury said in here last week after he'd just become a father again?'

'I know,' cried Eustace, 'it were "Drinks are on me."'

'That's very generous of you,' said Willie, laughing. 'Mine's a pint of the best.'

'Me too,' followed Arthur.

'Eh? What? You did that on purpose.'

'Did what?'

'Got me to say. "Drinks are on me."'

'By gum, you're generous tonight. Keep me one in Harry if Eustace's buying two rounds.'

'Nay, nay. I'm not. I'm only buying one round; you must think I'm daft.'

'You daft?' said Willie. 'Now what do you take us for? We wouldn't take advantage of you like that. We'll just have the one round for now, and the other later on sometime.'

'Oh, yes, right, er, have you ordered yet Arthur? What are you having?'

'A pint of best please.'

Arthur held the pint he already had, behind his back out of sight. Fat Harry, the club steward leaned over the bar and stared into Eustace's face.

'I wouldn't buy these two rogues a spoonful of arsenic never mind a pint each. You must be mad.'

'I'm not. I'm not. I'm not mad at all. I'm normal just like you lot. I'm not mad. I'm not.'

'All right, all right, go sit down and enjoy your drinks.'

Fat Harry could see Eustace working himself up to an epileptic fit, which he was prone to having when wound up to concert pitch, and not wishing to let an epileptic fit tarnish an otherwise quite uneventful evening, Harry decided to quieten the proceedings. Willie and Arthur being of the same mind as Fat Harry, took Eustace by the arm yet again, only much gentler this time taking care not to spill his half of bitter, and were guiding him to a quiet table away from the

23

bar, when Fat Harry spread his oversized beer-laden belly on to the top of the bar counter, leaned forward and bellowed at Eustace.

'Hey. You haven't paid for these drinks yet.'

'Shut up Harry and put them on his slate,' Willie shouted back.

'His slate's full, as is yours and Arthur's.'

'I haven't got one.'

'Exactly. It's so full it's never going to be opened again. So pay up now.'

'Later on, when we've had another round.'

'What do you mean when we've had another round? You lot have never ever had another round. You make one last all night, don't you. So come on pay up now.'

'Hold your noise a bit. We'll see you right later on.'

Fat Harry pulled his beer belly off the top of the bar and it sagged earthwards, turning part of the waistband of his trousers over in the process. He looked at the offending trio, sighed and shook his head in the full knowledge that matters could only get worse before they got any better as far as those three were concerned.

'Cold night tonight, isn't it. I say, isn't it cold tonight? It's warm in here though, warm isn't it? Lot of smoke about all over, smoke, isn't there? Lot of smoke.'

'Glad he works in the teazing room and not in the dyehouse,' said Willie.

'Aye. We couldn't do with that row all day long. I don't know how they put up with him in teazing.'

'What row? What row, Arthur? I cant here any row.'

Willie sat back in the hard wooden chair and reflected. 'You know, that idea of a Christmas club isn't so bad. We could do with having one at the mill, and then we'd happen have a bit of brass to chuff on next Christmas.'

'You mean have one of our own?' asked Arthur.

Eustace followed the words but not the gist of the conversation.

'Aye we could have one at the mill. We'd only need someone to run it, to collect the money and look after it and share it out at Christmas. It's simple.'

'Well seeing that you're so keen we'd best start and get one organised. What do you say Eustace?'

At the sound of his name, Eustace awoke from his trance like state. Just as if he'd been kissed by the handsome prince.

'What what did you say? Arthur? What did you say?'

Arthur grimaced and thought bad thoughts. 'A Christmas club at the mill and Willie could run it. We ought to have one didn't we?'

'Yes, yes, a Christmas club at t' mill and Willie could run it. We ought to have one didn't we? Yes, a good idea. Yes, can I join Willie? Are you going to run it? Willie? Are you? Yes, yes, a good idea. Can I join? Can I?'

He looked at Willie with eager anticipation as did Arthur.

Willie was still sitting back very relaxed and very reflective. For the first time in his life, someone had asked him to do something important and he wasn't going to let the opportunity slip by without giving it a good try.

'You're right Arthur, I'd better start and get it organised. How much a week are you each putting in?'

'Hey it's a bit sudden you know. I'll have to ask Jess about it. I know I can't afford much, for I haven't any spare to start with. What about you Eustace?'

'Er, me Arthur? Er, what about me Arthur? What do you mean?'

'How much are you going to put into Willie's Christmas club?'

'Hang on it's not just my Christmas club. It'll have to be for everyone at the mill.'

'Aye, I know that. Anyway what about it Eustace? What are you going to put in?'

'Well, I've been thinking.'

'You what?'

Eustace managed a feeble grin. 'Well I've been thinking, Willie. I have. I've been thinking I might put one pound a week in, just one pound, every week, one pound. How much will that be by Christmas Arthur? If I pay every week, Arthur. How much do you think I'll get? What do you think? Do you think I'll-'

He was cut short by Willie. 'I can't reckon that up at this time of night without a paper and pencil. It's a big sum is that.' He sat upright and began to make sniffing and snorting noises, snooking a ball of phlegm into the back of his throat, then propelling it, accompanied by a series of noises to the front of his mouth, then spat it out to land neatly by his foot. He completed the move by grinding it with the sole of his boot into the planked timber floor.

'Hoy! You mucky pup,' roared Fat Harry, who had been observing the stylish performance.

'Sorry Harry. Are you going to join our Christmas club?'

'Your Christmas club? You must be joking. I wouldn't come within a thousand miles of anything you lot were organising. I'd lose every penny I put in with you criminals in charge. It'd be like burning money.' He turned away roaring with laughter.

'I'll get him one day,' said Arthur. 'Anyway have you lot supped up yet, it's getting on for my bedtime.'

'Is it Arthur? Is it your bedtime already? Had we best go home now then? What time is it? What time do you go to bed, Arthur? Have I to finish my drink? Willie?'

Willie stood up and made for the door. 'Come on you lot it's another day tomorrow.'

'Aye you're right. Back to the dyehouse by seven. Come on Eustace.'

'Wait a minute Arthur. I haven't finished my drink yet, Arthur. Are you going to wait a minute whilst I drink up? Are you?'

'For heavens sake shut up and get on with it.'

'Yes Arthur, I shan't be a minute.'

Eustace guzzled the remains of his beer, almost choked, coughed until his face was the colour of a beetroot then sat back gasping for air.

'Come on Eustace.'

'Yes Arthur,' he mumbled, still gasping for air, 'I'm just coming Arthur.' He stood up still gasping, puffing and panting. 'Just coming Arthur. Are you ready Willie?'

By this time he was more or less back to normal and he made his way out of the club with the others.

Having reached the end of Gallipoli Avenue where Eustace lived, the other two stopped.

'What have you stopped for Willie? Just here? What for?'

'So we can point you in the right direction for your house.'

'It's up here.'

'Aye, we know that.'

'Well then, that's all right then. I'll go get to bed. Goodnight Willie. Goodnight Arthur. I'll see you tomorrow at the mill.'

'Not if we see you first,' Arthur muttered under his breath. 'He goes worse and worse.'

'Aye. Dafter and Dafter,' agreed Willie.

Soon they arrived at Cutside Cottages and Willie turned into his home, leaving Arthur the remaining three hundred yards to walk to his.

Inside number six, the fire was still glowing and the children were all tucked up in bed, as was Mrs Woofenden. Only Thelma remained up waiting for Willie.

'Shall I get your cocoa, love?'

'Yes please.'

Thelma went into the back kitchen to get Willie's bedtime drink. Willie stood with his back to the fire and had a good old belch. *Up yours Mrs Woofenden*, he thought.

Shortly after Thelma appeared with his drink. They climbed the stairs arm in arm, taking the cocoa with them.

'What sort of an evening have you had, love? Did you get the pigeons to the station?'

'Aye. Everything went off all right. Evans the station master was his usual happy self and we've spent the rest of the time at the club with Eustace, so it hasn't been bad. They're talking about having a Christmas club at the mill.'

'Who are?'

'Oh, one or two of them.'

Willie lay awake for a long time thinking how it might be nice to be the big boss of the Christmas club and though he thought and thought about it, he got nowhere at all with it and finally drifted in to his normal deep snoring untroubled sleep.

CHAPTER 4

At half past six the following morning Ted Smith, the night boiler man and watchman at Murgatroyd's Mill, performed one of the last chores of his nightly routine. It was to him the most pleasurable of his duties and quite the hardest for, since the introduction of automatic coal stokers and chain grates into the huge Lancashire boilers that raised the steam for the dyeing and finishing processes, not to mention warming the mill in winter, all the work had been taken out of his job.

This pleasure was to open the valve that let the steam run high up the pipe to the roof of the engine house and blow the mill hooter. The high pitched wailing sound that ran for thirty seconds and echoed up and down the valley, woke every living thing within earshot. It was rumoured by those with a more vivid imagination that it also awoke some of the dead in their graves, but this point had never actually been proven.

Generally speaking, Ted smith hated his job. Not just this particular job, but work of any type. So it gave him an immense feeling of power and satisfaction to be able to wake everyone in the neighbourhood whilst he was getting ready to go home to his bed.

The half a minute of hooter was almost over when Willie Arkenthwaite decided to open his eyes. It took him a further full five minutes to properly enter the land of the living and to make preparation to get out of bed. Thelma and the kids were awake, as they always were, but they habitually stayed in bed until Willie left for work because he usually wasn't fit to talk to first thing in the morning added to which his personal toilet habits defied description.

The pyjama jacket was removed to reveal an open necked, loose collared white Winceyette shirt with delicate pale red vertical stripes. The pyjama trousers were removed to reveal a pair of almost white Long Johns. These Long Johns were then covered by Willie's best pair of light grey working trousers, made from a fent from the mill that Thelma had sewn up for him. The braces were left dangling at the back until such time as Willie had performed his ablutions. To complete the scene, a pair of very well worn slippers were put on the feet and Willie, hands in pockets, plodded his way downstairs to the warmth of the living room.

The first job for Willie each morning was to rake out the glowing embers of the fire in the range, take out the hot ashes to the dustbin and stoke up the fire again. Willie enjoyed using the poker on the hot fire to rake out the ashes, for at every thrust and parry he muttered, 'Woofenden,' visualising driving a stake through the old lady's heart. Needless to say this was the best poked fire in Grolsby and it did him good to take it out of the old lady in this way. Having cleaned out the fire, he fetched a huge shovelful of coal, put it on the glowing embers then moved the kettle onto the grid to boil.

Soon, he was to take the kettle into the back kitchen where he poured the warm water into an enamel bowl in the sink and using a long since cracked mirror that hung on a nail over it, he proceeded to lather up his shaving brush and to cover his face in creamy carbolic froth. With a quick rub of his shiny cut throat razor on the leather strop, which hung on the back door, he then deftly shaved off the stubble from his face.

Packing up breakfast to eat at the mill was his next job. The kettle was back on the hob boiling merrily away and he brewed a pint of tea whilst contemplating the contents of his breakfast pack. Finally he settled for a buttered currant teacake with a sliced banana within. Having carefully constructed his sandwich he then lovingly laid it into his tin lunch box.

The next and equally important operation was to tear a piece of newspaper into three strips, put two heaped teaspoons of sugar into the middle of each strip, a heaped teaspoon of tea leaves onto the sugar in two of them and a similar quantity of coffee grounds onto the third one. The three mashings representing tea for breakfast, coffee for elevenses and tea for the mid afternoon break were then carefully wrapped into neat little parcels and placed in the lunch box.

Finally a medicine bottle, which somewhere in the dim and distant past had held a strong laxative, was filled with milk and the days refreshments were packed. The laxative bottle had been a source of constant amusement at the mill for many months past.

Having no pigeons to attend to, Willie sat back in Mrs Woofenden's chair to drink his pint of tea. Usually it went with him outside, but this morning, and until they re-stocked the pigeons, it would have to stop inside with him. Finishing his tea, Willie climbed the stairs to the bathroom, completed his morning toilet and returned downstairs. His clogs were on the hearth, where they had been all night, keeping warm and they felt very nice and cosy as he put them on. He took his coat and cap from the hook at the back of the front door ,wrapped his red striped scarf around his neck and, picking up his lunch box, he left the house just as the second hooter sounded at five minutes to seven, announcing five minutes to starting time.

Ted Smith, attired in cap- and coat really enjoyed operating the five to seven hooter as this was his home time and the second he let go of the lever that controlled the steam valve for the hooter, he was away home.

The biting north wind, blowing straight against the front of Cutside Cottages, caught Willie's breath as he left the warmth of his front room. There had been a very heavy frost during the night, the canal was beginning to ice over in small patches and his clogs made a crisp, fresh crunching sound as he walked on the frozen puddles of the tow path. As he exhaled, steamy breath disappeared just as quickly as it had appeared and the frozen air made him cough. The barge from St Helens, into which he and Arthur had peered the night before, chugged slowly by. The bargee, with a steaming mug of coffee balanced carefully at his side, gave Willie a cheery wave and Willie waved back. The lady of the barge was nowhere in sight and Willie correctly assumed that she had stayed below in the small cabin where it would be quite cosy and warm.

Ted Smith, the night watchman, came towards Willie and they met as usual at Coopers Bridge, a by now disused, cobbled, arched, turnpike bridge of many years standing.

'Morning Ted.'

'Morning Willie. Brass Monkey weather.'

'Aye and bloody cold to go with it.'

Ted stared at Willie, not appreciating his little joke.

'Have you left t' mill in one piece then?'

'Yes as normal, everything's as normal. Absolutely fed up with this boiler house routine. It's too hard a job for a man of my age. Going to find a lighter job.'

'But you've got a light job now.'

'Nowt of the sort. It's ruddy hard work.'

'Aye, it must be. Sleeping and getting paid for it.'

They were beginning to shout now for they hadn't stopped walking and were getting further apart from each other.

'I'll have you know I don't sleep at my work.'

'You're a liar,' came another voice.

Willie looked around at Arthur who had shouted the last few words from behind him. He turned around and hurried to catch up with Arthur. Ted shouted yet another reply, but the two friends were not listening to him.

'A right miserable sod is that one. Carries one half of the worlds problems on his shoulders and he does sleep at the mill,' said Arthur.

'Do you know,' said Willie, 'if I were as miserable as what he is, I'd jump in the canal. He has a bed behind the mill boiler, but it's covered over with old sacks during the day and it just looks like a dirty old pile of muck that hasn't been moved for years. One of these days Antony Murgatroyd is going to have that area cleared out and then the balloon'll go up.'

'Not before time. He is due for his cum-uppance and the sooner the better.'

'By-gum, but it's cold this morning,' said Willie. 'I think we ought to run to the mill to get us selves warm.'

'You run and I'll watch you. I'm quite prepared to freeze and get warm at the mill when I get there.'

'Nay it's always cold in yond dyehouse; it's not possible to get warm.'

'Aye I know, but it'll be warmer that what it is here.'

They hurried along to the mill and clocked in at the penny-hole door at dead on seven o'clock. They made their way to the dyehouse and exchanged caps and coats for the dyer's traditional thick, leather, waterproof aprons, which they both wore and which were provided by the mill as part of their uniform.

The first loading of the dyeing machines was always running by ten past seven. Willie and Arthur pushed in a cart of heavy, wet, woollen pieces and threw the first end of the top piece over the top of the huge wooden winch roller. They pulled the lever at the side of the machine which made the wide leather driving belt move from the loose pulley to the fast pulley, which in turn drove the winch roller and pulled the heavy fabric piece into the big timber vat that was sunk into the floor below them. They made sure that the head end of the piece was laid over the front edge of the vat and when the whole of the piece was in the vat, they caught the tail end and laid it together with the head end. They repeated the exercise six times then sewed each head end to its respective tail end so as to create six long continuous loops of fabric running over the top of the winch and into the vat. Having completed the first machine they shouted for the head dyer and moved onto the other five machines they looked after and fed them with cloth in the same way.

The Dyer, a man of some importance in the mill, distinguished from his labourers by the fact that he wore a khaki smock, emerged from his office on hearing Willie's shout. He carried a bucket of carefully mixed dye powder which he put down in front of the first dye vessel. The dyehouse foreman then came along and opened the cold water inlet valve from which he filled the vat. This submerged the cloth and then he opened the steam valve to boil the water. He put the bucket of dye powder under the cold water tap, half filled the bucket then transferred it to beneath the open ended steam pipe, to boil up the dye, before he tipped the bucket of ready mixed dye into the vat. He set the winch in motion with the control lever, leaving the coloured liquid to penetrate the cloth as it boiled. The bucket was returned to the dyer's office to be washed, dried and re-filled with dye powder. The Dyer was, in the meantime, mixing more powders to carefully prepared recipes for the next machine. And so the daily routine of the dyehouse moved into its full momentum.

There were eleven dyeing vessels in the room, six along one side and five along the other. At one end of the room, Willie and Arthur looked after three machines on each side, keeping them filled with cloth, and emptying them when the dyeing cycle was completed. Dick Jordan and Lewis Armitage looked after the five at the other end.

There should have been six, but one had been removed in preparation for one of the new fangled all stainless steel, machines with its own electric motor that was due to arrive any day soon.

Once all the machines had been filled and were running, it was breakfast time and the dyehouse staff sat around a rickety wood table in the centre of the room, where they could keep half an eye on the machines. Willie as part of his daily routine had to scald six pints of either tea or coffee. This was at breakfast only and the onerous routine was to collect the newspaper wrapped mashings from his workmates, take the six pots in a specially designed tray to the steam heated water geyser in the entrance to the big mill and scald the six pints. On his return to the dyehouse he put five pots on the table and delivered the sixth pot to the dyer's office, for the dyer, being a man of some importance, dined alone.

Willie sat down with the rest of the staff, opened up his sandwich box and extricated the currant teacake with banana. Walter Smith, the dyehouse foreman, stared at Willie's breakfast.

'Your Thelma stayed in bed again this morning, has she?'

'What does tha mean?'

'Well just look at that currant teacake. No woman alive would plaster a currant teacake with that much margarine.'

'I'll have you know it's best butter.'

'Never in this world. If that's best butter, then I'm the Emperor of China and I'm not, so it isn't.'

Willie, being quite used to this type of workshop banter, took no offence at the matter and began to trough by dipping the teacake into his pint of tea. This had the obvious effect of making the teacake soggy, but also leaving a considerable quantity of the margarine to float and melt into golden yellow globules in the tea. He then noisily sucked the soggy end of the teacake, took a bite and prepared to repeat the exercise.

Lewis Armitage who was eating a far more conventional marmalade sandwich asked, 'Have you ever seen a more disgusting sight than that?'

Willie grinned. 'Hey these currant teacakes with banana are fair grand. You should have one yourself Lewis.'

'No thanks, I'd rather die of starvation. It'd make me puke eating that.'

'Well it's not going to make me puke,' he said grinning again.

Arthur, who had been quietly eating his cold toast and dripping, said, 'Willie and me passed Ted Smith again as usual this morning. He's getting worse touchy about sleeping behind the boiler during the night.'

Dick Jordan, the fourth member of the dyehouse labouring team said, 'You know it's right. He sleeps all night here, wakes up in time to get steam up and then blow the mill hooter, then has his breakfast, waits until Walter Holroyd comes to take over for the dayshift, blows the five to seven hooter and then goes home. After that he waits until his wife goes off to t' Co-op, where as we all know she works, then he goes and beds down with Walter Holroyd's wife for a few hours, getting back home before his wife lands home from t' Co-op. Mind you he has to ruffle up the bed sheets to make it look as if he's slept all day at home, and it's rumoured that on more than one occasion, his missus has been a bit suspicious about the state of the bed, but he's had a lucky run so far.'

Willie belched out loud without any attempt either to conceal it or excuse himself, and then dipped what remained of the teacake into the tea. Finally, to round off a good breakfast he noisily slurped the remains of his pot.

'You know, he nearly didn't get away with it a fortnight ago,' said Lewis.

'How do you mean?'

'Well his missus had forgotten summat and when she were half way to t' Co-op she bethought her about it and went home to get it. Ted was as throng as hell, washing, shaving and sprucing himself up. "What are you getting all donned up for?" she asks him. Of course, as we all know, Ted can be a quick thinker when he wants to be, so he says, "I were just going off somewhere." So she says, "somewhere like where?" "It's a secret," he says. "What sort of secret?" she asks. "Well it's a secret and I can't tell you if it's a secret can I." Anyway like all good women she wheedles it out of him eventually that he's going off to look for a surprise birthday present for her and she believes him and goes off back to her work, leaving him to visit Margery Holroyd.

'So what's he going to do about her surprise present?'

'Well I don't rightly know what he's going to do and neither does he, except he knows he's going to have to get her something good and he also knows he cant afford to get her 'owt at all.'

'No, that's a problem we have at birthdays and Christmas,' Dick thought out loud.

'Aye well, Willie has a solution to that problem,' said Arthur

'What's that then Willie?'

'It's nowt much.'

'Come on then, let's know what it is you have in mind.'

Willie coughed, snooked up and spat a ball of phlegm into a nearby drain. 'Well it's like this. Arthur, me and Eustace were talking last night and we were saying we ought to have a Christmas club.'

'Not useless Eustace from t' teazin hoil?' asked Walter Smith.

'The very same.'

'Well if he's having 'owt to do with it, count me out from the start.'

'He's not having 'owt to do with it. Anyway we were thinking that we should have this club for anyone that wants to join, from the mill of course. So then we could all put a bit away each week then pay it back out just before Christmas.'

'Bloody good idea, count me in,' said Lewis. 'How are you going to organise it Willie?'

'Nay, it were only an idea like. I'm not going to organise it.'

'Why not? You should do, shouldn't he lads? It was your idea.'

The other three nodded their assent.

'Well that's settled then,' said Lewis. 'Tell you what, I'll help you a bit Willie.'

'Now hang on a minute lads, it were nobbut an idea. Somebody else ought to do it. Somebody what understands it.'

'Now look Willie,' said Arthur, 'it was your idea and you ought to do it. We'll all give you a helping hand with it.'

Willie was no longer listening to Arthur. He was having visions of grandeur at the head of a large organisation, with people putting vast amounts of money in his hand and him putting it in his pocket. He was brought back to reality by Arthur tapping his arm.

'Er, er, what Arthur?'

'I was just saying we ought to have a meeting in the canteen at dinner time.'

'Aye, well happen we did and there again happen we didn't.'

'Getting cold feet already are you?' enquired Lewis.

'No I am not. It's just that, doesn't tha think we should think about it a bit first?'

'No, there's no time like the present, so let's get on with it. I'll make a notice what we can pin on the canteen door, then all them that's there can join in and you can give a speech Willie.'

'Not on your Nellie.'

'But you'll have to.'

'Why me?'

'Because you are the secretary of Murgatroyd's Christmas club,' said Dick, with the satisfied grin of a Cheshire cat.

'Since when?' enquired Willie.

'Since just now,' said Dick and Willie, looking at the faces of his workmates, realised there was no future in protesting.

Arthur left the assembled throng and walked into the Dyer's office, where Seth Whitehead was enjoying his breakfast and newspaper in peace. He looked at Arthur just like a man who didn't want to be disturbed.

'What the hell do you want?'

'I want to borrow a big piece of paper and a pencil.'

'What for?'

'To write out a notice about us new Christmas club.'

'What new Christmas club?'

'The one what Willie's running.'

'I didn't know nothing about no Christmas club.'

'Neither did Willie until two minutes ago. Have you got a big piece of paper and a pencil that I can have, then?'

'You can use the back of one of them old daily piece recode sheets, there.'

He pointed to a pile of old sheets of paper that he had been indiscriminately thrown into a corner over a period of years so that they had formed an abstract heap that any modern art gallery would have been pleased to exhibit.

'Can I borrow your pencil as well?'

'You'll want me to write the bloody thing next.'

'You can if you want.'

'Bugger off out of it,' he shouted as Arthur made a hurried exit from the office, paper and pencil in hand and then as an after thought, 'Be sharp about it as well, it's almost time to start work again.'

Seth carefully put his foot behind the office door and savagely kicked it so that it swung to and almost travelled straight through the frame. He sat down, and closed his eyes, well contented with the pleasantries he had exchanged with a member of his staff.

Arthur sat down with the others and began to print in big letters.

MURGATROYDS CHRISTMAS CLUB
SECRETARY WILLIE ARKENTHWAITE
FIRST MEETING TODAY
MILL CANTEEN
QUARTER PAST TWELVE

Willie continued to protest, but the others just told him to shut up, and Arthur nipped across the yard and up one flight of stairs to the canteen which stood over the wool warehouse, where he pinned the notice on the door so that all attending diners would see it.

CHAPTER 5

As the morning ambled along, Willie's thoughts turned more and more often to the Christmas club. Usually he didn't have any coherent ideas worth speaking of, but this day was different. Each time he turned his attention to the club, his first thoughts were of a huge table laden with all the trimmings of a first class Christmas dinner, surrounding a huge turkey and a giant Christmas pudding sitting side by side in the middle. These two items were so large that they obliterated his view of his mother-in-law who was seated behind them. He could however see Thelma and all the kids well attired, all dressed up in party hats, boxes of crackers just waiting to be pulled, streamers, decorations, holly, mistletoe, presents by the score, a huge Christmas tree and everything that they had never been able to afford on Christmas day before.

Following the best part of the vision, he then began to focus on such things as when he would collect the money, how would he make a record of what he had collected, where would he keep the money, when would he pay it out again, how would he know how much to pay out and to whom? All these and another thousand questions went unanswered.

Dinner time came and Willie, following his well tried routine, dashed across the mill yard and hurtled up the canteen stairs to be first in the queue. He never washed his hands before dinner as this would make him miss the front of the line, a position he had held for many years, with only the very occasional miss, and one which he was not going to give up lightly. In order to make sure of pole position he didn't even remove the thick leather dyers apron, but dived out of the dyehouse like a fox being chased by the hounds.

His iron soled clogs made a ringing sound on the stone steps and sure enough he was there once again and able to read proudly the notice convening the meeting, which was pinned to the door outside the canteen. He was so engrossed in reading this notice that he was unaware of Sarah Anne Green, who was almost always second in the queue and the upwards of two hundred other people who were queuing behind them. It was only when one of the more impatient weavers dug his finger into Willies spine that he awoke from his dream like trance.

'Come on Willie, what's up with yer?' they were shouting from below.

'All right, all right, hang on a minute.' And still he continued to admire the notice.

Sarah Anne Green whispered in his ear. 'Take it down and pin it up against the servery, or else it'll get hidden at the back of the door and that will be the last you will see of it.'

In the midst of the cat calls, boos and shouts, Willie carefully took out the drawing pins and with the notice in hand he opened the canteen door and was propelled forward by the seething human tide towards the servery hatch.

Greasy Martha never opened the hatch until such time as the hungry mob made so much noise with banging and shouting that she was forced to do so. Her motto was, "Let em wait." And in true tradition the hatch was closed when the disorderly queue presented itself to be served. Sarah Anne Green showed Willie where to pin the notice for greatest effect, on a flat part of the partition that divided the preparation and eating areas, near to the serving hatch.

Willie agreed that it was a good spot and as he went through the motions of pinning it up again he asked, 'Are you going to join the Christmas club then?'

'I don't know. I can only afford half a crown a week at most. I'll have to see. I'll think about it whilst I eat my dinner.'

'What the bloody hell's that then and whatever it is you can take it down again right now.'

Willie and Sarah Anne had been so engrossed in conversation that they had not noticed the hatch open and Greasy Martha look out at them.

'Nay Martha love it's about the meeting here after dinner. It's about our new Christmas club and we're having a meeting here to sort out the job a bit like.'

'Well first of all William Arkenthwaite, I am not your love and secondly, you can take it off there here and now.'

'Nay. Aren't you going to join in?'

'What? Me? Join 'owt that you lot have 'owt to do with? Nay, credit me with some sense please.'

She snuffled, snorted and grunted to herself, making Willie, not for the first time, have visions of her and a lot more, round, pink bodied, short legged, curly tailed animals in a sty all together, with their trotters in the trough, lunching.

Her rasping voice awakened him from his dreams. 'What about this dinner? Do you want it or not? And get that poster off my wall.'

Willie picked up his dinner and moved away a few paces, then turning to face Martha. 'I'll move it when I've had my dinner Martha, love.'

'I've told you before I'm not your love.' But Willie was out of earshot, hurrying to the corner table.

Sarah Anne always sat with her cronies on the next table to Willie and when she arrived he was tucking into his plateful like there was no tomorrow.

'You'll have to move that there notice, Willie.'

'Nay, Sarah Anne, I shan't, just you wait and see.' He turned his attention to the more pressing matter of devouring his dinner. His eating habits and table manners were no better when he was out than when he was at home. He noisily guzzled what had been described as beef stew with boiled potatoes and carrots and by the time that Lewis Armitage arrived he was just in the act of picking up his plate to drink the gravy from it before licking it clean.

'Martha's playing hell about yond notice,' observed Lewis.

'Take no notice of the old bag. What's for pudding?' he replied in one breath.

'Manchester tart.'

'Eh great, one of my favourites, I'd best get into the queue.' Away he trotted to join the end of the by now diminishing queue where he came across his old friend Eustace who as usual, was last in line for the first course.

'Hello Willie, what's that notice by the serving hatch? What's for dinner? Are you playing cards after dinner?'

'Which question shall I answer first?'

'Eh?'

'Which question shall I...oh never mind. That notice is about the new Christmas club. We're having a meeting here after dinner, so you'd best get a move on and eat up.'

'A meeting, are we Willie? A meeting? What for? What about? Are you going to stand up and say summat Willie?'

A sudden horrible thought hit Willie like being smashed with a sledge hammer and then acute panic set in. 'A speech! A speech! I couldn't make a speech! What about? It's all Arthur's fault. Nay, I can't make a speech. Not in public.' He was awakened from his state of panic by the mellow tones of Eustace once again.

'What are you going to say Willie? Can I join Willie? Can I?'

Before Willie had time to answer they had arrived at the serving hatch and Eustace took his dinner. Willie gave Martha a nice smile.

'Now Martha, my dear, what's for pudding today?'

'You don't deserve no sweet, sticking notices up on my wall.'

'Come on now, fair do's, it's only until after dinner, then we're having a meeting, then it can come down again.'

'Who says you're having a meeting here? I've got to wash up, clear up and clean up. You're going to delay me and it's not good enough. I'm overworked now without any monkey business from you lot.'

'Aren't you going to put anything into this Christmas club then Martha? It'll be a proper do you know, not a two penny halfpenny affair.'

'It might not be a bad idea you know. That's if it's all above board and legal like. I'll think about it and see what happens at meeting.'

'Well whilst you're thinking about it, just cut me an extra big slice of Manchester tart, I aren't half hungry.'

'Was there ever a time when you weren't and anyway what makes you think you're entitled to a bigger slice than anyone else?'

'I've a lot to do, sorting out this here Christmas club and I need all the strength I can get. Besides which, I always do.'

Martha, grunting and grumbling, cut him an extra large slice of the tart and put it on a meat plate for him.

Dick Jordan put down his knife and fork and sat back, absolutely amazed at the spectacle before him. There was Willie with the biggest piece of Manchester tart he had ever seen, holding it up to his mouth, fingers in the cold custard and jam, thumbs supporting the pastry base from beneath, enjoying huge bites without putting it down or having time to enjoy one mouthful before the next was shoved in. As if this wasn't enough, the tart suddenly collapsed into one thousand bits and cascaded all over the table, the diners and the floor.

'Bloody Hell!' said Willie

'You nasty horrible little bugger,' said Dick. 'You must have left your manners in your mother's womb.'

Arthur Baxter was laughing uncontrollably and was in imminent danger of spitting out his mouthful of stew as he watched Willie collecting bits of Manchester tart from other people's dinners, from the table, and from the floor to assemble them on his plate, where he dived in again with fingers and thumbs.

'Why don't you use a spoon?'

'What for?'

'To bloody well eat your pudding.'

'Nay it's just as easy with my fingers.' With that, he continued to guzzle.

Whilst the others were fetching and eating their puddings, Willie was doing just that to his pint of tea which he slopped onto the floor on his way back to the table. Having arrived there he slurped as much as he could, on purpose, much to the disgust of those around him. They should have been used to it, but never quite were. Having emptied the pint pot and replaced it on the table; Willie proceeded to get the playing cards from the window ledge where they resided when not in use.

'Hang on a minute Willie, We've no time for cards today,' said Arthur.

'Why not Arthur?'

'Because…' then he pleaded, '…oh, give me strength. Because we're having the opening meeting of the Christmas club aren't we?'

'Oh aye.' Willie replaced the cards on the window ledge. 'Right. Let's get on with it then.'

'Wait till I've finished my dinner. I shan't be a minute now and then we'll have a bit of a try at it.'

As soon as he was ready, Arthur stood up and looked around at the assembled diners. Then he banged his pudding spoon hard on the table to get everyone's attention.

There was a spontaneous show of quietness by all there except Greasy Martha. Who called out, 'Oy, watch what you're doing with my spoon.'

She was howled down by the crowd and the silence returned as the attention of all turned back to Arthur.

'Er, ladies and gentlemen, er, friends, er, we, er, that is to say, Willie Arkenthwaite has proposed-'

'We hope you'll be very happy.'

'Who to?'

'He's already got one wife and a mother-in-law and a horde of kids.'

Arthur waited for the audience's comments to subside and began again. 'Ladies and gentlemen, Willie Arkenthwaite has suggested-'

'Nay. Shame.'

'The dirty old bugger.'

'I'm never going near him again.'

Once again the uproar subsided and Arthur continued. 'That we should have a, er, Christmas club. The lads in the, er, dyehouse think it's happen a good idea and, er, so, er, I give you Willie Arkenthwaite.'

A lone voice shouted, 'And we give him straight back to you.'

Arthur sat down to thunderous applause. He looked at Willie who studiously avoided his glance, but Dick Jordan, anticipating a problem, was already pushing Willie to try to get him to stand up.

Willie refused to move.

He sat stiffly, holding the edge of the table and just would not budge. The combined persuasive powers of Arthur, Dick and Lewis failed to move him. They pleaded, cajoled and threatened him, all to no avail. Even Sarah Anne Green came over and tried to reason with him without success. Eustace had a try, but gave it up before he had started properly, but then Arthur had a brilliant idea. He walked around the back of Willie, bent down and took hold of the legs of Willie's chair and pulled it hard from under him, taking the chair a fair distance away.

Willie came down to earth with a bump and lay flat on the floor, much to the amusement of the diners who responded to this fine bit of acrobatics with another round of applause. He then picked himself up and turned to face the crowd. Carefully he removed a dew drop from the end of his nose by wiping it on his shirt sleeve, then belched out loud, much to the amusement of the assembly.

Having taken a deep breath and realising there was no escape he began to speak. 'Ladies and Gentlemen-' He stopped and didn't know where to go from there. There were boos and catcalls at the delay, and even applause from one corner, and then he started again. 'Arthur says we want a Christmas club.'

'Nay it were your idea, not mine,' shouted Arthur.

'Well now, happen it were,' retorted Willie, who secretly liked to accept the thanks for putting up the idea in the first place. 'Well me and Arthur were talking last night and we thought as how we needed a Christmas club for all of us here at t' mill so we shan't be short next Christmas same as what we were this Christmas. So me and Arthur mentioned it to t' lads in t' dyehouse this morning and they thought it were a good idea too.'

He stopped to come up for air, and because he had dried up, but not for long.

'It's come on us a bit sudden like and none of us has any idea how to get along, so if any of you lot knows, let's be hearing from you.'

He sat down to tumultuous applause, as pleased as punch with himself. When the applause had died down and Arthur had finished congratulating him, there was a long pregnant pause, following which there quiet moans and groans as Daniel Sykes rose to his feet.

Daniel was a tall, thin, intellectual type of chap, who was the foreman weaver, thought he was God's gift to everything and was in fact a well known pain in the backside. Arthur had been known on several occasions over the years to remark that Daniel should have had a first class degree in boring people.

Daniel began to speak, 'It appears obvious to me that we should elect a steering committee to administer the affairs of the Christmas club. Even set up a trust in order that the full value of any tax advantage to be gained from such a move can be obtained for our benefit.' At which point he sat down and everyone stared in his direction.

'We aren't having him on t' committee,' Arthur hurriedly pointed out to Willie.

'No. He can have his own club,' Lewis replied.

Dick said, 'Hold on a minute though. He might have a point and know summat that we don't.'

Willie looked at them with a smile on his face. 'Well I think we ought to elect a committee, then ask Mr Antony Murgatroyd what to do next. He's bound to know.'

'You're excelling yourself today, Willie,' said Lewis.

'Aye it's that Manchester tart. I could just eat another big slice. Do you think there might be one? I think I'll just go and see.'

'Sit down and stay here,' said Dick. 'This is serious stuff we're at.'

Nothing much happened at all next. The four people at the centre of the discussion stared at one another and the rest of the room chatted amongst themselves. Eventually, after what seemed to Willie to be a lifetime, Sarah Anne Green stood up, banged her dirty pudding spoon on the table and bellowed for silence.

'By the look of things these men are a bit lost, as usual, with something a bit more complicated than normal, so I think we should take a vote to see if we want, or even need, a Christmas club-.'

She was rudely interrupted as Willie sprang to his feet.

'Yes, yes, that's it. Let's have a vote to see if we want a Christmas club. Now then all those in favour raise-'

'Hold on a minute Willie Arkenthwaite, shut your blathering and sit down. You wouldn't have known ought about having a Christmas club if I hadn't suggested it, so I'll carry on with it. All those in favour?'

There were a very limited few who didn't vote.

'All those against?'

Only Greasy Martha put her hand up. There were boos and cat calls, but she loved them all and rose to the occasion proffering a series of well aimed gestures.

'Well it looks as if we've got ourselves a Christmas club, or the beginnings of one at least. Now I'll hand you back to your mater of ceremonies Mr Arthur Baxter.'

Sarah Anne sat down to wild applause and Arthur slowly rose to his feet.

'Er, I would like to thank Sarah Anne for her, er, very valuable, er, contribution to the ,er, er, proceedings. Now, er, it looks like that we should elect a committee and I suggest that Sarah Anne Green becomes Chairman.'

There were murmurs of approval from around the room, except from Willie who began to see his chance of stardom slipping away from his grasp.

He tugged on Arthur's sleeve. 'What about me Arthur?'

'Oh, you can be treasurer. Yes, treasurer, that's the most important job of all.'

'Treasurer? Eh? Oh yes, treasurer.' A smile lit his face from corner to corner.

Arthur continued, 'Now we should, er, take a vote on Chairman, er, Sarah Anne Green, but first we should, er, ask her, er, are you, er, willing?'

'Of course she's willing, she always has been,' came a lone voice from the diners.

'Er, er, are you willing to become the chairman of Murgatroyd's Christmas club for the next twelve months, Sarah Anne?'

Sarah Anne stood up. 'Yes Mr Baxter, I am willing to become chairman for the next twelve months.'

'Mr Baxter? Who the hell's Mr Baxter,' came another shout from the crowd which was again ignored by the dignitaries.

'Now ladies and Gentlemen, er , can we have a, er, vote for Sarah Anne Green as Chairman. Those in, er, favour?'

Almost all of the hands present were raised.

'Er, er, those against?'

There were no dissenters.

'Er, right, Sarah Anne Green is elected, er, Chairman. Come over here lass, tha'd best take charge now. Come over here.'

Sarah Anne walked over slowly. She was a small woman with a grim determination and, with anything she did, she did work hard at it. She had had little thought that as she had read the notice at the top of the canteen steps that she could possibly be involved in the Christmas club and had as yet not quite come to terms with what was happening. However she put on a brave face and looked at the audience. She paused for a few seconds then began to speak.

'Ladies and Gentlemen. I would like to thank you for the confidence you have expressed in me, in electing me to be your chairman. I shall do my best to ensure that the club runs smoothly and that we do the best for all of you that invest your money with us. Now, in common with all other clubs we do need to elect a number of officials, namely secretary, treasurer and a committee. It would seem to be appropriate that Arthur Baxter and Willie Arkenthwaite should be involved as it was their idea in the first place. Lewis Armitage and Dick Jordan should I think be elected as they have been involved from the very beginning and probably two others from amongst you which would give us a good strong committee to sort out the club during the year.' At this point she sat down on the edge of Arthur's chair.

Arthur leaned on Sarah Anne and whispered in her ear, 'I say, Willie wants to be treasurer and I'll be secretary if it's alright with you.'

'It's alright with me as far as you are concerned, but I'm not so sure about Willie. Let's see what the rest of them say.'

She rose to face her audience once more. 'Arthur Baxter has kindly volunteered to act as secretary and Willie Arkenthwaite as treasurer. Now can we please take a vote on these two very important positions? Firstly for Arthur Baxter as secretary.'

She watched a unanimous show of hands.

'Thank-you, that was a total vote for Arthur. Now for Willie Arkenthwaite as treasurer.'

At this point the number of hands raised did not constitute a majority.

'Come on now friends, it was Willie's idea after all.'

More hands were raised than for the first vote.

'Those against?'

Greasy Martha's hand went up once more, but that was all.

'Motion carried. Arthur Baxter is elected secretary and Willie Arkenthwaite is elected treasurer.'

She sat down by Arthur again and whispered in his ear, 'What about Willie? Is he to be trusted to keep the books in order? He's not dishonest, I know, but when it comes to his ability to keep things straight…well quite frankly it worries me.'

'It worries me as well, lass. We shall just have to keep our eyes on him, that's all.'

47

'Right. We're running rapidly out of time, so we'd best get the election of the rest of the committee over and then we can get down to sorting out the finer details.'

She stood up again.

'Ladies and Gentlemen. We would now like to elect four committee members. As I said earlier, Dick Jordan and Lewis Armitage are willing to offer their services and therefore I would like you to vote for them. Those for?'

She watched as ninety nine percent of the hands were raised.

'Good, they are elected; now we need two more. Any nominations?'

Daniel Sykes stood up once again and addressed the gathering. 'In my opinion, for what my opinion is worth around here-'

'Here here,' came an interruption.

Daniel frowned in the direction of the lone voice. 'As I was saying, before I was so rudely interrupted, in my opinion the committee needs someone to join it with a knowledge of how business matters are carried out and one whose voice can carry some weight in various circles as and when it might be needed-'

'Does that mean someone what's a bit top heavy upstairs like?' came the same lone voice.

Daniel rose to the challenge 'If you mean someone with a good business brain then, yes I do, and furthermore I have much pleasure in offering myself for election as I am sure that I can be of real value to this committee.'

'There's nowt like a bit of cheek,' Willie observed to Arthur. 'What are we going to do now?'

'Nay. I don't know, except we shall have to fix everything before the meetings so that he's bugger all to do with owt when we do have a meeting and try not to have so many meetings either. What do you say Sarah Anne?'

'It will be very difficult with him, but we can't just ignore him. Let's get a vote taken.'

She rose again.

'Right Ladies and Gentlemen. Daniel Sykes has put his own name forward for election. Can we please take a vote? Those in favour?'

There was a mixed reception.

'Those against?'

Yet again a mixed reception.

'I think we'd better have a count, it looks pretty even to me.'

So they took a count with Arthur as secretary counting and he produced a majority of five votes in favour.

Daniel stood up again. 'I would just like to express my thanks to those who voted for me for the confidence you have shown in me. I will serve you to the best of my ability.' He sat down again.

Willie groaned, 'We're in for it now with him on t' committee, it should have been five vote t' other way.'

Sarah Anne whispered to Arthur, 'Now there's just one more to elect, who should it be do you think?'

'Well I know he's a bit daft, but I think that Eustace Ollerenshaw will do as he is told without question.'

'Let's see if there are any volunteers first,' said Sarah Anne as she rose to her feet yet again. 'Now we need just one more committee member. Have we any volunteers?'

She carefully scanned the blank, disinterested rows of faces in front of her and then turned to Arthur, 'Well, shall we ask Eustace?'

Arthur consulted Willie who was dozing off to sleep and awoke with a start. 'What about asking Eustace?'

'Asking him what?'

'Asking him if he'll be on t' committee.'

'Aye go on then. He'll be alright.'

Arthur turned to Sarah Anne, 'Yes ask Eustace.'

Sarah Anne faced the audience again. 'It has been suggested that Eustace Ollerenshaw be asked to join the committee.'

There was a low level of murmuring and a few laughs and sniggers were heard. Sarah Anne looked at Eustace and continued, 'Eustace Ollerenshaw, are you willing to stand?'

'He couldn't be willing if he tried,' came the interruption from the same source as before.

'I will ignore that very rude interruption and ask the question again. Eustace Ollerenshaw, are you willing to stand as a candidate for election to the Christmas club committee?'

Eustace from his nearby seat looked at Sarah Anne, then at Arthur and finally at Willie. 'On the committee? Me? On the committee? Yes, please, Yes, please.'

'Right Eustace Ollerenshaw is willing to stand as a committee member. All those in favour?'

There was a unanimous show of hands. Not because they favoured Eustace for the job, but more because they didn't want to be involved themselves.

'Eustace Ollerenshaw is elected to the committee.'

Sarah Anne sat down. She, Willie and Arthur held a short discussion and then she stood up again.

'Ladies and Gentlemen, the committee will meet within a very short time and we will put a notice up on the canteen wall to inform you all of the progress or otherwise that we have made and the method we shall employ to collect your money. Thank-you all.'

She sat down to a round of good, solid applause and the workforce of Murgatroyd's, who finished their lunch, drifted away in ones and twos as it was just about time to start work again.

'When and where shall we be holding the inaugural meeting of the committee?' enquired Daniel Sykes when the group of elected officers had all gathered around the corner table.

Arthur Baxter spoke up. 'Speaking as Secretary, I think we should hold a meeting in the working men's club at eight o'clock.'

'Women isn't allowed in,' Quipped Willie.

'They are into t' committee room and seeing as its Tuesday there'll be nowt on, so we can have it. I'll call and see Fat Harry on my way home and fix it up. Does that suit everybody?'

There were murmurs of assent except from Daniel Sykes. 'I am not altogether in favour of attending a meeting which will be held on licensed premises.'

'Well where would you have it then?' snapped Lewis.

'I don't exactly know. Probably the Church Sunday school, but I suppose I shall have to bow to the decision of the majority. Where exactly is the committee room in the club?'

'Yes, I was wondering that,' said Sarah Anne.

'First door on the left as you go through the front door of the club. You can't miss it. Anyway, I'll call for you Sarah Anne so that you won't have to go by yourself.' said Arthur.

'Thank-you. Right that's it, time for work again. See you in the club at eight.'

The meeting broke up and they all went back to their various departments.

CHAPTER 6

As Fat Harry moved sideways along the bar to serve Willie and Eustace, the polished edge of the bar counter became even more polished than it was before as his guts pressed against the edge of the wooden top.

'So they've dragged you onto this committee then have they Eustace? You'll have to watch em; they'll give you nowt but mugging jobs, mark my words. I've known them for a long time,' said Fat Harry in one of his more jovial moods.

'Oh I don't think...I, er, don't think they'll er-'

'Who else is on this committee then?' asked Harry.

'Er, er, er, oh yes, er, er, Sarah Anne Green, Willie Arkenthwaite, er, er, er, me and er, Arthur, Lewis Armitage, and er, Dick Jordan. Oh yes there's Daniel Sykes as well. That's er, let's see now, there'll be er, that's a difficult one. Willie, how many of us are there then?'

'Nay, Eustace, I haven't counted em yet. Let's see now there's me and you and Arthur, that's three and-'

'Seven.'

'Seven what Harry?' asked Willie.

Harry, very patiently for him, replied, 'Seven of you on this committee of yours.'

Eustace started talking again. 'Seven of us are there? Is there? Willie, seven of us on the committee. Hey won't it be good, won't it Willie? Eh, won't it be good?'

Fat Harry asked, 'This here Daniel Sykes, is that him what lives up Rougher Brow?'

'Aye,' said Willie.

'Not one of my better customers.'

'That's right.'

'Well known locally as a self opinionated twit. Thinks he knows everything there is to know about everything and its cousin?'

'The very same.'

'Knows nowt about owt when it comes down to it.'

'Exactly.'

'Heaven help the rest of you then. We shall just have to hope we can get him blind drunk by lacing his lemonade.'

'Not a cat in hells chance. He won't even drink a glass of free water for nowt.'

Arthur put his head around the door. 'A pint for me please, Harry, and a gin and tonic for the chairman.'

'Nay,' said Willie. 'We won't have any tonic. Nobody's wanted a tonic in here since goodness knows when.'

'Just a minute. Just a minute, William Arkenthwaite, I'll thank you not to make ill founded accusations on these premises.'

'What?'

'We do have some tonic, I'll have you know. Just a couple of bottles that we keep for visiting dignitaries and the like. And as your Chairman is one, she can have one.'

'How do you know our Chairman's a she?'

'Well none of you lot is fit to be chairman of owt, and anyway, I saw Arthur come in with her.'

'Well you've fair surprised me Harry. I've never seen soft drinks in here before.'

'You've got the club committee to thank for that. It was their insistence that we keep a few bottles for emergencies and that sort of thing.'

'Come on Harry,' urged Arthur who had come back into the bar. 'Can't keep a lady waiting like this; we need to make a good impression for our visitors.'

He took the two drinks from the bar after paying for them and looked at Willie. 'Are you and your friend coming into the committee room sometime tonight Willie? Or not?'

'Aye. We'll just have another one in before we come. Won't be a minute.'

Arthur disappeared with his drinks.

Lewis and Dick opened the front door and came into the warmth of the club from the freezing cold exterior.

'Cor, it isn't half cold out there tonight, proper brass monkey weather. Is everybody here?' asked Dick.

'All apart from Daniel Sykes. He's got three minutes to be late, and he won't be.

'Right we'll just get ourselves a pint and catch you up in a couple of minutes.'

Arthur entered the committee room for the second time that evening. It was a small room with a dark, brown, painted, panelled, oak bottom half and a dirty with age cream top half. In the middle was a table to seat eight people, sporting what had once been a good quality green baize cover. A large carved antique oak sideboard stood at one side of the room, holding old records, old minute books and other numerous articles concerning the club. There was a black leaded fireplace in the centre of one wall, with a huge fire roaring away in it, and over the top of it was a hideous clock with a monotonous tick donated to the club by a local widow in loving memory of her late husband, (sadly for the club's profits, departed this life), for the many happy hours, (and unknown to her, blind drunk hours), he had spent there, before she had finally put him to rest. Over the table was a single, dirty, sixty watt light bulb and the room was completed by a multitude of glass ashtrays. The overall effect, if one includes the threadbare carpet, was one of utter dinginess.

'Here you are Sarah Anne, one gin and tonic which, incidentally, took a bit of getting as we don't have many lady guests or soft drinks for that matter. Sorry about the state of this room and the hard chairs, but it's only used the odd night in any week at the most, and then, apart from the club annual general meeting, only for short committee meetings.'

'It's not too bad; it's just the smell of stale beer and cigarettes that make it uncomfortable. Still, it's better than nowhere, and at least we can get started here, although we shan't need many committee meetings during the year. It's really only at year end and pay out time that we need a proper meeting.'

Daniel Sykes walked in and took off his scarf, gloves, mac and cap. Having carefully stowed the scarf, gloves and cap in the pockets and sleeves of the mac, he carefully hung it on the sole hook that he found at the back of the door. 'It smells foul in here. I object to these sorts of stale odours, they numb your brain and give you a feeling of nausea. Can we have the windows open please and let in some fresh air?'

'No you can't,' said Willie who had entered the room very quietly, 'You can't because it's bloody cold outside and anyway, there aren't any windows in this room what'll open.'

'Well I think it's disgusting having to sit here, inhaling this sickening atmosphere all evening. It's not good enough.'

'Tha can always go home. Tha knows there's nowt to stop thee.'

Willie's hackles always rose when confronted by someone like Daniel Sykes.

'Now then you two,' said the chairman, 'give over bickering and let's get the meeting under way, it is eight o'clock.'

'Yes I believe we have a quorum present,' observed Daniel and with great satisfaction he stared at Willie knowing full well that he would not understand, only to be confirmed by Willie's next remark.

'Well where is it?'

'Where's what?'

'This here quorit thing what you're on about?'

'This here quorit thing happens to be a quorum. Now to explain in simple terms-'

'Hey, not so much of the simple.'

'I mean no disrespect to yourself Willie. I mean that so as to keep the matter the least complicated.'

'Oh yes. Very well then.'

'As I was saying, to keep it in its simplest terms, a quorum is when we have a large enough minimum number of eligible members present to run a meeting and take a vote. At present we have five out of seven which should be quite enough.'

'Actually we do have a full seven. Dick and Lewis will be here in a minute, they're just in the bar getting a drink,' said Arthur.

Daniel started talking again. 'I do think we should find a better meeting place than this, such as the Church hall or somewhere.'

'Are they licensed?' asked Willie.

'Certainly not.'

'Then it's a waste of time even talking about it.' Willie took the opportunity to have a loud belch, which everyone chose to ignore.

'Willie. Can you please go to the bar and ask both Dick and Lewis to come in so that we can start the meeting,' asked the Chairman.

'Aye, I can do that right now.'

He disappeared, to reappear two minutes later with the by now two late arrivals.

'Right,' said Sarah Anne, 'please be seated everyone. In order that we can keep the meetings as informal as possible I will not stand up to speak. Arthur have you got pen and paper at the ready to take notes for the minutes?'

'Yes I have.'

'What's he got to take a note of the time for?' asked Willie.

'Some committee this is going to be,' said Daniel.

'Now Daniel, please keep all personal remarks to yourself in future, and Willie the minutes are nothing to do with time, they are a write up of the meeting so that a record of proceedings can be kept by the secretary. It's a bit like a history of the meetings.'

'What do we want a record of the proceedings for?'

'So that we can refer to them from time to time if we need to, and so that, as time goes on, a true record of all that has taken place with the Christmas club can be kept.'

Daniel Sykes sat quietly sulking, having been ticked off by Sarah Anne.

'Now as duly elected Chairman of Murgatroyd's Christmas club, I declare the meeting open at 8.10pm.'

Arthur made a note on his pad and Willie leaned over to see what he was writing.

'What have you written 8.10 there for Arthur?' he whispered.

'So that I can write it in the minutes.'

Sarah Anne ignored the interruption and continued, 'I have worked out a short agenda so as to give us a basis to work on, starting with who is eligible for membership of the club. Has anyone any thoughts on this matter?'

Lewis was the first to speak. 'Well seeing that it's Murgatroyd's Christmas club it seems only right and proper that only folks as works at the mill should be able to join.'

'Yes,' said Daniel Sykes, 'this is a very good idea and very much along the lines that I was thinking. It would make administration that much easier than if folks from far and wide were to join.'

'What happens if Fat Harry or some of the lads from the Club want to join, or someone from the pigeon association, or-'

'Now, Willie. As chairman I have to tell you that as treasurer it will be your job each week to get all the money in, and it will be a hard enough job at Murgatroyd's without a lot of outsiders to think about as well.'

Eustace, who had up until now uttered not one syllable, dozing as he was not able to follow the conversation, suddenly came to life. 'Will it? Will it? Willie? Will it be your job to collect all the money every week? Will it? Hey won't that be grand?' Thereupon, having made his first worthwhile contribution to the event, he went back to his dozing.

Arthur then had his turn.

'I agree with Lewis and Daniel, we should only admit people who work at the mill. It's not fair for strangers from far and wide to join and as Sarah Anne says Willie, you've enough on your plate at the mill without making more work for yourself.'

'I weren't talking about strangers joining, just folk what we know.'

'I used the word strangers to cover folk that we know that don't work at the mill.'

'Oh yes, but there might just be a few of us mates that might want to join, like Fat Harry and them.'

Sarah Anne addressed Willie, 'Have you actually asked Fat Harry, as you call him and whomsoever your mates might be, if they want to join?'

'Not yet. I was going to do that later tonight.'

'And what if they don't?'

'Don't want to join our Christmas club? Nay, they'll never not want to join.'

The secretary said, 'Well now, I think we should put it to the vote.'

'Yes.' Said Daniel Sykes. 'It's about time we stopped all this useless chatter about Fat Harry and got on with something more positive.'

'Right,' said the Chairman, 'the motion is "All those in favour of keeping the Christmas club to the employees of Murgatroyd's only." All those in favour?'

There was an almost unanimous show of hands, then Willie reluctantly raised his. About this time, Willie began to have an urgent need to snook up and spit out.

'Good. Motion carried. Right now the second item on the agenda is-'

'Hang on a minute. I can't write that fast,' said the secretary.

'Willie belched noisily and said, 'Time for another round I think.' He stood up and walked over to the bell push that was set in the wall adjacent the sideboard. He leaned on the push button for longer than necessary.

'Fat Harry'll just be saying, "There's no peace working at a club like this. Why can't they hold a meeting without me having to walk around there and fetch them another round of drinks." Then he'll come clomping around the bar and walk down here, clomp, clomp, clomp, any time now. Listen for him. Here he comes, clomp, clomp, clomp.'

Sure enough the door opened and Fat Harry's huge, beaming face appeared around it. 'Did you ring sir?'

Willie was just about to make his usual reply of 'no, it was probably a giraffe having a fart what disturbed you, but now you're here we might as well have another round' when he remembered that there was a lady present and checked himself. Instead he said, 'Yes please Steward, we'd like another round of drinks please.'

'Hey? Yer what? You've never asked for owt politely before.'

'No,' agreed Willie. 'But you see steward; we've never had a lady present before either.'

Fat Harry turned his head and let his gaze rest on Sarah Anne, at which his manner changed visibly.

'Well, Sarah Anne Green. I haven't seen you in years. Nobody told me it was you that was coming to this meeting. Well, I never did. How are you my love?' and he stood with a broad grin on his face, staring at Sarah Anne.

She, being in her early forties and still carrying a model like figure, felt herself slowly turning the colour of a well pickled beetroot and was for once lost for words. 'Er, er, hello Harry. I didn't know that you were the steward at the club.'

'This could prove to be more than interesting,' whispered Lewis to Dick.

'What did you say Lewis?' enquired Eustace. 'I couldn't hear you. What did you say?'

'I coughed in French.'

'How do you do that Lewis? How do you cough in French? Can you teach me to do it? Can you Lewis? Can you?'

'What on earth possessed you to bring along an imbecile like him?' asked Fat Harry of no one in particular.

Daniel Sykes rose to his feet and addressed the meeting. 'As you are all aware I was against this meeting being held on licensed premises, but seeing that it is, can we please get on with it.'

Sarah Anne had by this time composed herself again. 'Yes, everyone wants the same drink again, can you please bring another round Harry.'

'Certainly. For you Sarah Anne, with the greatest of pleasure,' and he left the room.

Sarah Anne now took complete control of herself and the meeting. 'We have already decided that Murgatroyd's Christmas club will be open only to those who are directly involved as Murgatroyd's employees. So the next item on the agenda is how's best, and when to collect the money that members will pay into the club.'

'Well I think I shall put it in an old biscuit tin. I can happen get one from t' co-op.'

'That is exactly the type of stupid remark that one expects to hear from our treasurer,' said Daniel Sykes.

'Oh, and what's wrong with what I said Mr ever so High and mighty, pray?'

'All right you two. That is enough,' said the Chairman. 'We are not here so that you two can have a verbal battle, we have a job to do so can we get on with it please. The next question is when to collect the money. Has anyone any suggestions to offer?'

Eustace, from whom, no one in the room expected any sensible contribution to the debate, suddenly came to life. 'Friday dinner time. Yes that's it, Friday dinner time, isn't it? Isn't it? Friday dinner time, yes, that the right time. Friday.'

The other members of the committee were gob smacked and sat staring at him in total silence. Only Arthur had the presence of mind to pull himself together and stop what might otherwise have been a very long utterance.

'Why Friday dinner time?'

Eustace looked blank for a few seconds and Arthur asked the question again. 'Why Friday dinner time?'

'Because I've just been paid and I'll have enough money to pay with, shan't I Arthur? Shan't I? Just have been paid and I'll have some money, won't I Arthur? Won't I?'

'Yes Eustace, you will, and so will everyone else in the mill as long as they've been to collect their wages from the penny hoil, after the hooter's gone.'

'It looks like Friday dinner time in the canteen might be the right time,' said Sarah Anne and, looking around, it seemed that everyone was in agreement. 'Good that's settled. Now about the-'

'Hang on a minute. What about them what goes home for their dinners?' asked Dick.

'They'll have to come back a bit earlier than usual come up to t' canteen to pay their dues,' replied Arthur.

'Yes, there's no reason why they shouldn't return to the mill five minutes earlier than usual to pay up,' confirmed the Chairman. 'Now, how to collect the money. Anybody got any bright ideas?'

Willie could contain himself no longer, the ball of phlegm had been waiting its turn to be removed for ages and so he snooked it up into his mouth. The chairman remonstrated with him. Through the phlegm, Willie made a noise that sounded like an apology, and then he got out of his seat, walked over to the fire and spat the contents into it, where it sizzled merrily away. The Chairman remonstrated with him again.

Daniel Sykes made a discreet coughing noise which drew everyone's attention. 'If Willie was to be seated at the table by the piano, those that were intending to pay could form an orderly queue past the servery hatch, where he could deal with each of them in turn, collecting their money and making an entry in his book.'

'I haven't got a book.'

'A minor detail. You only need something very basic and straightforward, either one page per week or one page per person. Something that is easy to control. I think one page per week would be easiest, in fact, if it were sorted out properly on a large sheet of paper, you could probably organise three or four months at one time on the one sheet.'

Willie looked baffled. All this talk of pages per week, pages per person and three or four months per person had made him think that possibly he had bitten off more than he could chew. His thoughts, such as they were, were interrupted by the arrival of Fat Harry carrying a tray of drinks.

'Now, here's your G & T Sarah Anne, love.' He placed the glass in front of her, very carefully and exactly where it should be. 'Do you know it's done me a power of good seeing you again after all these years. I hope you'll have a lot more meetings here. No doubt you have got married since last I saw you.'

Sarah Anne, although colouring up again, remained as calm as possible, concealing the flutterings and stirrings inside her. 'Yes Harry, happily married with two teenage children. How about you?'

'No not me, a bachelor by profession. Matrimony never came my way. Still there's time yet and I live in hopes that-'

He was interrupted by, 'Aye, and we all live in hopes that we might get a drink sometime,' from Willie.

Harry dropped the tray in the middle of the table with a loud bang, stared threateningly at Willie and shouted, 'Right who's paying for this round then?'

There was a deathly hush, not a sound from anywhere, until Arthur spoke out. 'Don't worry Harry, I'll sort it out and let you have the money when we've finished.'

'Right-oh, you know how much it is, so make sure you bring the right amount.'

With a wicked grin and a wink at Sarah Anne, he clomped out. They all sat quietly drinking their pints of beer. Willie was picking his nose and devouring the contents thereof, when Sarah Anne enquired, 'Not had enough tea tonight Willie?'

'Yes, plenty, we had bacon and egg with black pudding, and acres of fat to dip up, and tons of bread, it were great. Why?'

'Nothing really, it was just with you eating again now that I wondered if you hadn't had much tea.'

'I weren't eating, only drinking my beer,' he said very seriously.

'What were you eating Willie?' enquired Eustace.

'Shut up,' said Lewis.

'Can we please get on with the meeting and then I can return home. As you know I make nothing of having to attend licensed premises.'

'Why don't you go home then,' said Willie, but Daniel chose to ignore him and not reply.

Sarah Anne, by now composed yet again, took the meeting in hand. 'We were discussing ways of recording the amounts of money paid into the club each week, and I think it would be an excellent idea if we were to let the secretary and treasurer sort it out between them and arrive at the best method of dealing with it.'

'Hear, hear,' said Daniel Sykes. 'Now the more important question to my way of thinking-'

'Which way is that?' enquired Dick Jordan.

'Why I ever got myself involved with a bunch of ignoramuses like you lot, I'll never know.'

'Who are you calling an ignoramus? I've a good mind to come around there and alter the shape of your face.'

'Now, now,' said the Chairman, 'we cannot sort out matters of importance with all these senseless interruptions. Now please sit down Dick and let us hear no more of this stupidity. Please carry on Daniel. You were saying.'

'I was saying that the more important question is what to do with the money once Willie has collected it.'

'Yes, that was the next item on the agenda. Has anyone any inspiration on this matter?'

'I were thinking of taking it home and keeping it in a tin under the bed.'

Arthur frowned at him. 'Nay lad. I should think we ought to put it in the bank.'

'Daniel put his spoke in again. 'Very definitely, the bank is the place to keep the money. We can use the Northern Counties Bank down Station Lane.'

'Do you bank there Daniel?' enquired the Chairman.

'Er no, that is, I, er, don't possess a bank account.'

'Does anyone have a bank account?' she enquired.

There was no response. Then Willie, suffering a minor brainstorm said, 'We could ask Mr Anthony what to do about a bank account. He goes regularly to the Northern Counties.'

'How do you know?' asked Lewis.

'Because I've seen him when I've been dashing on to Sweeny Todd's to get my hair cut at dinner times.'

'I'm surprised you bother going to Sweeny Todd's with the bit of hair you've got,' continued Lewis.

'Yes he does, he does bank at the Northern Counties bank, he does, he goes regularly. I've seen him when I've been to Sweeny Todd's. Haven't I Willie? Haven't I.'

Sarah Anne decided that she had better bring the meeting back to order, before it got completely out of control.

'Well now, what about the money? It seems to me that Willie, as treasurer, had better get in touch with Mr Anthony and ask him if he will fix us a meeting with the bank manager so that we can open an account. All those in favour?'

All present raised a hand.

'Very good, motion carried. Willie, will you make the necessary arrangements please. Now if there is no other business, it's half past nine and time for home. I declare the meeting closed. Arthur, how much do you want for the G & T?'

'Nay, Sarah Anne. If I can't buy you a drink then I don't know.'

'That's very nice of you Arthur, thank-you. At least you do it from a gentlemanly and friendly angle and not because you're a lecherous leering lout like Harry Howard. Are you coming along home or are you staying here drinking with the rest of them?'

'No, I think I'll walk along home and make sure you are all right. You should be safe enough through the village, but you never know, and in any case, I could do with an early night myself.'

They were just about to go and fetch their coats when Daniel Sykes walked over to them. 'Ah, Sarah Anne, please allow me to escort you home on this most horrible of nights. It can't be very pleasant for a lady to be on her own in the dark.'

A cold shiver ran down Sarah Anne's back but she managed a smile.

'Well that's very good of you Daniel, and I appreciate the thought, but Arthur's going to drop me off on his way home, and anyway, it is out of your way to come past our house.'

'Yes I know, but I just thought I might be of assistance, so, seeing that I can't, I'll bid you all goodnight.' He proceeded to wrestle with his coat to be finally reunited with his cap, scarf and gloves which he very carefully placed on his person in the correct position, precisely, shouted, 'Good-night,' and left the room to a chorus of 'Good-nights' which were soon changed by a lone voice shouting 'Flipping good riddance.'

'Willie, please do not get personal again,' begged the Chairman.

'Well, he's a pain up the-'

'Willie, give over. Live in peace with your fellow man,'

'But he's not my fellow man. He's not even a man at all.' Following which he belched out loud, without apology, and Sarah Anne, half smiling, said, 'No, and neither are you at times.'

'Come on Sarah Anne, get your coat and we can go.'

She put on her coat that had been resting on the back of the chair throughout the meeting. Arthur collected his coat and cap from one of the hooks in the cold draughty corridor and they both prepared to enter the bitter cold outside.

'Are you lads coming with us?' ventured Arthur.

'Nay, not on your Nellie. There's a good hour's drinking yet.' replied Lewis.

'Come on then Sarah Anne.' So, to a chorus of good-nights, they left the club.

*

Arthur and Sarah Anne walked quickly in the bitter, frosty air.

'Thank goodness I got out of the club without Harry Howard seeing me. No Doubt he'd have been trying to be all over me again.'

'Yes, he can be a bit of a nuisance. I think he's harmless enough. In fact I'm sure he is. But you never know, do you?'

As they walked through the village centre Sarah Anne stopped outside Mossop's electrical and radio shop. Staring at a wireless set, 'You know, that's what I'd like to get with my Christmas club money next Christmas. It doesn't say how much they are though, does it? I'd best remember to go and ask on Saturday and I'll not bring Bill because he might not approve.'

'Why? I would have thought that Bill would want a new wireless set, like we all would.'

'Yes, he probably does, but he'd sooner buy himself a new set of wooden bowls.'

They walked on, talking and laughing together. Arthur left Sarah Anne at her garden gate and made his own way home.

*

Back in the club, the remains of the committee made their way into the bar.

'Weren't a bad meeting,' said Willie as they were selecting their dominoes from the face down pack on the table. 'Mind you, I couldn't understand a lot of it.'

'Couldn't you Willie? Couldn't you understand it? Couldn't you. I couldn't either.'

'It was simple enough,' said Lewis. 'Surely you could follow what was going on. Who's got double six?'

'Not me,' said Dick. 'I understood it perfectly. There was nowt not to understand, it was all very straightforward.'

'Aye, but it were all that about how to book it down and what to do with the money that's left me a bit flustered. Anyway, happen Arthur'll help me when the time comes.'

'Time'll be here by Friday, it's not so far away,' said Dick. 'Have any of you decided how much each week you're going to put into the club yet? I think I shall go for five bob.'

'Five bob?' queried Lewis in astonishment. 'I were nobbut thinking, oh, half a crown. It's a lot brass out of our pay is five bob.'

Fat Harry came over to the table where the four friends were getting the dominoes session under way. 'Has him with the constipated gob gone home then?' he bellowed.

'Who's him with the constipated gob then?' enquired Lewis.

'Him from Rougher Brow, Sykes, tha knows, him what's been to your meeting. The lemonade king.'

'I wouldn't say he had a constipated gob.'

'No, more like verbal diarrhoea he's got. It's a bloody purgative he needs rubbing on his throat, not a laxative,' Confirmed Willie. 'Knows all there is to know about everything. There's nothing in the whole wide world he doesn't know, but he hasn't got a bank account, and he didn't know a right lot about banking either. That shut him up in double quick time.'

Eustace, who had been sitting quietly, contemplating space, and not following the conversation too well, suddenly came to life. 'What do you want to rub his neck hoil with a laxative for Willie? Hey, Willie, I say, what do you want to rub his neck hoil with a laxative for?' He looked to Willie for an answer.

'You dunderhead. It was a purgative, on his throat to stop him talking, not a laxative on his neck. A fat lot of good that would have done; it would probably have made his clack drop out. Come to think of it I might just nip into t' weaving shed tomorrow and rub a bit of laxative on his neck hoil. That might shut him up for good.'

Fat Harry bellowed again, 'Where's Sarah Anne Green?' Has she gone home? By gum, she's a bonny lass if ever I saw one. Could do a man good she could. Why didn't you bring her in here with you when you came in?'

'You're a randy old sod,' said Lewis.

'Not so much of the old if you please. Randy I might be, but old I definitely am not.'

'That's a matter of some opinion,' said Willie.

'Now listen here you. I'll sling you straight out of here and over yond hedge in the back if I have any more of your lip.'

'Come on then, come on,' shouted Willie getting excited, 'come on then.' He stood up shadow boxing with clenched fists.

'Sit down for heaven's sake, and both of you, act your age,' said Lewis. 'You're both as daft as each other, and can we please get on with the dominoes?'

Fat Harry laughed. 'Can I join your Christmas club then?' he asked of no one in particular.

'Just a minute,' said Willie sternly and trying to look efficient. 'I am sorry to have to inform you, as treasurer, that it was this evening decided, under rule three, that no one who does not work at Murgatroyd's mill can join the Christmas club and furthermore, seeing that you do not work at all, but spend all day lounging about here, drinking beer, talking and polishing the bar top with your fat guts, you are definitely not allowed to join.' He completed the speech with a good loud belch which true to form he did not excuse.

There followed a stunned silence during which four pairs of eyes were trained on Willie.

The silence was eventually broken by Fat Harry. 'You big, stupid, foul mouthed-'

He was interrupted by Lewis, 'Willie's right Harry, in as far as if you don't work at Murgatroyd's, you can't join. About the rest of the speech, I am not in a position to express an opinion and by the way steward, we are all ready for yet another round of your most excellent ale, so be a good fellow and cut along to your bar where you may prepare and serve the said beverages.'

Harry opened his mouth then closed it again, stared at Lewis, then Willie, then Dick and finally Eustace. Only Eustace wasn't staring back at him. The others were levelling their gaze straight at him without expression, so he stomped away to the bar.

As soon as he was out of earshot, the four friends broke out into loud uproarious laughter.

'How the hell did you manage to speak like that Willie?' asked Dick.

'Nay, I don't know what came over me. It were simple like when I concentrated a bit.' Willie sat back, letting forth yet another ear shattering belch.

'Why don't you get your over generous mother-in-law to tip a bob or two into the club each week Willie?' asked Dick.

'Cos it's not allowed under rule three,' Willie replied sarcastically. 'There again that's probably as good a reason as there is for me not to bother asking the old cow. Mind you, if I could prize a trifle out of her it might not be a right bad do. I might have words with our Thelma and see what she can do about it.'

'Aye, you want to, the more you put in, the more you'll have to come next Christmas. I'm going to try mine for a contribution,' observed Dick. 'How about you Eustace?'

'Oh, yes, er, oh, yes, er, how about me what, Dick?

'How about getting your mother-in-law to put a bob or two into the Christmas club each week?'

'But she can't, can she Willie? Can she? She can't, you said so, didn't you Willie? Didn't you say she can't? Nobody can't do what doesn't work at Murgatroyd's.'

Willie, who had been sitting quietly chewing his finger nails, muttered under his breath to Dick, 'See he does listen sometimes and that proves it.' Then aloud to Eustace he said, 'If you get the money from her each week, add it to yours and pay it into the club in your own name, no one will know the difference and you can sort it out with her next Christmas. Can't you?'

'Oh yes, I see, yes that's it, at least I think it is, isn't it? Yes, yes, that's it.'

'Thank God for that,' said Lewis to no one in particular.

Willie turned his attention to the bar and shouted, 'Steward. Steward my good fellow, kindly trot this way with our tray of liquid refreshment. We're bloody parched.'

But the only response he got was bellowed back, 'Shut your noise and wait your turn you stupid little twerp.'

The attention of the whole club was focused on Willie as they waited for his reply, but he disappointed everyone by not taking the bait. Instead he remarked to anyone who would listen that it was nice to know they were all still in good hands at the club.

The remainder of the evening passed off much as usual. A few more pints, more coarse humour, dominoes, senseless comment, farting and belching and finally, Fat Harry's well know cry at eleven o'clock, 'Right you can all sod off home. I'm shutting.'

At this time he slammed down the new rolled shutter front of the bar and herded all the flock into the bitter cold outdoors. They all wended their weary way home, some to be met by wives already asleep in bed, others by wives sitting up waiting with supper prepared or for explanations as to where they had been and why, but irrespective of the greeting they got, they all crawled into bed, contented and tired.

CHAPTER 7

Mr Anthony Murgatroyd made two tours of inspection around the mill each day. The first at about half past nine in the morning after dealing with the post and seeing to the incoming orders so as to be back in his office by half past ten to take coffee from his silver service. The second tour was made sometime after lunch as and when it became convenient, but usually between three and four o'clock. Many a time, Mr Anthony would be accompanied by visitors who were, more often that not, buyers from the great British fashion houses and occasionally from abroad.

The tour of inspection always took on the same form. Out through the back door of the office block, across the yard and into the lift then ascending the six floors to the top of the big mill. Here were to be found two long pairs of spinning mules with their hundreds of gleaming spindles, flashing in the light as they revolved at hundreds of revolutions per minute, drawing out the thick woollen carded sliver into a strong thread.

Then a slow walking descent of the mill, through the various floors, passing more mule gates, then lower down the big heavy carding machines with their giant flat belt pulleys hurtling around, driving the fancy rollers, swifts, hopper feeds, condenser belts, peralter burr crushers and other magical pieces of machinery associated with the carding of wool. The carding engines were in places so close together, that it was necessary to turn sideways to safely pass between the revolving pulleys. All these machines were driven from overhead line shafts, by wide, flat, leather belts, the drive to each floor being by a vertical shaft up the outside of the mill wall, through giant, noisy, cast iron bevel gears, running in huge bronze bearings covered in oil and grease.

From the big mill, the next shed to be visited was the blending department, a step backward in processing order but more convenient in terms of the tour. In here were found people walking about covered in fibre and hair from the wool being processed, looking for all the world like giant teddy bears on off-white days. Huge bales of wool, already dyed to shade were emptied by hand and put into large hoppers, from where the fibre was sucked and blown down long circular fans to the blending room. Here it was mixed with dyed wool of other shades and qualities, then sucked by fans into the Willying machines, Garnets and Fearnaughts, all with big sharp teeth on revolving drums, which one by one mixed the various colours and qualities even further to produce an entirely new and special blend to go to the carding department.

Next the tour went through the weaving shed, with rows and rows of noisy looms clattering away creating both plain and fancy cloths of all colours and designs. Here, some of the looms had been converted to the new electric motor drives but the majority were still driven by the overhead line shafts. The tour concluded by passing through the greasy piece warehouse, the piece dyehouse, the wet finishing and the dry finishing departments to end back at Mr Anthony's office by way of the finished piece warehouse and despatch.

Throughout the tour, Mr Anthony would stop and pick up a handful of wool or feel at a piece of cloth. He would look at it, smell it and rub it between his fingers, for he was one of a rare breed of men, a wool man who knew wool inside out and upside down. What he didn't know about wool wasn't worth knowing. He would stop and talk with all the departmental managers and foremen, both about cloth and socially. He would also stop and pass the time of day with any of his workforce that happened to be around, for he always took a deep interest in the well-being of his employees.

On the day following the inaugural meeting on the Murgatroyd's Christmas club, Mr Anthony was on his morning tour, walking through the dyehouse with a visitor, when Willie saw him. Dick saw him as well and nudged Willie, 'Go on, go and ask him whilst he's here.'

'Nay I can't, he's got a visitor with him.'

'Go on. Get a move on, else he'll have gone.'

Willie watched Mr Anthony and his visitor as they took hold of a sopping wet piece of cloth that was going round and round in a dye vessel, to make a close inspection of it. The dyehouse foreman, Walter Smith was with them and Willie was not so sure about interrupting them.

'Go on Willie, move yerself.'

Dick pushed him towards the little group where he stood, hovering, indiscreetly. The group took no notice of him, and he swayed, changing the weight balance of his body from one clog to the other. He put one hand behind his back and scratched his bottom, and then he pushed the same hand backward and forwards across his bald head. He stuck his finger in his left ear and cleaned out the wax which he rubbed onto his leather apron and then he turned around to look at Dick who was motioning him forward. He was just about to start picking his nose when Walter Smith saw him.

'What do you want, Willie?'

'Want a word wi' Mr Anthony like.'

'Cant you see Mr Anthony's busy?'

'Aye, but I've need of a word with him.'

'Well you can't just interrupt him. This here's a very important customer and you'll have to come back another time when he's not so busy.'

'Aye, but tha sees, it's like this.'

'Now look Willie, I'll tell him you want a word with him, so get back to your work.'

Willie walked back to Dick and the round of pieces they were just changing over. 'He hadn't time to see me. It's no good; we'll never get this job going.'

'Hang on a minute Willie, Mr Anthony's all right. He'll see you when he has the time. I'm sure of it.'

They got on with loading and unloading the machine.

*

The same afternoon, Anthony Murgatroyd came into the dyehouse and walked straight over to Willie.

'Now then Willie, Walter Smith told me you wanted to have a word with me this morning, but unfortunately I was tied up with a very important prospective customer at the time. Anyway, I'm here now, so what is it all about?'

Actually coming face to face with Mr Anthony to discuss something serious, completely flustered Willie and he was not quite coherent when he began to speak.

'Well it's about the bank account, like.'

71

'The bank account?'

'Er, yes, can you help us get one?'

'Who's us?'

'The committee. It's us what needs it.'

Mr Anthony was well known for his patience and he realised that he would need all that he could muster. 'Which committee?'

'Murgatroyd's Christmas club.'

'So. We have a Christmas club, have we?'

Willie wanted to belch but didn't dare. 'Aye and we need to have a bank account like.'

'Willie. Come with me to the private office where it's quiet and let us sort out just exactly what it is that you want.'

Willie had never been to the private office before. He'd been to the enquiry window in the general office a few times, but never, ever to the private office and, until this moment, had never expected to either. So it was, with some awe and trepidation, that he followed Mr Anthony. They walked through the back door of the office block and Willie's clogs made a peculiar ringing noise on the linoleum covered floor. They made even more noise on each tread as they climbed the stairs and finally they made no noise at all as they walked side by side along the thick carpeted, oak panel lined corridor to the office which said PRIVATE in big black letters on the door.

All the time that they had been walking, Mr Anthony had been talking to Willie, enquiring about Thelma and the children, the prospects for Grolsby AFC in the local league and about the trouble that Willie had been having recently with a neighbour over his back garden always been fouled by the neighbours dog. They talked so much that, by the time Willie was motioned into a comfortable leather chair, he was much more relaxed than when they had set off.

Willie had heard of the boss' private offices before and on the way up the stairs he had imagined that he would be taken into a very large room with a roaring fire, a desk in the middle that looked as if it stretched into the village, large crystal chandeliers, very deep pile carpets, a private bathroom concealed in the oak panelling, a large well stocked bar and a very pretty young secretary to welcome him. Instead the reality was indeed very different. It was a very plain room, small with an average executive desk, a couple of steel filing cabinets and half a dozen well worn leather chairs. A single light bulb hung on the end of a flex in the centre of the ceiling and the carpeted floor had holes here and there. The desk was strewn with papers, as were the tops of the filing cabinets, two of the chairs, the windowsill and various parts of the floor. The only luxury was a large painting of Mr Anthony's grandfather, the founder of the firm, himself called Anthony and another painting of his father Mr Joseph Murgatroyd. Of the pretty young secretary, there was no sign. Willie looked around, surveyed the scene and eventually spoke. 'Well tha's fair sloughed me and no mistake, Mr Anthony. I always thought that you'd a right posh office up here with big cocktail cabinets and a private bathroom and great big comfortable armchairs and you've nowt, no cigars, no whisky, no nowt at all.'

'I'm sorry to have disappointed you, Willie, but you see I only use this office when I'm bound to. I prefer to spend my time either in the mill or in the sales office and anyway I can't thoil to spending hard earned brass on a lot of frivolous and fancy gadgets for an office. Now what's this about a Christmas club?'

'Well it's like this. A few of us have got together and decided that we ought to have a Christmas club here at t' mill, for them what works here.' He stopped to cross and uncross his legs. 'We had a meeting in t' canteen the other dinner time regarding the proposed club and they made me treasurer, Arthur Baxter secretary and Sarah Anne Green Chairman, and then we had a few on t' committee. I think that's seven of us altogether.'

'Yes, I heard from Martha's nattering and grumbling that you'd had a meeting regarding the proposed club.'

Willie had taken the opportunity of Mr Anthony's interruption to poke his ear, uncross his legs, play with his trouser belt and generally fidget.

'Aye well we had a meeting at the club last night to settle some details.'

'Was Sarah Anne Green there?'

'Yes.'

'What? Actually inside the club?'

'Aye. Why not?'

'Why not indeed, but a very brave yet foolish woman.'

'How come?'

'Not exactly the place for a lady I would have thought.'

'Well, we only let her into the committee room, so everything's sort of settled now.'

'Good, good. So what do you want from me?'

'Eh?'

'What have you come to see me for?'

'About the bank.'

'What bank?'

Willie decided that Mr Anthony must be just a little bit stupid, so he thought he had better explain it in detail.

'Well it's like this. We decided that we need to be able to put the money, what I collect on a Friday dinner time, into the bank so as we know where it is like. I said I'd keep it in a tin under my bed, but they weren't having none of that. Instead I've got to take it t' bank.' He stopped for breath and to collect his thoughts.

Mr Anthony intervened, 'So where do I come into it?'

'For flipping crying out loud,' shouted Willie. 'We want you to get us a bank account.'

'Why me?'

'Because none of us knows owt about bank accounts.'

'Ah I see now. You want me to use my good offices to help you to open an account at the bank.'

'Aye. That's about the strength of it.'

'Right. I'll do it tomorrow morning when I take the cheques in. Incidentally, can I join the Christmas club?'

'Of course you can. You work here don't you?'

In order to prolong the agony of the interview no longer, Mr Anthony suggested that it was time for work once again and the two of them walked back together to the dyehouse, he promising Willie that he would let him know what happened at the bank as soon as he arrived back at the mill tomorrow morning.

*

The next day, Mr Anthony followed his well tried morning routine of opening the post, checking the order book and then touring the mill. He made an unscheduled stop at the counting house to tell the company secretary not to take the cheques to the bank as he had to visit there himself shortly. The secretary gave Mr Anthony the paying in book and thanked him for saving him some time so as to attend to other pressing matters.

Immediately Mr Anthony was out of earshot of the counting house, all hell let loose as the company secretary kicked the living daylights out of whatsoever or whosoever he could find to kick, as part of his daily pleasure was to get away from the mill for a short while to place the odd bet or two and to spend as much time as possible in the company of many of the ladies of the village with whom he was well acquainted. Today, through no fault of his own he had been denied that pleasure.

*

It was an extremely cold and frosty morning, and it didn't take Mr Anthony long to walk from the mill, through the village and halfway along Station Lane to arrive at the Northern Counties Bank. The building stood out as a fine and perfect example of the soundness and rock solid nature of the bank. Even though by city standards it was indeed tiny, it still imposed itself on Station Lane and made all the other buildings, including the station itself and the Railway Hotel, come a very poor second. Mr Anthony conducted the mill business at the counter and then enquired if the manager was free.

Douglas Sharples, the manager of the Grolsby branch, was always free for Anthony Murgatroyd. He might not have been free for anyone else, depending on whom that might have been, but with Anthony being a near neighbour, their families being very friendly and not to mention that Murgatroyd's were his best customer, he was very free.

As a general rule, Sharples was a man of few words, most of which were very much to the point and he was blessed with the idea that he was a few degrees better than anyone from the West Riding of Yorkshire with certain exceptions. Anthony Murgatroyd being one of these. Sharples was ex-Shropshire, ex-public school, ex-army and proud of his own capabilities.

Mr Anthony entered the ornate office.

'Come in; come in, nice to see you. 'Anthony took the outstretched hand of Douglas Sharples and shook it warmly. 'Sit down, won't you. How's the family?'

'Well, Douglas, thank-you. Well. How's yours?'

'Just the same thanks. Now, are you here on business or pleasure? Bloody good party up at Johnston's last Saturday night, eh? My word his daughter isn't half developing into a desirable young woman, couldn't keep my eyes off her.'

'Yes, she's a pretty little thing isn't she? Turned a few heads, she did.'

'Not so little either. I managed to get myself wedged in a doorway with her, face to face as it were. I wish I was eighteen again. So what was it you wanted, eh?'

'I'm only here to do a favour for some of my workers. A few of them have decided to run a Christmas club ready for next Christmas and they intend to collect the contributions each Friday lunchtime after we have paid the wages, then bank the money straight after lunch.'

'So what has that got to do with you?'

'Well they asked me if I could fix it for them to have a bank account and I promised to see what I could do to help them, hence why I am here. Of course, you must understand that I want, and I want you, to do the best possible we can for them.'

'How much money are we talking about?'

'That is the question of the year. Let's see now, we have close on two hundred and fifty employees. If they all put ten shillings a week in and they won't all, and a lot of them won't join, then think of the number you first thought of, helped along by a following wind and the moon in the third quarter. Let's say sixty to seventy pounds a week, perhaps, but I could be miles out.'

'Three to three and a half thousand a year, a tidy little sum. The best thing we can do is to let them have a special high interest savings account. It is supposed to be for fixed monthly or weekly investments and we can assume that if the club is working correctly, the weekly amount will be fixed. We need one month's notice of withdrawal, but we can fix that now or when the account is opened or near enough anyway. I have the power of discretion in cases like this to allow a cheque book on a savings account, and that can be dealt with, leaving only the question of who is going to run the show or sign the cheques or pay in the money etc. etc.'

'As far as I can tell you, Willie Arkenthwaite is.'

'Who?'

'Willie Arkenthwaite.'

'Never heard of him. Not one of our clients.'

'Definitely not, but you will have heard of him by the time you've got him sorted out.'

'Who is he?'

'He lives in Cutside cottages on the canal bank, halfway between here and the mill. He's been elected treasurer of the club, but how he's going to go on with it, I do not know. I've always found him to be extremely honest, but he's very difficult to hold a serious conversation with, as he can't follow most normal matters. Anyway, you'll have to judge him as you find him.'

'One of those, eh? Would you say you could describe him as being a bit thick?'

'As good a description as one could have asked for. Mind you, he's all there when he wants to be.'

'Yes, I know the type, leave him to me. When can I have him here?'

'Today after lunch? Say two o'clock.'

Sharples consulted his diary. 'Yes that will be just fine. Thanks Anthony.'

'No problem, Douglas. No problem at all.'

The two men rose from their padded chairs and Douglas started to talk again. 'Are you going to pay into the Christmas club then Anthony?'

'I haven't given it much thought, although I might just risk a half a crown a week.'

Anthony Murgatroyd stared aghast as Douglas Horatio Sharples laughed out loud, for in keeping with many of the more formal bank managers of the day, Sharples made it a solemn rule never to laugh during working hours.

'You've laughed during office hours.'

'Sorry, couldn't help it. It was the thought of you shelling out half a crown every week. You'll only have about six quid by Christmas at the most. You could afford six pounds a week and not notice it. It's well worth a laugh during office hours. Just wait until I tell the chief clerk about it.'

'Now then Douglas, do you want to chip into the club?'

'No, not at all. I can't afford anything at all on my salary.'

This time they both burst out laughing and as Douglas escorted Anthony to the front door, many people noted and talked for several years afterwards about the day that Douglas Horatio Sharples laughed during office hours.

Mr Anthony arrived back at Damside mills, so known because his grandfather had built the mill at the side of an existing but redundant mill dam. This towering mill was erected much to the consternation of the owner of the mill on the opposite bank of the dam, because old man Murgatroyd had managed, by means never disclosed, to get a right to draw water from the existing dam rather than build himself a new one nearby and in the process of doing so had saved himself a fortune.

The owners of Tasmania Mill, on the other side of the dam, had never forgiven the Murgatroyd's and three generations on, there was still and uneasy calm in their relationship.

After leaving the bank paying in book with the company secretary, Mr Anthony took a walk down to the dyehouse where he sought out the foreman dyer, Walter Smith.

'Now Walter, you know this business about a Christmas club and Willie Arkenthwaite's involvement in it?'

'Yes Mr Anthony, I'm going to join the club on Friday.'

'How much are you going to put into to it, Walter?'

'I don't exactly know. I've been trying to figure it out all morning. Happen ten bob a week. I don't know exactly just yet. I'd better ask the wife tonight.'

'Yes, you would more than likely be better to ask your wife before making a decision of that sort. Anyway, Willie's going to need a bit of time off every Friday, just after lunch, so that he can take the money to the bank. It will only take him the odd half hour or so, can you spare him?'

'Oh yes, I can cover for him for half an hour, no problem.'

'Good, good. Now he needs to go to the bank this afternoon to set up the account, so I suggest we let him go straight after lunch to let him smarten himself up somewhat and then he should be back here by three o'clock. Can you manage that?'

'We'll have to won't we.'

'Yes, you will.'

He made his way over to Willie, who ever since he had seen Mr Anthony enter the dyehouse, had been on tenterhooks; waiting to see if would be allowed to go to the bank.

'Now Willie, I've had a talk with Mr Sharples the bank manager and he wants to see you at two o'clock to discuss matters appertaining to the Christmas club money. He suggests you put the money into a special high interest savings account, so that the fund will increase in value as the year rolls along.'

'Very good, Mr Anthony. I'll go when I've had my dinner.'

He had no idea exactly what Mr Anthony was talking about.

'Yes Willie, that's fine, but do pop in home and put something more suitable on. You're not exactly dressed in bank visiting attire and Willie.'

'Yes?'

'Do try to speak a little more refined when you get to the bank.'

'Eh?'

'Speak posh in the bank.'

'Oh aye Mr Anthony, I will.'

Willie was once again in his usual place at the head of the dinner time queue, with Sarah Anne Green right behind him.

'Have you seen Mr Anthony, Willie?'

'Yes I have, I had a talk with him this morning in the private office, then he went t' bank and saw the manager, and now I've to go see the manager after dinner at two o'clock. I've got to go home and get myself washed and changed and I've got to talk poshish, like, and he were going on summat about high interest what I couldn't understand and-'

'Hang on a minute Willie. Is Mr Anthony letting you have time off to go to the bank this afternoon?'

'Aye.'

'With pay?'

'Well, well, nay, I don't know. Well now you mention it, I never thought to ask him.'

'Here, save my place in the queue a bit, better still get my dinner for me whilst I come back. Here's the money.'

She thrust a two shilling piece into his hand and disappeared down the canteen steps, pushing past the queuing throng. She ran over to the office block and asked the young girl receptionist if she could see Mr Anthony on a matter of some urgency. The young lady, who on getting the job of receptionist had instantly risen four steps up the social ladder, looked at Sarah Anne and spoke in a snotty haughty manner. 'And whom shell Ay say desires to see Mr Anthony?'

Sarah Anne was not put off by such people and blasted forth. 'Now look here young woman, you know who I am as well as I do, and I'll thank you to mind your manners when you speak to me or I'll have a thing or two to say to your mother and father when next I see them.'

The young lady blushed, mellowed and ran out of the room in one and the same breath. She did not appear again, but Mr Anthony was not long in coming into the reception area.

'Now Sarah Anne, what brings you to my humble domain?'

'It's about the Christmas club. You know I'm chairman and Willie Arkenthwaite, for all his sins, was elected treasurer and I understand he's been to see you about going to the bank and, in fact, he tells me he's going after dinner.'

'Yes, that's right. I have made arrangements with the dyehouse foreman to cover for him whilst he goes about his weekly duties connected with the Christmas club and also for him to go to the bank this afternoon.'

'Are you going to pay his wages whilst he's doing his treasurers duties?'

'Do you know, I've not given the matter as much as a second thought yet. Should I, do you think?'

'Well, we are sort of doing it voluntarily for the benefit of those who work here and only those that work here, not anyone else and I think you should pay his wages if I guarantee to keep his activities to the bare minimum each week.'

'Sarah Anne, of course I'll pay his wages for that period each week. I think it's a good thing for the mill and I'm looking forward to being able to join. When are you collecting the first instalment?'

'Friday this week, in the canteen, at dinner time.'

'Good, I'll be there and please tell Willie that all will be alright with his wages.'

'Thank-you Mr Anthony. I'll go and tell him and get my dinner.'

She made her way back to the canteen, half walking, half running.

Meanwhile at the canteen, Willie was having just a little bit of trouble. Firstly, with Greasy Martha, in trying to convince her that he really did want Sarah Anne's dinner as well as his own and then secondly, trying to work out how he was going to carry two plates of dinner and two lots of cutlery over to his table. However, he was soon relieved of any further worries by the reappearance of Sarah Anne who was able to carry her own food and utensils.

'By gum I'm glad you're back, I were just wondering how I were going to carry all this over to the corner table. Did you see him?'

'Yes. He says it's all alright. He'll pay your wages whilst you attend to the duties of the Christmas club, providing you don't overdo it.'

'Good then I can have my dinner and geroff t' bank.'

Willie sat in his usual seat at the corner table and was joined by his three pals from the dyehouse. He ate with his customary, well known zeal and noise, using knife and fork occasionally, fingers regularly and tongue finally to lick the plate clean, stopping only for a loud customary belch. He headed back to the servery for his pudding which again he dispensed with in his own inimitable style. Having consumed the pint of tea in one long swallow he got up to leave, belching loudly yet again.

'Hold on Willie, it's card time,' said Dick.

'Nay not today I'm off to the bank.'

'Come on you can go after we've played. We can't properly play a three hand.'

'Well get somebody else to play for me today. How about Eustace?'

'Nay, we'll not play if it's got to get that bad.'

'Well suit yourselves. I'm off to the bank. It's a very important job what I'm doing.'

With that he walked away leaving the other three staring after him.

Willie went back to the dyehouse to remove his thick leather apron, replacing it with his cap and coat and then away to leave the mill through the arched front gate. The gate was closed as it was only opened at twelve noon to let those who went home for dinner out in a hurry, and then closed until a quarter to one when it was opened again to let them back in again. In order to get out at any other time it was necessary to go through the penny hoil corridor, or gate lodge, so named because it was where the gate keeper or penny hoil man paid out the wages through the little opening window or penny hoil, each Friday tea time.

George Schofield had been the penny hoil man at Murgatroyd's for as long as anyone could remember. It was part of his duty to stay at his post throughout the mill dinner break and keep his eyes on the comings and goings through the gate. In summer, he would stand across the road, leaning on the wall overlooking the canal, but in winter he had a roaring coal fire in his office and he usually took the opportunity of the lull in dinner time traffic to have forty winks.

As Willie approached the penny hoil he could see George, slumped back in his chair, with his feet resting firmly on one of the open drawers of his desk. The fire was blazing away and George was fast asleep. Willie gave over hurrying. so that his feet stopped clonking, and instead he was to be observed making a very careful and stealthy approach to the penny hoil. He opened the door without a sound, crept inside very quietly, closed the door, then slowly and stealthily made his way over to George Schofield's feet resting on the drawer. He took very careful aim and quickly kicked the drawer back into its housing, causing George's feet to crash to the floor and George to sit bolt upright at far too great a speed for a man of his age.

'Oh you are still alive then George? I thought you had gone to meet your maker when I walked through the passage and saw your lifeless form lying there.'

'You bloody, dozy, stupid sod, you could have killed me. I could have died of heart failure; you might have set my palpitations off again. You can make folk have a growth with a physical shock, you can make them lose their memory, it is possible to do.'

'Now George, it was just my little bit of fun.'

'Bit of fun! Bit of fun indeed. His mood changed instantly, for the worse. And what the bloody hell were you doing in my office anyway? My inner sanctum is off limits to all and sundry except for the chosen few and management.'

'Like Mary Barhead?'

A slight reddening around the cheekbone was to be observed. 'That's got nothing to do with you, William Arkenthwaite. Who comes in here is my affair and my affair alone.'

'Yes well that's what I was saying, it is your affair with Mary Barhead, and anyway my name's not William, it's Willie, but a nod's as good as a wink to a blind horse, so I'll be on my way.'

'If it's not a rude question, and I've no doubt it is, where are you going?'

'To the bank.'

'What for?'

'Same as thee, it's my affair and my affair alone, but mine's not called Mary Barhead.

With this, Willie escaped into the cold, half foggy midday January air and half walking, half running he made his way to number six Cutside Cottages.

Willie opened his front door to be met by Mrs Woofenden sitting almost in the fire.

'Is that you our Willie? Thelma, your Willie's home. Whatever can have happened? What are you doing home at this time? Have you had your dinner? Is t' mill on fire? Have you had an accident or summat?'

She stopped only long enough for a sharp intake of warm air, giving Willie no time to reply then started screeching again at the top of her voice. 'Thelma, your Willie's home, where are you? Come and have a look, what can have happened? Has t' mill engine run out of control?

Willie chose to ignore the old lady and to make his way upstairs to find his best dark grey three piece suit. Thelma opened the back kitchen door, came into the living room and confronted her mother.

'Now what on earth is all this noise about?'

'It's our Willie. He's come home.'

'Well, where is he? He's nowhere in sight.'

'He's gone upstairs.'

'Well, what's it about?'

'I don't know. You know what Willie's like, he never said a word. Just walked in and went upstairs. I told you not to marry him, you could have done so much better for yourself, but would you take any notice? No you would not, you would only do-'

She gave over as she realised that she was talking to four walls and a fire. However, she was highly delighted as she had got her spoke in about her son-in-law, once again.

Thelma entered the bedroom to find Willie busily getting changed. 'What are you doing?'

'Going t' bank to see about the new Christmas club.'

'But you should be at your work.'

'Mr Anthony's let me go and he's paying my wages. I've got to go see the manger at half past one to see about our new account so I can bank all t' money every Friday after dinner.'

'So what are you getting changed for?'

'Well, Mr Anthony said I wasn't fair well enough dressed to go before t' bank manager in my dirty working clothes and I'd best go home and change.'

'You don't need your best suit; you could put your sports jacket on and your new brown trousers. It's not a funeral or a wedding.'

'No, but it's a bank manager and I'd best look right and then.'

'Why are you going?'

'I am the treasurer of the Christmas club and in my official capacity I have to go see the bank manager about our money.'

'Are you sure you know what you are doing?'

'Well, no. Well, happen I know a bit about it and I shall have to learn the rest as I go.'

'Well do take care love, it's a lot of money you'll be handling and it's somebody else's and Willie-'

'Yes?'

'Do try to be civil to my mother. She's very upset that you walked in and ignored her and wouldn't tell her why you were home.'

'Well you know what she's like, straight into the attack, spitting fire and venom as soon as I walk through the door. It's easier to say nowt than have a row with her.'

'I know it's difficult, but you could try. It makes life so difficult for me. She'll go on all afternoon about it.'

'Specially for you, I'll be nice to her when I go downstairs.'

Thelma left Willie with a hug, a kiss and a smile and he continued to change into his best white shirt, red polka dot tie, grey suit and highly polished black shoes. He then applied a very generous helping of hair cream, combed it straight, put on his best grey overcoat, new cap and scarf, that he'd had as Christmas presents, and descended the stairs.

'Coming with me then Mrs W?' he said with a grin as he faced his mother-in-law.

'You know very well I can't, my back's playing me up something shocking. If I'd been a bit younger there'd have been no stopping me. Anyway, where are you going?'

'To see the bank manager about Murgatroyd's Christmas club.'

'What's it to do with you?'

'I'm Treasurer. I'm in charge.'

'There's no answer to that.'

Thelma straightened Willies cap and ran her hand over his collar. 'Come on love, you'll be late. It's almost a quarter past one.'

'Yes alright, I'm on my way. So long.'

'Good luck,' shouted Thelma as he walked along the canal tow path.

She closed the door to the strains of 'Shut that door, the cold's going through my back like the blade of a sword cutting it. You'll have to keep your eye on him you know, there'll be no good come of this Christmas club, just you mark my words. I told you not to marry-'

'Oh for heavens sake shut up mother.' Thelma stormed into the back kitchen and slammed the door hard, tears in her eyes.

Mrs Woofenden stared at the fire with an expression that was blacker than the coal that was burning on it.

Willie walked quickly towards the village in the sure knowledge that he had half an hour to spare to pop into the Club and have a quick drink before his meeting with the bank manager. He passed the canal wharf where a barge was unloading huge bales of wool and on through the village past the shops, most of which were closed for lunch, and on to the club. He carefully hung his outer garments on the hook rail in the entrance hall with the other few coats, that were there from the usual small lunchtime crowd, and he entered the bar.

'Awe my gawd! What do we have here?' rang out the dulcet tones of Fat Harry. 'Is it a well dressed dummy from fifty shilling tailor's window, or is it the fairy that has just fallen of the Christmas tree? No, no. It must be the new representative from the brewery that we haven't met before. Good afternoon sir, somewhat cold for the time of the year, even the brass monkey's put his clothes back on. What can I get you to drink, sir?'

'Give us a pint.'

'A pint. Certainly, sir.'

He poured the drink, chuckling under his breath but saying nothing. When the glass was full of the frothing bronze liquid he handed it over the bar to Willie.

'That will be one shilling and sixpence if you don't mind, sir, please.'

'Get stuffed.'

'I beg your pardon, sir.'

'Get stuffed. You invited me to have a drink, so you can pay for it. I only came in here to show you that I do have a best suit, just to prove to those of you that have so often claimed differently that I do in fact have one. So thank-you for the drink.'

'I shall take the greatest of pleasure, sir, in walking to the end of the room there,' Harry pointed to the far end of the bar, 'turning through ninety degrees, walking four paces forward, turning through ninety degrees yet again, walking up to the position you are currently occupying, leaning upon my recently very highly polished bar top sir, picking you up by the ears with my left hand whilst at one and the same time, with my right hand, sir, helping your teeth to rapidly pass through you body if you do not, sir, pay for that pint bloody quick.'

Although Fat Harry was much taller, rounder and wider than Willie, he did not make any impression on his well dressed client who replied, 'Thank-you, my man, I'll not forget your generosity in a long time,' and he went on drinking his pint, adding a rather loud fart to close the proceedings.

'That doesn't suit one that is dressed like a right dandy. Have you made a will yet?'

'Have I heck. I've nowt to leave to nobody and anyway it's personal, it's nowt to do with you.'

'It's everything to do with me. I need to know that your Thelma and the children are well provided for before I rip your insides out slowly, piece by piece. By the way what are you doing here dressed like a dog's dinner when you should be grovelling to your master up at Murgatroyd's?'

'I'm going to the bank at two o'clock.'

'What for?'

'To see the manager.'

'What for?' shouted Harry.

'To see about the Christmas club.'

'What about the Christmas club?'

'We need an account.'

'Why?'

'To bank the money.'

'So what's with the new look Willie then?'

'Anthony Murgatroyd said I'd best get changed and look posh for the manager.'

'Ah, well. Good luck. Do you want another pint in there which I am definitely not paying for?'

'No, not just now. I'd best stay sober for the manager, and anyroad, it's time I were on my way, it's ten to two and I don't want to be late.'

'Well take care. Are you coming in tonight?'

'Might. Might not. See how the mood grabs me.'

'You know you will. You never miss. Are you going to pay me for that pint or not?'

'Not and thanks.'

Willie closed the door behind him, reapplied his outer garments and went out into the bitter cold. It wasn't far to the bank, perhaps three hundred yards, and Willie set off at a brisk pace. He was passing the end of Mafeking Street when he stopped dead in his tracks as he observed what he took to be Daniel Sykes trying to make his escape from a house half way up the street. It was obvious that he didn't want to be seen and gave furtive glances in all directions, but he didn't see Willie.

'Couldn't be him. He should be at his work.' thought Willie. 'But it was him, I'm sure it was. I wonder who lives there and what he were up to? Aye I wonder.' He wondered all the way to the bank.

CHAPTER 8

The Grolsby branch of the Northern Counties Bank was a majestic building standing between the railway station and the railway hotel. It was built of local millstone grit, not the common rough finished house stone, but carefully machined and bevel edged, so popular with those architects who worked with clients who had a money-no-object building fund.

To Willie Arkenthwaite it represented something akin to a prison or courthouse or somewhere to beware, as he stood before it and viewed it on this particularly cold and drab winter's day.

He decided he would not be a coward and miss his appointment; he therefore counted up to three, then three and a half, and then started again. Two and a half, two and three quarters, three and he marched smartly straight towards the revolving front doors.

Willie pushed the nearest segment of the door with more than necessary force and in so doing he helped one of the bank's regular customers to exit the bank at a far greater rate of knots that they would otherwise have done.

He looked round the building he had entered and stood back dumbstruck, admiring the majestic beauty and luxury of the interior. Never in his wildest dreams had he imagined the thick pile carpets, the large ornate chandeliers, the marble columns, the central heating and the air of quietness and calm. It is fair to say that he had not known what to expect and he stood back for a few minutes to take it all in.

People came and people went. Some queued at counters, others went through various doors and he could see people working, sitting at desks behind the counters. No one bothered him or talked to him, they just left him alone to study his surroundings.

Eventually a young lady that he almost recognised said 'good afternoon' to him as she walked past and he returned the greeting, but she did not ask him what he wanted or why he was there. So he began to look around for someone to ask as to where he might find the manager. Seeing no one who looked important he ventured a little walk around to see what he could find. His wanderings eventually brought him into contact with a small opening window at the far end of the counter which displayed a notice that announced ENQUIRIES. At the side of the window was a brass bell push with a small notice that said PUSH FOR ATTENTION. Willie was just about to press the bell push when he began to have cold feet about how much noise the bell might make. He looked around carefully to see if anyone was watching and finding no one, he plucked up courage and leaned hard on the brass button.

Nothing happened; there was no sound at all.

He decided that perhaps it rang in a place that could not be heard from the counter and so he decided to wait for a few seconds before leaning on the button again.

Once again there was a painful silence.

Willie could see people walking about behind the barrier that separated the public from the private section of the bank. He wondered what to do to attract their attention. He could have hammered hard on the window with his fist, but even to Willie, who wanted to belch but dared not, this did not appear to be seemly behaviour. He could have done his locally famous monkey impression but decided that the bank was not the place for that type of exhibition.

He finally decided to try and repair the bell. It was almost a dead certainty in his mind that the trouble lay with the bell push, because he could see it and he could not see the bell. Willie fumbled in his back trouser pocket until he found his twenty seven implement Swiss Army knife that he always carried with him. He selected the medium width screwdriver blade from the three available and carefully removed the cover plate of the bell push, which also removed the push contacts as well. The screwdriver blade was then folded away and the multi purpose file opened. He carefully polished the contacts with the file, having first of all probed them to make sure they were low voltage then polished away with the file until the contacts were bright and shiny.

He worked quietly away, concentrating hard on the job in hand and did not notice the enquiry window open quietly. He almost leapt from his skin when a voice close to his ear enquired, 'And what do you think you are doing?'

'Mending your bell. It's bust. Nobody came when I rung it, twice, and it hadn't rung, so I decided it were bust, so I thought I'd mend it for you, then ring it again.'

The spotty faced youth said, in a haughty manner, 'This is a most unusual state of affairs. We do not usually allow this type of occurrence in the bank you know. A further question, sir, whilst I am here, what business do you have with the bank?'

'Eh?'

'What do you want?'

Willie smiled proudly. 'I've come to see t' manager.'

'Have you an appointment, sir?'

'Aye, of course I have lad. Why else do you think I'd be stood here?'

'What is your name, sir, please?'

'Willie.'

'Willie who?'

'Arkenthwaite.'

'Right Mr Arkenthwaite, what did you wish to discuss with the manager?'

'It's none of your business, and if it were, I wouldn't tell you, cause you ask too many damned questions for my liking. So be a good lad and trot along and tell him I'm here.'

The smartly dressed, spotty faced youth stood back and gave Willie a good coat of looking at. Never in his short career at the bank had anyone spoken to him in this manner before. He just stood and watched as Willie finished cleaning the contacts of the bell push and began to screw the brass top plate back into position. He grimaced as Willie snooked up aloud and then looked for somewhere to spit out the phlegm, finally swallowing it, and then jumped in surprise as Willie pressed the bell push and it rang loudly all over the bank. Then frowned as Willie belched out noisily without an apology. Willie looked up and observed the young man standing staring at him.

'Get on with it then. Give over staring at me and go and tell t' gaffer I'm here.'

The young man turned and walked away. Willie pressed the bell push again, just to prove a point and the bell rang out loud and clear again. The young man turned back to Willie who shouted, 'And get a move on. I haven't got all day to wait whilst you ponsy lot dawdle about. I've some work to do.'

The young man glared at Willie then went towards the manager's office. Once out of sight he turned to where Willie was standing and generously pulled out his tongue at the unseeing new customer. He knocked on the manager's door, waited for the customary shout of 'come in', and then he opened the door and entered.

'Mr Sharples, there is a most uncouth and ill mannered person to see you by name of Willie, sorry, Arkenthwaite, who says he has an appointment with you. A most unsavoury character if you want my opinion.'

'Quite frankly, I do not want your opinion and for what it's worth, this Mr Arkenthwaite is soon to become one of our clients. So show him in and bring me the file you opened this morning after Anthony Murgatroyd had been in to talk about the Christmas club. Mr Arkenthwaite is the treasurer of the club and as such will be in here banking the club funds at least once each week from now on.'

'Very good Mr Sharples, but I would not trust him with my last farthing. I do not like the look of him at all.'

With that the young man closed the door and walked back over to the enquiry window where Willie was waiting patiently and watching the young ladies working behind the counter.

'Mr Sharples will see you now Mr Arkenthwaite. Please go across to the door marked PRIVATE at the opposite end of the counter where I will meet you and escort you to his office.'

'Ah telled you ah'd an appointment lad,' said Willie in reply.

He walked across the carpeted floor to the door marked private. He was wishing he was out on the street again for he was getting all sorts of unwelcome feelings in his body. The door opened and Willie entered a long oak panelled corridor. The young man walked silently in front of him until they came to a large solid oak door bearing the sign MANAGER in big gold letters. He knocked discreetly and opened the door announcing as he did, 'Mr Arkenthwaite, sir.'

'Nay lad you needn't call me sir after my name, thanks all the same.'

'I was referring to Mr Sharples as sir. Not you.' Having closed the door he once again enjoyed the luxury of sticking his tongue out at Willie, with the door firmly between them.

Mr Sharples rose from his chair, walked around the desk and shook Willie warmly by the hand, much to Willie's surprise. 'Hello Mr Arkenthwaite, I'm very pleased to meet you. Anthony Murgatroyd has told me a lot about you. Please sit down in that chair.' He motioned to a large black leather padded armchair in front of his desk.

Willie was by now a little nonplussed by all these posh speaking people and he blurted out, 'Hello, Sir Sharples, I'm pleased to meet you as well.'

'No, not Sir Sharples. I haven't hit the dizzy height of knighthood just yet.'

Willie had not grasped the basic fundamentals of this conversation and as he was sitting down he said by way of apology for something he didn't understand, 'Nay, yond young lad called you sir and I got a bit flummoxed.'

'The term "Sir" is used by staff to managers in the banking profession.'

'Oh yes, I see,' said Willie, trying to sound convincing.

'Now I understand you are intending to run a Christmas club for the benefit of the employees of Murgatroyd's mill.'

'Aye that's right.' Following which they stared at each other, Willie waiting for Mr Sharples to continue his questioning and Mr Sharples waiting for Willie to elaborate on his plans.

Mr Sharples watched Willie who was staring all over the room and decided to break the silence. 'Can you briefly elaborate on your proposals for the initial organisation of the club?'

'Eh?'

'Er, can you er, er, can you tell me how you are going to run the club?'

Mr Sharples had, whilst they were talking, been slowly and quietly opening a drawer in his desk, standing upright a half bottle that had been lying down. It was flat in appearance and contained a deep golden bronze, French, seventy per cent proof liquid and in his well practised method, so as not to arouse the suspicion of the client, he had been unscrewing the cap. Whilst Willie was thinking of a suitable reply to the last question, Mr Sharples ducked down behind the desk out of sight of Willie and took a quick slurp from the bottle, replaced the cap and lay the bottle flat down and closed the door, then surfaced again only to find Willie, leaning over the desk watching him.

'Are you alright Mr Sharples?'

'Er yes, I er, er, just dropped something, but I have located it now thank-you. Are you ready now to tell me all about the club?'

'Oh yes, it's simple. Me and Arthur'll -'

'Who is Arthur?'

'My mate Arthur. He's secretary.'

'Yes, but Arthur who?'

'Arthur Baxter. He works in the dyehouse with me and Lewis and Dick. Anyroad, as I were saying, me and Arthur'll collect all t' brass every Friday dinner time in the canteen, then I'll bring it straight on here and give it to you.'

'Well now, you won't exactly give it to me, you will have to hand it over to one of the clerks behind the counter. What will be the subscription rate each week for the members? No, no er, how much will each member pay into the club each week?'

'Well that depends on what they can afford when it's time to pay. It might be different each week depending on how skint they are.'

He was stopped by Mr Sharples. 'Skint?'

'Short, tha knows. Short of brass.'

'Oh yes, please carry on.'

'Well, like I were saying, it might be different every week but I shall keep a record of what they all put in, in my little red book. It's got lines and columns for cash, you know. Myself, I shall put three pounds a week in when I have it to spare and nowt at all when I haven't.'

'What do you know of banking procedures?'

'Nowt at all.'

'Do you not even know how to go about paying your money into a bank account?'

'No. I was just going to give it to you.'

Mr Sharples ignored this last remark and continued in a business like manor. 'Firstly we need to open an account for the Christmas club. We did that in anticipation this morning after Anthony Murgatroyd had been in to see me, and all that we need to do now, to complete that particular part of the operation, is for you to give your specimen signature on this card, just here, so that you may legally transact the business of the club.'

Willie gave Mr Sharples a funny look. 'Why do you want me to pee into a little bottle?'

'I beg your pardon?'

'Well the last time I was asked for a specimen was at the doctor's. I had to pee into a little bottle, and it dint half take some hitting the hole. But I can't think why you want that for at the bank.'

'It's a specimen of your hand writing we want, not a medical specimen,' roared Mr Sharples, who by this time was becoming visibly upset.

'Now don't you go on having a bad turn, Mr Sharples, it were just a little misunderstanding on my part.'

Mr Sharples passed the card over to Willie for signature and at the same time began to slowly open the drawer in his desk again, for medicinal purposes. Willie took a grubby pencil from his pocket, licked the lead, to make it nice and juicy for writing smoothly and was about to write his name in his best possible hand when Mr Sharples intervened, 'Er no, Mr Arkenthwaite, in ink if you please. Here, use my pen.'

He took from his pocket a fine gold fountain pen which was his pride and joy, and which certainly looked expensive, or at least Willie thought it did as he lovingly felt it, rubbing his fingers up and down it in and staring at it in disbelief .A diplomatic cough from Mr Sharples, brought Willie back into the land of the living once more and he began to carefully write his name. He managed the 'W' without too much difficulty, but then in forming the 'A' he somehow twisted the two points of the nib, scratching the card, producing a blot the size of a garden pea and in the process, permanently damaging the nib.

'Oh my God,' shouted Mr Sharples, 'my best gold pen. You've ruined it. Ruined it. It will cost a fortune to repair.'

'Nay it were nowt. It only wants twisting back into place again. Give us your pliers, I'll do it now.'

'No, no, you may not. That pen requires very special attention.'

'Suit yourself. Give us a Biro. I'm not used to a fountain pen.'

So, Willie, believing that Mr Sharples was making a lot of fuss over nothing, took the proffered ball point and after being given a new card, completed his signature without any further incident.

'Next you will need a paying in book which is here.' He held it aloft for Willie to see. 'I have had your current account number written onto the front cover to make it easier for you, and-'

He was rudely interrupted, 'What's a current account number?'

'It's the number of Murgatroyd's Christmas club current account so that we can keep a check of, and record, all transactions and make an observation on the name and number of each transaction as a cross reference. Every bank account, anywhere from Timbuktu to Jeguf has a number. It makes the posting of entries so much easier for the staff.'

Willie was floundering again with this explanation, so he had a little belch and asked a question in a different direction.

'What's t' paying in book for then?'

'The paying in book is for you to use every Friday when you pay your money into the club account. You fill in all these columns, including the account number and total the money in this square here.' Mr Sharples pointed to all the relevant sections in the book whilst Willie took a half hearted interest.

'When you have paid over the money to the cashier and handed him the book, he will stamp this small section known as the counterfoil, then sign it and that will be your record that we have received your money. The transaction will then be entered into your account by one of the staff, on the accounting machine, so that each payment is recorded on a very large sheet, which is our record of your account. Once a month we shall send you a statement of that account.'

'What's a statement?'

Mr Sharples was rapidly becoming seriously exasperated but he counted to ten and took himself in hand. At least he would have if Willie hadn't had a good old loud belch. 'What did you say?'

'Ah didn't say nowt. I were waiting for you to tell me about this here statement thing.'

Mr Sharples composed himself once more. 'The statement gives details of all the money you have paid in during that particular month and then gives you a total of all the money that you have got in your account. It is, of course, in your own interest to check the statement with your paying in book to ensure that all payments to your account have been entered and recorded. Now, about the cheque book. It is usual in such cases as this to have at least two signatories to a cheque so that there can be no fraud. Furthermore, it is advisable to have a third signatory if either of the other two should be ill or away from home at a time when the cheque needs signing.'

Willie had been about to ask what a signatory was when he had a flash of inspiration and realised the answer.

Mr Sharples continued, 'Now, have you any nominees?' He observed Willie frown and look up. 'Can you tell me who the other signatories are to be?'

'No. I'll have to think about it.'

'Well please let me know as soon as possible. The cheque book will be about a fortnight in being prepared, so I suggest you ask for it at the counter about that time.'

Mr Sharples felt that he was well overdue for another nip from his bottle, so he carefully opened the drawer again, whilst appearing to sit perfectly still. He stood the bottle upright, unscrewed the cap, and stared straight at Willie who was staring straight back at him. A short diversion was necessary.

'Have you seen that rather fine print of the Canaletto hanging on the wall behind you, Mr Arkenthwaite?'

Willie turned to look at the painting. Sharples knocked some papers onto the floor and dived down behind the desk for a quick swallow of the brown nectar, put the cap back on the bottle, laid the bottle down again, slammed the drawer to very quietly, picked up the papers and sat back again, just in time to see Willie turning back to face him.

'Do you mean that painting there?' asked Willie pointing to the Canaletto print.

'Yes.'

'It's horrible. I wouldn't give it t' wife's mother for her birthday, it's that bad. Is there anything else then?'

'Yes. Anthony Murgatroyd has suggested that you should open a deposit account so that you can, for the benefit of your members, accrue the maximum possible interest before next Christmas.'

'What does that mean?'

'For every pound you have invested, we will pay you four and a half per cent worked out on a daily basis. That means we will pay you eleven pence in the pound. You will need to hold an audit before you pay out the club funds because you could be liable for tax on the interest depending on just how much interest you have received. This of course depends on the current interest rates to depositors and by the way, when I use the term you, I mean the club and not you personally, if you know what I mean.'

Willie didn't. All he wanted to do now was to get himself out of the situation he found himself in and away to the big outdoors where he could have a good old belch. He sat quietly for a few minutes then he asked, 'Do we get this eleven pence for nowt?'

'Yes in one sense and no in another. The bank lends your money to someone else who in turn pays interest for borrowing it and the bank then gives you some of the interest it has received as a payment for lending it to us in the first place.'

'Well I don't know so much about that. If you're going to lend our money to someone else, how do we know we'll get it back again?'

'Your money goes into a big pool and we lend it out of the pool. Your money is always available to you on demand, no problem in that respect. The big advantage is that all your members will get back more than they paid in when you have your Christmas pay out. We have made arrangements to leave fifty pounds in the current account and to put the rest on automatic transfer to the deposit account. If you find it necessary to have more money in the current account, you will have to come in and see one of the cashiers to make the necessary arrangements by signing a transfer form. Now is all that perfectly clear?' Mr Sharples secretly hoped and prayed that it was.

'Aye I think so.' said Willie very unconvincingly.

'Well in that case, here is your paying in book. We shall expect to see you on Friday with your first payment and don't forget two things, to collect your cheque book and to nominate two more signatories.'

With that Mr Sharples rose to his feet, walked around the desk to Willie, who stood up, and they both walked out of the office together, down the long corridor and back to the customer's side of the counter.

'When you come in with your money on Friday, just take it to one of the windows and give it over to one of the cashiers. Goodbye, Mr Arkenthwaite, and thank-you for calling.'

'Goodbye, Mr Sharples, and thank-you.'

They shook hands and Willie walked out of the bank into the cold air. He snooked up a big ball of phlegm and spit it out onto the pavement, carefully killed it with the sole of his shoe, turned to face the bank, stuck out his tongue, farted as loud as he possibly could and muttered, 'up yours, Mr Sharples', and feeling much relieved he headed for home.

Back in the bank, Mr Sharples dashed back to his office in desperate need of several nips of brandy to calm his shattered nerves.

CHAPTER 9

Banking matters were soon forgotten as Willie passed the bottom of Mafeking Street.

'Hey up, hey up,' he said to himself as he turned up the street, but when he got to the house out of which he thought he had seen Daniel Sykes come, he couldn't decide whether it was number seventeen or number nineteen, but he was certain it was one of them.

He retraced his steps to the main road and was soon back at the club, where, there still being a good quarter of an hour official drinking time left, he went in without hesitation, work ignored.

'Good afternoon, sir, yet again once more, sir. It's not often we have the honour of welcoming you to our humble institution twice in the same afternoon, sir. Particularly when you should be slaving your guts out at the mill, sir, instead of being on the razzle, sir.' Fat Harry had a grin as wide as his stomach.

'Shut your gob and give us a pint.'

'Certainly, sir. Well not exactly certainly, sir.' His grin got even wider and his polite attitude continued. 'If sir will kindly show me the colour of his money, I will oblige.' Then he roared, 'Because you're not having another bugger till do and that is a fact.'

'Just pour one and I'll pay. Come on, I've got one hell of a thirst and so would you if you'd been to see that Sharples fellow.'

'He's alright. Just a high-foluting miserable sod. He can't help it, there's nowt wrong with him really.' He gave Willie his pint. 'At least no worse than any other bank manager.'

Willie's countenance changed into a wicked grin. 'I say Harry, who lives at either number seventeen, or nineteen Mafeking Street?'

'Don't know. Why?'

'Well, when I left here before, to go to t' bank, as I crossed the bottom of Mafeking Street, I saw Daniel Sykes come out of one of them two, but I couldn't tell you just which, and he should have been at t' mill and he doesn't live there.'

'No, no. You're right, he doesn't live there. Now let's think a minute, is it the new painted one, seventeen, or is it the one…hey I know it's yond blonde woman.'

'Not her, what's?'

'Aye, her with the big-'

'Well I'll be blowed…and Daniel Sykes.'

'Aye,' said Harry. 'Daniel Sykes. Daniel holier than thou Sykes. A walking encyclopaedia of useless information. Never put a foot wrong in his life and now having his wicked way with her. Are you sure it was him?'

'Well I thought it was, but I'll try and check when I get back and talking about getting back-'

'Hey, you can't go yet. What about Daniel Sykes?'

'I never thought I'd live to see the day! I wouldn't have thought he were capable of owt like that. By gum, wait until his missus finds out, there won't half be one hell of a row and three quarters for she's got one hell of a temper, or so they say on at Strict and Particulars where she's the boss. I wonder if he knows what to do when he gets behind her locked door?' asked Harry.

'He might just, because he's got three children. I wonder what excuse he's given at t' mill for not being there. I bet he hasn't got a proper one like me. Anyroad, I'd best be on my way else I might not have any excuses left.'

So Willie left the cosy warmth of the club and ambled steadily along the main street towards the mill. The street was filled with shoppers all going about their business, many stopping to speak to Willie then stepping back to admire and question the smartly dressed man they normally never saw.

Len Charrington, the local retail purveyor of high class meats and home cooked pies, brawn a speciality, known to one and all as Porky, observed the smartly dressed figure of Willie across the street and went to the shop door to shout across. 'Hey Willie. Come over here a minute.'

Willie crossed the street and entered the shop. 'Can't stop more than a minute Len, I'm on my way back t' mill and I'm late already.'

'Why? Where have you been?'

'To the Bank.'

'What for?'

'Eh?'

'What for?'

'To arrange about the Christmas club.'

'Which Christmas club?' Len's ears picked up.

'Ours up at t' mill.'

'What's it got to do with you?'

'You have the honour to be speaking to the honourable Treasurer.'

'What you? How the hell did you get that job then?'

'I were voted on. Anyway it were my idea to start with.'

'It was?'

'Well me and Arthur and one or two others.'

'So you're in charge then?' said Len thoughtfully. 'Running it, like?'

'Well it isn't starting until Friday, but you could say that I were in charge. Yes.'

Len looked around to make sure that no one was eavesdropping. 'Listen Willie,' he talked in a hushed voice, 'I might just be able to do you a very big favour in return for another one from you, seeing that you're in a privileged position as it were, and it'll put a few bob into your pocket.'

Willie's ears picked up at this half whispered information from Len. 'Oh aye. Tell me more.'

'Well if you can persuade your club members to come shop here for all their Christmas meat and turkeys, and I'll offer a five percent discount to encourage them, then I'll give you an extra five percent in pound notes or meat on all that they spend. The only thing is, no one has to know bout the last bit and it depends on you bringing me a fair bit of extra Christmas trade. So remember, and very important, keep it to yourself.' Len pointed to the side of his nose. 'So, what do you say?'

'Sounds alright to me,' said Willie 'How much will it be worth?'

'How many members have you?'

'Nay I can't fair tell you that because we haven't started properly yet. I can happen let you know on Friday, when we've had a bit of a do at it. I can let you know on my way to the bank.'

'Well let me know how many as soon as you can and then I'll tell you how much you can expect. Now don't forget, mum's the word.' He pointed to his nose again.

Willie pointed to his own nose as he left the shop. 'Might just be a bit of alright this here Christmas club,' he thought as he made his way along the village, snooking up here, spitting there and occasionally breaking wind.

He was deep in thought. So deep in fact that that he didn't know that he had said out loud, to no one in particular, with a huge grin on his face. 'By gum I never knew Len Charrington had such a big nose.'

Len Charrington never knew either why a little old lady, not one of his regular customers, spent the whole of five minutes staring intently at him through the shop window.

'Be sharp and shut that door! There's a right draught when it's open and it gets into my bones, right through to the marrow. This cold weather will be the death of me yet.'

'I ought to leave it wide open,' thought Willie, but he shut it just like Mrs Woofenden knew he would.

'Now how have you gone on at the bank? What's the manager like? Have you sorted him out and got your Christmas club sorted out? Are you going back to your work again? We can't afford to lose an afternoon's pay. Have you-' She gave over as she realised she was interrogating an empty room.

Willie went into the kitchen to Thelma. 'Have we a mantrap what'll fit your mother?' he enquired.' I nearly left the front door open wide to let the cold air get through to her marrow. She's had the bloody cheek to tell me to get back to my work because we can't afford to lose a full afternoon's pay. We could if she contributed a bit towards the running of the house. It's not fair, I've kept her for more years than I care to think about and she's kept me poor all that time.'

Willie had a good loud belch.

'Willie!'

'Sorry, love. That was for you mother. Have we owt to eat, I'm starving.'

'You can't be starving by the smell of your breath and you can manage till teatime without. Now I know it's difficult and I know she goes on a bit, but can't you try to live in peace with her? It does make life awkward for me. As soon as you've gone back to work she'll be on at me about how she pleaded with me not to marry you and so on.'

'It's just like living with the Gestapo. Anyhow, I'd best go and get changed and get back to the mill, they'll be wondering where I am. Hey, do you know what? You know Daniel Sykes? I saw him coming out of number nineteen Mafeking Street where yond blonde woman lives.'

'Which blonde woman?'

'You know her what always wears low cut dresses and uses a lot of make-up. Nice figure, different feller every night whilst her husband's away at sea.'

'How do you know so much about her?'

'I hear folk talking.'

'Are you sure that's all, only hearsay?'

'Aye that's all. I don't know the woman personally.'

'Not Daniel Sykes. Why wasn't he at the mill?'

'Nay I don't know. But I'm sure as hell going to find out when I get back.'

Willie went upstairs to get into his working attire again. He returned to the kitchen to give Thelma a kiss, then into the front room where he stopped in front of his mother-in-law who was tuning up for a good squawk.

'Well it's about time. I thought you were never-'

'Shut your foul gob for a minute and listen to me.' Willie was amazed by his own courage.

Mrs Woofenden looked somewhat startled if not angry.

Willie continued, 'If you say one word about me to Thelma after I've gone back to my work, when I get back home again, I'll have you out of that door and on your way for good as fast as its bloody well possible. Do you understand?'

She thought about replying, but, thinking he just perhaps meant it, she decided to turn the tear taps on at full flow instead. Willie straightened his cap, opened the front door, went out into the icy, biting half fog and set off with a determined stride towards the mill. Leaving the front door wide open. He heard her shouting, 'Thelma, Thelma.', quickened his pace and laughed out loud.

The big wrought iron gate was open but Willie made a slight detour through the penny hoil to speak to George Schofield who saw him coming.

'Oh, it's you again.'

'Hey, that rumour that you sleep in here all day isn't true then?'

'Huh?'

'Now then. Has Daniel Sykes come back yet?'

'No and he won't be. His mother's popped her clogs for the last time and he's off sorting the funeral arrangements. Anyway, what's it to you?'

'Nowt. I just saw him in the village when he should have been here and I wondered what he were doing. Well thank-you for your assistance, my man. You may go back to sleep now.'

'Bugger off and get some work done.'

Willie made straight for the dyehouse.

'How've you gone on then?' enquired Arthur as soon as Willie had put on his leather apron.

'Not bad. Not bad. I've sorted it out with Sharples the bank manager. I just have to take the money every Friday after dinner and that's all there is to it. Hey, guess what, I saw Daniel Sykes coming out of number nineteen Mafeking Street.'

'So what, apart from why was he there when he should have been here?'

'His mother's died.'

'So what?'

'Well he's out making arrangements for the funeral but I saw him coming out of number nineteen Mafeking Street.'

'What is so significant about number nineteen Mafeking Street?'

'She lives there.'

'Who's she?'

'That blonde woman with the big attributes, her what's husband is a sailor and her what displays her favours all over for any man what'll have her.'

'Aye, I know who you mean. Happen she's related?'

'Never in a month of Sundays. Not a miserable sod like him related to a woman of easy virtue.'

'Why not?' asked Arthur.

'Well it doesn't seem right, him being like he is and her being like she is, they couldn't be related.

'Happen it's her husband?'

'What is?'

'Happen it's him that's related.'

'I never thought of that. It's more likely, cos them two can't be off the same breed. It's just not possible.'

'Hey up,' said Arthur, 'we'd best get some work done. Walter's coming over. Let's ask him about it, he might know.'

Walter Smith hurried over to see why the two friends were not working. 'Have you two got nowt to do?' he bellowed.

'Hey Walter, come over here a minute,' said Willie motioning him to attend, which he did. 'You know yond blonde woman what lives at number nineteen Mafeking Street?'

'What about her?' asked Walter beginning to redden up around the neck.

'What relation is she to Daniel Sykes?'

'Nay, I don't know and anyway what is it to you?'

'I saw him coming out of her front door when I went t' bank.'

'His mother's died. Perhaps they are related and he'd gone to tell her. Still, I don't think they are related; in fact I'm fairly sure they're not. So what would he be doing there at that time of day?'

'I wonder,' said Arthur.

'I've been wondering ever since I saw him.'

Walter intervened, 'Give over worrying about Daniel Sykes and get some work done for a change.'

They started work again. Arthur poured a bucket of black dye liquid into a dyeing machine and Willie dragged a big cart load of cloth pieces up to another dyeing machine. As he passed Arthur, Willie stopped briefly and said. 'Did you notice how Walter began to blush when we mentioned her what lives at number nineteen Mafeking Street?'

'Yes I had noticed. It makes you think doesn't it?'

'Aye, it does that.'

'It makes you think,' said Arthur repeating himself, 'that we ought to go round to Mafeking Street on our way to the club. If we go there, that is, just to see what, if owt, is happening.'

'Aye we could do. It might make life interesting for a change.'

So the late afternoon's work in Murgatroyd's dyehouse continued at its usual hurried pace. Willie confided in Arthur that he would probably be in terrible trouble when he arrived home, following his brush with his mother-in-law and Arthur interrogated Willie closely on what had transpired at the bank. Not that he managed to get a lot of sense out of Willie about the matter.

As Willie, Arthur and Eustace were walking home at five o'clock; the ice was crunching under their feet as they walked on top of the frozen puddles which lay perpetually through the middle of most winters in the ruts and troughs of the canal towpath.

'Now are you sure that you are fully prepared for the first session on Friday dinnertime?' Arthur asked Willie.

'First session of what?'

'First session of people bringing money for the Christmas club.'

'Is it on Friday? Is it Arthur? Is it on Friday? First time is it?'

'Yes, Eustace, it is. Have you decided how much you are going to pay in?'

'No, no, not yet. I've no idea, none at all, no, none at all. I don't know how much to pay in, I don't know. How much do you think I should pay in?'

'Well I can't answer that for you, but a pound wouldn't be a bad idea.'

'A pound, I might, a pound. Yes, I might. How much would that be at Christmas?'

'Well, how much is fifty times one pound?' Willie asked him.

'Fifty times one pound. Fifty times one pond, that's a difficult question to answer. I don't know. Now lets see, it's er, er, er, er, er, fifty.'

Willie and Arthur walked on in silence as Eustace wrestled with the mathematical problem, discussing it with himself.

'It's a bit of a poor do when you can't reckon up something as simple as that,' observed Arthur

'Aye it is,' agreed Willie, who was having serious private doubts about his own ability to cope with the task that lay ahead of him. 'Mind, you've got to be daft not to be able to reckon up a simple sum like that.'

'Fifty pounds, Fifty pounds. It was easy wasn't it? Wasn't it Willie? Easy wasn't it?' Eustace walked on with a very contented smile.

They arrived outside Willie's abode at Cutside Cottages, but both Arthur and Eustace lived nearer the centre of the village.

'You coming to the club later Willie?'

'I think I'll go now. Look she's staring out of the window, sat in front of the fire. She won't ever let Thelma draw the curtains until I get in from the mill. Mind you, that's only so she can nosey. What she can see in the pitch black dark from where she sits, I do not know. I think I might go and move her onto the towpath where she can freeze to death and then there'll be peace in our house. Anyroad, I'm having no more of her nonsense ever again. I've made my mind up. So, I'll call for you at half past eight.'

'Make it nine will you. She wants a bit of a shelf putting up in the scullery.'

'Can I come to the club? Can I, Willie? Can I? Can I?'

'Yes Eustace, you can come with us. Of course you can. You be at the club at a quarter past nine.'

Arthur and Eustace moved off towards their respective homes, leaving Willie standing staring at his front door. He took a deep breath and marched smartly up to the cottage, forcefully opened the front door and marched in, slamming the door hard behind him.

'You're late again,' cackled Mrs Woofenden.

'Shut your gob and don't ever interfere with me again.'

'Willie! Don't you ever speak to my mother like that,' shouted Thelma from the back kitchen.

He gave his mother-in-law a look of utter contempt then turned his attention to the kitchen door, walked smartly over to it, put his head through to see Thelma preparing tea and said in a voice loud enough to carry back to his mother-in-law, 'Now, listen here, I've just about had my bellyful of your mother. I've had enough of her moaning and groaning about her bad back and the cold getting through to her bones. There's nothing wrong with her back that a dose or two of hard work wouldn't put right and she's not as starved as she makes out either.'

'But Willie-' Thelma started but he silenced her.

'But Willie, nothing. You just hold your noise a while and listen to me. She has sat in front of the great big fire now for that long that she can't do without it, but it's all her own making, so starting tonight, you can start and cut down on the amount of coal that we burn. She sits there in front of that fire day in and day out, never contributing a penny piece to the running of this house. She expects us to wait on her hand and foot and there's nowt wrong with her. She has an appetite like a horse, eats like there's no tomorrow, but never pays for any food. She never gives the kids owt except something and nothing at Christmas and Birthdays and finally she's a rotten, miserable, tight fisted old hag.'

Willie was delighted with his performance so far. He turned away from Thelma, who had stopped preparing tea in the face of his tirade, and returned to the front room where he addressed himself to the old lady.

'I hope you heard that lot Woofenden.'

It was obvious she had for a tidal wave was issuing from her eyes.

'I see you did. Right you can stop scriking right now and listen to me. I have had enough of your moaning, groaning and interfering, so you can agree to stop it here and now, immediately and for good, or you can pack your bags tonight and leave my house for ever.'

'Where will I go? I've nowhere else to go.'

'That's up to you. But in addition to all that, if you are stopping and deciding to behave, you can start paying your way. Five pounds a week will do nicely for a start.'

'Five pounds a week? Five pounds a week? I can't afford five pounds a week.'

'Well you can and I know you can, so you can start this Friday. In fact I'll put one pound of it into our new Christmas club every week.'

Josie and the other younger children had been watching the proceedings with awe. They had, on very few occasions, seen their father as cross and masterly as he was now and they were very frightened of him, because they knew that when he was in this mood, he meant every word he said, so they kept very quiet. Even Josie, who was very prone to getting involved in any domestic argument that was going on, kept herself well out of this one.

Willie continued his tirade at Mrs Woofenden. 'You can also start and help Thelma around the house. It's wearing her to a frazzle looking after all of us, so I'll give you twenty four hours to decide. Either you do as I say, or you pack your bags and get out of my house for good.'

'It's not your house. It belongs to the mill-' she began.

'I might not own the house, but it's still my house and if I say so, you will go. I only need to mention it to Anthony Murgatroyd and he'll make sure you're gone.' He turned to face the kitchen and asked, 'what's for tea Thelma?'

Thelma looked at him, and then decided she'd better answer. 'Sausage and chips.'

'Good. Now get it ready and on t' table. I could eat an elephant.'

They ate tea in a somewhat strained atmosphere, almost in silence except for the sound of Willie and his performing table manners. He, for his part, enjoyed his tea more than usual.

After tea and a couple of hours pottering about between the kitchen and the now empty pigeon loft, Willie went upstairs to get washed and changed to go to the club. Thelma came upstairs into the bedroom, put her arms around Willie, and gave him a big hug and then a long loving kiss.

'Thanks, love,' she said and went back downstairs again. Willie smiled, glowing inside, knowing he had done what he should have done a long time before.

Willie knocked at Arthur's door promptly at nine o'clock. It was opened by Arthur's wife Jessie, a good natured, well built woman who always made Willie feel at home.

'Come in, Willie. Arthur's not hardly ready yet. He's been fixing me a new shelf in the back scullery and it's taken him a bit longer than he thought. He gets a bit muddled with a job like that. He's very good at decorating but he's not at all clever with woodwork and bits of repair jobs.'

Arthur came through from the scullery in time to save his reputation from any further demolition, already changed and ready to go.

'Now behave yourselves you two. Are you taking Eustace with you?'

'Yes, he said he'd come along,' said Arthur.

'Well don't lead him into any trouble, you know he can't cope.'

'Don't worry, Mrs Baxter, we always look after him.'

'When will you start to call me Jess?' she asked Willie.

'I've told you before, it doesn't sound right,' he replied.

'Well I wish you would. I hate Mrs Baxter from a friend.'

'Right oh, Jess,' said Willie grinning. 'Come on Arthur, let's be having you.' The two of them set off walking to the club.

On the way, Willie said, 'Why don't we go round by Mafeking Street and see what's doing at number nineteen?'

'It's too cold,' said Arthur.

'Aye it is, bit it's not far out of our way, just to see if she's in mourning or not.'

So they walked along, Willie playing football with a stone, imagining himself playing for Manchester United in their front line and he helped in along with a belch here and a spit there. Arthur, being by this time somewhat worried as to what might happen on Friday lunchtime when they opened the Christmas club, tried his best to cross question Willie about just exactly what he might be intending to do, but as usual he could get not a lot of sense out of him and he was no wiser when they arrived at Mafeking Street.

'We can't just walk up here and back for no good reason or folk that see us will think we're potty,' said Arthur.

'We have a good reason.'

'Yes, but you know what I mean.'

'Aye, but we can look like two plain clothes beat bobbies. Nice and steady like, about their speed.'

So they walked steadily up the hill to the top, past the terrace of neat clean houses, all with well scoured front steps and neatly kept gardens. Number nineteen was a blaze of light. There were lights upstairs and in the front hallway, but no one came and nothing happened. When they reached the top of the street, Arthur moaned about how cold it was and how it would be a lot warmer in the club, but Willie insisted on walking slowly back down the street. They passed the front of number nineteen again and Arthur, moaning again, nattered about what a waste of time it had been and it was only when they were a couple of houses further down the street that they heard the sound of a door opening and people talking.

They turned immediately around to observe Walter Smith coming out from within. Unfortunately for Walter there was a very bright street light just outside and, as he made a quick and furtive glance up and down the street, his eyes came to rest on Willie and Arthur.

Walter stepped back inside quickly and slammed the door.

'That's flummoxed him,' said Willie. 'Quick, round the back.'

'There's a through passage two houses up,' said Arthur, before they set off running like rats out of a trap towards the back door, arriving there just in time to see Walter step out, observe them and step straight back in again.

'What now?' asked Arthur, who had stopped moaning and was starting to enjoy himself.

'Nay, I don't know. Which door do you think he'll try next?'

'I don't know. Tell you what, you stop here, and I'll nip around the front again.'

Arthur set of running just as fast as his little legs would take him and arrived back at the front door just in time to see Walter look out and slam the door again. Willie observed the curtains at the back of the house part and Walter look into the black darkness of the icy night. It was beginning to snow. Just a few light airborne flakes, but enough to tell Willie that it was time to go to the comfort of the club. He walked back through the passage to the front of the house to tell Arthur that it was time they were going.

'Hold on a minute,' said Arthur, 'we've got him trapped in there. We could make him very late home and in certain trouble with his missus.'

'Didn't I tell you he blushed when I mentioned Daniel Sykes being here? By gum we couldn't half have some fun, but I reckon we'd best let him be for now, so let's get off t' club.'

'Go on then, it's not fair to leave him there and, just think, we can hold it against him for the rest of his life.'

It smelt warm and cosy when they opened the front door of the club and even warmer when they went into the brightly lit bar.

'My word, well look who's here for the forty-third time today. Can't keep away. It must be my overly pleasant personality that pulls him in. It can't be the beer, nor the decorations, so it must be me. What will you be purchasing for your own consumption this evening, oh truly valued customer?'

'At the next club committee meeting I'm going to recommend a new steward.' Arthur whispered to Willie.

Willie took up Fat Harry's challenge. 'It's not the beer, it's not the decorations and it's certainly not you foulbreath. It's because it's warm in here and the landlord at the Wool Sack will only put a little bit of coal on his fire, and that's why we're here.' He took a breather to break wind, causing much coarse comment from those sitting in the air stream, but contrary to the threatening, no one moved away.

Fat Harry was the first to react. 'They reckon there's going to be a farting contest over in the hills this summer. Can I enter you Willie as the club's official farter?'

'Nay I think not, I'll have enough on my plate with this here Christmas club.'

'So what are you having to drink, you and your side kick here, eh? And your other sidekick that's just walked in.'

They turned to see Eustace approaching.

'Sorry I'm late, Arthur, Willie, sorry I'm late. My mother wanted a few jobs doing and they took me a bit to do, they did, they took me a bit of doing Willie.'

'You're lucky; you've just come in time as it's your turn to buy a round,' said Arthur.

'Is it? Is it my turn to buy a round? Is it Willie, my turn to buy a round? Is it?'

'Yes it is Eustace,' said Dick, who, accompanied by Lewis had crept in behind the other three.

'Well what yer having then? Triple whiskies all round?' asked the steward.

Eustace was just a little taken back by this last announcement. 'No no, not whisky. No, not whisky, no, no, not-'

'Go on, treat us all,' said Dick.

'No, no, just a pint each, just a pint. Can't afford whisky. No, no, can't afford, not whisky, just pints, yes, just pints.'

Fat Harry pulled the pints and Eustace, after searching through several pockets to no avail and having been offered the job of cleaning out the none too salubrious lavatories in exchange for the drinks, found some money and paid.

Willie began to tell the tale he'd been dyeing to tell. 'Saw Walter Smith on the way here.'

'Oh aye,' said no one in particular very uninterestedly.

'Aye, he were coming out of number nineteen Mafeking Street.'

'Where that blonde tart lives?' asked Fat Harry. 'Her what-'

'Aye her.' Amid uproarious laughter Willie related the events of his and Arthur's visit to Mafeking Street earlier in the evening.

Dick said, 'Wait until I get to work tomorrow.'

'Nay, don't say nowt to him at all,' said Arthur. 'Let's see what he says to us first of all. So don't none of you say owt at all to him, not nowt at all.'

'You can hold it against him for the rest of his life,' said Lewis. 'You two should be able to have a right nice steady carry on from now on. You want to make the most of it.'

'Ee, I never thought about that, but we'll work on it, won't we Arthur. Hey, you lot I've had a right do with t' wife's mother. I've told her she can either get off her fat backside and get some work done, pay her fair share and burn less coal on the fire or pack her bags and get gone.'

'Did you Willie? Did you? Did you tell her that?' Eustace smiled with admiration.

'What did she say?' asked Dick.

'Nowt. She just sat there blubbering and wailing.'

'Good lad Willie. I'm proud of you,' said Fat Harry.

There followed a chorus of praise for him, but privately they all assumed he was lying and it was just wishful thinking again.

CHAPTER 10

Friday morning arrived with a heavy snow that lay three or four inches deep on the canal towpath. Wearing their Wellington boots, Willie and Arthur trudged towards the mill, head on into the driving snowstorm coming on the back of a North East wind.

'I hope it won't be so deep by ten o'clock that they can't fetch our wage money from t' bank, or else we shan't be able to start the Christmas club at dinner time. Nobody'll have owt to put into it. Where's Eustace?' said Willie all in one breath.

'Nay, I haven't seen him this morning, probably digging a path from his front door to the gate.'

'Aye, that's the beauty of having a front door straight onto the towpath. I've nowt to dig.'

'Yes, you're right. It's taken me ten minutes to dig out. I can't have Jess late for her work. Willie, have you brought a book or anything to write down who pays us what, when you collect the money?'

'No, I never thought about it. Do I need one do you reckon?'

'Of course you do, a book and a pencil, so that you can write down who pays what and then after the first week you can make up a series of columns across, with names in the first vertical and the amount they pay. It will be very simple after that and then any of us can do it of you can't for any reason.'

Willie was once again floundering in understanding Arthur's very straightforward explanation but said, 'Yes I'll do that, happen I can borrow a piece of paper from Walter Smith, it's the least he can do under the circumstances.'

'Yes, it wouldn't do him any harm to give us a piece or two.'

They arrived at the penny hoil; where they went in to clock on and say good morning to George Schofield.

'Brass monkey weather,' said George dryly.

'It is that,' agreed Willie. 'Just the day for taking your pet elephant ice skating.'

'Don't be so daft. I can't afford skates big enough to fit my elephant and anyway it can't skate.'

Eustace arrived decidedly out of breath. 'I've run all the way in the snow. I have, run, all the way, in the snow, all the way.'

Willie looked at him and said, 'George's elephant can't ice skate.'

'Can't it George? Can't it? Can't it ice skate? Your elephant, can't it? Can't it?' He paused for a few brief moments then said, 'Which elephant George. I didn't know you had one. Have you? Have you an elephant? Have you George?' He paused again then smiled. 'You're having me on, aren't you? Having me on, aren't you George.'

Arthur interrupted the proceedings by saying, 'Come on or we'll be late.'

'It's alright, he can't say nowt,' said Willie.

'Who can't say nowt?' enquired George Schofield.

'Walter Smith.'

'He can't because he hasn't clocked in yet, but why can't he say anything?'

'It's nowt to do with you. Are you putting owt into our Christmas club? It's at dinner time today, you know.'

'Aye, I do know and no I'm not. You're not having any of my brass and that is for sure. I'll never see it again if you lot get a hold of it. You won't have seen Ted Smith on his way home this morning, will you? He's had to stop behind and help Walter Holroyd dig a load of snow off the coal stack, or else we shall run out of steam later. He won't half cop it when he gets home more than late.'

'Do him good to cop it,' said Willie. 'Come on let's get that dyehouse into life.'

They hadn't been working for long when Walter Smith walked in. Willie beamed at him, saying, 'We've got things moving alright so you needn't have worried about it.'

'Thanks Willie. I wasn't worrying anyway. No problems?'

'Well me and Arthur haven't any. Can I have a piece of paper?'

'What do you want a piece of paper for?'

'For our Christmas club what we're starting this dinner time. Are you putting owt in?'

'No, I can't afford just now. I've a lot of commitments at home you understand.'

'Oh aye, I understand alright. Can I have a piece of paper then?'

'Yes. How big a piece do you want?'

'Oh, er, a big one and a pencil.'

'And a pencil?'

'Aye. I've got to write down a list of them what's paid and how much.'

'How many are you expecting to join?'

'Nay, I haven't a clue. Can I borrow a pencil then?'

Walter, having decided he was very lucky to get away without a cross questioning regarding last night's activities, went away to get Willie his paper and pencil.

When morning break time came around, Willie, Arthur, Dick and Lewis were talking about number nineteen Mafeking Street. Walter must have heard the uproarious laughter, as he turned around from his mug of coffee and newspaper several times to stare at them. Dick was more than surprised that Walter had said nothing of the affair to any of them.

'He could have apologised for his behaviour or played war with you two for spying in him or summat, but to say nothing at all, it's brazen.'

They chatted about the same subject throughout break time without getting it any further, just turning it over and over.

Dinner time arrived and Willie was half way up the canteen steps when the hooter sounded. Sarah Anne Green, who not for no good reason was worried about Willie, was close behind him.

'Hello Willie. Have you got everything prepared?'

'Aye, I think so. I've got a big piece of paper and a pencil.'

'And what are you going to do with the paper and pencil?'

'Going to write down everybody what pays and how much they pay.'

'Then what?'

'Then I'm going to t' bank with t' money, then I'm coming back here to my work.'

'What are you going to do about making a permanent week by week record of the payments?'

'Eh?'

'What are you going to do about making a list that you can use every week so that it's easier for you? A bit like school register, only for money.'

'Well me and Arthur talked about it and we're going to do it after today and before next week.'

'Where's the paying in book?'

'What paying in…? Oh hell I've gone and left it at home. Mind you that's nowt because I shall pass our house on my way to the bank so I can get it then.'

Fortunately for Willie, the serving hatch opened and Greasy Martha stuck her ugly head out. 'Fish.' She stated or possibly asked.

'What about it?' asked Willie.

'Do you want some or not? It's all the same to me.'

'Aye I might as well as not. Has it got worms in it?'

'Do you want parsley sauce? Worm's good with parsley sauce.'

'Well in that case, happen I'd better have some. Put plenty of chips on I'm starving.'

'I've never known you not to be.'

'Is there any parsley in the parsley sauce?

'No, it's my own special recipe made with fresh green mouse droppings.'

'Great stuff. Shove a huge dollop all over it. It's a long time since I had green mouse dropping sauce called parsley.'

Willie walked over to the corner table carrying an unusually generous helping which he devoured at great speed, partly with his fork, partly with his knife and partly with his fingers, making more than his fair share of noise in the process. He had almost finished his meal when the others arrived with theirs and they had no sooner started to eat than Willie was on his feet heading for the dirties trolley to stack his licked clean plate. He was quickly at the back of the queue to the serving hatch, those in front of him still waiting for their first course. As Willie arrived at the hatch he was handed a plate of fish and chips.

'Bloody funny pudding.'

Martha looked at him and said, 'Oh, it's you is it? By gum you've pigged that lot. Sweets isn't ready yet.'

'Well get a move on. I've a lot to do this dinner time.'

Martha continued to prepare for serving the sweets. 'Are you ready for the big rush then?'

'Do you reckon there's going to be a big rush?'

'Yes, there well might be. There's a lot of talk about joining. Anyway, your sweet's ready.'

She placed the dish of Manchester tart in front of him and then gave him the huge jug of custard so that he could pour on as much of it as he liked. In the meantime, Martha dodged out of sight to have a quick drag of her cigarette and a cough.

On the way back to his table, Willie passed Eric Tanner who was half way through his first course.

'One of them, aren't you Eric?' said Willie at the top of his voice.

'One of which?' retorted Eric in a very offended manner.

'You know, one of them there,' said Willie as he winked at Eric.

Almost at a scream, Eric shouted, 'One of which? I don't know what you mean I'm sure, and I'll sue you if you say any more, and anyway, what are you talking about?'

'One of them from Manchester.'

'Yes. So what?'

'So we're only having your pudding. That's what.'

'What sort of pudding?'

The whole of the canteen was by now watching and listening to the proceedings.

'Manchester tart. You were brought up on it and that's why you are as you are.'

'I've a mind to give you a good hiding.'

'No fighting in here,' shouted Greasy Martha from the servery. 'Outside the pair of you if you're going to fight. I've got to clear up after you.'

Eric Tanner turned his back on Willie in the hope of offending him, but Willie wasn't in the least bothered. He had upset haughty Eric and that was enough for him.

Willie's portion of Manchester tart was soon dispensed with in a few deft movements of spoon, fingers and tongue to lick the remaining custard from the plate. The pint of tea was downed as if it were a spoonful and his dinner was rounded off in time honoured tradition with the usual good loud belch which everyone present expected and ignored.

Soon after Willie had finished his dinner, Sarah Anne Green came across and asked, 'Are we just about ready?'

'Yes, I think so. Just as soon as Arthur's finished eating.'

'Won't be two minutes,' he replied.

Sarah Anne sat down at their table to wait for Arthur and as soon as he was ready, she rose to her feet and banged on the table with Willie's dirty spoon. Eventually, some sort of order was established and she began to give the assembled diners a short lecture.

'Ladies and gentlemen, as you all know today is the first payment day for the Christmas club. Willie Arkenthwaite will take your money, here at the corner table, ably assisted by Arthur Baxter. Thank-you.'

She sat down on a free seat nearby, making ready to watch and assist if required.

The rush to join was slow to start, in fact for a few minutes it was non-existent. Then slowly, first one, then another, then a few more, and finally a lot more, until there was a sizeable queue weaving in and out amongst the canteen tables, all wanting to give Willie their money.

Willie carefully laid his piece of paper on the table, got out his pencil, licked the lead, began to write down the name of the first person in the queue and promptly broke the point. There was a short delay whilst he took out his Swiss Army knife and sharpened the pencil and then he began to write again. He carefully wrote down the name of each person that paid, and the amount they paid, as well as taking the money.

Arthur began to realise that it would take them far longer than the allotted dinner break to deal with the queue, so he started to take the money in order to speed things along and to give Willie more time to deal with the writing down operation.

In order to speed up the system even further, Willie began to note some people by initial only, then he lost control of the situation completely by getting some names in full, some by initials missing out the money they had paid, noting the money but not the name and slowly losing track of what was happening.

Mr Anthony Murgatroyd appeared at the head of the queue and passed over a five pound note which Willie handled longingly, before Arthur nudged him and removed it to add to his ever growing pile.

By the time that the mill hooter sounded again to herald the start of the afternoon work session, they still had a sizeable queue, but they continued to work until they had dealt with every one of them.

'Right,' said Willie, 'that were right good do. We've had loads of them, and money, so now I'll get off to t' bank.'

'How many have we had?' Arthur asked.

'A lot. A right lot.'

'Yes but how many's a right lot?'

'Well, I'm not right sure. I got a bit confused halfway through, so I don't know just how many we had.'

'Haven't you got a full list?'

'Well nearly, but I missed a few. Anyway, we can get them next week.'

Arthur examined Willie's piece of paper. 'Who's that?' he asked pointing to the initials J.C.-10/-

'J.C. That would be, er, let's see now, er, it would be, er came with er, lets see now, it would be, er-'

'Jasper Collins.'

'Yes. That were him, Jasper Collins.'

'How many more like that?'

'Like what?'

'Initials. No name.'

'A lot.'

'Do you know who they all are?'

'A few of them and there's some with just name and no money.'

'I'd best come around to your house tonight to see if we can sort this lot out before we go to the club. It's a good job Sarah Anne's gone back to her work. Now you'd best take all this brass to the bank.' He handed over to Willie a mountain of coins and notes.'

'What am I going to carry all this lot in and how much is there?'

'You'll have to count it, then roll the notes up and put them in your pocket along with the change.'

'I'll count it when I get home,' said Willie, then he made a scruffy roll of the notes, pushed them into his trouser pocket and went off to find his coat, scarf, cap and gloves.

'Where are you off?' shouted George Schofield from the warmth and comfort of his little office behind the penny hoil.

'What's it to do with you?' came the reply.

'Nowt. I were nobbut asking. Mind you, I couldn't care less and in this weather you'd be a fool to go anyway.'

'Well in that case, I'm telling you nowt at all, except that I'll be back later. So long.'

He went, just hearing George's shout of, 'So long.'

The snow was still falling heavily and there was a deep covering by the time that Willie left the mill for his cottage. There had been no-one along the canal towpath for ages, and certainly the local snowplough had not, as it never did.

He struggled gamely through the deepening snow, each footstep being an effort and getting worse by the minute. As he approached the cottage, he assumed that his mother-in-law would still be sitting by the huge roaring fire and he resolved to give her another talking to on the subject. He was not at all surprised when, on entering the front room, she took the initiative and attacked him.

'Thelma! Our Willie's home,' she screeched and then she turned her attention to him. With a self satisfied smirk on her face, she asked, 'Have you come home to get changed to take the money to the bank? And you needn't ask before you do, because I've been up on my two feet all morning helping Thelma. I've only just sat down for a rest and I'm tired out, so you trot off wherever it is you're going and I'll just have a short sleep to recover all that lost energy.'

Willie said nothing but walked into the back kitchen where he took hold of Thelma and gave her a big hug and kiss.

'Stop it, mother'll be watching, and anyway what are you doing home at this time again?'

'Have you any idea what I've done with the paying in book?'

'No, none at all. Have you lost it?'

'Not so much lost it as I can't remember where I put it. I forgot to look for it last night, so I didn't take it with me this morning. Hey we've had a heck of a lot joined and I've stacks of money to take to the bank.'

'How much have you then?'

'Don't know. I haven't counted it yet, thought I'd count it at t' bank.'

'If you don't know how much you've got, how do you know who has paid and if so, how much they've paid?'

'It's all on a piece of paper what we got from Walter Smith.'

'I wonder he's even talking to you after last night.'

'He's no option. Anyway, Arthur's coming round after tea to help me sort out a proper list of members. So where's the paying in book?'

'Did you ever take it out of your best suit when you'd been to the bank the other day?'

'Hey no, it might be there, mightn't it?'

He dashed upstairs to try to find the missing book and returned to the kitchen with it a couple of minutes later.

'Has your mother been good? Behaved herself and helped you like I told her to, and like she says she has?'

'Yes, she's washed up and done some ironing. Mind you it's tired her out.'

'It would have tired you if you'd done nowt for more years than you could remember, but at least she must have taken heed of my warning.'

'You scared the living daylights out of her. I'd a terrible time with her when you'd gone back to your work. You'll never know, or care, how much you upset her. Anyway, are you going to fill that paying in book in?'

'No. I'll fill it in at the bank. So long, I'll see you at tea time.' He had no need to speak to the old lady as he passed her for she was fast asleep in front of the fire.

Willie had taken no more than two strides into the ever deepening snow when Thelma called from the front door. 'Willie love, it's too deep for me to go out, fetch me two pounds of sugar from the co-op please.'

Willie waved and nodded, and then he heard her voice again. 'Oh and Willie, don't forget, straight there and then straight back to the mill.'

'But of course my dear,' he said mockingly and went on his way.

The club looked strange with no-one in it. The big fat steward was half asleep, lolling on the bar counter, and there was a general air of gloom about the place. Willie crept very stealthily and silently to the bar where the grotesque form of Fat Harry lay. He thought, just once, about picking up the soda siphon and squirting it in Harry's ear, but then decided that it might be very unsafe to do so, taking into account Harry's size and temper.

The next thought was for him to pour himself a pint without Harry finding out he'd got it, but also decided against that idea for more or less the same reasons, plus the fact that Harry was leaning on the pump handle didn't help. He looked around for some other form of mischief and suddenly an idea entered his head. The sheer brilliance of which amazed him and he spent a few moments in silent congratulation. He would pull out the peg that held up the roll shutter in front of the bar and this would come clattering down making a terrible noise and narrowly avoiding Harry. He walked around the bar to where he could see the peg above his head and began to outstretch his hand. At this moment in time, Willie had his back to Harry and he jumped a mile as he heard a ghostly whisper in his ear. 'Now listen very carefully fart face, if you as much as touch that peg, they'll find you hanging from the end of the bar.'

'Pour us a pint, Harry.'

'What the hell are you doing here again, disturbing a bloke going about his legal duties?

'Taking the Christmas club money to the bank. Will you help me count it?'

'You mean you haven't counted it yet?'

'No, it was a bit busy when they were paying it over and there was a hell of a lot of them, so I thought I'd count it here or at t' bank.'

'Come on then, let's have a pint each and count it. It's dead in here, glad you came in; there's been nobody at all. It's only in weather like

124

this. It's usually busy on a Friday dinner time, It's rotten when it's quiet. Where's the money then?'

Willie tipped out a hugging of coins from his left trouser pocket, then another from his right side, a few from his jacket and then a big roll of scruffy notes.

'Is that it? By gum, there's a lot. Do you know how much there should be?'

'Nay, they were coming that thick and fast that it were getting out of control, so we lost track a bit and me and Arthur's going to sort it out tonight. I'd best pay for that pint whilst I bethink me.'

'Nay, nobody will ever know, give over bothering, get it supped and say nowt.'

'You're a good pal, Harry. Now let's get this money counted so that I can get on to the bank before they close.'

It didn't take them long to count it and arrive at a grand total of sixty four pounds three shillings and sixpence.

'Good do,' said Harry. 'There's a good few paid.'

'Yes, over a hundred and fifty people, I bet.'

'Not so many. There can't be a lot more than that as works there.'

'There's over two hundred goes there every morning, but how many of them actually works is a good question.'

'You silly beggar. You know what I meant.'

'Aye, I do. About two hundred.'

'Well isn't it time you were off. They'll wonder where you are if you don't turn up.'

'Yes, I'm just going. I'll finish my beer first though.'

Willie made another scruffy bundle of the notes which he put back in his trouser pocket. He put all the coins in his jacket pocket and took his leave of Harry.

'Go straight to the bank. Do not pass go. Do not collect two hundred pounds and do not go up Mafeking Street.'

Harry heard the 'shut up' part of whatever it was that Willie replied and then the door slammed, leaving him to go back to sleep after the welcome interruptions.

A rather large, fussy, pompous lady was at the head of the queue in the bank. She wore a fur coat and a fur hat and spoke posh. She was arguing with the cashier in a very loud commanding voice that her account was not overdrawn, and under no circumstances whatsoever had the young girl ever to say so again. In fact she wished to see the manager immediately and if she did not see the manager immediately she would close her account and take it elsewhere. Willie was inclined to shout some words of encouragement to the woman to take her account elsewhere and quickly but feeling a bit like a fish out of water, he kept quiet and waited for his turn to come.

The young lady behind the desk said, 'Yes sir?'

'I've er, er, brought the, er, money.'

'Yes sir. Well are you going to pay it over?'

'Er yes, er, here it is.'

Willie put the scruffy bundle of notes followed by several handfuls of coins onto the counter then stood looking absent-mindedly at the girl.

'Have you got your paying in book please, sir?'

'Yes. Here it is.'

'But you haven't filled it in, sir.'

'Have I got to fill it in then?'

'Yes sir. Haven't you paid in any money before?'

'No, and I don't know how to fill the book in.'

He didn't like to admit it to the young lady but he realised that he had no alternative, as she was very bright and much cleverer that him. So the young lady painstakingly gave him a lesson in the finer arts of filling in the various boxes and columns, including sorting out the various denominations of notes and coins.

'It's going to be a hard job is this, every Friday. Have I got to sort out all these different things?'

'Yes, sir. Every time you pay some money into the bank.'

'Well it's going to take me a long time. I shall never get back to the mill before finishing time.'

'You can come in here and sit at one of those small tables to sort it out.' She indicated a couple of tables under the window behind Willie.

'Very nice. Yes I'll do that,' said Willie as he watched the young lady stamp the page and counterfoil before tearing the page out of the book and returning it to him.

He could not decide whether or not to go back to the mill. However after a quick debate with himself, common sense overruled his heart and he headed back through the snow which had started again in earnest after a brief respite.

Not given to being a deep thinker, Willie was somewhat surprised to find himself thinking about the mess he had made of listing people's names and the monies that they had paid to him. So deep in thought was he that he could remember nothing of the events leading up to his head feeling cold and wet, his body being splayed out in the snow and a warm, rough tongue licking his left ear. Several of the inhabitants of the village who were within earshot well remembered the 'bloody hell' they heard floating down the main street that horrible snowy day, and Willie remembered well enough the number of hands that picked him up and brushed the snow off him. He also remembered hearing the voices around him.

'Who is it?'

'It's Willie Arkenthwaite.'

'What's he doing out hear in the middle of a Friday afternoon?'

'You'll have to look after this here dog better than that Sam.'

About this time, Willie had recovered enough of his senses to look around and see a collection of familiar faces gathered around him, along with Sam Garside and his Lakeland Terrier.

Willie stared at Sam. 'What the hell happened, Sam?'

'Nay, it were thee. I said "good afternoon Willie" and yer took no notice, just walked on with yer head down as if yer hadn't heard me, and then bang, yer walked straight into t' dog lead and went straight over it with yer head in t' snow and yer arse uphill. Josh here took a liking to yer ears and kept 'em warm for yer. What's up wi' yer? It's not like yer to be like yer were.'

'Sorry Sam. I'd my mind on other things. Is the dog alright?'

'Oh aye. There's not up wi' t' dog. He had many a worse do ner that. Anyroad what were yer thinking about? Is it this here Christmas club what rumour had it yer t' big boss over?'

'Aye, summat like that, just a few problems. Anyway if your dog is alright, I'm alright, so there's no harm done and I'd best be on my way. I'll see you later. In fact when I do see you, you can buy me a pint for causing the accident.'

'Nay it weren't that bad an accident, not worth a pint it weren't and any road it were yer fault.'

'So long, Sam.

'So long, Willie.'

Willie trudged away, heading for the mill, fuming with inner rage at his own stupidity. The onlookers had moved on, one by one, all laughing at him behind his back and it was this that was making him angry. He vowed not to tell a soul about his fall and after carefully observing what he could see of himself and removing a few lumps of snow that was stuck to his clothes; he kept on walking with his mind firmly attached to the monetary problems.

He passed through the penny hoil passage without even looking in to see George Schofield who was looking out and staring at him aghast, for never, ever, in all the years that they had both worked at the mill, had Willie passed by without a few words of idiotic wisdom. It wasn't until Willie had vanished from sight around the corner of the big mill that George gave over staring after Willie, and even then it was quite a while before he resumed his normal gormless expression. He then began to muse as to why Willies coat had been covered in lumps of snow.

'Has tha been rolling in t' snow then?'

Willie ignored, or maybe didn't hear, this proffered gem from the far side of the dyehouse. Similarly the 'hey up, he's back. By gum lad, you were nobbut just in time, we were about to send the St Bernards out looking for you,' didn't receive the verbal return it should have.

In fact no one could get a word out of Willie for the rest of the afternoon. He buckled down and worked harder than usual, ignoring everyone around him.

When five o'clock came, Arthur asked him, 'What time shall I come round to your house?'

'Straight after tea. I'm a bit worried about this money business.'

'You're not on your own. I'm scared stiff over it. I'll be round at half past six.'

'Thank heavens for that.'

The two of them, and Eustace, struggled together to Willie's cottage. Eustace was most concerned about Willie and Arthur tried his best to explain the difficulties they were facing to sort out the club money. They parted company outside Cutside Cottages with their customary 'see you later' and 'at the club Willie.'

'The club, are you going to the club? Arthur? Are you? Are you going-'

'Shut up Eustace.'

Arthur and Eustace plodded on through the deep snow, still arguing.

CHAPTER 11

The warmth of the front room at number six Cutside Cottages relieved Willie's sombre mood somewhat. Mrs Woofenden was at her usual post in the corner and the young children were playing on the peg rug in front of the fire. Josie was laying the table for tea and Thelma was busy in the kitchen. Most of the snow had melted from Willie's Wellington boots into small pools on the front room carpet by the time he got to the kitchen where he gave Thelma his usual hug and kiss.

'Willie, have you let all the snow from your boots melt on the living room carpet, as usual?'

'Sorry, love.'

'Where's the sugar?'

'Oh sorry, I forgot to get it.'

'Oh Willie! I wanted to bake tonight. Can you go now and get it?'

'Co-op shuts at half past five, it's too late. Mind you, Freddy Nevershut will still be open. I could go there, only his sugar is a halfpenny dearer than t' co-op's. Hold tea up for ten minutes and I'll go get a bag.'

He went out into the bitter cold night again and headed for the village. The wind was easing a little and there was a steady downpour of big white flakes.

The bell over the door sounded as Willie entered the emporium of Freddy Nevershut.

'By gum, it's Willie Arkenthwaite as I live and breathe. You haven't graced your presence in my establishment since I don't know when. How are you?'

A quarter of an hour later, Willie was still sitting on the edge of an upturned lemonade crate telling the tale with Freddy.

'Before I forget, can I have two pounds of sugar? I'd best not go home without it.'

'Is that all you've come for on a night like this?'

'Yes, our Thelma hasn't been out today.'

'She wouldn't have been in here if she had.'

'No, she likes her divvy from the Co-op. Er, Freddy, getting back to our Christmas club, what's in it for me if I try and get as many as I can of 'em, to get their Christmas orders here? Can you do stuff a bit cheaper for them and what can I get out of it for nowt?'

'Nay, Willie. That's corruption! You know full well that I'm an upright and sober, law abiding citizen and a true Christian…pop back in a fortnight and I'll have had time to think about it.'

'Thanks Freddy. Give us a quarter of aniseed balls for the kids. How much do I owe you?'

Willie picked up the sugar and sweets, paid Freddy and trudged off into the deep snow again. The bargees were tying up a barge at the wharf when he went past and he stopped to exchange a few words with them before returning to the cosiness of his cottage.

'Well, now that I'm back, what's for tea?'

'Neck of mutton stew and dumplings with bread and butter pudding for afters,' said one of the youngsters who had as big a liking for food as his father.

'Great stuff,' said Willie rushing to wash and find his slippers.

He sat down at the table, just in time to observe Josie take a big, steaming, time blackened pan from the hob of the range and carry it to the table, where she proceeded to serve the contents into a pile of hot dishes.

'Put plenty of dumplings on mine, Josie,' he ordered as he got up from the table and walked over to stand with his back to the fire to get warmed through before he began to eat. He was still standing there when Thelma came out of the back kitchen to ask her mother and the children to come and sit around the table.

'Come on Willie, love, your tea's out.'

'Nay, I can't, I shall have to get warm, it's the weather you know, it cuts through my bones, I'm starved to the very marrow.'

Mrs Woofenden looked at Willie, then at Thelma, shed a tear or two, and then said, 'Thelma lass, tell your Willie to stop imitating me will you?'

'See Willie. You've upset my mother again.'

'Not half as much as I shall if ever I hear any more of her trouble,' he said and, with a smile of great satisfaction, he sat down at the table again where he gave a demonstration of troughing with accompanying sound effects of which any right thinking pig would have been proud. The youngsters were struggling to finish their big bowls of stew and Willie suddenly had an idea how to get them to eat it all up.

He said, 'I've got a very special present for after tea and those who don't eat all their stew can't share at it.'

'What is it?' came the chorus.

'Wait and see.'

'Oh Dad, come on, tell us.'

'No, you'll have to eat all your stew and dumps first.'

'Oh Dad, come on, tell us what it is.'

'No. Eat your tea.'

The children tucked in again, resigned to that fact that they would have to eat all of their stew before they could enjoy their surprise. Thelma, who had joined into the spirit of the events, doled out large portions of bread and butter pudding, skipping Willie's usual pudding mountain in favour of the children. He realised why and didn't complain, just ate with his usual fervour.

As soon as the pudding was eaten and all plates were empty, the children started again. 'Come on Dad, let's have our surprise now.'

'No, not yet. I want my mug of tea first. In peace.'

'Oh go on. Now, now,' the chant began, 'now, now, now-'

'All right,' he said and smiling, he went into the kitchen to retrieve the bag of aniseed balls from his coat pocket transferring it immediately into his trouser pocket. He walked back into the front room to sit at the table again picking up the pint pot of steaming hot tea that had been put there by Thelma in his absence.

The children stared and shouted at him, 'Dad, dad.'

'Oh go on then,' he said as he handed them the bag of sweets. 'Give one to your Mum and Gran.'

'Super. Thanks dad. Do you want one mum?'

'Don't talk with your mouths full,' said Willie, happy in his children's joy.

'You shouldn't spoil them like that,' said Mrs Woofenden.

Willie looked her straight in the eye and she retreated into silence again.

'Now you youngsters, Uncle Arthur's coming around tonight because me and him's got a lot of office work to do and we need some quiet whilst we work. So I want no noise whilst he's here. So if you want to play, you'll have to go into the kitchen. Okay?'

'Yes Dad.'

Half past six arrived and Arthur, with his usual promptness, knocked on the door.

Josie opened it wide and beaming at him said, 'Come in Uncle Arthur, out of the cold snow. Here let me take your coat and hang it up. How's aunt Jess?'

'Jess is fine, just fine. Where's the young 'uns?'

'They're playing in the kitchen.'

Arthur walked through into the back with the greeting, 'Hello Thelma. Hi kids.'

'Hi, Uncle Arthur.'

'I haven't seen you all since Christmas. Did you have a good time? What did Father Christmas bring you?'

'He brought me a new dolly and a pram for my new dolly,' said little Margaret, who was seven and Peter who was ten joined in the conversation with 'he brought me a clockwork train set, but that's upstairs in my bedroom. Do you want to come upstairs and have a look at it?'

'Later on, when me and your dad's finished our business. Now what about you Thelma, what did you get from Father Christmas?'

'You know full well what I got from Father Christmas, don't you? A couple of pairs of nylons same as last year and the year before and the year before and-'

'What did you get Uncle Arthur?' asked young Peter.

'A bag of coal and a string of onions,' he said laughing.

'What have you got in your case?' continued the ever inquisitive little boy, for Arthur had brought along his briefcase.

'Dolls eyes, mill chimneys and other things for grown-ups,' he said seriously.

'Can I have a look please?'

'No, not until you're a big man like me.'

'Now, now Peter,' scolded Thelma. 'Let Uncle Arthur and your Dad get on with their business.'

Arthur returned to the front room and sat down at the table with its cloth cover, where Willie joined him. He proceeded to open his case and take out a foolscap pad. Willie placed his single sheet of paper on the table in front of him and stared at it, waiting for Arthur to begin. Arthur then picked up Willie's piece of paper and studied it for a while.

'I can't make head nor tail of this. There's a few names with money, there's a lot of initials, there's a lot of amounts of money, we know how much money you took to the bank, so let's try and make a sensible list of the members for a start. We know there were a heck of a lot of folk who paid, don't we, so we might take quite a long time to sort the list out. Now then Willie, let's write down on my pad, a list of names of all those that paid.'

He took from his waistcoat pocket a very expensive looking fountain pen.

'By gum, that's a very fine pen,' said Willie gazing at it jealously.

'Yes. Jess gave it to me for Christmas.'

'Can I try it out to write the list?'

'No you can not. You should know that a fountain pen's a very special pen and only its owner should use it. Haven't you got a pen of your own?'

'Aye, I've got an ordinary pen and a bottle of ink what we use for special occasions, but I usually use a pencil. Anyroad a pencil'll do this job.'

He walked over to the range and took a pencil from the mantle shelf.

When he was seated again, Arthur enquired, 'Are you ready now?'

'Yes, I'm ready. Let's get cracking.'

Willie carefully wrote out the list of names that he had written out in full earlier in the day, as Arthur looked on. He was painfully slow and Arthur was almost losing patience with waiting for the list to be written out in almost joined up handwriting.

'Good, now what about these, here?' Arthur pointed to the original dinner time list. 'These initials here, do you know who they all are?'

'Some of them.'

'Right. Write down those that you know out in full, then let's see if we can decide who the rest are.'

'Cant we stop now? My writing arm's tired.'

'No, we can not, not for a long time yet, not until we've sorted everything out.'

'But I'm not used to all this writing and it's rotten difficult.'

'By heck, but you're a lazy sod William Arkenthwaite. Come on, get on with it or we shan't get a drink tonight.'

So Willie studied his list of initials and wrote out the names of those that he could remember, adding twenty one names to the list. Making twenty seven in total. He sat back, heaved a huge sigh of relief and for good measure, farted fortissimo.

'There's a hell of a lot of initials there yet,' said Arthur as he began to count them. 'Thirty Seven yet left there. Don't you know any of them?'

'No. I can't think of one more.'

'It's a good job I got a full list of employees from Tom Sykes this afternoon. He was a bit reluctant to let me have it at first, but when I explained to him what a cock-up you'd made of the official list, he almost begged me to take it.'

'I didn't make a cock-up of it. It were just all them folk what came too quick for me. I couldn't keep track of them. Anyroad, let's have a look at this list you've got. Where is it?'

Arthur in his amateur clerical/administrative roll, always the perfect professional in these matters, opened the briefcase with a flourish of arms and wrists, busied himself pretending to search for the piece of paper, found it, snapped the clasp of the briefcase firmly closed and laid the piece of paper smartly on the table.

Willie observed the exhibition with interest and said silently to himself and anyone else who might just happen to be passing by, 'Bloody show off.'

'Right, let us examine the matter more closely.' Arthur carefully unscrewed the lid of the new fountain pen and began to point to each name on the list which were in alphabetical order. Willie followed with keen interest. Not the names, but the fountain pen, and his mind strayed onto owning such a device. He was awakened from his daydreams by Arthur's raised voice, 'Well has he or hasn't he?'

'Er who?'

'Sid Beaumont. Did he pay us any money?'

'Yes, Sid did.'

'How much?'

'Well if he isn't on the list and his initials aren't down either we can't tell, can we?'

'But you're sure he paid?'

'Yes I'm sure.'

'Okay, so we've got one Sidney Beaumont with no known amount of contribution, so let's put his name on a separate sheet of paper and see how many names we can list.'

It was a good half hour before they had a comprehensive list of names and all initials were crossed off except one. For Arthur it had been a difficult half hour trying to keep Willie's mind on the job. For Willie it had been a very boring half hour with his mind constantly straying to any subject other than the name listing. For Mrs Woofenden, sitting in her corner chair by the fire, it had been an amusing half hour confirming her thoughts that Thelma was far too good for Willie and for Thelma it had been a very routine half hour darning and mending the children's clothes.

'Now, who's the owner of this last pair of initials that we can't find? I just can't understand it; we've no one that fits GM at all.'

'Well I don't know,' Willie replied half interestedly. 'Oh yes I do. Hang on a minute, it's Greasy Martha.'

'Greasy Martha? What's her proper name?'

'Who's Greasy Martha?' Thelma enquired.

'Fag ash Lil from the canteen. Her what slops fat all over the place and drops fag ash in us dinners,' replied Willie.

'I know, she lives down Ashbourne Road,' said Thelma. Her real name's Martha Gregson.'

Mrs Woofenden put her two pennyworth in, 'That doesn't sound right. If I'm not mistaken Gregson was her maiden name and if you'd written the GM as MG you would have had no problem with that one.'

'She's never married. Nobody would ever marry her.'

'Our Thelma married you.'

'I've warned you already tonight,' said Willie, but this time she did not shed a tear, instead she sat quietly, pleased and contented.

'It's Martha Sykes,' said Thelma. 'You know, she married Hector George Sykes. His mother kept the sweet shop by the Church for years and years.'

'Oh, you mean Horrible Hector. Well they didn't spoil two couples did they?'

Arthur was beginning to get professionally agitated again. 'Can we please get on with the matter in hand? This idle chatter is getting us nowhere at all.'

'It is, we've got the answer to GM.'

'Well time is pressing on, so let's get this job finished. Now we've still got a list of names with no money against them and a list of monies with no names. So where do we go from here?'

'How about the club?'

'First sensible suggestion you've had all night,' said Arthur.

'You're both raving mad in this weather,' said Mrs Woofenden.

Arthur maintained his professional manner, packed away the papers into his briefcase, and then they both put on their outdoor clothes and disappeared in to the horrible night.

Mrs Woofenden started onto Thelma again as soon as Willie and Arthur had vanished through the front door. 'I told you not to marry Willie Arkenthwaite. I warned you, I did my best, but you would take no notice. No brains, that's his trouble. He's got this Christmas club into a right mess and it isn't above started proper yet. You'll live to mark my words yet, he's no good, not one bit of-'

She was rudely interrupted by young Josie, who had just had enough of her Grandma's vicious tongue. 'That's my dad your talking about and I'll be obliged if you'll give over right now. You never have a good word for him, in fact, you never have a good word for anyone and I for one am fed up of hearing you. He's provided you with a good home, to which as we all know you never contribute one penny piece. You are the most ungrateful woman I have ever met or ever want to meet. He's my dad, my favourite Dad and I won't hear another wrong word said against him.'

She stood staring straight at her Grandma, shaking with rage and frightened of the consequences of what she had just done.

A tear or three came to the old lady's eyes. She looked at Thelma and then said appealingly, 'Are you going to sit there and let your Josie talk to me like that?'

'Yes mother, I am, because like the other two, I also am fed up to the back teeth of hearing you moan and groan. You are making this into a very miserable house. We were a very happy family until you came to live here and now you are rapidly driving a great big wedge between us all, making us all very unhappy. So I think it's high time you began to think about things a bit and keep quiet whilst you do so.'

Thelma nudged Josie and they went into the kitchen to join the other children. The old lady sat by the fire wetting her handkerchief as she wiped her red eyes.

Willie and Arthur trudged along the towpath through the deep snow.

'Do you reckon they'd sentence me to death if I threw the old cow into the canal with a weight tied around her neck?'

Arthur's reply was immediate, 'I reckon they'd be bound to.'

'Even if I explained to them that it was a mercy killing?'

'How can you possibly make it out that it's an act of mercy?'

'Well it would be very merciful on me and Thelma. Summat'll have to be done about her, she's been staring me out all night.'

'Aye, I noticed she never took her eyes off you, not even for one second, and they are evil eyes, horrible evil staring eyes that bore right into you. It makes a shiver run down your spine thinking about her, doesn't it? Yes you've a right problem there and no mistake. Anyway, let's change the subject. It seems to me that we've need of a committee meeting. We ought to have it on Wednesday evening in the club; there'll be no one in the committee room that night. I'll fix it up tomorrow. We just need to review progress so far and to see if anyone has any bright new ideas.'

Willie nodded in agreement as he always did when Arthur was speaking. However his mind was on two more imminent pressing matters. The first was to have a good belch, the second was to suggest that they should go to the George Inn rather than the club, it being a lot nearer in the bad weather, and they had no particular reason to go to the club. Arthur readily agreed, looking forward to seeing one or two people they hadn't seen for quite some time.

The George Inn was named after George IV, in the days when it had been a large elegant posting inn on one of the many turnpike highways that ran between Lancashire and Yorkshire. Many a wealthy traveller and many a highwayman had graced its portals in years gone by, but now it was somewhat different. Instead of a thriving wayside inn it was now a local pub frequented not all that frequently, by a largely lethargic and apathetic clientele. It was dowdy and drab in appearance. There were concert and meeting rooms, lounge and public bars, a tap room and a snug, but only the lounge and public bars were in use. No one ever held a meeting or a concert there. A few brave ones drank there regularly and occasionally people, like Willie and Arthur, would visit when for no particular reason they couldn't or wouldn't find anywhere else to go. Just before and during the war it had been a very popular place to drink, but the present landlord whom the brewery had installed, had seen to it that the regulars and therefore the sales had dwindled.

They stood on the doorstep and surveyed the dismal scene. 'Ten past nine and not a light in sight,' Willie said laughing a little.

'Door's locked as well if I know owt about it,' said Arthur as he tried the handle.

Willie stood back and looked up. 'One miserable low light in the far room, yonder.' He pointed. 'The skinflint bugger can't even put a decent size bulb in his own living room.'

Willie read the sign over the front door. 'James Richard Wood, licensed to sell intoxicating liquor etc. He ought to be licensed to hang for crimes against the human race and drinkers in particular. Ring the bell Arthur.'

Arthur pressed the bell and waited for rather a lot of nothing to happen. Willie enjoyed himself picking his nose. Arthur pressed the bell again and waited. Willie snooked up and aimed a ball of phlegm into a street grate, being well satisfied with his directional control. Arthur leaned on the bell and remained leaning on it.

Two minutes later an upstairs window opened and a curler bedecked head poked its way out. A coarse female voice screeched, 'Shut that bloody racket. What the hell do you want?'

'What the hell do you mean, what do we want? We want a drink, that is what we want.'

'What time is it?' she enquired.

'A quarter past nine. It's nearly closing time.'

'You'll have to wait a couple of minutes.'

The head disappeared ad the window slammed shut.

'Ignorant cow,' observed Willie. 'She makes it sound as if she's doing us a bloody great favour opening up.'

'Yes, it's a sad reflection on what a good pub it was when we were under age drinking all those years ago.'

'Aye, it were a good pub for under age and after hours drinking were this.'

By the time that various locks and bolts were withdrawn, three more people had gathered in the doorway to wait. They rapidly dispersed for a brief interlude when Willie broke wind, but they were back again by the time the door opened.

James Richard Wood himself personally opened the door to let his guests into the cold depressing public bar. He slouched away in front of them, heading for the back of the bar. He was wearing a loose shirt with no collar, part of a two tone suit, black trousers and a brown checked waistcoat. His well used carpet slippers slid across the floor in a steady mechanical motion, he kept his hands firmly in his pockets and his head was bowed all the time.

'Can't think why you lot can't let a fellow have a bit of peace. Didn't think there was anyone daft enough to come out tonight. Bloody cold in't it? What do you want?'

Willie didn't know which question to answer first, so he plumped for the sensible one. 'A pint of bitter and a pint of common, and can we have em served outside where it's warmer?'

'What do you mean outside where it's warmer? It's perishing out there.'

'Aye it is, but a brass monkey would be hard done by to survive in here. Haven't you lit the fire today?'

'Couldn't see much point in it. Can't see why you lot had to come in here tonight.' He continued to serve the other customers still muttering. 'There was me looking forward to a nice cosy night in front of the fire, listening to the wireless, then a nice early night. Then you lot come along. It wouldn't be so bad if you were regulars but you only come in here when you can't be bothered to go as far as the club. You haven't half upset the wife; she'll go on at me something awful when you've gone home. Life won't be worth living then.'

'I can't think why your good lady should be upset,' said Arthur. 'After all, you wouldn't have taken any brass at all if we hadn't turned up.'

'There's others here as well you know. I haven't opened up just for you two.'

'No,' said Willie, 'but they wouldn't have rung the bell like we did.'

Just then a vision of loveliness, still wearing her curlers in her hair, torn cardigan, dirty dress and worn out slippers shuffled in behind the bar and surveyed the gathered throng.

'All that bloody fuss just so that you two can have a drink, I might have known. Why couldn't you go to the club like you usually do?'

'Don't worry Edith, we will tomorrow,' said Willie.

'Yes, I think you can assume that we shall not grace your hovel with our presence again for many a long night to come,' said Arthur.

Edith looked at them both and made an unladylike noise accompanied by a gesture directed at them and disappeared again to the upstairs living quarters where it was much warmer.

'Good riddance to bad rubbish,' said Willie.

'Don't you speak about my dear wife like that behind her back Willie Arkenthwaite,' said James Richard.

Willie stared him straight in the eye and belched as loud as he could.

'You've got the manners of a bloody pig,' said James Richard.

Willie downed the rest of the pint in one swallow, stared yet again at James Richard and belched even louder. Concluding the performance with a solitary fart and one solitary word. 'Arseholes.'

'Time for an organised retreat I think,' said Arthur.

'Yes let's go somewhere where we are more welcome,' said Willie and just for good luck and in a loud voice, 'and somewhere where it's warm.'

James Richard had the final word. 'Just to use one of your well know phrases or sayings., good riddance to bad rubbish.'

He might have had the last word but not quite the last of the noise as Willie responded with yet another loud belch and a gesture. Finally, just for good measure, he broke wind as loud and as forcibly as he possibly could.

Unknown to the two of them, James Richard did have another final word.

The snow had abated a little by the time the two pals emerged from the pub and on to the street.

'Come on, let's go and have one at the club for good measure,' said Willie.

'Right. You're on, and you're paying.'

They trudged on the few hundred yards to the club. There was no more talking, it was too cold.

'Am I glad to see you two,' boomed out Fat Harry.

'Well, that makes a change for a start,' Willie replied.

'Why what's up?' Arthur enquired.

Harry pointed into the corner of the room. They turned around to observe Eustace, sitting bolt upright at a table. His usual happy countenance looking every inch like death warmed up. They stared at him for a few minutes then turned back towards Harry.

'What's up with him? And two pints please.'

'Please? Please. Coming from you William Arkenthwaite. There's nowt so queer as you acting a bit proper.'

Fat Harry proceeded to pull the two pints and go on talking. 'He came in here just after seven and started heavy drinking, pint after pint. It's not like him. He's said nowt to nobody, just gone on drinking, it's not like him, he's got me worried.'

'Well when Mr Arkenthwaite has paid for these two pints, we'll go over and have a word with him.'

'Oh yes,' said Willie as he reluctantly handed over the money.

They picked up the two pint glasses and ambled over to the table and sat down, one on each side of Eustace, who remained motionless, staring into his beer. Willie gave a rather loud belch that produced a frown from Arthur, but had no effect on Eustace.

'I've just won two hundred quid,' Willie announced to no one in particular and still there was no response from Eustace, just another frown from Arthur.

Arthur then tried with more success, taking hold of Eustace's hand he said, 'What's up old friend? We don't like to see you down in the dumps like this.'

Eustace looked up, his eyes were watering.

'It's rotten Arthur, it is, it's rotten, absolutely rotten, Arthur, Willie, it is, it's-'

'What's rotten Eustace?' he enquired.

'It's Claribell, that's what it is, it's Claribell, she did it, she did, she bloody well did it, the stupid little twit. That's what she is, a stupid little twit, that's what, a stupid tw-'

Willie interrupted, 'It must be bad; your language is shocking for you. Who the hell's Claribell and what did she do?'

'I'll ring her ruddy neck if ever I get hold of her, wring her neck, aye, that's it, wring her bloody sodding neck, that's it, I'll wring..'

'Pardon,' said Arthur, 'this is not the Eustace that we know well and love. Who is Claribell and what has she done to get you into this state?'

'The bloody cat, our bloody cat, the stupid sod, our cat, the stupid cat, she's only gone and eaten Tweety Pie.'

'Who the hell's Tweety Pie?'

'Tweety Pie, Tweety Pie, my old pal, my beautiful budgie, Willie, Arthur, my old friend. He could say "Hello Eustace, Hello Eustace." He could say that Arthur, he could Willie. Trained him myself I did, trained him, I did, trained him, took me years and years, it did, years and years, always said "Hello Eustace, Hello Eustace." Then that bloody daft cat, it's eaten him, all of him, just left a few feathers and bits, just a few feathers, eaten him all, she has, Willie, all of him, a few green and yellow feathers on the table, that's all, just a few green and yellow feathers, that's all. Nothing left, eaten all of him, best pal a fellow ever had, a real pal, a real friend and he's been eaten. It's that bloody sodding stupid Claribell, that's what it is, it's-'

'Well Eustace, we are really sorry, 'said Arthur.

'I hope it gets indigestion, Willie, yes, indigestion, no, diarrhoea, yes that's it diarrhoea, so bad that it blows its brains out.'

'Not to mention other parts of its anatomy,' Willie added.

'Where did you learn a big word like anatomy?' Arthur enquired.

'It's nowt to do with you,' replied Willie, who just for good measure and, bearing in mind the effect the recent conversation concerning diarrhoea had had on him, ended with a loud fart.

'I'm going to give it to next door's dog. That's what I'll do, give it to next door's dog, that'll teach it, that'll learn it a thing or two, it will Willie, Arthur, it will. There'll be nowt but skin and claws left of it, nowt but skin and claws, just like my darling Tweety Pie. It's buggered, Willie, it is Arthur, proper buggered.' Following which, Eustace crawled back into his own little state of depression.

Willie stared at Eustace then observed, 'Well there's a how-do-you-do and no mistake.'

'Yes it throws our little problem of names, no names, money and no money into complete insignificance. By the way Willie, whilst I'm talking it's your round.'

'Nay, it's not my round again. It can't be, not yet, I've only just bought a round. Are you sure? Nay, it's not; I bought this round what we're just finishing.'

'So you did, Willie, sorry it is my round. I'll hail the steward and we might get waiter service if we're lucky.'

Arthur turned to the bar. 'Ahoy there steward.' There was no response so he tried again. 'I say there, bar steward.'

Fat Harry looked up.

'Two more glasses of your best ale for me and my friend over here if you please.'

Fat Harry mouthed an answer and went back to reading his paper.

'What did he say?' Arthur asked.

'I don't exactly know but I don't think you're going to get the service you want.'

Arthur walked over to the bar and quietly clattered the two glasses on the counter top. 'Two pints of the usual.'

Harry grinned. 'Not so much as an, if you please, by your leave or even kiss my-'

He was cut short, 'Now then Harry, there are deeply troubled people in here tonight who can well do without your coarse humour.'

'Have you found out what's up with him?'

'Yes, it would appear that his pet budgerigar, answering to the name of Tweety Pie, has fallen victim to a dark, foul and dastardly deed.'

'What happened to Tweety chuffing Pie then?'

'He has met his maker in a most unfortunate fashion.'

'Eh?'

'He has been the subject of a feline's refectorious delight.'

'Eh?'

'Claribell's eaten him.'

'Ho, ho, ha, ha, ha,' Fat Harry's huge frame roared with laughter. 'Flippin' heck, who the hummary's Claribell?'

'Their cat.'

'Ho, ho, ho, best I've heard this week. Come over here you lot and listen to this.' He waved to the other customers.

'I think, drink up and get poor old Eustace home.'

'Yes, you're right,' agreed Willie. 'Come on, sup up. Last to finish buys tomorrow's first round.'

'You've no need to bother racing, I can't win against an ale can like you, Willie.'

Willie grinned and emptied his glass in one long swallow. He was at the door with Eustace before Arthur had finished drinking.

They took Eustace home and left him by his front door. Conversation was not in evidence and little was said after they had left Eustace other than for Willie to remind Arthur who's turn it was to buy the first round tomorrow.

145

CHAPTER 12

The committee meeting was finally called for the Wednesday evening in the committee room of the club, at half past seven sharp. It had to be Wednesday, as it was the only night of the week that the room was free from other functions.

Willie, having had a heavy tea of home made steak and kidney pudding with chips and peas, followed by apple roly-poly pudding and custard was in good form as he called for Arthur. Jess opened the door after Willie had just about flattened it with the big brass knocker. She gave him a big broad welcoming grin and said, 'Come on in out of the cold. How's Thelma? Arthur tells me your mother-in-law is being her usual obnoxious self.'

'If you want to have a few minutes pleasant conversation whilst we wait for Arthur, please do not mention her again.' Jess looked startled and Willie continued, 'Sorry if I were a bit sharp, but tempers at our house are just about at breaking point over her. Even Josie played war with her yesterday. She'll have to go, there's nowt but trouble and strife in our house with her there, and it used to be such a happy place before she moved in.'

'I saw Thelma today and she told me all about it. You're having a rough time of it just at present.'

'Yes, I might not be the world's brainiest bloke, nor the richest, but we've a nice little cottage and a right grand family. We were all very happy until she arrived, sticking her oar in, complaining about me and how her Thelma should have married someone better. That's all that she does, complain and moan. If it's not one thing it's another.'

Jess decided that it was time to change the subject. 'When are the new pigeons coming?'

'We haven't decided yet, probably when the weather gets a bit better. New birds'll settle quicker in warmer weather and then they'll have bags of time to get used to their new house before it's racing season again.'

'I'll be glad when they do come,' said Jess, 'Arthur's beginning to get a bit irritable without his favourite hobby. Mind you, this

146

Christmas club is taking his mind off them and talking of Christmas clubs, where is he I wonder?'

She walked out of the living room to the bottom of the stairs and shouted up them. 'Arthur, Arthur, are you ready? Willie's here.'

Willie took a good look around the living room, as he always did when he was there, and felt his usual pang of jealousy. The room was very similar to his, very neat and tidy unlike his, with no children to make a mess and best of all, no Woofenden.

Jess reappeared saying, 'He's lost his clean socks again.'

'Has he lost them before?'

'He loses them almost every time he wants them. You men are quite incapable of looking after yourselves. I wonder where you'd be without us women?'

'I wonder,' said Willie. 'Particularly one in particular.'

Arthur descended the stairs, well groomed as usual for an evening out.

'Do you want to borrow a pair of my socks or have you found your own?'

'Up yours,' said Arthur with wide grin.

'Now now, you two,' said Jess, 'please leave the club talk to the club, this is a clean and respectable house and we're keeping it that way. Come on now, you'll be late, especially if you're calling for Eustace.'

'Calling for Eustace, are we? Are we? Are we Arthur, calling for Eustace? Are we? Are we? Are we Arthur, Are we?'

'Willie, that really isn't very kind of you to mimic Eustace like that,' said Jess.

'No, but it's good isn't it?'

'Come on let's be having you on your way. There's a good programme on the wireless that I want to listen to.'

She gave Arthur a peck on the cheek and he carefully tucked the end of his scarf into the smart v-cut of his thick tweed overcoat. Jess opened the door to let in the icy cold North wind. Arthur picked up his brief case and they exited into the night, heading for Eustace's abode.

It meant a slight detour to collect Eustace but, as the snow had by now been cleared from most of the streets and all of the pavements, it was an easy walk.

Eustace lived in the middle of a long terrace of stone houses which Willie always reckoned must be the longest terrace in the world, in view of how long it took to walk from one end to the other. The road behind the terrace had not been cleared and the snow was still very deep, much of it flattened into hard packed ice because of the number of people that had walked over it. Willie knocked on the back door which faced the road and it was answered promptly by Eustace's dragon-like wife Joan.

'Come in, won't you. He'll be ready in a minute.'

'Yes, thank-you.'

'I can't think what use he can be to you on a committee; he's no use to me around the house, completely useless. Are you ready yet? Arthur and Willie are waiting,' she bawled upstairs.

Arthur ventured some polite conversation. 'I understand that the cat has eaten the budgie.'

'Best thing that ever happened to it. It was like him, sitting there going tweet, tweet all day long. At least it's shut that horrible row up.'

Arthur didn't try polite conversation again and there was then a very pregnant silence for two minutes. Willie thought that Eustace was a poor sod with a wife like the woman who was standing with them, then because he couldn't think of anything better 'poor sod' he thought and he was just about to think it again when his thoughts were disturbed by-

'Hello Willie, hello Arthur, isn't it cold outside? Isn't it? Have you got your Wellington's on? Have you? Arthur? Willie? Oh yes, yes you have, I'll put mine on. Yes, I'll put mine on. Where are they Joan? Where are they?'

'Cor, you'd lose your head if it were loose. They're in the back pantry, where you left them.'

It always took a couple of seconds for things to dawn with Eustace, so, seeing that he wasn't going to move immediately and get the Wellington's she said, 'I'll go and fetch them, it's no good bothering waiting for you.' She stomped off into the back pantry and returned in a trice, Wellington's to hand. 'Here. Get them on and get going, you'll be late. All of you,' she added.

The three men almost got themselves wedged into the front door opening in their eagerness to get out. Even the cold night was preferable to being any longer in the company of Joan Ollerenshaw.

'Are we going to be late Willie? Are we?'

'Not so you'd notice, Eustace. Is your Joan always in such a bad frame of mind? She always is with me and Arthur.'

'Oh, it's not just you two, it's not, it isn't. She's gone off men in general, she has, off men, she is Arthur. She reckons, she does, reckons that they cause her more bother than their worth, she does, she does, she definitely does.'

'Aye, we've noticed we're nowt better than a nuisance to her, several times now,' said Arthur as they made their way slowly along the front of the terrace. 'I take it she's a bit more gentle with other women.'

'Not a lot, not a lot. They get in her way as well, they do, get in her way. Come to think of it, it's only that bloody stupid sodding cat that doesn't, just that bloody stupid sodding cat. It's always "who's mummy's little pet then?" It is, it is Willie. "Who's mummy's little pet then?" and then, "Come to mummy little darlikins." It is Arthur, it's "come to mummy little darlikins" all day, all sodding day long. If I just get the chance, just the chance, just once…' a wicked gleam came into his eyes as he said, 'I'd shove its little darlikins right up its little-'

'The thought's too horrible to contemplate,' said Arthur. 'Though, it's not that I don't entirely agree with you.'

'Speaking personally,' said Willie, 'I might come along and help you.' He was sore at the verbal mauling he had received from Joan. 'Anyway, here we are at our number two residence.'

It was twenty five past seven when they walked into the club, so they went first of all into the bar for a drink.

'Your round Eustace,' said Willie.

'Is it? My round? Is it? My round?'

'Put your money where your mouth is,' shouted Fat Harry. 'It's good to see you're better and not maudlin like you were on Monday night. I thought you were a gonner or at least on a slow decline, thought we might be having to have a collection for a wreath. As it is, here you are again, all hale and hearty and talking again with a vengeance. Three pints is it?'

'Yes please Harry, yes, three pints, yes, yes Harry please, that's it, three pints, yes, best bitter-'

'Coming up,' said Harry with a smile, cutting off Eustace in mid sentence, for as anyone in the club could tell you, if you didn't cut him off he might just go on until closing time.

'Committee room's ready for you gentlemen, given it a special quick flick over seeing that we're going to have a lady present, and talking about ladies, here she is.'

Fat Harry's grin broadened perceptively. 'Hello Sarah love. What can I get you to drink?'

'I'll have a gin and tonic if you're paying, Harry.'

Arthur leaned over to Willie. 'Just look at him playing up to Sarah Anne, the big stupid fool, she thinks no more about him than she does the station platform.'

'Aye, but he's smitten. Just look at him.'

The fact that Fat Harry was smitten with Sarah Anne would have been obvious to anyone who was there at that time, by the way he was prancing about behind the bar, wiping the bottom of her glass with a clean tea towel rather that the filthy one he usually used, the way he kept on making short smiling glances in her direction and the change in his general attitude.

Eustace very bravely enquired as to when he might expect to get served, but Harry just whispered in his ear, 'Shut your gob and wait your turn.'

'Right you lot. It's half past seven,' Arthur announced to the assembled throng, 'time the meeting began. Can we please move into the committee room?'

'I've lit the fire so that you'll be nice and warm in there. Here you are Sarah Anne, your very good health.'

He gave her the gin and tonic, so out of politeness she stayed to have a few words with him.

'What about my three pints?' Eustace enquired.

Harry turned to face Eustace and was just about to tear a verbal strip off him when Sarah Anne said, 'Yes please Harry, get him his drinks, we should start the meeting on time.'

Arthur led the procession along the corridor, unintentionally at funeral pace. Sarah Anne was next followed by Willie, Eustace, Dick, and Lewis, in no particular order.

Willie piped up from the rear to no one in particular, 'What time's the interment?' But Arthur wasn't to be drawn and carried on walking.

Eustace, who wasn't normally to be credited with being observant, asked, Where's Daniel Sykes?'

Dick Jordan, who was quick on the uptake, said, 'Probably still feeding the lions.'

'What lions, Dick, which lions?'

'The lions in the den, from the Bible. You know Eustace, Daniel in the lions den.'

'Oh yes,' said Eustace, only to be agreeable.

Sarah Anne as Chairman stood up and called the meeting to order. 'Good evening gentlemen and thank-you all for coming along on this most horrible of nights. Have we any apologies for absence?' She looked around but there was no response.

'That's unfortunate,' Dick whispered to Willie. 'He must be coming.'

'Right then, if there are no apologies we will get straight onto the second item on the agenda. The reading of the minutes of the last committee meeting held here at the club last week. Arthur, can you oblige please?'

Arthur rose to the occasion, 'Yes, certainly madam chairman.'

He stood with the minute book in hand like a soloist at a concert, read the minutes and sat down.

Sarah Anne rose again. 'Can we have a proposer and a seconder for the minutes please?'

Three or four hands went up and Arthur made some notes.

Sarah Anne continued. 'Now for the reason we are here tonight, a report from Arthur and Willie to give us an up to date picture of events so far. Which of you would like to begin?'

As the others were waiting for some response from either the secretary or the treasurer, the door was opened with some force and Daniel Sykes dashed in, gasping for breath, trying to say something.

He remained firmly grasping the door handle whilst he regained his composure.

'Have you been running then?' enquired Willie.

'Yes, yes of course I've been running,' he said very crossly, then he smiled at Sarah Anne 'My apologies for my lateness Madam Chairman.' He removed his thick tweed coat and sat down.

'Now can we please begin this report from, oh yes, the secretary? I think.'

Arthur rose slowly to his feet. 'Er yes, well as you know, the initial response to the Christmas club was somewhat overwhelming and took both myself and Willie by surprise. In fact we were totally unable to cope with the onslaught. There were so many people wanting to join the club that we lost control of the situation. We managed to get the first few names and the money they paid, then we fell behind and finished up with a list of names without how much they had paid, a list of money without names and we had some more money without either names or amounts.'

'I think it is absolutely disgraceful that you could not cope with the situation,' interrupted Daniel Sykes.

'Please allow the secretary to continue Daniel Sykes, without interruption. You can have your say later.'

'Thank-you very much madam Chairman. You will all be delighted to know that we have rectified the situation by asking almost everyone who works at the mill if they did join the club and if so, how much they paid. Now you could be forgiven for thinking that it is almost impossible to get the truth from everyone regarding money, especially where there is an opportunity to be on the make as it were, but without any problem we have been able to match names with money, to account for all the money that was paid in and to balance the first week's accounts.'

Daniel Sykes interrupted again, 'Well that's an improvement but I still say that the whole matter is absolutely disgraceful.'

Sarah Anne didn't bother to intervene again.

Arthur glared then continued, 'We have now been able to devise a system where we can tick off each persons name against our master list as they pay and that side of things should run smoothly hereafter. That concludes my report for this meeting.'

Eustace gave a solo performance of clapping and then said, 'That was good Arthur, it was, it was good, it was Arthur, good, it was-'

Daniel Sykes interrupted him, almost shouting at Sarah Anne, 'Madam Chairman, I would be very much obliged if you would kindly ask our treasurer to refrain from picking his nose and eating the contents thereof. I can think of nothing more revolting and despicable than to sit here watching him carry out this vile and indecent act.'

Willie stared at Daniel Sykes. Sarah Anne was too embarrassed to comment.

Finally Willie spoke directly to Daniel Sykes. 'Do you want a lick then? It's right good stuff, nice and salty, super quality.'

'You nasty little man,' was all that Daniel could reply in his rage.

'Now then, you two. Let's have some order to the meeting.'

Sarah Anne was about to ask Willie for his contribution when Dick Jordan put his four pennyworth in. 'Can we please get on and have the treasurer's report?'

'Yes, I was just about to deal with it. Willie, please.'

Willie stood up and stared right through the wall opposite. He played with his pencil and finally after an indeterminable pause, said, 'Er, er, aye well er, yes, well, it's like this, we, er got everything sorted out like.' He stopped and another long pause followed then he said, 'Oh aye, I went to t' bank.'

He was saved from further immediate embarrassment by Fat Harry opening the door and walking in with a large tray of drinks.

'Now Sarah Anne, love,' he said with his usual smile. 'I thought as how you'd all be thirsty by now, so I brought you another round of drinks in just as the last.'

'Are these on the house?' enquired Lewis Armitage.

'No, they bloody well are not,' said Harry and looked at Sarah Anne in embarrassment. 'My apologies for the foul language.'

He carried on placing the drinks carefully on the green baize cover of the committee room table until he arrived at Daniel Sykes. 'Hey up it's the Lucozade king himself. What will you be drinking then? Seeing that you sneaked in here without buying a first round.'

Daniel Sykes turned five shades deeper of purple and looked ready to burst, but restrained his anger and ordered a tomato juice.

Willie took the opportunity of Harry's timely intervention to ask Arthur what he should say next.

'Tell them about your visit to the bank, how much money you paid in, how many paid and anything else that's relevant.'

'I didn't think I'd have to speak.'

'You'll have to give a report at every committee meeting, just like anyone who has a special job.'

'If I'd have known, I wouldn't have had a special job.'

Willie lapsed into silence, meditating as to how he had got himself into this mess. He had served on committees before at the club. He'd been on the management committee one year and the racing trip committee another time, but only as a general member, not anything special as it were, and now here he was, treasurer of Murgatroyd's Christmas club. He came back to life as Sarah Anne was digging him in the ribs.

'Come on, Willie, it's time to continue with your explanation of events.'

He looked around. Where was Fat Harry? He must have gone, everyone had a drink including Daniel Sykes. He must have been far too deep in thought for far longer than he thought he had. He stood up again, picked up his pint glass, took a long, slow, swallow and with difficulty stifled an urge to belch, especially in the direction of Daniel Sykes. He began to address the meeting once again.

'Nah then, we had a bit of a rush on Friday dinner time, but when it were over and we'd had time to reckon up, we'd had one hundred and twenty seven people paid.'

'Eeh, that's marvellous,' said Dick Jordan and a low murmur of voices accompanied by a nodding of several heads agreed with him.

Willie was glad of the short break to collect his thoughts before continuing, 'We took sixty three pounds three shillings and six pence, all of which I took to the bank.'

At this point he began to dry up again.

'Er, we, er, well, we, er,' and then he had what for him was a brilliant idea, so he steamed on again at top pace. The highest amount of money what we took from one person was five pounds and I might as well tell you who it were.'

He was interrupted by the Chairman who stood up and said to him. 'Willie, I don't think that it's quite ethical to divulge the details of individual members' payments to the committee.'

'Eh?'

'You mustn't tell who pays what. It's confidential.'

'Aye, but this five pound one doesn't matter because everybody knows anyway that it were Mr Anthony himself.'

Sarah Anne gave over trying and sat down again.

'And the lowest what we had were half a crown. Mind you, we'd a few of them and I'm not telling who they all are. Now, er, er, I can't think of anything else to say except that next time it'll go like clockwork.'

He sat down well contented with his performance.

Sarah Anne rose to her feet yet again. 'I can't think that we can take this matter any further tonight except to thank Arthur and Willie for what must have been a far more difficult task than we had appreciated last Friday and to wish them luck with future collections. Now is there any other business before I declare the meeting closed and we adjourn?'

Daniel Sykes, to the accompaniment of several moans and groans stood up and began to address the meeting in his familiar, somewhat austere manner. 'Madam Chairman. If we are to bank the princely sum of sixty four pounds, three shillings and six pence each week except for holiday week until the week before Christmas, this is going to mean something like two thousand nine hundred pounds being banked by that time. Now can I, through the chair, ask the treasurer whether this money is being kept on current account?'

Arthur dug his elbow into Willie's ribcage to awaken him with a start from his own private little world.

'What?'

'Answer Sykes's question.'

'What Question?'

'Just answer yes.'

'Yes.'

Daniel continued, 'It seems to me that it would be advisable to transfer this money into a deposit account where interest could be gained on the capital. With there being a regularly increasing capital it is more than difficult to estimate the final yield over the year, but every little helps and the interest could be divided up at Christmas, pro rata to the amount that each member has paid in. Could we please have the treasurer's thoughts on this most important of issues?'

Sarah Anne and Arthur were the only two people in the room that had understood Daniel's point. Willie was baffled, Eustace had been baffled even before Daniel had started to speak, Dick had a mild interest in the subject, but Lewis couldn't have cared less.

Arthur whispered in Willie's ear, 'Go on then, get up and answer him.'

'Answer him, I couldn't even begin to understand him, let alone answer him. You answer him.'

Arthur stood up. 'Madam Chairman, may I please answer the question on behalf of the treasurer?'

Sarah Anne was very relieved to see Arthur stand up as she had been dreading Willie's answer. She was just about to nod her assent when Daniel Sykes got there first.

'Why can't he answer for himself?'

'Because he has asked me to answer on his behalf.'

'He can't because he knows nothing about it. He's thick, he is, thick. He's not fit to be our treasurer.'

Willie, who had been trying his best to stifle the almost overwhelming urge to break wind for a long time now, lost both his temper and the wind - loudly, looked at Daniel Sykes and shouted, 'I'll come over there and smash your gob straight through your teeth and down your throat and out of your arsehole if you say one more wrong word about me.'

'Willie. Please control yourself,' ordered the Chairman.

'Well he's always picking on me and I'll pick on him with my fist if there's any more of it.'

'May I continue?' Arthur enquired looking at Daniel Sykes whose silence was taken as confirmation that he could. 'Thank-you. Now the idea of banking the money on deposit or some other form of interest bearing account must be one that appeals to us all. I do believe that everyone in this room tonight would support a motion in favour of such a move, but there is the small matter of taxation to consider. We have not before talked about this matter but it would appear to be worthy of some further consideration and I would like to thank Daniel Sykes for bringing the matter to the attention of the committee. Might I ask Daniel if he has any thoughts himself on the taxation of the interest?'

Arthur sat down, very pleased with his oration as was the Chairman.

Willie was bored, this conversation was going over his head and his glass was empty. He yawned and stared into space, then just as Arthur sat down, he said to no one in particular, 'I could do with another pint.'

Sarah Anne looked around to find several empty glasses and observed that five minutes break wouldn't go amiss, but only five minutes and quicker if possible. The room emptied as if the plague had entered when the announcement of the break was made. Even Daniel Sykes went off for a comfort stop.

Around the bar the conversation between Dick, Eustace, Lewis and Willie centred around the fact that the intricacies of high finance were beyond them and with the exception of Willie they might just as well not be there or even on the committee for that matter. However, Willie, who was in need of moral support, persuaded them to stick with him, so they returned to the committee room suitably refreshed and replenished.

Sarah Anne opened the proceedings once more. 'Daniel, you were just about to give us your thoughts on the problems of taxation that we may face if we open a deposit account.'

Daniel rose to the occasion. 'Quite frankly, madam chairman, the fact that the interest we would receive from a deposit account could be liable to taxation had not crossed my mind at all. However, as I have had time during the interval to give a brief thought to the problem, initially it would seem that the interest would be treated as unearned income and therefore liable to taxation, thereby causing a problem, albeit a minor one. On the other hand it could be that the income is so small when broken down into individual payouts that it would be negligible in taxation terms. I would not like to see any of us become embroiled with the Inland Revenue, with long meetings and arguments ensuing, but like any other man not wishing to look a gift horse in the mouth, I would very much welcome a sum bonus as it were on my contributions. So my advice, for what it is worth, and I hasten to add for the benefit of those who know me well, not a course of action I recommend lightly, is that we place the money on deposit and completely ignore the tax man. If we get done by him later, we get done, plead total ignorance and pay up.'

As Daniel sat down, Eustace began to clap and the others joined him. Daniel was visibly moved.

Sarah Anne asked, 'Can we please have a proposer and a seconder for the motion that all contributions to the Murgatroyd's Christmas club should be put into deposit account?'

Daniel proposed the motion, Lewis seconded it and it was carried unanimously.

The chairman continued, 'Right Willie. Will you please make the necessary arrangements?'

'Eh?'

'Give me strength,' she muttered. 'Willie, will you please go to the bank and make the necessary arrangements to open a deposit account and keep the money from the Christmas club in this new account except for the few pounds we need in the current account for contingencies'

Willie leaned towards Arthur and asked, 'What's contingencies?'

'Well let's see now, it's like if you were just going to buy the last pint of the night and you decided not to, instead putting the money back into your pocket to save it for if you might need it for something else.'

'But I never do.'

'Well if you did it would be.'

'What?'

'A bloody contingency.'

The rest of the committee turned to look at Arthur's raised voice.

'Oh yes, I see,' Willie said trying to sound convincing.

'Willie?' asked Sarah Anne.

'What?'

A note of exasperation sounded in Sarah Anne's normally calm voice. 'Go to the bank and open a deposit account.'

'Yes I will, but I'll have to get Mr Anthony's permission.'

'I'm sure he'll allow it. Right, if there isn't any other business, I'll close the meeting, leaving you gentlemen with plenty of drinking time and it's home for me.'

'Won't you come and have a quick drink before you go?' Arthur asked her.

'No, not tonight. I've some housework to do.'

With that the meeting, with the exception of the chairman and Daniel Sykes, adjourned to the bar.'

Fat Harry, as usual, was first off the tee with his sarcastic wit. 'Where is he then?'

'Who?'

'Why the Lucozade King, of course.'

'Gone home to be miserable there because he's better being miserable there than here.'

'He might have gone to nineteen Mafeking Street,' said Willie.

'Well she's welcome to the miserable sod. Never could abide him and his supercilious attitude,' observed Harry.

'Why don't you pour some ale and keep your customers happy?' asked Arthur.

Harry decided to change the subject. 'Are you feeling better Eustace?'

'Me? Feeling better? Me? I haven't been poorly, not me, no, not me Harry, no, not me, no not-'

Harry was beginning to regret his mistake. 'No, but you were a lot off it when you were in here the other night. You sat in that corner and said nowt to nobody all night. Even the terrible two couldn't get a word out of you. It were just as if you was dead, or nearly dead.'

'That was after Claribell had eaten Tweety Pie, poor old Tweety Pie, she had, she'd eaten Tweety Pie.' Eustace shed a tear. 'My poor little bird's gone, gone, he has Harry, he's gone. Eaten by her ruddy stupid sodding cat. Eaten by-'

He was rudely interrupted by, 'Give him another pint Harry.'

Willie had cut him short to the relief of the customers in the bar. Harry pulled a pint and passed it to Eustace, who accepted it without any sort of acknowledgement. He sat down in the corner next to the bar and quickly drank the pint, looking down in the dumps and lost in his own little world of budgerigars, cats and very domineering wives. The others watched him and Lewis bought him another pint.

'Nobody's offered to pay me for yond last pint yet, but I'm not forgetting who ordered it in a great hurry.'

'Here you are,' said Willie as he handed over the money, 'don't let me be the cause of your distress. It's bad enough having one distressed person here without any more.'

The evening rolled on and the conversation followed its usual pattern of football, weather and sex. Daniel Sykes featured largely in the latter subject, particularly the bit about Mafeking Street and as usual, several rounds of beer were consumed except for Eustace. He drank considerably more than the others, at their expense, right up to and beyond closing time at which time he began to serenade the crowd with an endless and tuneless rendering of Nellie Dean.

Fat Harry donated a double whisky as a nightcap for Eustace, working on the theory that it was a very rare occasion when he could be seen to be drunk and it would be a good idea to help him on a little.

Arthur was ready for home by this time and pointed out to Willie that they couldn't very well leave Eustace at the club in his present condition, so they agreed to take him home although it meant a short detour for them both.

'The club won't miss another drop of whisky will it Harry?' Willie asked.

'Not if it's for a good cause. Here fill his glass to the brim.' He passed the whisky bottle over the bar to Willie who filled Eustace's glass right up to the top. Eustace needed a little encouragement to finish this final glassful for he was in such a state that he was having difficulty locating his mouth and he needed assistance from the others.

When the glass was finally empty, and not much of the liquid was spilled on his jacket, Willie and Arthur helped him to stand up. They didn't have to help him to sit down again quickly and they lifted him up again. They then, all four of them, struggled to put on his scarf, coat, gloves and cap. It wasn't that he was uncooperative; it was more that he was just like the India rubber man with no control over his movements. He was ushered outside and it was when the cold night air hit him that the trouble really started. Nellie Dean was rendered at full volume, it wasn't in tune, pitch or time, but it was loud. They tried to quieten him but to no avail. Dick, in a mood of desperation, put is hand over Eustace's mouth but removed it with a loud scream as he studied the teeth prints in it.

Willie and Arthur managed, by each taking hold of one of his arms, to drag him along home. Dick and Lewis came along for the fun of it. As they made their way along the road, past rows of cottages and houses, the very loud, tuneless strains of Nellie Dean caused windows to open, curtains to twitch, dogs to bark and cats to flee. They came to an abrupt halt outside Eustace's abode.

'What shall we do now?' Willie asked.

'You go knock on the door,' said Dick.

'It'll happen be best if you do it,' Willie replied.

'Yes, go on Dick,' said Arthur, 'we'll just continue to support Eustace whilst you get the door open.'

As it happened, Dick didn't need to go and hammer the knocker, for two reasons. Firstly, Eustace began to fight with Arthur and Willie to free himself of their support. They let him go and he immediately attempted to force his way through the neatly trimmed privet hedge that surrounded his garden rather than take the more conventional route of through the gate and up the path. Secondly, the door opened anyway and Joan, disturbed by the kerfuffle outside, looked out. With the exception of Eustace who was still fighting the privet hedge and singing, no one moved a muscle and no one dared to speak.

Joan was the first one to break the deadlock.

'What are you lot staring at?' she snarled.

'We've brought Eustace home,' Arthur said lamely.

'Why couldn't he bring himself home?' she demanded.

'Well er, well er, well it's like this. He's had too much to drink and he's not in a fit state to see himself home.' Arthur was never so glad in his whole life to finish a little speech.

'No thanks to you lot I imagine.'

'Now look here, it wasn't our fault.' Stroppy women were beginning to get to Willie. 'I don't mind being blamed for something I have done, but I strongly object to being accused of what I haven't.'

Joan realised that in Willie, there might be someone who, unlike Eustace would face her and argue her out, so she pulled in her horns and looked at Eustace.

'Leave him there; I'll deal with him later.'

They left Eustace still fighting the hedge and hurried away along the road before she changed her mind or something. They hadn't gone far when they heard the singing stop, the plaintive cry of a drunken man as a woman's heavy hand descended hard upon his head, the rough end of a woman's tongue and more cries from the man.

CHAPTER 13

Mrs Amelia Smythies, (with a Y), changed her voice from third gear to top, 'And furthermore, I have been on this earth a long time.'

'Nobody could argue with that,' agreed Willie.

She glared as only a woman of breeding can glare and continued, 'But never, ever, have I had the misfortune to meet such a horribly rude, disgusting, filthy, mannerless little man as you. What Gerald would have said if he had been here, I shudder to think.'

Gerald Smythies, (not bothered about the Y), was the president of the cricket club, the bowling club, chairman of the brass band, member of this, sponsor of that, churchwarden, rural district councillor, junior school governor, and the list went on, and when he found the time, he ran his old family firm of corn millers and agricultural supplies distributors.

Mrs Smythies was also a member of every association, committee and gathering of which she could in some way wheedle her way into becoming a member. She was one of that peculiar breed of women, who could possibly have been quite good looking in her early twenties, but now forty years on, she was fat, bloated and ugly. Her extravagantly superfluous mode of dress, combined with her extra loud, commanding voice, made her to be very well known, if not on a personal level, in every nook and cranny throughout the length and breadth of the village.

The shopkeepers of the village lived in dread of her next visit because, unlike the vast majority of the local female upper crust who were pleasant enough people to deal with, Mrs Amelia Smythies was a sod. She carefully examined every piece of fruit or vegetable in the greengrocers before consenting to purchase. The butcher was in danger of suffering a double strangulated hernia from lifting carcases of meat from fridge to slab, in order for her to find a suitable piece of meat for her Sunday roast. She watched Freddy Nevershut weigh out each pound or half pound of whatever it as she was buying to make sure it was not underweight. Her favourite saying was, 'You have to try and monitor the activities of the local tradesmen, you know, as they are sure to try to profit from your visit.'

It was precisely this extra careful control of her weekly grocery order, that Freddy's lad had to deliver once approved, that was occupying her mind so intently when Willie entered the shop, belched out loud and farted at the same time without apology or excuse.

Amelia Smythies had just finished her tirade at Freddy about the quality of last week's cheese when the offence happened and it was at that point that she turned her attention to Willie with the verbal barrage.

Willie attacked saying, 'Your Gerald wouldn't have given a monkey's chuff if he had been here. He wouldn't have cared less.'

'My husband would have been distraught.'

'Dis-what?'

'Distraught.'

'Oh yes, that what I thought you said.'

'Your command of the English language isn't very good either, is it?'

'What?'

'Pardon, my man. Pardon.'

'Why? What have you done? You must have done it quietly, I didn't hear it. Did you Freddy?'

'I beg your pardon,' she screamed.

'Nay, I just wondered if you'd had to fart as well.'

'I have never, never, never, ever, been so insulted. Well that does it; I'm not stopping here one moment longer whilst he's here. I will be back later to complete my order, when this specimen is gone. Good day, Mr Ogley.' With that and a long stony stare at Willie, she left. The bell on the shop doorway clanked, the door slammed hard and all was once more at peace in the little shop, which true to its nickname, very rarely shut.

Freddy Ogley looked at Willie who was looking a little bit sheepish.

'I suppose you'll be a bit cross with me, Freddy?'

'Well I ought to be absolutely livid, but to tell you the truth I fair enjoyed it.' Willie relaxed somewhat at this unexpected answer and Freddy continued, 'That woman, if that's what she is, gets on my wick. She spends a fair amount of brass in here every week, but, boy oh boy, she doesn't half put me through it. "Just another couple of currants to make the pound up, I think Mr Ogley; please make sure make sure you close the sugar bag tightly, one and a half grains came out last week because you had not taken sufficient care", and so it goes on, week after week after week. She's so ugly as well. I sometimes think she might petrify me when she stares hard.'

'Aye, she's a face a bit like a camel's bottom,' said Willie who was busying himself poking the wax out of his ear with his little finger and wiping it on his trousers, 'and she dresses like no one I've ever seen before or want to again.'

'Yes, how her Gerald puts up with her, I'll never know.'

'Oh, he doesn't, he's never in to put up with her, neither is she for that matter.'

'Anyway, Willie, what can I do for you this bright and merry evening?'

'There's nowt bright and merry about this evening. It's bloody freezing out there and blowing a howling gale. It's cold enough to freeze a monkey's, tonight.'

'A monkeys what?' Freddy enquired.

'A monkey's you know what. I called in to see if you had had any more thoughts about what we were talking about last time I called.'

'You mean about the Christmas club?'

'Aye, that's it.'

'Well, it all depends like. How many members have you?'

For once in his life, Willie had come prepared with all the facts and figures he could muster to do with the club. 'Well we had one hundred and twenty seven members paid the first week, but then we had six more join the second week and another thirteen joined last week so that makes a total of one hundred and forty six. Mind you we reckon there might be a few more join yet.'

'That's not bad, not bad at all,' said Freddy, more than suitably impressed. 'How much money are you banking each week?'

Willie exaggerated the figure just a little, thinking, and rightly so, that Freddy might be even more impressed. 'About eighty pounds.'

'About eighty pounds, eighty pounds eh! Very good, very good indeed. That's about four thousand in the year.'

Willie was pleased that Freddy knew it was four thousand so quickly, because he wouldn't have been able to reckon it up without a paper and pencil, and then only slowly.

'So, hey, that's all right, that is. How much do you reckon you'll be able to get them to spend here then?'

'Nay, that's a daft question if ever I heard one. You'll know far better than me how much folk spend here. How much do you reckon then?'

'Not enough, however much it is. You see food's usually the main item at Christmas, that and presents, say half and half happen. Hey, that wouldn't be bad, two thousand, that would boost my takings alright, by gum it would that, eeh well I never thought, hey it might be a right good do yet.'

He continued to enthuse and Willie began to enjoy it, because for every word that Freddy uttered, Willie began to feel far better about the whole job. Then suddenly Freddy went quiet and his countenance changed.

'Hey some of that brass'll have to go to other food shops, butchers, greengrocers, bakers and the like, so that's going to cut it down a lot, by at least half again. Still, one thousand isn't bad, in fact it's good.'

Willie's good and warm feelings had rapidly vanished at Freddy's temporary change of mood but they began to come back again.

'It'll probably be a thousand more that I would have had if I hadn't, if you see what I mean?'

'Dead on there, Freddy lad.' Willie was absolutely baffled. 'So what do you reckon then?'

'What do I reckon about what?'

'About what it's worth to me and the committee if I promote your shop at the club?'

'Well, it's got to be done proper like. Official you know. None of this, behind the backs of the committee. It's more than my future trade's worth if any smell of anything a bit dodgy gets out.'

'No problem.'

'Right then, five percent discount for all Christmas orders for all paid up club members as long as I have their orders two weeks before Christmas and a free box of groceries to yourself, to the value of twenty five pounds.'

Willie was over the moon. 'Twenty five pounds, eeh, that's great. I'll get them all to come. Eeh, that's smashing.'

'There's just one thing however, there's nowt doing under five hundred pounds. I'll still give the five percent discount but your free box of groceries won't be there if they don't spend a minimum of five hundred pounds.'

'I'll make sure they spend far more than five hundred pounds.'

'Excellent. You still having bother with the wife's mother then, Willie?'

'Not hardly as much as what I were. I put my foot down with a firm hand with her and it's certainly quietened her off a bit. She's still a nasty, old bugger, but quieter with it. Anyroad it's time I weren't here, my tea'll be ready, so I'll see you later.'

He headed off to the warmth of his cosy cottage and more importantly, his tea.

Willie had, as requested by the committee at its second meeting, was preparing to organise the deposit account at the bank. He had asked Walter Smith for permission to be absent for longer than usual that Friday afternoon whilst he went to the bank and this had been readily granted, especially when Walter learned that he might get a bit of Divvy on his Christmas club money. Willie and Arthur had collected the money properly from the members in the canteen. Willie had collected the actual money whilst Arthur with his new list had made a note of who had paid what. He had also added the new members to the list and they had got through the entire procedure in not much longer than the allotted time. Even Greasy Martha had been in an affable mood and had not tried to clear them out of the canteen before they had completed the task in hand.

'We'll balance it later,' Arthur had advised Willie when the last member had paid and Willie had pushed and shoved the money into various pockets.

The only balancing that Willie had ever seen was at the Palace Theatre as a young lad when his parents had taken him to the music hall, where he had sat riveted to his seat watching the feats and antics of the balancing act on the slack wire. So he couldn't quite work out what Arthur was on about, about balancing.

167

He plucked up courage to ask, 'Balance what?'

Arthur couldn't work out whether to strangle Willie, or just ignore him, but being a peace loving sort of bloke he asked Willie to wait until after tea for an explanation. He also pointed out to Willie that it was time for him to be heading for the bank.

The Club held for Willie what was to become a regular Friday early afternoon magnetism. It was always quiet at this time of the year and over the next few months. It was also to become a quick counting house for the Christmas club money, with liquid refreshment.

'Hey up, make way, Lord moneybags is here again to thrill us all once more with one of his Friday displays of knowledge and dexterity in the world of high finance.' This solemn announcement was made by Fat Harry from behind the bar as Willie entered. It was to no one in particular as there was almost no one there to hear it.

The reply came swift and sure, 'Piss off.' Then as an afterthought, 'Give us a pint.'

Harry's almost permanent grin broadened at Willie's reply but then he looked solemnly back and said, 'No sir, as usual I will not give you a pint. I am not a charitable institution. However, and seeing that it is you, I will sell you a pint for the usual small consideration.'

'Small what?'

'Pay up and enjoy it.'

'I might pay up, but I shan't enjoy it.'

'How dare you say you will not enjoy a glass of our best bitter beer?'

'I shall enjoy your beer. It's paying for it.'

'What is?'

'What I shan't enjoy.'

'Oh.'

Two minutes later there was money all over the bar counter as Willie emptied his pockets, narrowly avoiding mixing his own half a crown piece with it. He and Harry carefully counted it all, separated it into various denominations and entered it into the paying in book, this being a job that required a degree of concentration. Willie subconsciously belched and farted his way through it. He finished his pint, re-pocketed the money picked up the paying in book and headed for the bank.

There was a long queue inside the bank, composed mainly of local businessmen and shopkeepers all attending to their usual business, with the odd local wealthy widow asking long and awkward questions of the staff. There were just one or two other people who, like Willie, were there for slightly different reasons.

After what seemed to be a whole afternoon of waiting, Willie's turn finally arrived and across the counter he faced a smart young man, who sat smiling waiting for Willie to make the first move. Willie stood expressionless, staring blankly at the young man, waiting for him to kick off.

It was a few moments before the young man decided to speak and then it was only 'Yes, sir?

Willie, who was delighted to have won the war without words, answered, 'Ah've come to pay in.'

There was another somewhat pregnant pause before it dawned on the bright young lad that this could be Mr Arkenthwaite from the Murgatroyd's Christmas club about whom they had been lectured long and hard by Mr Sharples, so he decided to act dumb and play it by ear.

'What have you come to pay in, sir?'

'Money.' Then as an afterthought, 'From the Christmas Club.' Then as a final afterthought, 'From Murgatroyd's mill.'

The young man's worst fears were realised, but he carried on calmly and correctly. 'Where is the money, sir?'

Willie pulled out the handful of crumpled notes from his right hand jacket pocket, two handfuls of coins from his left hand jacket pocket, a few coins from his left hand trouser pocket, followed by a huge amount of coins from his right hand trouser pocket. Accompanying this he extracted his own half a crown, a sometime white, filthy handkerchief and his Swiss Army, twenty seven blade penknife.

The sight of the handkerchief was just about enough to put the young man's lights out for ever but he composed himself and carefully counted the money and put the coins into one pound piles.

'Can I have you paying in book please, sir?'

'Oh aye, here it is, all correct. Tha'll have no need to count it. It's right, sixty eight pounds, seven shillings and six pence.'

'Sixty eight pounds, seven shillings to be exact, sir.'

There followed a long and bitter argument which was won by the young man, counting the money again and still arriving at the same answer. Willie reminded himself not to forget to thump Fat Harry when next he visited the club.

The paying in book was returned to Willie and the young man was pleased that Willie's turn was finished, looking forward to his more normal type of customer to come next in line, when his hopes were short lived.

'Now then, we want to open one of them other sort of accounts.'

The young man began to look crestfallen. 'Which sort of account, sir?'

'One of them what pays us to use it. You know a what-do-you-call-it? A doings, a, oh hell, I can't remember what you call it.'

'A deposit account, sir?'

'Aye, that's right, a deposit account.'

'I'll get the necessary forms, sir.'

'Ta lad,' he said and belched loudly.

The young man winced and left Willie leaning on the counter, staring at his surroundings. He was not normally known for making a detailed study of his immediate environment, or anything for that matter, but having nothing to do he began to look around. The very delicate and ornate plasterwork of the central ceiling rose was the first thing to take his attention, closely followed by the not so ornate spiral effect around the perimeter.

'By gum, Albert Absolom had a good do here,' he said to himself. 'Mind you it'd be beyond him would good stuff like this.'

From end to end, he next investigated the floor covering. 'Better bloody carpet than what we have at home.' He would have been heard to mutter, had anyone being listening.

He turned his attention to the fixtures and fittings behind the counter and was about to give himself a few more mutterings when a sharp pain struck him between the shoulder blades making him gasp for air as his head pitched forward towards the counter top.

''Ow do, Willie,' said a deep rich Yorkshire voice.

Willie gasped his way back into sufficient life to turn and observe the smiling face of Joshua Greasly, the proprietor of the local newsagents, books and fancy goods shop. 'Haven't seen you in weeks how are you I've seen your Thelma when she comes in to pay for your papers, her mother's alright I hear, what are you doing in here, have you come into brass or are you borrowing?'

Willie was trying to get a few words in to tell Josh in very un-bank-like language what he thought of people who knocked seven bells out of him without letting him know what was coming, but he couldn't even get a word in edgeways as the non-stop verbal tirade continued unabated.

'Ow's things at the club, I haven't been for weeks, too busy you know, it's a ten day a week job is running a paper shop, and nowt for it at the end of the day, nowt at all, if yer make owt government takes it, up early, to bed early, up tired all day, nobody in their right mind would have a paper shop, still it's a job, hey up, it's my turn, well I'd best get on, been nice talking to you, see you sometime.' He turned his attention to the counter clerk at the position next to Willie.

All this time Willie had been recovering his breath in short sharp gasps and was just about back to normal, having broken several lots of wind owing to the shock he had received, when the young man returned.

'Well, all we need is your signature on the form and everything is sorted out.'

There was no response from Willie and the young man looked up to observe him, fairly red in the face and still gasping for breath, although much improved by now.

'Are you alright Mr er,er,er?' he asked and looked at the paying in slip. 'Arkenthwaite.'

'Aye, lad.' He pulled himself up straight. 'Aye, right as rain, thank-you.'

The form was pushed over the counter to Willie who signed it and pushed it back.

'Now, Mr Arkenthwaite, how much do you wish to open it with?'
'What?'
'How much do you want as an opening deposit?'
'What do you mean?'
'You have just opened a deposit account on behalf of the club and you must therefore be desirous of putting a sum of money into it.'

'Oh, aye. That's right.'

'Well how much?'

'Don't know.' The young man was becoming exasperated. 'Well nobody said. Why don't you ask your manager? He's a friend of Mr Anthony.'

'You mean Mr Sharples?'

'Aye, that's him. Him what drinks a lot?'

'I don't think that Mr Sharples is a heavy drinker.'

'I didn't say he were. He just drinks a lot.'

'I don't think we need to disturb him with such a minor problem. Now it seems to me that you would need to put all of the money you bank each week into this deposit account so that you can earn as much interest on it as possible, right up to Christmas. What do you think Mr Arkenthwaite?'

Willie was just about to agree when his train of thought was disturbed by an interruption. 'Are you having nowt but a lot of bother Willie?' Joshua Greasly had finished his business and not waiting for a reply he went on. 'Don't let this lot in here give you any hassle, give em more that you get back if necessary, play hell with em, sort em out, you're the customer, you're the master of the situation, put your foot down with a firm hand, well I can't stop here gossiping all day, must be off customer's will be waiting, they're my masters, see you, Willie, so long.'

The young man was waiting patiently for Willie's decision and Willie was wishing that he was the master of the situation. Finally he decided. 'Yes.'

'You mean we bank all of the money into the deposit account each week?'

'Aye.'

'Right, we shall have to fill in a standard automatic transfer form. You pay into the current account each week as you have done today and we will then automatically transfer this money into your deposit account, leaving a working balance in the current account of say ten pounds, for contingencies.'

Willie was about to enquire as to what were contingencies yet again, but having decided not to show his ignorance signed the form, left the bank and went back to the mill.

On his return to the dyehouse, Willie immediately sought out Arthur, reported on the progress he had made at the bank and asked one very important question. 'What's contingencies?' Arthur just shook his head.

Meanwhile back at the bank, the young man was busy consulting his colleagues as to their knowledge of their manager's heavy drinking habits.

It was so cold on that Friday evening, as Arthur and Willie hurried home from the mill, that they didn't stop to exchange the usual pleasantries with their workmates. Neither did they say much to each other. It was only when they reached Cutside Cottages that Willie asked, 'Club tonight?'

'Of course,' his best pal agreed.

'I'll call for you,' Willie shouted.

'By gum, mend that fire sharp, Josie, for it's a cold 'un.'

'Aye it is dad; I've been frozen all day at school.'

'Where's your Grandma?' he asked as he suddenly realised there was something missing from the room and particularly from the corner by the fire.

'She's poorly, my mum's upstairs with her now and tea's a bit late on account of her being ill.'

Willie, who liked to get his priorities in the correct order first of all enquired, 'What's for tea?' And secondly, 'What's up with her? Nowt serious I hope,' hoping it was something very serious.

'She's been sick all day and she's got diarrhoea as well.'

'Oh, a both ends job, eh?' Then under his breath he said, 'With a bit of luck she might pass herself away.' Then out loud, 'Well then, happen I'd best go and look at her.'

He climbed the narrow staircase with the bend at the bottom and went into her bedroom. He was met with a scene of buckets and towels all over, Mrs Woofenden in bed and Thelma mopping up the bedclothes. The air was heavy with the stench of vomit.

Willie pulled his face at the smell then looked at his mother in law and said, 'Coming out of both ends at once by all accounts, isn't it? You won't know which direction to go first, will you?'

Stephen Bailey

Mrs Woofenden burst into floods of tears.

'Willie!' shouted Thelma, 'it's bad enough having to cope with the situation without your stupid comments.'

Willie ignored Thelma's rebuke. 'How long will tea be?'

'Oh, you go and have yours with the children and I'll have mine later when I can find the time.'

Now Willie for all his faults worshipped his family and liked them all to sit together for tea. 'Nay I shan't lass. I'll wait for you until you've done. Have you had the Doctor to her?'

'No, not yet, she's only been like this for about an hour.'

'Well, happen you'd better, she might disappear up her own what's-it at this rate.'

Mrs Woofenden heaved and brought back the remains of some meal or other into the bucket at the side of the bed.

'Just like the Vomitorium at Throstle Park this is. I see you had carrots for dinner.'

Willie returned downstairs to the children, pleased that he had been able to get a bit back at his mother-in-law, even if she was at a disadvantage.

'What's for tea Josie?' he enquired.

'Stewed liver and onions with mash and cauliflower followed by chocolate pudding and custard.'

'Aye, that'll be fine if we ever get it.'

'Do you want yours now?'

'Nay lass, I'll wait for your mother. If her's has to be ruined, then mine can be too.'

'It'll not ruin, Dad, but the custard might get a thick skin on it.'

'Good, I like custard skin. Listen, we'll never get our tea again by the sound of that lot.'

They both looked up at the ceiling to listen to the sounds of a very poorly old lady which was penetrating into the downstairs of the house.

Tea was eventually taken after Thelma had settled her mother and got her off to sleep. There wasn't much conversation over tea except for a couple of very useful comments from Willie, both of which brought a stern rebuke from both Thelma and Josie.

174

'Why don't you take your mother a big dish of stewed prunes up for her tea? And 'I reckon the undertaker will have one hell of a job getting a coffin around that bend at the bottom of the stairs.'

Willie didn't stay long at home in view of the circumstances. He quickly washed, changed and disappeared to Arthur's. Jess, as usual, made him welcome and when he had explained the situation at home she was soon putting her hat and coat on to go see if she could help Thelma. The two men arrived at the club somewhat earlier than usual.

They hung their outer garments on the hooks in the corridor and walked into the bar. Arthur stared, as Willie took up the pose of a Christmas fairy, standing almost on tiptoe and holding his hands above his head. He advanced into the room singing to the tune of the Blue Danube waltz.

'Honk honk honk honk honk puke puke puke puke. Honk honk-' and continued right up to the bar.

Fat Harry observed his arrival at the bar with an unusually sombre expression. 'If that's the best you can do then I'm not entering you for the talent show at the summer fête. Next door's cat could give a more polished performance.' Then he burst out laughing, asking, 'Have you gone off your crock or something?'

'No, it's the wife's mother.'

'There's no answer to that.'

'There is,' said Arthur and he took up the tune, 'honk honk-'

'Shut up, it's early yet and I for one cannot stand this racket any longer. It's a rotten job is this, having to put up with you lot, I don't know how I do it on my rate of pay; any lesser mortal would have perished by now. Anyway what's up with your wife's mother?'

'She's just a little bit sick.'

'A little bit sick and you're making all that stir?'

'Well not just a little bit sick, a bloody hell of a lot sick, acres and acres of vomit, honking and puking all over the place. They had carrots for their dinner. Coming out of both ends at once as well. Delightful smell in our house and the noise she's making whilst she's doing it, never heard anything like it.'

'Aye well, she's had a good tutor at the noise bit, hasn't she?' said Harry.

'Who?' Willie asked.

'I can't think,' Arthur replied.

'So, what's the form then? You stopping here till the early hours so as not to get involved or what?'

'Don't know. Mind you, if she goes on going like she were going when I came out, there'll be nowt left of her by the time it comes closing time - I hope.'

'Come over here and I'll explain again about theses contingencies,' said Arthur as he began to make his way over to the table by the fire, where the other three were getting the dominoes out ready to start a game.

'What contingencies?' asked Harry innocently.

Willie looked at him and tapped the side of his nose with his forefinger.

'Bugger off.' said Harry and Willie went, laughing.

Willie snooked up and spat a rounded ball of phlegm into the fire, where it sizzled.

'Bullseye,' he was heard to remark, then he sat down. 'Now, what about these contingencies?'

'Now, I explained all about them last week.' said Arthur. 'Don't you remember?'

'Can't say as I do.'

'What's a contingency Arthur? What is? A contingency, what is it Arthur?' Eustace enquired whilst Dick and Lewis abandoned the dominoes to listen in.

'A contingency is like an insurance, it's as if, er, let's see now, as if you were going to spend the night in a tent on a mountain and you had only enough rations with you for one evening meal. Rather than eat it all, you would save a part of it for breakfast, just in case you couldn't get back to base in time. That's an insurance, a contingency, it's like being prepared for what you hoped might not happen. Does that explain it to you?'

'Well aye,' said Willie, 'except that I wouldn't go onto the mountain without enough food in the first place.'

'I don't understand, Arthur, I don't Willie, I don't understand it at all. None of it, not any of it, I don't Arthur, I don't,' Eustace bleated.

Arthur was well into the process of making a monumental decision, whether or not to try to explain the matter again to Eustace, when the decision was made for him.

'Good evening, brethren, it is very inclement outdoors. May I join you to share the benefits of this splendid fire which our host has kindly kindled for our comfort?'

They all turned to observe the tall, round figure of the Reverend Clifford Tunstall MA, vicar of St Cuthbert's-on-the-Hill, the local parish church.

'Aye, sit yourself down vicar,' said Dick who was well acquainted with him as his wife was a regular worshipper at the church.

They all hutched up to make room for another chair that the vicar fetched from the next table then with a broad jovial beam; he put his pint glass on the table and sat down.

'I am given to understand, by Mr Anthony Murgatroyd who, as you are all aware, unlike present company, is a regular worshipper at my church, that you have opened a Christmas club at the mill.'

'Yes, that's right vicar,' said Arthur. 'In fact we are holding one half of a committee meeting right now. Mind you we are seven eighths of the way through it.'

'How does one hold a half of a committee meeting?'

'Willie answered, 'Why you daft bugger, sorry vicar, there's nobbut half of us here. Well no, we're nearly all here, but two main 'uns' missing. Sarah Anne Green, who's chairman, and that well known self-opinionated twit, Daniel Sykes, who'll do nowt but moan if he isn't here to criticise whilst we make the decisions.'

'You are probably right, Willie, I am a daft bugger, I should have realised what Arthur meant. Now, Daniel Sykes, is he the one that visits that well known lady up Mafeking Street?'

They looked at one another then back at the vicar.

'Yes, that's him,' said Dick.

'Can't say that I know the said gentleman, but his reputation goes before him.'

'Anyway what brings you in here, vicar?' Lewis enquired.

'Well it's Friday evening, we have no meetings or socials at the church demanding my attention, for a change, so I decided to come out to the club for a drink and to see how the other half of my congregation, that I never see on a Sunday, is faring. Now don't get worried, Willie. I am not here Bible thumping, just gently recruiting without ramming it down anyone's throat. By the way, my glass is empty. Does anyone need a refill and perhaps afterwards we could have a game of dominoes?'

Ten seconds later, the vicar, who was well known for his generosity, ordered six pints and when he returned with a tray of pint glasses, the dominoes were shuffled.

'Shall we play for a shilling a corner?' asked the vicar, whose skill with the dominoes was also well known.

'No thank-you, vicar. We don't gamble,' said Arthur

It wasn't long before the vicar had won the first game and as the evening progressed, almost every other game as well.

'I think the almighty has guided me this evening,' he was heard to remark.

'Nowt o' t' sort,' said Willie, 'you win every time. You're a ruddy professional.'

'Well no, Willie, not a professional, but I do confess to having some small skill at the game.'

As well as winning, the vicar consumed copious quantities of best bitter which they allowed him to buy for himself, as none of them could keep up with him. He was drinking three to one of theirs.

'Well, shall we just try one last hand?' he enquired.

'No vicar. I think we've all had enough for one night and may I say that I for one am glad that we've not been playing for money,' said Arthur.

'Yes, no doubt you are. Now, Willie, how's Thelma and the rest of the household?'

Dick nudged Lewis, whispering, 'Wait for it, round three.'

'Thelma's as right as rain, so are the kids, but her mother, she's not well, honking and puking all over the place, coming out of both ends at the same time. Can't tell whether to sit on the lavatory or stick her head down it. Smells awful in the house and noisy with it too, belching and farting as well in between. Thelma's looking after her, don't know how she copes with it.'

'Perhaps she'll be better when you get back. Well, it's half past ten and high time that all good men of the cloth were tucked up safely in bed, so I'll just have a quick whisky chaser to see me home.' He hurried off to the bar.

Arthur watched him go. 'You couldn't ask for a better vicar even if you wanted one, equally at home with us here as he is with Anthony Murgatroyd and his set. Very posh and proper, but no side on him at all.'

Clifford Tunstall MA returned from the bar and stood with his back to the fire, sipping his double malt whisky night cap.

'Now, Gentlemen, what chance is there of a poor vicar like me joining your Christmas club?'

Eustace was the first to answer. 'Are you a bit short of money like we all are? Are you? Are you vicar? Short of money? Are you?'

'Well no, not exactly short, but I thought it might be an interesting exercise.'

Willie was the next to speak. 'Sorry, vicar, you can't. The clubs for them what work at the mill and no one else.'

'Oh I see.'

'Yes,' agreed Arthur, 'Willie's right, it's only for us and it's only fair to refuse you as we've already refused others.'

'Oh well, never mind, it's time I was away to prepare the communion wine.'

'What for Sunday?' asked Lewis.

'Yes, it takes a lot or preparation. Well goodnight.'

He finished warming his back, walked over to the bar and had a few words with Harry, bid everyone goodnight and left.

'I can't understand why he has to prepare the communion wine on a Friday night, can you? Can you Dick? Can you understand it? I can't. Can you Arthur?'

They all turned to look at Eustace. Was he having a brainstorm or what? He normally didn't think enough not to understand anything.

'Course I can understand,' Said Willie. 'He wants a nightcap. Mind you I wouldn't fancy communion wine after what he's supped in here tonight.'

'How do you know whether or not you'd fancy communion wine, you've never tasted it in your life,' said Dick.

'Well I wouldn't fancy wine after all that beer and whisky. Anyway I'm ready for a pint of tea. Shall we have one for the road before we go?'

'No, I'm skint already and it's only Friday night,' said Lewis. 'I've spent enough for one night.'

'You shouldn't hand over all your wage packet unopened to your wife every Friday teatime.'

'It's alright for you; you get subbed by your mother-in-law.'

'I've told you before, it's nowt to do with you what I get from her, and talking about her, I wonder if she's still honking and puking all over the place. I'd best stop here all night. Still I'd happen better go and see how Thelma's coping with her.'

The gang of five left the club to the vile farewells from Fat Harry and suitable responses from themselves and as usual parted company arranging to meet at the club the following evening.

Willie arrived home to witness a scene of domestic chaos. Josie was washing Mrs Woofenden's bed sheets in a bucket in the kitchen, the fire in the living room was almost out and Thelma was upstairs with her mother. Willie climbed the narrow stairs after examining the size of the tight bend at the bottom and wondering if they'd be able to get a coffin both up and down. He put his head around the old lady's bedroom door, the room was still heavy with the stench of illness, Thelma was bust tidying the bedclothes and his mother-in-law was sitting up in bed looking extremely poorly.

'Still performing then, are you?' Willie enquired.

She burst into floods of tears. Thelma came around the bed and escorted Willie downstairs where she scolded him yet again for his callous behaviour towards her mother.

'Come on, let's have a pot of tea and some cake, then we can go to bed,' he said and Thelma dutifully brewed up.

They drank it and retired to bed in anticipation of a rough night ahead with the poorly old lady.

CHAPTER 14

The horrible depressing cold weather of Winter slowly turned in to the more temperate days of Spring and Summer. With it, the gang of five's thoughts turned to bowls and cricket. The long Winter evenings spent in the club were by now a thing of the past and were spent either on the super turf of the crown bowling green behind the club or at the other end of the village at the cricket field when there was anything worth watching.

The Christmas club rolled uneventfully along with the seasons except for a few new members joining. Willie had become a regular Friday dinnertime visitor to the club, where he and Fat Harry counted the money before he deposited it at the bank, where the new normal procedure was to pay the money straight into the deposit account.

The strife between Willie and Mrs Woofenden rolled along apace with everything else, the old lady becoming slowly more bed-ridden and Willie becoming more and more stroppy with her. Thelma despaired of the situation and she became equally more crotchety.

As well as the time spent on his interests of bowls and cricket, Willie also put a lot of time and effort into his fairly large garden at the back of the cottage. Vegetables were his primary interest, potatoes, beans, peas, carrots, cabbages, cauliflowers, Brussels sprouts and onions were all to be found growing in profusion in neat orderly rows. Willie had won several prizes over many years at the local flower and vegetable show. Josie helped her father in the garden, whilst Arthur and sometimes Eustace were to be found sitting on an old garden seat watching Willie at work and giving moral support.

It was on such an evening in May that Willie was busy weeding and hoeing his vegetables. It was not long before Whitsuntide and the youngsters of the village were looking forward to the Whit Monday walks from the various churches and chapels, culminating in the village meet, tea and junior sports at the cricket field.

Arthur was in a quiet and happy contemplation with the rest of the world, sitting on an old upturned bucket, leaning back against the pigeon loft and smoking a pipe of twist. He was staring at Willie, but seeing through him as his thoughts wandered from this, to that, to the other.

Eustace was sitting on an orange box next to Arthur, not leaning back and relaxed, but hunched up forward and fidgeting. He rubbed his hands together, scratched his ear, ruffled his hair, rubbed his hands again and was never still, for Eustace was never still, never relaxed, never at ease.

'What on earth's that?'

Arthur had arrived back into the land of the living very quickly, still staring at Willie, who was holding a very large orange-brown squelchy object between the thumb and forefinger at the end of his outstretched arm.

'What is it Willie? What is it? Tell us Willie, what is it?'

'You had your tea Eustace?' Willie enquired

'Yes Willie, I've had my tea, why Willie, why?'

'Just thought you might like this delicious morsel, with a bit of salad.'

'Why what is it? What is it, Willie?'

Willie walked over to Eustace, who, on observing a giant, fat, juicy, orange -brown slug approaching, got up and hurriedly removed himself to the bottom of the garden.

'You know I don't like slugs,' he shouted, 'you're horrible trying to frighten me like that. You know I don't like them, you're horrible you are, rotten with me you are, rotten, rotten. You know I can't stand slugs and creepy crawlies like that.'

'That'll do your cabbages a power of good,' said Arthur as he observed Willie laying the slug on the ground and cut it in half with his spade so that all its inside came oozing out as a black slimy liquid.

'It'll not do them a lot of harm,' said Willie.

Eustace shouted, 'Has it gone?'

'Yes, it's fallen in bits.'

'How can it have fallen in bits? How can it? How? How can it have fallen in bits? It can't have. Can I have a look? Can I?' He walked slowly over to look at it. 'Gosh it's horrible; I think I'm going to be sick. I am, I am going to be sick. I am, it's horrible it is, it is, it's all over, I think I'm going to be sick.'

Get over by the river,' said Willie. 'You aren't getting on with it so quick. If you are going to vomit, get on with it, and get it over and done with.'

'I'm feeling much better already, much better, I am, I'm feeling much better.'

He was sitting down again, leaning on the shed this time, his pale white face contrasting with the dirty old creosote of the shed wall.

'When's the new Pigeons due?' asked Willie.

'Could be any time now. I'm expecting to hear about them very soon,' said pigeon secretary Arthur.

'Are you getting some new ones? Are you Willie? Some new ones?'

'Yes Eustace and tell you what, I aren't half ready for the twice yearly battle of wits with Owen Evans at the station when we go and fetch them. Anyway Arthur, is it time we were Spring cleaning the pigeon loft?'

'Yes, let's do it one night next week. Now then if you've finished, let's get along to the club.'

'Willies cut a great big slug in half Harry, he has, cut it into two. It was all over, oozed out it did, all over. It made me feel sick, sick it did, sick.'

'Did you vomit in Willie's garden then?'

'No, no, I didn't, but I felt like doing, I did, I did-'

'Was it all liquidy and sticky and nasty? Did all its inside come oozing out, just like puss out of a sore?'

'Give over Harry, you are making me feel sick again, you are, you're making me feel sick.'

'Well don't bloody well throw up here. Get off to the gents and put your head down the pot and don't forget to flush it before you get up again.'

'I can't Harry, I can't reach the chain, not if I'm bending down, I can't Harry, I can't-'

Arthur chipped in. 'You should have seen him Harry, as white as a virgin bride's wedding dress he was. It's a wonder he wasn't sick, just like death on legs.'

'Talking about looking like death Willie, how's your mother-in-law, we don't seem to have heard a lot about her recently.'

'Confined to bed, she is. Not a lot to tell. Very quiet, she is. Both Thelma and Josie are worn out trailing up and down stairs after her. She's still very demanding, its "fetch me this, bring me that, carry me the other," still eating as much as two pigs, forever knocking on the bedroom floor with her stick. There's not a lot of peace with her around.'

'What's exactly up with her then?' asked Lewis who had been at the club when they arrived and was two pints up on them already.

'Clapped out and knackered.'

'Has she long in yet, then?' asked Harry

'Don't rightly know. Doctor's more or less given up on her. Her legs have gone but she's not lost her appetite or her temper and she's still a martyr to her back.'

'So you don't reckon it'll be long now before you and your Thelma's very rich then, eh?'

'Nowt o' t' sort. She has no brass. That's the trouble.'

'What is?' asked Arthur.

'Oh, for crying out loud. Why the hell don't you take some notice when I'm talking to you? What I said was she has no brass to leave and that's the trouble.'

'Just as I said. What is? There is no trouble, what you've never had, you'll never miss, will You?'

'Well yes and no. Yes, you're right, but no, I've always had high hopes of having a bob or two to make us a bit more comfortable when she's gone and it'll be a big let down to find that there's nowt.'

'But that's what I've been saying,' said Arthur, 'it won't be such a let down if you know she has nowt before she departs this life, will it?'

'No, but it's not fair is it? We've looked after her all these years and cared for all her needs, even the little nasty unmentionable ones and how has she repaid us?'

'With bags and bags of coal,' chimed in Harry. 'She's kept you snug and warm every Winter for ever.'

'I've told you before she hasn't paid for the bloody stuff.'

'I'll thank you to moderate both the tone and volume of your language in this establishment, but begging your pardon, you have historically informed us that the old lady has purchased all of your coal, so either you are a liar or your are demented.'

'Demented. Anyway, she has nowt and never did have owt. Mind you we keep on living in hopes that a miracle might happen.'

'Did her husband leave anything?' asked Lewis.

'Not him, only the trousers he stood up in, drank all he ever had. Seem to remember we had to pitch in to give him a decent burial, so there's nowt left from that direction either.'

'Never mind, Willie, have another pint on me to drown your sorrows,' said Arthur.

'Is everything prepared for tomorrow night's committee meeting?' Lewis enquired.

'Is Sarah Anne coming here again?' asked Harry with his usual big broad grin at the mention of her name.

'Yes she is, you lecherous old bugger,' Arthur said. 'So you can start polishing the glasses right now and clearing up the committee room.'

'It'll be a pleasure.' He hummed away to himself with the grin still evident and began the task of polishing the glasses.

The rest of them, including Eustace, who had been having some difficulty following the conversation, went outside into the late evening sunshine and played bowls until they could see no more.

The following evening, Arthur, as secretary of Murgatroyd's Christmas club, was in the committee room of the Grolsby Working Men's Club Affiliated shortly after seven o'clock, preparing for the committee meeting. Just exactly what he was doing was difficult to determine, as the room was always kept in a high state of alertness, ready for any hastily arranged meeting. All he was doing, Harry had been overheard telling some of the regulars, was fussing, about nowt in particular. Just fussing and making a right meal of it.

The other drinkers in the bar could at the same time be overheard discussing Harry's current mode of dress.

He looked smart. He was even wearing a tie, his shoes were highly polished and his hair brushed straight. Not the Harry they knew and loved, but there again they didn't have to ask why, for as one of them observed, 'He's in cloud cuckoo land. His favourite bird is coming to the committee meeting.'

Sarah Anne Green was the first to arrive, not long before half past seven and soon she was enjoying a large gin and tonic, a gift from the steward. In fact, a gift from club funds, but what the Club committee never knew, never hurt them. Fat Harry was all attention for her, wiping her seat before she sat down, wiping the table before she put her drink on it and generally frolicking about like a lamb at springtime. Sarah Anne was secretly enjoying it, but trying to appear not to notice it, for she had a soft spot for Harry which was becoming softer with each subsequent visit to the club. The other committee members were lapping it up, trying not to stare too hard at them.

Dick and Lewis arrived together followed closely by Willie who immediately lowered the tone of the meeting by farting loudly. Harry was just about to make a crude observation about farting in public when he remembered that he had a distinguished visitor present and so checked his tongue.

He had to keep his opinions to himself again shortly afterwards when Willie, having had several quick swallows of beer, belched out loud.

Arthur appeared in the bar, called the members to order and preceded them at funeral pace, along the corridor to the committee room. Eustace just scraped in at the last moments of the procession.

Sarah Anne as chairman opened the meeting and asked if there were any apologies for absence. There being none, Willie enquired as to where the hell Daniel Sykes was, and the only suggestion that came back was Mafeking Street.

'Right, let's get on,' said the chairman, not wishing to prolong that particular subject, 'secretary's report, please.'

Arthur slowly rose to his feet. 'Not a lot to report madam chairman. Everything is going to plan. The membership has increased since the last meeting and is still doing so in penny numbers.'

'In what?' asked Dick.

'Just an odd recruit now and then. We have now got the banking of the money very well under control and that concludes my report.'

'Thank-you, Arthur. Can we now have the Treasurers report please, Willie.'

Willie stood up then sat down again as a very out of breath Daniel Sykes rushed in.

'Sorry I'm late, madam Chairman,' he blurted out as he gasped for air. 'I was very unfortunately delayed.'

'At Mafeking Street?' Lewis enquired quietly.

Daniel heard him. 'I will not stand for this type of insinuation.'

'Well sit down then and let's get on with it,' said Arthur.

The chairman intervened saying, 'Yes Daniel, do sit down please and let us get on as quickly as possible. The chair accepts your apology for lateness. Now Willie can we begin your report please.'

Willie had been reading up on procedural matters in the library and he was determined to present his report very correctly. Daniel Sykes' untimely entrance had somewhat unnerved him but Willie composed himself sufficiently to begin by the time that Daniel was seated.

'Madam Chairman, it gives me great pleasure-' He stopped as the door opened and the beaming face of Fat Harry surveyed the meeting.

'I thought you might be wanting a refill by now. Mind you, some of you late comers will be wanting to buy your first drink of the evening.'

Daniel Sykes, who was just about to argue the point about his having walked into the committee room without buying a drink, was quietly cautioned by Sarah Anne.

'Harry,' she said, 'will you quickly get your orders then leave us to get on. We'll pay you for the drinks when we have finished.'

'Certainly, Sarah Anne. It will be my pleasure.'

He flitted, surprisingly deftly for his size from one member to another, collecting their dirty glasses and taking their orders.

'Willie, please continue with your report.'

For the third time, Willie rose to his feet. 'Madam Chairman it gives me great pleasure to present the treasurers report. The club continues to function well each week. Arthur and I collect the money in the canteen every Friday dinner time and then I take it straight to the bank. We've now got the weekly takings up to seventy one pounds four shillings. Mind you, I don't think we shall get many more new members now as it's coming up to the middle of Summer.

However, I do think we would get more members if we ran the club for a second year. Now I have an important announcement to make-'

He was rudely interrupted by Daniel Sykes, 'You don't know anything important to announce. You never did.'

'I do. At least I know which house I go to bed in, which is more than some folk do.'

'Are you accusing me of sleeping around?'

'Nay lad, I'm not accusing nobody of nowt, but if the cap fits, wear it.'

The chairman intervened yet again, 'We all know what you were saying Willie. Now will you please both be quiet and let us get on.'

Willie had taken the opportunity of Sarah Anne's little speech to remove a particularly annoying obstruction from his nose with his finger and wipe it on a very dirty handkerchief.

'Just look at him now, not fit to be called a human being, ought to live in a sty with the rest of the swine.'

'Oh, for heavens sake, you two, sort out your differences after the meeting and Willie will you please get on with it and make your important announcement.'

Willie took a very noisy slurp of beer.

'I don't know exactly how to begin. I had the idea that we might do a bit better for ourselves than just have a Christmas club, so I asked one or two of the local trades-people if we could get a bit of discount for club members with their Christmas orders. For instance, I asked Freddy Ogley, you know Freddy Nevershut, what he would do for us if we were to give him a fair lot of Christmas orders and he said five percent discount on owt we order providing there's a minimum total of five hundred pounds spent there and he'd want to know two weeks before Christmas.'

Daniel Sykes interrupted, 'My wife shops at the co-op and she'll not want to change, neither will a lot of them because they all want their divvy.'

'Aye, but you can get five percent at Freddy Nevershut's you know.' He leaned over to Arthur and whispered, 'What's five percent?'

'What do you mean, what's five percent?'

'You know, how much in the pound?'

'Oh yes, I see. It's a shilling.'

Willie stood up straight once more and addressed the meeting. 'It's one shilling in the pound. Co-op divvy's nobbut seven pence, so my idea's better.'

'Yes but it's only five pence better. I still prefer the co-op.'

'So you go to the so and so co-op and let's see what anyone else thinks about it.'

'Which other establishments have you arranged discounts with, Willie?' asked Sarah Anne.

'Well there's Mouncy the greengrocer, he said he'd do five percent on orders up to five pounds and seven and a half percent on orders over that providing we put a notice up at the mill recommending him. Mossops the electrical shop said they might but they didn't think it would make any difference to their trade.'

'It's still the co-op for me. Haven't you asked a butcher?'

'Of course I have. I were coming to that. I asked Len Charrington what he could offer us and he said he'd knock a penny a pound off turkeys and two pence a pound off pork and sausages, but there again his minimum is two pounds for each order. Ted Hardy at the newspaper shop said he give us five percent if we could get him one hundred pounds of extra orders from the club. So you see if we can sort it out right, there's no problem, everyone can win, plus of course the interest on the deposit account. It should be good Christmas all round.' Willie sat down to a round of genuine applause and he drained his pint glass and began to speak again.

'I think we'd better recharge our glasses.'

'Yes,' said the chairman, 'it's getting warm in here. I could do with a long drink this time and anyway it's my round. You're always buying me drinks so I'm going to stand my corner tonight. Press the bell for the steward please, Eustace.'

Eustace got up and fumbled with the bell push which refused to return to its proper place of rest.

'Oh dear, it's stuck. It is Willie, it's stuck, it is, Arthur, Lewis.' He was beginning to panic. 'It's stuck alright, stuck. What shall we do Arthur? What ever shall we do?'

Sarah Anne was about to ask Arthur to assist when she was upstaged by the door bursting open and Fat Harry come panting in.

Stephen Bailey

'What the hell's going on? Is there a fire or summat?' Then he looked at Eustace, the bell push and then Eustace again. 'I might have known, you bloody daft lummock, you aren't fit to be let out. Come out of the way and let me have a look.' He pushed Eustace roughly to one side and began to fiddle with the bell push, to no avail as it was still stuck and the bell refused to give over ringing.

The meeting temporarily broke up in confusion with five willing pairs of hands trying to stop the bell ringing by leaning on the bar and Eustace whimpering to himself. 'I'm sorry Harry. I am, it just stuck, it wouldn't come out, it wouldn't, I am sorry, I am.'

Willie took the opportunity to relieve himself of certain elements of flatulence that had been gathering in the four corners of his body for some time, making him feel very uncomfortable. Sarah Anne took the time to confide in Arthur that they could do with replacing both Daniel Sykes and Eustace on the committee with two more amiable and right thinking people. Arthur pointed out that if they were to run the club into a second year they would have to hold an annual general meeting in January and that would bet he right time for a change.

Sanity eventually prevailed, the bell was silenced, a round of drinks was served, the meeting was reconvened and brought to order by the chairman.

'Now as I see things, we are in the enviable position where we can obtain discounts from selected village shops if we can produce a guaranteed volume of trade in the week leading up to Christmas.'

'Yes, that just about sums up the situation very nicely,' said Arthur

'So how do we know who is going to buy what and how and when and where and if?'

'Well to answer all of your questions as I see it, we are going to have to ask each member about his or her shopping intentions,' said Willie.

'That is a gross intrusion into their private lives which has nothing whatsoever to do with us,' Daniel Sykes argued.

Willie replied, 'Act your age, you silly bugger, we only want to get them to the same set of shops for one week of the year.'

'Well, I'm having nothing to do with it at all. In fact, I think I shall go home as I can see no useful purpose being served by my staying.'

There was a chorus of 'hear, hear.'

190

'Well if that's how you all think, I shall go,' he shouted and got up to leave.

'Shall I help you on with your coat?' asked Willie.

'Certainly not. It's Summer. I don't wear a coat in Summer.' He stormed out slamming the door behind him.

'Good riddance to bad rubbish,' said Willie.

'Well well,' said Sarah Anne. 'That takes the biscuit. Anyway has anyone any ideas how we can put the matter into practice? Or even if we want to? Would someone like to make a formal proposal on the issue?'

'Yes, I would.' Arthur was on his feet. 'As you all know, I had prior knowledge of Willie's suggestion and subsequent investigations and I have been giving the matter a lot of thought. I do envisage some difficulties ahead, but even so, on balance, I have no hesitation in proposing that we adopt the scheme. I would, however, like to hear more ideas from other members before we propose it for a vote and I do think that Willie should be the proposer as it was his idea in the first place.'

He stopped and the chairman intervened.

'Alright, Arthur. I think that the committee as a whole can accept that, but can you give us some indication as to what lines you are thinking along?'

'Well, it's difficult. On the one hand we have a series of local tradesmen all willing to offer us discounts if we can attain a minimum order level. On the other, hand we have a club full on members who all shop at different establishments, who would not wish to tell us what they are going to buy for Christmas or tell us how much the are willing to spend, whether in total or broken down into groceries, green groceries, meat and so on. However, I do think that the only way we can get the scheme off the ground is to put it to the members and ask them the questions we think they won't answer, then see what happens. But how we actually question them I do not know.'

'We could just ask them when we see them,' said Lewis.

The chairman answered again. 'No, I don't think that would do. For one thing we never see most of them from one Friday to the next and for another, they won't know the answer when we ask them without thinking about it for a few days.'

191

At this point in the proceedings, an unknown spark of hitherto unexplored imagination suddenly reared its ugly head as Eustace pronounced, 'We could, yes we could, we could you know.' Following which he became silent again.

'We could do what?' Willie shouted.

Eustace began to speak again. 'We could, yes we could, we could pin a notice up in the canteen, a notice, in the canteen, we could, on the wall, where everyone could read it, Willie, they could, they could read it, near the serving hatch, that's it, near the serving hatch, they could read it, we could, near the serving hatch, we could-'

The committee in general had been so taken aback by this outburst that it was a little while before any of them recovered sufficiently to reply, but Sarah Anne decided that it was time to put an end to Eustace's tirade which was still continuing, getting no further than pinning a notice on the wall by the serving hatch, but nevertheless he was still talking, so she tactfully intervened.

'Well, Eustace, thank-you for your suggestion. I think we can probably discuss it more detail now.'

Eustace became quiet, happy with his idea and he sat contentedly with a broad grin on his face, looking around the room at the other members.

Sarah Anne took the initiative, asking, 'Has anyone anything to say about Eustace's proposal? Personally, I think it merits serious consideration.'

Lewis was the first to reply. 'I think it's a good idea. We could put it up as soon as possible and give them all time to think about it.'

Willie said, 'There's just one big snag.'

'What's that?' asked Lewis.

'Greasy Martha. The silly cow will not let us put up a notice on her canteen wall. She'll be as awkward as possible about it.'

'Now,' said Arthur, 'the problems associated with Greasy Martha and her cantankerous ways are too varied and difficult to be discussed here tonight. However, I do think that if we were to enlist the help of Mr Anthony, most of the problems associated with her would disappear quickly. After all he is a member of the club.'

The chairman spoke next. 'Now there's another good idea. I now think that it is time that I gave a resume of events so far, and then we can take a vote on the issue. Basically, Willie has proposed that we adopt a scheme where bulk buying from local tradesmen with our Christmas orders means that certain financial inducements of benefit to us all, can be had. Secondly, Eustace has proposed that in order to test the feelings of club members on this issue, we should outline the scheme on a notice to be pinned on the canteen wall and await comments. Thirdly, Arthur has suggested that we enlist the help of Mr Anthony Murgatroyd in overcoming the difficulties that will arise in pinning the notice on the canteen wall.' She paused for breath. 'Has anyone any alternative suggestions for consideration?' She paused again. 'No? Good. Any objections?' She paused again. 'No? Again, therefore I think we should consider all three items to be carried by the meeting for further discussion and adopted as basic principles for the committee to work on. Well, Eustace, are you pleased with the result of your suggestion?'

'Yes Sarah Anne. Yes, yes I am, very pleased, yes, pleased, very pleased, good idea, yes, pleased-'

Willie decided that it was his turn to speak. 'Talking about basic principles, I think it's time for another round.'

'Hold on a minute,' said Arthur. 'These motions have not been officially passed.'

'No, you have a point.' said the Chairman.

'Right then. I'll propose them, you second them Eustace. Sarah Anne, can we have a vote please.'

All hands were raised.

'Unanimous. Motion carried. Now what was that about a drink, Willie? Ring the bell please.'

'Nay, let's have a stretch and walk into the bar for five minutes, just to clear my head of all this technical stuff.'

There being no objection to this proposal either, the room emptied at a gallop, not at all like the earlier sombre entrance.

'Meeting over then?' enquired Fat Harry. 'Miles and miles of hot air gone up the chimney. Can't see what you've got to talk about with a Christmas club, except how to line your own pockets without the rest of the members finding out.' Then his attitude changed. 'Here Sarah Anne, love, sit yourself down on this bar stool here. What will you have, another G and T?'

'Yes please, Harry.'

'My pleasure, all my pleasure,' he said as he hurried about his business, as happy as a pig in clover. 'Won't be a minute. You'll be needing this after dealing with that lot I reckon. Well, it's grand to see you again, fair grand; I hope you're going to hold your meetings here more often.'

He was interrupted by Willie, 'Hoi get a move on, we haven't got all night to wait for you flirting with our chairman.'

Harry fired a stare at Willie and walked over to him putting his nose end one thousandth of an inch from Willie's nose end. 'I shall tell you once, and once only,' he whispered, then he bellowed, 'shut your gob and wait your turn.'

Then he turned his attention back to Sarah Anne.

Willie leaned on the bar, idly picking his nose, Sarah Anne sat back well content with life and the others stood looking glum waiting patiently in the hope of a drink.

The door of the bar opened and Mr Anthony Murgatroyd walked in. He was very smartly dressed not at all in keeping with the company in which he found himself. He walked over to the bar and ordered a whisky and dry ginger.

'Be with you in just a moment Mr Murgatroyd, sir, got a bit of a rush on. Don't usually see you in here, nice to see you though.'

'Thank-you Harry. I heard on the grapevine that there was a committee meeting of the works Christmas club and I thought I would like to see for myself what progress is being made. That's if no one objects.'

Sarah Anne said, 'No Mr Anthony. You're very welcome.'

'Have you already completed the formal part of the evening? Am I too late?'

Harry presented Mr Anthony with his whisky and dry before he served Willie and friends, much to their disgust.

'Nay, Mr Anthony, we're only half way through. We just stopped for a drink, that is if we ever manage to get one,' answered Willie.

'You'll get one right over you in a minute if you don't shut up,' boomed Harry as he prepared their pints.

Mr Anthony turned to Willie. 'I'm sorry if I jumped the queue, Willie. I had no idea you were waiting.'

'Think nothing of it. It weren't your fault. It were this fat lummock behind the bar.'

'I think we ought to be getting on with the meeting,' said the chairman.

'Yes,' replied Arthur, 'time, being the proverbial enemy, marches on. Bring your drinks.'

Once again he led the procession to the committee room where they all took their seats. 'You might as well have Daniel Sykes' chair, Mr Anthony, as he's taken the huff and buggered off,' said Lewis.

'Why?'

'Because he's of low intelligence and a loony,' said Willie.

'Oh, I can't believe that of him.'

'Well actually,' said the chairman, 'there has been an on going clash of personalities between Daniel and some members of the committee, Willie in particular, which came to a head earlier this evening. As Lewis has said, Daniel took umbrage and left, since when the atmosphere in here has warmed considerably.'

'Yes, I can see that a better atmosphere can come into being without Daniel. Not the easiest of people even at the best of times.'

'Well now,' said Arthur, 'I think that for Mr Anthony's benefit and our own, it would be sensible if I were to outline progress so far.'

He proceeded to give a detailed resume of events up to drinks time. When Arthur had completed his eloquent delivery, Mr Anthony was about to speak when Willie got his spoke in first.

'Can you do owt about Greasy Martha then, Mr Anthony? Can you have her tongue cut out so that we can put the notice up in the canteen without having a big argument?'

Mr Anthony looked at Sarah Anne. 'With your permission Madam Chairman?'

She nodded and he continued. 'Firstly, let me say that I have not come here tonight to interfere in any way in the affairs of the Christmas club. I have come out of a sense of interest only. If you do not wish me to stay, you have only to say the word and I will go, without being offended in any way. On the other hand if I can be of any assistance, I shall be pleased to give it to you.' He stopped momentarily as Willie belched and the strangely for him apologised. 'Now as regards putting anything on the canteen wall, there is no problem at all, in theory. However there is, as you rightly point out, a problem with Martha Sykes. How to get around this problem is more often that not a problem in itself. However if you leave this one with me, I will see if I can sort something out for you.

You seem to have got the club well organised on a sound basis. I particularly like Willie's idea of obtaining the Christmas provisions and a cheaper rate than normal and I look forward to making full use of these facilities myself, so you can be sure of at least one supporter. If I were you, I would hammer the trades-people for even more discount or shop around until you can find the best available deal by playing one off against the other.

I think I have stolen the show for long enough now, so with your permission Madam chairman, I will sit back, shut up, enjoy my drink and listen to the remainder of the meeting. Thank-you for listening to me.'

Sarah Anne was the first to speak. 'Thank-you, Mr Anthony, particularly for your advice and encouragement. If you feel like joining in again, please feel free to do so. So, Willie, seeing that it was your original suggestion, how do you feel about talking to the other shopkeepers in the village about their discount rates?'

Willie extracted his finger from the nostrilectomy he was performing and stared at Sarah Anne for a while. 'Well yes, yes, why not? I can ask them all in the village then play them off against each other until we've got the best deal we can.'

'Might I suggest,' said Arthur, 'that we discuss this matter with as many people as possible then select the best ones nearer Christmas.'

'All very well is that,' said Lewis who was just beginning to get over his fear of opening his mouth in front of Mr Anthony, 'but folk'll want to know where they are going to get their Christmas stuff a long time beforehand and if we don't make a decision for weeks and weeks, it'll happen cause a problem.'

'Aye, we'll have to do it quicker than that,' said Willie.

'Than what Willie? Than what? Quicker than what Willie? Willie, quicker than-'

Anthony Murgatroyd intervened, 'I think, Eustace, that what they are trying to tell us is that the shopkeepers will have to be contacted very soon now if the committee is going to recommend a particular shop where the provisions are going to be very cheap at Christmas, before various members put their orders down elsewhere. Does that explain it for you?'

'Yes, Mr Anthony, thank-you Mr Anthony yes, thank-you, yes, yes-'

Arthur decided to quieten Eustace. 'What about the notice for the canteen wall?'

'Forget about it now until such time as we have a clearer picture about where we are heading,' the Chairman advised. 'Is there any other business?'

No one spoke for a while then Mr Anthony said, 'Has any thought been given to the distribution of the money?'

'What do you mean?' asked the treasurer.

'When and how are you going to pay out the funds?'

'Well I expect that we shall be ready to pay out the money at dinner time on the last Friday before Christmas. Mind you, Mr Anthony, I shall have to have an hour off to go get the money from the bank.' He tried to speak correctly to Mr Anthony.

'That isn't quite what I had in mind when I asked you the question. I had been thinking that it might be a very good idea if we were to have a big Christmas party for all the members of the Christmas club, at which we could distribute the money. I must apologise to you all for the use of the "we" bit. It doesn't infer that I wish to interfere or to press my will on your committee but I thought it might be a good gesture to the members.'

Mr Anthony looked around at a somewhat stunned audience.

There was a very long period of silence and then Sarah Anne spoke. 'I quite like the idea. What sort of party had you in mind and where would we have it and who would organise it and how much would it cost and what would…oh, I don't know what. It's all come out of the blue, so sudden like.'

Arthur said, 'Well I think we should discuss whether or not we want a party to start with and then, if we do, sort out the details later.'

'A very good idea, Arthur. Do you mind if I continue to sit here and join in the discussion occasionally?'

'No, we don't mind at all, you are more than welcome Mr Anthony and anyway it was your idea in the first place, so you should stop and see it through.'

'I think it's a bloody good idea.'

'Language Willie. Language,' cautioned the chairman.

'Sorry, but I do think it is a bloody good idea.'

'Right, the motion is do we want to hold a party? I will propose it; can I please have a seconder?'

'Yes,' said Willie.

'The committee therefore proposes that a Christmas party be held at which club funds will be distributed. Those in favour?'

All hands were raised.

'No need to ask those against to vote, we have a unanimous vote in favour. Motion carried. Where and when is it to be held?'

Arthur had been studying the situation. 'It seems to me that the Friday night before Christmas would be best. We could get the money from the bank just before it closes and seeing that Christmas day is on a Wednesday this year, it just fits right.'

'What about Saturday?' asked Lewis. 'Saturday's always best for a party.'

'No, we should have far too long to look after the money because the bank shuts at midday on a Saturday. No, Friday's best.'

Dick agreed. 'Friday's fine with me and if we give em plenty of notice, they'll all be able to come.'

'Any objection to Friday?' asked the chairman.

No one offered any objection, so 'FRIDAY NIGHT IS PARTY NIGHT.' became the slogan of the committee.

'So where shall we have it?'

'Here,' replied Willie without a second thought.

'Yes, here.' chorused the other members.

Even Anthony Murgatroyd nodded his assent.

Arthur, being the only Working Men's Club official present at the meeting, aired his views on the subject. 'We could use the Club Room. We'd probably get two hundred and fifty or so to the party and they'd all fit in there without any problem. I can use my influence to hire the room for that night.'

Sarah Anne spoke again. 'Well now, we've had a very long meeting tonight and a very fruitful one. However, it is getting late and I for one am weary. I think we can settle the details of the party later and if there are no objections, I will declare the meeting closed.'

Mr Anthony stood up. 'Before we go, I would like to thank you all for putting up with me, so much so that I would like to offer a contribution towards the cost of the party. You all know I like a good party, so if no-one objects I would like to be invited to the meeting that fixes the party details. If that is possible?'

'Well, Mr Anthony, as chairman of the Christmas club committee, I would like to thank you for and accept your most generous offer. I would also like to say that you are more than welcome at any of our meetings. I declare the meeting closed.'

'Come on, let me buy you all a drink,' said Mr Anthony.

Willie farted, belched and sang half a chorus of 'for he's a jolly good fellow.'

Fat Harry was his usual subservient self when Anthony Murgatroyd ordered the drinks. It was, 'Yes Mr Anthony, sir, no Mr Anthony, sir, three bags full, Mr Anthony, sir' and 'Yes, Sarah Anne love.'

'Just listen to the big fat twit,' Willie whispered in Arthur's ear. He's got both Mr Anthony and Sarah Anne to bow and scrape to. We've certainly got the all singing and dancing model tonight.'

Anthony Murgatroyd was standing at the bar next to Eustace who was feeling very uncomfortable standing next to the boss and not knowing what to say. However he didn't need to worry as Mr Anthony spoke first. 'Well now, are you looking forward to the party Eustace?'

'No, Mr Anthony, no I'm not, not. Mr Anthony, no I'm not. It's my Joan, shows me up in public she does, my Joan, shows me up in public. I'm not looking forward to it at all. I might not tell her about it, might not, then it'll be better, be better if I don't tell her. Mr Anthony then she won't know will she?'

'But you voted for it!'

'Yes, Mr Anthony, it's a good idea, a very good idea, I like it, I do, but not with my Joan, not with her, no, not with her.'

Mr Anthony realised that it was no use pursuing this particular line of discussion, so he asked, 'Will you come to the party yourself Eustace?'

Oh yes Mr Anthony, oh yes, I will, yes, but not with Joan, no, not with Joan, no not with her, but I'll come, I'm on the committee I am, yes I am. I'll come.'

Anthony Murgatroyd decided that he'd had enough of Eustace for one night so he quickly finished his drink and said goodnight to all concerned.

Willie looked at Arthur and Sarah Anne. 'Not a bad sort our Anthony, is he, not a bad sort at all. Blooming good do a party, eh? Just what we need, a right good do.'

Sarah Anne laughed and said, 'Yes Willie, let's have a right good do.'

Arthur had the presence of mind to go and examine the club appointment book. With good luck he found that the Friday before Christmas was free and so he pencilled it in as Murgatroyd's Christmas Club Party. From seven o'clock. He also as a mark of respect mentioned it to Fat Harry who's only comment was, 'Will Sarah Anne be coming?'

'Yes, with her husband.'

The only reply from Harry was, 'Oh.'

They all departed the club by eleven o'clock. Dick and Lewis escorted Eustace home. Arthur and Willie walked Sarah Anne to her house where they got a mug of tea and then they took themselves off to their respective dwellings, both delighted with their evenings work.

'How's your mother?' Willie asked Thelma as they got into bed.

'Just the same, love. No better.'

'Good, good,' thought Willie as he fell asleep.

CHAPTER 15

'England six, Wales nil,' Willie shouted through the station office window although he could see no-one inside.

There came back a suitable, but completely unintelligible, reply in pure Welsh from somewhere within. There was a shuffling and muttering, then a pointed face appeared at the window.

'Oh, it is you two comedians, is it? Hang on a minute and shut your gobs won't you.'

Evans searched for his keys to lock the booking office door and join the two friends on the station platform from where they had come to collect their new pigeons. It was the height of summer, and light until late, which accounted for why they had not arrived at the station until eight o'clock.

'Late tonight you are, isn't it?' observed Evans.

'Not shut, are you?' enquired Arthur.

'No. Last train's half past ten to Manchester. Got to stay open until she's been through. Come on with me, boyo. Pigeons are waiting on number two platform, been doing a bit of train spotting they have, waiting for you two. Been here since yesterday morning, knew you'd be coming, so I didn't sell them. Gave them a few biscuit crumbs this morning, so they're bound to be ravenous by now, though. Holiday week next week, isn't it? Going away are you?'

'No,' said Willie, 'can't leave Thelma's mother, worst luck.'

'How about you Arthur?'

'Scarborough.'

'By train, I hope?'

'Of course.'

'Change at York. No through trains. Where'll you be staying?'

'A nice little boarding house behind Peasholme Park. What about you Evans?'

'As ever, back to the valleys, land of my fathers, change at Stockport and Cardiff.'

'Free rail travel,' said Willie. 'Sponging on the relations. Free holiday in fact.'

'That's right, boyo. Can't beat it, can you? Well here they are. Little beauties aren't they? Hope they'll be back for flying later on.'

'Yes they will, just as soon as we've trained them locally.'

Arthur and Willie picked up the pigeon baskets and began to carry them out of the station.

'Thirty bob,' said Evans.

'Thirty bob what?' enquired an incredulous Arthur.

'They arrived carriage forward, so it's thirty bob you owe me. Well not me, British Rail.'

They put the baskets down again.

Willie looked at him. 'Carriage forward rubbish, we've never had to pay for them before.'

'Well, whatever, it's thirty bob and that doesn't include the biscuit crumbs that I gave them out of the goodness of my own heart.'

'I can't believe my own ears. Are you absolutely sure?' asked Arthur

'As sure, as sure's sure.'

Arthur found the one pound ten shillings they owed and paid it over.

'Thanks. British railways biscuit crumbs come free.'

They left the station wishing each other a good holiday and just as they were leaving, Evans enquired as to the health of Willie's mother-in-law. He didn't quite catch the reply he got back. But he took it to mean that she wasn't very well.

Willie spent the holiday week gardening, playing with the children, watching the barges on the canal and occasionally giving Thelma a helping hand with her mother, who was slowly getting worse but mellowing a little as old age and illness took a tighter grip on her. He was missing his annual trip to Blackpool, he was missing Arthur in Scarborough, Lewis in Bridlington, Dick in Morecambe and Eustace who had been taken to Llandudno and had been told that he was going to enjoy it whether he liked it or not.

He enjoyed the break from the mill but wished that he had gone away on holiday. He took Thelma for a drink to the pub on three nights that week but he also missed the certainty of his normal everyday life. Inevitably, his thoughts turned to the Christmas club and the contribution to be made by Anthony Murgatroyd that possibly might mean free drink. As ever, left to his own thoughts, he had not made any firm plans, just daydreams of more, and even more, free beer. The formulation of precise plans was left until a committee meeting in early September.

It was during the latter part of August that Mrs Woofenden put her clogs under the bed for the last time. Thelma was overcome with grief. Willie had mixed emotions, for the old lady had been ill for such a long time that Willie eventually held some compassionate feeling for her. But on the other hand, he was pleased that his house might now return to the peaceful place he had almost forgotten existed. For the children, this was their first taste of death, funerals, grieving relations, and darkened rooms with drawn curtains all day, preparations for the traditional ham tea, and they were quite overawed. Even Josie, who could just remember one other grandparent's funeral, did not know what to expect next.

The old lady plagued them even after departing this life, with Sedgwick the local undertaker having a more than difficult time getting the coffin around the narrow bend at the bottom of the stairs when they came to fetch the body. Even more so when they came to carry it back downstairs with the body in it. Willie had to give them a hand to get it into the front room and Sedgwick whispered to him that he should not let anyone else die upstairs in that house of he could get himself a different undertaker.

Events leading up to the funeral had found Willie having to stop in during the evening, much to his disgust, in order to comfort Thelma and to greet the never ending number of people who called to express their sympathy to the family. There were, as ever, the genuine ones and then those who were noseying, who wanted more than anything to have a look inside Cutside Cottage, and who inevitably left saying that they were sorry but for some drummed up excuse they would not be able to come to the funeral and that 'By gum she were a grand 'un were Mrs Woofenden.'

'Two faced buggers,' were Willie's words to them from behind closed doors, when they had departed.

There were also a few morbid ones who came to look at the body.

'Doesn't she look at peace with herself?' or 'he does a good job on body does Sedgwick, doesn't he?'

Taken all in all, both Thelma and Willie were relieved when the funeral time arrived. Sedgwick was very much the professional at his job. The two funeral coaches led by the hearse came smoothly and quietly to a halt outside the cottage. Thelma, Willie, Josie and Aunt Bertha, who was Mrs Woofenden's spinster sister, travelled in the first coach, with another aunt and three cousins in the second one.

There was also a private car belonging to lifelong friends of the old lady. Arthur and Bess travelled in that car, Arthur being one of life's professional mourners who could make himself available at the first scent of a death.

Aunt Bertha described the service at the chapel as 'very moving' and produced copious quantities of tears throughout. She continued with the sobbing right through to the graveside and only gave over when the funeral tea was mentioned.

As the parson had scattered the handful of earth on the coffin, Willie had felt obliged to assist him, over zealously in fact, as he threw a rather large handful of stones and soil which rattled on top of the wooden box, making all those present stare at him for a couple of seconds. However the parson continued and the incident was more or less forgotten except by Thelma, who, at the first convenient moment gave Willie an earful.

They returned home to a ham salad, trifle and cake tea, at which, as is usual, they ate the old lady down, only finishing when the table was bare. Willie observed that the parson had eaten far more than his fair share and certainly far more than was good for him. However, he was well known for performing this trick at all such functions and it really didn't cause much comment.

After tea, which they had eaten at three o'clock, they settled down for a long chat. The cousins from Sheffield did not need to catch a train until half past seven and Aunt Bertha would go with them as she only lived a couple of stops down the line.

Willie listened half-heartedly to how well they were all doing in steel city, how well they were going to do and how Willie would do well to move there. He would do a lot better for himself if he moved there than if he stopped where he was and it wasn't surprising that at seven o'clock, with five minutes walk to the station, Willie said, 'It's time you wee getting ready to catch the train.'

'Oh no, there's plenty of time yet, Willie, love,' said Thelma.

'Aye, but they don't want to miss their train do they?' Arthur butted in because he also had had enough of their boasting.

In the end, the argument about train times and how long it took to walk to the station carried on until it was time to go. The children who had been exceptionally well behaved, thanked their relations for the sweets and treats they had brought, then Willie, Thelma, Arthur and Bess walked with them to the station to wish them all a safe journey home.

Owen Evans expressed his sympathy to Thelma and stayed talking to them for while; holding what was for him, a very rare type of sensible conversation.

As they walked back along the village, Willie said to Thelma, 'By gum, but your cousins are a boring lot with all their airs and graces. I wasn't half glad to see the back of them.'

'They're not that bad. Anyway come along into the Crown and Anchor and I'll buy you all a drink up to my mother's will.'

'Why? She had nowt at all,' said Willie.

'That's more than you know,' said Thelma as she guided a somewhat inquisitive and bemused Willie into the snug. Arthur and Bess, who had been walking behind had not heard the conversation but nevertheless followed on. It was a pub they didn't frequent very often, but none of them were too proud to refuse a drink if someone else was paying.

*

The next committee meeting was held at the club in September, as arranged. Willie was sporting a new cap, which drew comment from everyone there including Anthony Murgatroyd who ventured to enquire as to whether or not Willie was really spending his mother-in-law's inheritance. This in turn prompted Lewis to use one of Willies by now famous phrases. 'She couldn't have, she had nowt.' Willie turned a blind eye to this comment as he had been doing throughout the weeks since his mother-in-law had passed on.

The meeting took its, by now, usual form. Drinks at the bar with Fat Harry dancing attendance on Sarah Anne and Mr Anthony.

Arthur's procession to the committee room at funeral pace, all members in attendance. Willie being his usual foul self, belching, farting, scratching his bottom, picking his nose, getting the wax out of his ears and any other thing that he could think of to absent-mindedly amuse himself.

The agenda for the meeting took the well tried route. Apologies for absence, minutes of the last meeting, matters arising and then the proposed Christmas party.

'I've written down a list of items I think essential for a successful party,' said Sarah Anne. 'I'll read them out if no one has any objections. One - venue. Two - band. Three - food. Four - drink. Five-distributing club funds. Regarding the venue, are we all agreed that the club room here will be as good if not better than anywhere else?'

Only Daniel Sykes dissented, for in his view, they should use the Church hall where there would be no alcoholic drinks served, but this suggestion was ignored by the rest of the meeting.

Willie confided in Arthur, stating, 'Daniel Sykes should be taken to a brewery, chained to a chair, mouth forced open and beer poured into him continuously for hours until he converted to a human being. Mind you, they'd have to put the chair into a big tank, because if it's going in continuously at one end, it's coming out continuously at the other.'

So it was agreed that Friday the twentieth of December, in the club room, at the club, would be the date of the party, starting at half past seven. Arthur had already cleared the date with Fat Harry and everything was in order.

The next item to be discussed was the band. Unfortunately none of them had given any thought to this item. It was suggested that a gramophone with a selection of Victor Sylvester's ballroom records might be the answer and one of the committee could put on the records.

'Malcolm Siswick has a set of drums,' said Lewis. 'All we need is a good pianist to play with him.'

'That's no good. What we want is a right band.' Willie was very emphatic.

At this point Eustace had one of his more than rare brainstorms. 'What about Sid Sidebottom and his Sextipating Cynctet?' What about them eh? Sid Sidebottom's Sextipating Cynctet? What about them? Sid-'

'What the hell's Sid Sidebottom and his Sextipating Cynctet?' asked Dick.

Willie thought for a minute. 'I think he means Sid Sidebottom's Syncopating Sextet and there's only five of them now, anyway.'

'They used to be a good little band at one time,' said Mr Anthony. 'But I haven't heard of them for years.'

Arthur, being better informed than his colleagues on this subject informed them, 'I think you will find that they are in fact now a quartet and play only occasionally nowadays, but as Mr Anthony says, they used to be good and for anything I know, they still are. As well as that they used to be reasonably priced. I think we should investigate them.'

This item was accepted by everyone, even Daniel Sykes and it was left with Arthur to sort it out.

'Food now,' said Sarah Anne.

'Potted meat sandwiches and jelly and custard and trifle and pork pies and cakes and-'

Sarah Anne ignored Willie's outburst and continued, 'I had been thinking that perhaps we should ask the club ladies committee if they wanted to cater.'

Arthur soon countered this suggestion by stating rule thirty-two, 'The Club will cater for its own functions only and all other users must provide their own catering by whatever means they may decide. The club facilities will be available to them during the period of use. In other words, no, and we can do whatever else we want.'

Lewis said that his wife and Dick's could cater as they were well known for catering for small functions, but as there would be rather a lot of people there, it would be asking rather a lot of them.

Anthony Murgatroyd suggested a faith supper.

'A what?' asked Willie, who by this time was listening again.

'A faith supper. You know, everyone brings something, just enough for themselves. Say if four people were coming from one house they would bring sandwiches for eight or pork pies for eight, or trifle for eight, or cakes for eight or something for eight, put it all out on a table and at supper time everyone eats what they fancy. It would need sorting out into half doing savouries and half doing sweet things, then perhaps the committee wives could make the tea and coffee. That way it wouldn't add much to the price of the tickets.'

'What a bloody good idea,' said Willie, 'I'll have half a dozen.'

Fortunately everyone ignored him yet again and the Chairman wisely suggested that Lewis and Dick along with their respective wives might like to take on the job of catering. They agreed readily to this suggestion and the Chairman moved swiftly onto the next item. 'Drink now. I think that this item will answer itself. No doubt the steward will arrange the bar. Arthur?'

'Yes, all taken care of madam Chairman.'

'Can we get an extension until eleven thirty?' Mr Anthony enquired.

'I haven't asked about it, but I will. I don't foresee any major problem; we've done it many times before.'

Mr Anthony spoke again. 'Well, if that is the case, my contribution to this party will be to partly pay for the drinks. In other words, a free bar until supper time. After that it will be a paying bar again.'

'Well this is most generous of you Mr Anthony. On behalf of the Christmas club, thank-you.' Sarah Anne sat down, to hear a lot of murmuring of thanks from around her.

Daniel Sykes was sulking, wishing he could give a tirade on the evils of the demon drink, but with his boss at the meeting, he didn't dare.

'Next item, the distribution of club funds. Over to you Willie.'

'Well, well.' Willie had come to the meeting totally unprepared. 'I don't know really, I haven't thought about it yet, I er, well, I, er-'

'Fortunately madam Chairman, I have given the matter a lot of thought,' Interrupted Arthur and Willie gave a silent prayer of thanks. 'Mind you, I haven't got very far except to realise that we've got to have the money here for the party and we've got to have it distributed in an orderly fashion before we go home.'

Sarah Anne put in her spoke. 'You do realise that every member of the club will know exactly what he or she is entitled to on pay day, so surely that will make life a little easier, or maybe not as the case might be.'

'Yes, but we do have the money in a deposit account and they will all be getting more than they had reckoned on and half of them will argue it's wrong.'

Willie belched and farted.

Anthony Murgatroyd decided that it was his turn to interfere. 'Now it seems to me that there are only a few problems with the money, all of which are very easily solved. Number one, the money has to be fetched from the bank. This is no problem as both Willie, without belching, and Arthur can go to the bank just before closing time, with my permission, collect the money and bring it round here to the club. Number two, the money has to be looked after at the club until distribution time. This is no problem as Willie, without farting, and Arthur can sit here with my permission and guard it. Is there a safe here?'

'Yes, Mr Anthony, there is, in the office behind the bar.'

'Even better, then you can lock the money in the safe and stay to look after it. Number three, the money has to be distributed. Even yet, no problem. Whilst Willie, ,not picking, his nose…' Willie gave over '…and Arthur are looking after it, they can also be counting it and putting it in to wage packets which they can get from the wages office, with my compliments, if they care to climb the stairs at the mill and ask for some. All your problems are solved easily.'

'Well, Mr Anthony, that sounds most acceptable and speaking from the chair, on behalf of us all present I would like to offer you our most grateful thanks.'

'Hear hear,' said Willie, followed by the rest of the committee and a loud belch for good measure.

'I said without, Willie!'

Willie gave him a knowing grin.

'Has anyone any other business?' asked the chairman.

Daniel Sykes had. He had a lot to say on the evils of drink, on the bad influence Willie's manners had on the proceedings and on the fact that Mr Anthony was in some way aiding that bad influence, but he dare not for he reckoned it was more than his job was worth.

'No, then I declare the meeting closed at half past eight. A sensible time to close a meeting and just the right time for an early night cap if it isn't too busy in the bar.'

'What influence does the size of the crowd in the bar have on your decision?' asked Anthony Murgatroyd.

'It's a men's club. Not quite the place for a lady, but if it isn't too crowded I might just have a quick one before I go home.'

'Come on, you'll be alright, and anyway, I'm going to buy you all a drink. I for one am highly delighted with the way you have all buckled down and worked so hard to get this Christmas club off the ground. Margaret and I are both looking forward to the party night. It's a long time since we had a social event at the mill.'

'Are you coming to the party then? asked Dick in astonishment.

'Of course I am. I wouldn't miss it for the world. Don't forget I pay into it and I shall want my fair share of the proceeds like anyone else.'

As the rest of them made their way to the bar, Arthur held Willie back in the committee room.

'Where's the safe key? As far as I know it's been lost for years. No-one knows where it is or anything about it.'

'You know it's no good asking me. I know nothing about it; I'm not on the Club committee. We'd best ask fat Harry about it.'

They went along to the bar and were each presented with a pint of best bitter by Mr Anthony. They couldn't get near to Fat Harry as he was engrossed attending to the wants and desires of Sarah Anne at the opposite end of the bar. Arthur just for one fleeting moment thought he saw them holding hands across the bar, but decided he had been seeing things and dismissed it from his mind.

Arthur eventually called Fat Harry over. 'Where's the safe key? And leave Sarah Anne alone,' he added as an after thought.

'Man has to take his pleasures where and when and how he can get them,' said Harry with a wicked smile. 'Now, about the key. I've no idea, that safe hasn't been opened in living memory so, don't know. There's a big bag of keys that no one knows what they are for in the drawer under the bar. Do you want it?'

'Yes, let's be having it and we'll give them a coat of looking at.'

They took the bag of keys into the small Club office that stood between the bar and the committee room and they emptied the contents on to the desk.

'There's dozens of them,' observed Willie. 'We shall never find the right one.'

'Shut up moaning and show me a safe key. These small ones will be no good.' Arthur sorted out all the small ones and put them back into the bag. 'There's keys here that look to be hundreds of years old. Look at this big one here.' He held aloft a giant tarnished brass key. 'Church clock winder I shouldn't wonder. Ah, here's one that might do the trick.' He selected a medium sized, age blackened, iron key and gave it to Willie, who tried to fit it into the keyhole, but it would not go.

'It's too big. Let me have another look.' He picked one up that looked to be the right size and tried it. It went into the hole but wouldn't turn. They tried three more without success, then Willie, partially in desperation tried to turn the safe door handle. It would not turn, but as a last defiant gesture he tugged the door and almost fell over as it swung open towards him. He only remained upright by hanging on tightly and swinging out with the heavy opening door. They both stared at the wide open safe, then cracked out laughing.

'After all these years, it wasn't bloody well locked. Well I never. The trouble it's caused! Well I'll be blowed.'

'Not as much as you will be next,' Willie walked over to the safe and picked up a bright shiny key from the top shelf. He held it up for Arthur to see, and then he closed the door, inserted it into the keyhole, turned it, locked the safe and gave the key to Arthur.

'Well I'll be buggered. I wonder who was responsible for that. I've been treasurer here for eight years now and we've never been able to find the key. Probably during the war when it was done. The poor old sod that did it's more that likely in a box in the cemetery by now. Open it up again and let's see what's inside it.'

Willie opened the safe again only this time properly with the key. Arthur reached inside.

'By gum. Just look at this!'

He picked up a cup and read out the inscription, 'Eli Seddon Memorial domino Cup. Presented to The Grolsby Working Men's Club by Mrs Elsie Seddon in fond memory of her Husband Eli, killed in action September, 1916. Hey look here, last presentation was Herbert Halliday, 1941. It must have been in there for over ten years. What else is in there?' Willie removed a pile of old books and papers that he gave to Arthur.

'Nothing but old Club records and accounts. Come on let's take the cup next door.'

'Well, I'm fair flabbergasted,' shouted the Club Steward. 'We thought that were a goner. Well I never did. I take it you found the key.'

'It wasn't locked.'

'It what?'

'It wasn't locked.'

'Nay. Not after all these years. We knew there were nowt important in it; else we'd have had a professional safe breaker at it before now. But fancy, not locked. We shall look a right load of nuppits when that tale gets around.'

'Best to say nowt about it and just start the dominoes competition up again,' said Willie.

'Committee decision is that,' said Arthur.

Harry agreed.

Willie didn't. 'To hell with the committee, let's get it set up and going again soon.'

Fat Harry enquired as to what else had been discovered in the safe and having been informed that there was nothing else of value except old club records, he swallowed his pride and made the magnanimous decision to buy Willie, Arthur and Sarah Anne a little drink by way of celebration. Shortly after, Willie and Arthur left the club for home but Sarah Anne declined their invitation of an escort home.

'I foretell just a little bit of trouble brewing there.'

'Aye but who for?' asked Willie.

*

A few days later, Willie was pushing a fully-loaded dye barrow full of dripping wet pieces along the dyehouse to the wringing machine, when Arthur stopped him and suggested that they should go and find Sid Sidebottom and his Syncopating Sextet as soon as possible. They agreed on the next evening and Willie enquired if Arthur knew where they might find him and Arthur replied that he did.

The following evening, Thelma demanded of Willie as to why he was getting ready to go out so early. She was missing the company of her mother and she tried to keep Willie at home as much as she could.

'Me and Arthur's off to find Sid Sidebottom and his Sextipating Cynctet for the Christmas club do.'

'You're off your rockers, the pair of you. Sid Sidebottom's Syncopating Sextet as it was properly known, died with the outbreak of war and it was a poor band then.'

'Willie took a leaf out of Arthur's book for his reply. 'It's a committee decision. Anyway, it's Arthur's problem. I'm just going with him for moral support.'

'Alcoholic support, more like.'

'Well perhaps just one quick one on the way back.'

'Quick five or six more like. Don't be late.'

Willie escaped as soon as he could, thinking perhaps that having the old lady living with them might have had its compensations after all, and beginning just a teeny weeny bit to mourn her passing.

The terrible two walked briskly through the village and were approaching a densely populated area when Willie nudged Arthur and pointed ahead to the figure of Daniel Sykes going in the same general direction as they were, Mafeking Street, number nineteen.

'A pound to a penny,' said Arthur. 'Let's keep well back, then put a spurt on to catch him up just before number nineteen.'

As Daniel turned the corner into the street, Willie and Arthur ran as quietly as they could, on tiptoe up to the corner, and then marched smartly into the street. Daniel heard them, turned to look and quickened his pace, as did the other two. They didn't quite get to sprinting as Willie, who was very unfit, stopped to recover his breath.

'You're puffing just like a little tank engine, totally out of condition, just look at you. Dr Baxter will have to prescribe a course of exercise with a restriction on the copious quantities of food and alcohol that you consume.'

'Nowt o' t' sort.' Willie continued to take in some deep breaths and to make a few ungentlemanly noises as well. 'It was well worth it,' he said puffing and laughing. 'Is he still running?'

'Yes.'

'Let him go, it'll do him good. He'll never speak to us again. How much further is this house we're going to?'

'I think it's about two more streets further up. It's a smallholding on Badger Hill.'

They walked along slowly. Partly for Willie to completely recover, and partly to keep an eye out for Daniel Sykes again. They were however out of luck on the second item and they didn't see him again that night.

'Here we are.'

'I'm not going in there,' said Willie as he hesitated outside a broken down hovel which had at one time been an idyllic country cottage. Some of the windows were broken or boarded up; the remaining whole ones had not been cleaned in generations. The front gate was hanging by a thread to the lower hinge, the other being rusted away, the front lawn lay eagerly awaiting hay-making time and the paintwork had the appearance of waiting for the invention of colour. In fact there was a general air of gloom, despondency and dilapidation about the whole place.

'I'm scared to go in, it gives me the creeps. You never know what might happen to you in a place like this.'

Arthur put on a brave face. 'Come on, I'm going in. Are you coming?'

Willie followed on behind as Arthur resolutely strode over the remains on the gate, picked his way through the forest that had been a front path and knocked on the rotten front door. Willie moved right in behind Arthur as what sounded like a giant brute of a dog tried to tear the front door out of its frame, barking, snarling and scratching. There then followed a heated exchange between the dog and its master, before the dog was silenced and the door opened to reveal a shabbily dressed man, standing in a half-lit entrance hall with doors to left and right, completed by a set of stairs ascending behind him.

'Who is it and what do you want?'

'Sid Sidebottom?' asked Arthur.

'Who wants him?'

'Arthur Baxter and Willie Arkenthwaite.'

The man peered at them for a while. 'By gum, the terrible two. Haven't seen you in years. Didn't just recognise you for a minute. Come in won't you? Don't mind the dog, he's a big softy, wouldn't harm a fly. Just pat him as you pass him to show that you are friendly, like. Mind the hole in the hall floor; just follow me, keeping to the right.'

He led the way into the living room. The terrible two gingerly patted the dog as they walked past it, but all it did was to ignore Arthur and give Willie a big lick. Willie gasped and coughed as the stench in the living room took his breath away. He looked around at his surroundings. There was filth everywhere. The very old black-leaded range was blacker than black but not with lead, paper was peeling from the walls in places, there were piles of dog dirt, cat dirt and every other possible sort of dirt all over. The furniture was battered and bruised and the carpet was half holes and half threadbare. There were three hens wandering about and Cissy Sidebottom lolled in a chair, dressed in filthy rags and a cigarette hanging form her bottom lip. There was one forty watt bulb hanging on the end of a flex in the middle of the ceiling, well not exactly a ceiling, more like religious plaster.

'Sit down, boys, sit down.'

He pushed a mountain of newspapers off the settee onto the floor and made room for them. As they sat down a fog like cloud of dust rose up around them.

'I'll just put the kettle on and we'll have a good old cup of tea and then I can find out why you're here.'

'No thanks,' said Arthur. 'We've only just finished our teas and we've an, er, er meeting to go to and we're late already. We've just come to see if you and your band can play at a dance and Christmas party at the club on Friday twentieth of December.'

'By Jove, yes. There's only five of us now, you know, but it will be alright, there aren't as many dances nowadays, but I'm sure we can play for you. What do you want, old time or modern sequence? We can do both, a mixture will be best. Christmas melodies as well, we can even have carol singing, if you want we play in evening dress, you know, and we charge twenty pounds for the night until midnight and only one interval. Mind you, we expect a good free supper and a few drinks to oil the windpipes. Is the piano OK at the Club, because we need one? I play saxophone, Dennis Shires on trumpet, Maud Lindley on piano, Jack France on percussion and Hubert Shaw on double bass. Not a bad collection eh? We practice Wednesdays in the band room for an hour or so at about eight, if you want to refresh you memories of our talents before you make a firm booking.'

Sid Sidebottom paused for breath and Arthur just managed to get a word in.

'That sounds fine, just fine. So that's a deal is it? Friday twentieth of December, start at half past seven, finish at a quarter to midnight, at the Club. Is that OK? Good, now we'll have to be going as we are running very late.'

They both rose quickly, but decorously, and took their leave of Sid and Cissy. She, having contributed absolutely nothing to the conversation, hardly even acknowledging their presence.

'Flippin' heck,' said Arthur as the hovel door closed behind them.

'Twice,' said Willie. 'What a pong. How the hell does he survive in there? It smells rotten.'

'I thought he was never going to give over talking. I know we agreed to have him and his band but I wonder what they are really like. I think we'd better go to the band room next Wednesday night.'

'Let's go to the Club, I could murder a quick pint.'

They forgot about Daniel Sykes and joined Eustace and Dick in the Club for a drink.

'Where's Lewis?' asked Willie.

'His missus won't let him out. She won't, she won't let him out. He's got to decorate, he has, he's got to decorate, to decorate. The lounge. Poor sod.'

Willie farted and ordered two pints.

'Who's your friend?' Fat Harry enquired of no-one in particular.

'We've just been to the dirtiest, smelliest, rottenest, most broken down hovel in Grolsby,' said Willie.

'You've not been to Cissy Sidebottom's?'

'How did you guess, Harry?'

'Well known fact. They've won the Nations cup for the muckiest house in the free world for the last five years running. Mind you, his band's still first rate. Are we having them at the Christmas party?'

'Yes, we are, and hey you'd better behave yourself that evening because Sarah Anne's bringing her husband to the party as I told you the other day.'

'Aye, I know. Still I might talk her into helping me behind the bar from time to time.'

'Helping you do what behind the bar?' Willie enquired.

'That's for me to know and you to wonder about.' Harry gave them a knowing grin.

'I hope you're going to wear a tie that night.'

'Best dressed man that night. Evening dress only behind this bar. By the way Arthur, I shall have to have a lot of assistants for the big do.'

'Daniel Sykes could help you along with her from number nineteen. By the way we saw him up there tonight.'

'Did he just go in as bold as brass?'

'No, we ran him a couple of blocks before we gave him up.'

'Tell the truth Willie,' said Arthur. 'You ran out of steam and we had to give up the chase whilst you got your breath back.'

Willie decided that it was time to change the subject so he addressed himself to Eustace. 'Your wife helping out at the party?'

'Well I don't know, don't know, I haven't asked her yet. She might, yes, she might, yes, yes, she might. I don't know, I'll have to ask her, I will, yes, I will. Will you ask her Willie? Will you? Will you ask her? She'll come for you, she will Willie, yes, she will. Not for me, no, not for me, but she will for you, yes she will.'

'It's not up to me to ask her, that's your job. You're on the committee like the rest of us.' He had memories of a large nasty tempered woman that he daren't ask either. 'I'll see if Thelma will, it might be better coming from her, woman to woman.'

'Thank-you, Willie, thank-you. Oh, that is a relief, it is, a relief. She wouldn't have come for me, not for me, no not for me.' He sighed and sat quietly with his own troubled thoughts.

Willie had walked back into his nice, warm and cosy cottage by half past nine. He looked around the neat, clean living room, and then he looked at Thelma and thought about Eustace and his particularly bad domestic circumstances. He walked over to Thelma and gave her a big hug, a squeeze and finished with a long loving kiss.

217

'What was that all about?' she asked somewhat surprised at his impromptu action.

'Nowt really, love, just for you being you.'

It took him a long time that night to properly explain his action.

Considering the very amateurish state of the committee, the whole process of forming the Christmas club and general events so far, had gone very smoothly. In fact it looked as if it would continue to do so until Arthur enquired of Willie if he had fixed up proper arrangements with the shopkeepers who were going to supply the discounted goods at Christmas to the members of the club.

'What do you mean?'

'Have you got them all properly sorted out? Who's going to supply who with what at what price, then who's going to order what from whom and where and why and when and how much and, oh heck, there are no more questions left.'

'Eh?'

'Is all under control?

'Well, er, let's see now, well, er, well, happen, er, yes, happen it is and there again happen it isn't, it all depends.'

'Depends on what?'

'On what you mean?'

Arthur was rapidly becoming more than exasperated so he decided to try a different approach.

'Have you for instance been along to Freddy Nevershut's and given him a list of what everyone wants in their Christmas order?'

'No.'

'Have you actually got a list of what everyone wants?'

'No. I haven't.'

'Well don't you think it's about time we bloody well did have a list then? It was your idea and it's high time you did something about it. We've only just got over eleven weeks left to our pay out day.'

'Er, yes, well, to tell you the truth, I really do not know what to do about it. Do you?'

'Yes, but not right now. They were in the canteen at dinnertime, just getting ready to play cards. 'I'll come around to your house tonight before we go to the Club. Ask your Thelma to get the coffee pot on about eight o'clock.'

Arthur stood with his back to Willie's roaring fire trying to get the first chills of early winter out of his system. He was holding a steaming hot pot of Thelma's coffee.

'Now that I'm comfortable, Willie, let's begin. How many shops have you been into?'

'Let's have a see. Grocers, greengrocers, butchers, toyshop and electrical shop and that's enough.'

'Well, er, yes, you are probably right. It's enough for you to cope with and it's enough for asking questions of the members. When are you going to ask your members what they want and how are you going to note it down?'

Thelma, who was sitting by the fireside darning Willie's religious socks, intervened with her womanly intuition, 'You can sort out all these problems without doing anything about them.'

'We can?' Arthur asked her.

'Yes it's simple. Just go to each of the shops that you have chosen and arrange with the shopkeepers to keep list of orders from each of your members who orders. Give the members a list of the shops they can get discounts at and you have cracked it.'

Willie enthused, 'Aye, we have, it sounds a great idea to me. Thanks a million, love.'

'It would to you, but we'd have to give each shopkeeper a list of members so that there are no trespassers, as it were,' concluded Arthur after a heavy thinking round.

'There you are, all settled simply. Why don't you get off to the Club and leave me in peace with my darning.'

The terrible two ambled peacefully onto the Club discussing the Christmas club and the work they had yet to do for it. The party was now less that three months away and really, other than talk, they had done precious little about it apart from collect the money each Friday dinner time.

'On Saturday, you'd better get yourself into each of those five shops and tell them to expect a visit from our club members and to note down their requirements so that they can have all prepared in time for the big day. Oh, and whilst you are there, just check that the previously negotiated discount rate still applies.'

'Yes I will,' Willie said half heartedly.

On Saturday morning, Thelma asked Willie to help her with one or two of the more arduous household chores and to take a look at the bathroom that was in need of a fresh coat of paint.

'Sorry, love, got to get myself around the five shops and prepare them for the onslaught that is to come.'

'But they're all open until six on a Saturday, so you've plenty of time. You can stay home and help me this morning.'

Willie studied carefully and realised he had no good reason or alibi to get him away from the house, so he succumbed to female pressure, pottering about outside when he could escape for a few minutes.

After a dinner of fish and chips, which was the time honoured tradition at number six Cutside Cottages on a Saturday lunchtime, Willie walked into the village, and in particular, to the emporium of Freddy Nevershut Ogley.

'Third time you've disgraced these humble premises with your presence since last Christmas, William Arkenthwaite. It's beginning to become a habit.'

'It's because I can't resist the overpowering, friendly welcome I get when I do call.'

'Well now you are here, what do you want?'

'Told you it was the friendly welcome that attracted me.'

'Your Thelma sent you out from under her feet so that you can be under my feet, has she?'

'You know this discount for the Murgatroyd's Christmas club?'

'Oh, that.' He had been hoping that they had forgotten about it.

'Well, we are about eleven weeks away from payout time so we are going round telling everyone in the club that wants to buy groceries with their money to come along and give their orders in to you as soon as they can. I'll give you a list of members so that you'll know who to expect. As well as that, we are going to tell them to make sure that you know they are club members.'

'That's real good of you, Willie, real good. Just what my profits want is all this discount. Real good of you.'

Willie sensed an air of something brewing somewhere in Freddy's attitude, so, giving the customary belch, he said, 'We can always go to the co-op you know.'

'No, no, don't bother; I'll do it, no problem.'

'Are you sure?'

'Yes.'

'Absolutely sure?'

'Yes, yes, bloody yes. Now go away, I've a lot to think about.'

Willie went on his way, extremely pleased with his performance, some of which he had been secretly rehearsing for the last few hours. He next called at the butchers, then the electrical shop. The same message, that was received by both proprietors with about the same enthusiasm as Freddy Nevershut had displayed earlier. To all of them, the idea had seemed good at the time of conception but not so good in the grey light of dawn when it came to crunch time.

The last shop to be visited was the toy shop of Herbert Chew. Willie had made the arrangements with him in the months before as he had with the others. The problem was that Herbert Chew had the only toy shop in the village and as such held a total monopoly of the local trade which led him to believe he didn't have to discount his goods to the club. The other problem and almost as bad as the first one for those trying to set up such a deal was that Herbert Chew was almost stone deaf. He left serving in the shop to his wife Agatha whilst he did the administration. This deafness did not help matters along when it came to a discussion, particularly when it was one he didn't want to have anyway. It had taken Willie a long time on his first visit to persuade Herbert that the Christmas club should have some discount and although he thought that Herbert had agreed, he wasn't exactly sure.

Willie opened the front door and entered the very old fashioned, poorly lit shop. An extra loud bell that was hit by a striker attached to the door frame, alerted the entire neighbourhood to his arrival and he could just hear a female voice coming from the back room at the close of a conversational shout. She shuffled into the shop, her threadbare slippers making a scraping sound on the stone flagged floor. Her slow appearance had given Willie the time to look around the shop. It was crying out to be repainted. The old dark brown paint was peeling all over and it was ready for a much lighter shade, Willie decided.

'Hello, Willie. How are you?' She stopped for a cough and splutter and Willie took the opportunity to do something similar. 'How's Thelma and the children? Growing up by now, I suppose. Haven't seen them in a long time. Tell Thelma to pop in for a chat sometime will you?'

'No fear,' thought Willie. For Agatha Chew had three Olympic Gold medals for scandal mongering and only wanted Thelma to call so that she could extract as much information as possible from her. This would then be redistributed as venomously as throughout the whole village.

'I've come to see about Murgatroyd's Christmas club.'

'You'll have to see him. He's in the back. Go through.'

Willie walked around the back of the counter and passed from one depressing room to another. It was a typical village store back room. Filled with boxes, some full, some empty, reject toys, dolls at the dolls hospital, two chairs in front of a roaring fire, a small kitchen area, a workbench with tools of the trade and an antique bureau full of papers at which was seated Herbert Chew pouring over a set of invoices. He had not heard Willie come in and almost jumped out of his skin when Willie poked him on the shoulder.

'You daft bugger. What do you want to go and do a daft thing like that for? You could have made me have a heart attack.'

'You'll never have a heart attack; you're made of stronger stuff than that. Anyway, how are you?'

'What?'

'How are you?'

'Yer what?'

'I've come about the Christmas club'

'What?'

'I've-come-about-the-Christmas-club.'

'What about it?'

'About the discount.'

Herbert heard the last word.

'Discount. What discount?'

222

'The discount of five percent you said you'd give to club members for their Christmas orders from Murgatroyd's Christmas club.'

'What?'

Willie repeated his small speech very slowly and very loudly.

'Don't know. You'll have to talk to the wife.'

'She said I'd to talk to you.'

'What?'

'She-said-I'd-to-talk-to-you.'

'Oh, she did, did she? We'll soon see about that.'

He stormed into the shop where all hell let loose between him and his wife. Willie remained in the back room standing with his back to the fire, keeping warm and enjoying listening to the row that no-one was winning. From what he could hear however it was becoming more and more apparent that neither of them was prepared to deal with the matter and as far as they were concerned there was no discount.

The row ceased abruptly and Herbert Chew stormed back into the back room.

'There's nowt doing and that's my final word on the subject, and hers as well. Bloody woman. So that's it. Goodbye.'

He turned his back on Willie and resumed his seat at the bureau.

'So you're not going to give us the discounts like what you promised?'

'What?'

'Oh, nowt. I'm going.'

The greengrocers was quite amiable about the discount but a very disappointed Willie went home thinking about Angela Chew. He walked into the cottage, grabbed Thelma around the waist, giving her a big hug and a long loving kiss.

'What was that for?' she enquired, somewhat taken aback.

'Again, just because you are you.'

Once again it took him a long time to explain his actions.

CHAPTER 16

The day of the party and payout was drawing nearer. It had been decided that one more committee meeting was necessary to finalise all arrangements. Before that day, Willie had, not without an enormous amount of difficulty, formulated a notice to put up in the canteen, to inform everyone about the arrangements for discounts available to club members.

He had pondered about the wording of it for many a long hour, both at work and in his times of leisure. He had even smuggled a piece of paper and a pencil into his garden shed one evening in order to write it out. Thelma wouldn't suspect anything as he went every night in winter with his hurricane lamp to look at the pigeons and his shed.

Willie lit the lamp in the back kitchen as he always did, carefully pumped it up to its correct pressure, or near enough, then took it down the garden into his shed where he put it in its usual position at the end of the bench. Having then assessed the mess on the rest of the bench, he decided that he had better have a good tidy and sweep down before he could even attempt to write on the paper.

The job of picking out the various screws, nails and other sundry remains of months of pottering was going to take at least a good hour before he could start to write his notice. He therefore thought it prudent to forestall any intervention that might possibly come from Thelma in view of the length of time he would be missing from the house, so he began to tidy the bench. After a little while, he thought of a good excuse to go and get warm again, so he went back up the garden into the house. He found Thelma sitting in front of the fire knitting.

'What are you knitting, love?'

'A new cardigan for Josie's birthday present, but it's a secret and she hasn't to know about it, so I've got to knit it when she's out or after she's gone to bed.'

'Where is she then?'

'She's gone with Christine and Pauline to a new Youth club they've started at the Church.'

'But she's a Methodist.'

'I don't think that'll have much effect on Josie. Anyway it's good for her to get out a bit.'

'Have you a spare empty jam jar anywhere that I can have to sort out my nails and screws?'

'Yes, there is one under the sink. Don't you think you'd better wait until its light at the weekend?'

'Aye, you're right, but I'll just make a start then finish it on Sunday.'

He took the jar back to the shed and put a few screws into it, just as a token gesture, which effectively, with a little help from a good push to one side of the remains on the bench, made an area large enough for his piece of paper. He then swept the dirt and dust into an empty space on the floor, dusted the bench top with a rag and carefully placed the already crumpled piece of paper into the middle of the clean area. He took the pencil in hand with a flourish and a fart, licked the point and stared into space.

After a few minutes he wrote at the top of the paper, 'NOTICE', and then after a further long time, 'MURGATOYD'S CHRISTMAS CLUB.' He had been thinking about the wording of the poster for days, so without much hesitation he continued to the next line, 'DISCOUNT SCHEME.'

At this point his mind became a huge void as his thoughts had never got any further than here. The more pressing problem was what to do with the piece of paper to keep it out of everyone's way until he could muster up some ideas to put on it. He eventually hit on the idea of emptying the tool drawer and putting the paper on the bottom of it beneath the brown paper liner he had had there for more years than he cared to remember.

Willie emptied the drawer, put the piece of paper under the brown paper and replaced the tools. This had given him the opportunity to clean out the contents and discard one or two broken items that had been waiting to be disposed of for a very long time. In fact he did himself a very big favour, or so he told himself.

When he got back to the house, Thelma was still knitting.

225

'I think I'll just go to the club for a quick pint.'

Thelma agreed with him as she wanted to do as much knitting as possible in peace.

'Are you calling for Arthur?'

'No, he's doing some work in the kitchen for Jess tonight.'

'What sort of work?'

'Mending a broken hinge on a cupboard door and that sort of thing.'

'Thank goodness for that. I couldn't quite see him rolling out the pastry.'

Willie got washed and changed then made his way to the club where the only occupant other than the Steward was Philip Perry, or Pee Pee as he was well known in the village.

'Hi, Pee Pee. How goes it?'

'How goes what?'

Pee Pee had no sense of humour and was one of those people who believed that the world owed them a living. He was a permanent moaner and carried a huge chip on his shoulder.

'How goes everything and life in general?'

'He's full of the joys of Spring,' said Fat Harry

'I'm fed up.'

'Fed up, what with?'

'Everything. Everything and nothing.'

What are you going on about? Everything and nothing?'

'Well I'm fed up with anything and I'm fed up with nothing. I'm just fed up.'

'I'm a famous trick cyclist and I'm going to analyse you,' said Willie.

'You're a famous what?'

'A trick cyclist.'

'I think he means a psychiatrist,' said Harry

'Now, when I say a word or a few words, you say another word or words back, the first thing that comes into your head. Black pudding.'

'Dinner.'

'Very good - knickers.'

'Mavis.

'Who the hell's Mavis?

'Wife's friend.'

Very good. Even better,' said Willie thinking that he had possibly stumbled into some scandal and also thinking he'd better probe deeper.

'I think there's something here we don't know about but that we ought to be knowing,' said Fat Harry.

'No, no, it's nothing like what you're both thinking.'

'How do you know what I'm thinking?'

'You only think one way. No, it's just that she wears them modern French knickers. I know, I've seen them on her washing line.'

'A likely story. However let's get on. The next word is bunker.'

'Golf course.'

'Very good, in fact excellent, you are making good progress. Now, hole-in-one.'

'Drinks all round in the clubhouse.'

'Mine's a pint,' said Willie.

'Hang on a minute, I didn't invite you to have a drink.'

'You said drinks all round.'

'But that was because we were playing at trick cyclists.'

'Yes but when you said drinks all round, that's just what it means.'

'I'm fed up.'

'Aye, you will be,' said Willie. 'But thanks for the drink anyway.'

Harry poured the round, and then with a great deal of difficulty, extracted the money from Pee Pee.

'Won't be long now until the big day arrives, Willie, will it?' asked Fat Harry.

'No, it's getting here quicker than I'd like.'

'What big day's this then?' enquired Pee Pee

'Pay out day for Murgatroyd's Christmas club.'

'So, why's that a big day then?'

'We're having a big do in here. That's why.'

'What sort of a do?'

'A dance and supper, with Sid Sidebottom's Sextipating Cynctet.'

'I think you mean Syncopating Sextet.'

'Yes, that's it but there's only five of them.'

'Does that alter the spelling then?' Pee Pee asked.

'Eh?'

'I thought he were dead and disbanded.'

'No, still going strong.'

'Can anyone come?' he asked hopefully.

'Not on your nellie. It's strictly members only. Mr Anthony is coming with his wife.'

'So what?'

'Hey, it'll be a good do when he comes, free booze and the like.'

Dick and Lewis walked into the bar. 'Bloody cold, Harry. Put some coal on the fire.'

Willie farted.

'That'll keep us all nice and warm,' observed Harry. 'Thank-you for your contribution, Willie. If I put any more coal on that fire we shall be sending for the fire brigade and they can't come tonight cause its half day closing, so I'm not. Anyway stand with your backs to it and warm your brains. If you were to place an order with the bar for liquid refreshment, I may just bring it over to you. There are two good reasons why I may bring it over. I'm short of exercise and I'm fed up of standing here listening to Pee Pee moaning.'

Dick asked, 'Are you going to trim the club up for the party Harry?'

'Am I what?' Predictably he roared, 'Am I hell as like. You can decorate your own room and we'll have the artificial tree on the end of the bar as always.'

'Very charitable indeed. Very nice of you. A good time is going to be had in here by all, I don't think, with that attitude.'

Harry, who had been walking back to the bar, spun on his heels, charged back and stopped with his nose about a quarter of an inch from Dick's. He was purple faced and about to boil over. Dick, who wasn't given to panicking and took everything in his stride didn't move but stared straight into Harry's eyes, waiting for the tirade to begin. He didn't have to wait more than a split second.

'I'm not bloody paid to bloody put bloody decorations up. The governing committee pay me only a paupers wage and that's not surprising when you look around and count how many people there are in here right now. Furthermore you wouldn't let me join your piddling little Christmas club, so I'm not bloody helping you. Got it?' He stormed back to the bar.

Dick lit a cigarette and said, 'You're right Harry; it's not a bad fire you've lit.'

'I can do something right then can I,' he shouted back.

Willie, Lewis and Pee Pee had been cowering and pondering whether or not they might have come to Dick's assistance, or if indeed it might have been best just to quietly go home and leave Dick to Harry's tender mercy. As it was they were more than delighted when the all clear was sounded.

'Have you got the booking for next week's committee meeting in the diary?' Willie asked in a fit of inspiration.

'Yes, that's in alright. Mr one hundred and one percent put it in after the last meeting.'

'Who's Mr one hundred and one percent?' asked Pee Pee.

'Arthur, never put a foot wrong, Baxter.'

'Oh aye, he's on the ball alright when it comes to efficiency is our Arthur.'

'Are you related to him?' asked Dick.

'No, why?'

'It was just the way you said, our Arthur.'

'Just a term of adherement.'

Fat Harry suddenly brightened up and changed the subject.

'Will Sarah Anne be coming?'

'She'd better be, she's the Chairman.'

Harry smiled. 'Good, good,' he said.

Dick looked at him and an idea crept into his head. 'What about that long dollop, Sykes the sod. Is he coming?'

'Well he should be, he's on the committee even though he's a pain,' said Willie.

'He's about as bad as Sarah Anne is good. I think I might ban him from ever entering the club again and then get Sarah Anne to come here every night.'

The remainder of the evening drifted by with a few more members arriving for a late drink and a convivial atmosphere continuing until closing time.

When Willie arrived home, Thelma had put the knitting away and made supper.

'Anything happen at the club tonight?'

Not Particularly, Fat Harry murdered Dick, then killed him dead, then shouted at him, but nothing special.'

On Saturday morning, Willie was up bright and early, just as it was coming light, and immediately after he had finished his bacon and eggs, away he went to his shed to retrieve his notice. He stared at it for some time then went for a walk around his garden and then returned to the shed.

He looked proudly at the notice and in particular the title, 'DISCOUNT SCHEME'. Then, he walked around to the pigeon loft where he spent some time talking to the birds. The next time he returned to the shed he was feeling distinctly cold and the lure of the fire indoors was like a magnet to him. He decided that there was only one thing for it; he would have to swallow his pride and ask Thelma to help him complete the notice.

He took the piece of paper into the warm glow of the house.

'Any chance of a coffee, love?'

'You'll have to get your own. I'm just a bit busy knitting this cardigan whilst the kids are out at Sunday school. What's that piece of paper you're trying to hide behind your back?'

'Well, it's like this, shall I go make the coffee?'

'When you've told me what that paper is for.'

'Well it's for your idea,' he blurted out.

'For my idea?'

'Yes, you said we should tell the shopkeepers who the members are and the members who the shopkeepers are so that they can all sort themselves out.'

'Yes I did, so what's the paper for?'

'For the notice.'

'What notice?'

'The notice to hang in the canteen to tell them who the shopkeepers are.'

'Oh is that all,' said Thelma who was losing interest and putting her attention back into her knitting.

'Yes, well, I've been doing it in the shed, you see.'

'Yes, I see, and?'

'Well, it's like this, you see, I've got stuck.'

'What do you mean you've got stuck?'

'Well I don't know what to put on the notice.'

'Go and put the coffee on. It won't do you any harm to brew up for once. Do you know where the kettle is?'

'Yes.'

'Water?'

'Yes.'

'Coffee, milk, sugar, mugs, spoon?'

'Get on with your knitting.'

'Well go and do it then, there's a love. I could just do with a mug of coffee and I'll do your notice as soon as I've finished Josie's cardigan. I've only got to sew on the left sleeve and the buttons now.'

Willie studied the contents of the kitchen. The coffee grounds were in a jar at the back of the cupboard. They weren't often used and he couldn't think why he fancied a mug of coffee, but he did. The trouble was that coffee grounds got in your teeth, you swallowed some and the remains made a right mess in the bottom of the mug.

Arthur's missus Jess always drank coffee, never tea. She brewed it in a jug and let it settle a while before pouring it through a sieve. They didn't have a sieve, but he thought he would try the jug method anyway.

When he finally delivered the mug of not so hot coffee to Thelma, he was extremely pleased with the results of his effort. Even Thelma was full of praise and immediately promoted him to coffee brewer in chief, with his promise that he would try and get it hot next time.

'Now what's all the fuss about this notice?' she asked.

'Well I've got as far as the title "MURGATROYD'S CHRISTMAS CLUB. NOTICE. DISCOUNT SCHEME" and that's all.'

'Sit at the table with your pencil ready and a new sheet of paper from my writing pad. We'll make a sort of mock up before we do the real thing.

Thelma carefully wrote

NOTICE
MURGATROYD'S CHRISTMAS CLUB
DISCOUNT SCHEME

in capital letters at the top of the paper, then in her best handwriting, put. 'The shops listed below have offered a discount on your Christmas orders. Every shopkeeper has a list of members of the club. All you have to do is to give your name in with your Christmas order to get your discount.'

'I think we should ask Josie to do the proper notice with her paint set. She can make a very nice coloured poster for you; she's very good at doing that sort of thing. She'll not be long before she's home and you can ask her as soon as she lands.'

'Aye, a very good idea,' replied Willie and for the third time in recent living memory gave Thelma a hug and a kiss.

'What was that for?'

'Thanks. That's all.'

Willie went out into his garden again. It was dinner time when he next returned to the house, having passed the time pottering and talking to the pigeons.

'Dinner ready?' he asked of no one in particular.

'Almost Dad, but you'll have to wait for a few more minutes yet until I've finished your poster so that we can clear away and lay the table.'

Normally, Willie would have remonstrated that his dinner wasn't ready and that it was half past twelve, but because today, Josie was doing something special for him, he kept quiet.

'There now, it's finished. Do you want to have a look?'

Willie smiled at her, walked over, put his arm around her and looked at his poster. It was bold, brightly coloured and clearly gave out the required message.

'Ee, that's fair champion,' he said and gave her a hug and a kiss, then, as an afterthought he said, 'Thanks love that's brilliant.'

The traditional Yorkshire pudding was served and Willie ate his with more than his usual relish, which created more than the usual amount of flatulence. This was followed by roast beef and for pudding, jam roly poly, swimming in acres and acres of custard. Finally the meal was washed down with a pint mug of tea. Willie then sat down in front of the fire, put his feet on the mantle shelf and fell into a deep sleep whilst the younger children cleared the table and washed up.

Wednesday dawned fine and clear and stayed that way until the evening when Murgatroyd's Christmas club committee was due to convene at the Working Men's Club at half past seven, prompt.

They were all there in the bar, on time, except Daniel Sykes. Fat Harry was flirting with Sarah Anne, Eustace was lost in his own little world and Arthur was pacing up and down with a pile of papers in his hand, trying to look important. Willie and the others were enjoying a pint and a chat. There was a very convivial atmosphere.

Arthur brought them all back to reality with an announcement. 'Well Ladies and Gentlemen, it is now just hafter half past seven and hi would like you hall to make your way to the committee room so that we may commhence the meeting forthwith.'

'Has he been having elocution lessons?' Dick enquired quietly.

'More like posh gob lessons,' said Willie.'

Dick caught up with Arthur. 'By gum, that were well put Arthur old Mate.'

'Yes, yes,' replied Arthur, his face turning to a broad grin. 'I have been giving hay little private hattention to may public delivery recently.'

'I told thee it were posh gob lessons,' said Willie before adding a few posh noises of his own.

'Can we please get the meeting under way?' Arthur demanded again.

'Are you on a promise or something?' Willie enquired.

'Yes, as a matter of fact, I am on a promise to put some curtains up for Jess as soon as I can get home. So come on you people, let us get the show onto the road.'

'What show Arthur? What show? What road? What-'

'For goodness sake, shut up Eustace.'

The meeting duly sat down, everyone on suitably supplied with alcoholic refreshment. Arthur nudged Sarah Anne into stopping talking and opening the meeting.

'Good evening, everyone, and thank-you for coming along this evening to what I hope will prove to be the last committee meeting before we pay out the money and hold the party. We have a lot to get through, so I suggest we begin with-'

'Oh bugger,' thought Willie, 'we're here for the duration.'

'-the item that is customary on these occasions the reading of the minutes of the last meeting. Arthur, can you please oblige?'

'But hof course madam Chairman. Minutes hof the committee meeting hof the Murgatroyd's Christmas club, held hat-'

He was interrupted by Eustace who was having one of his rare brainstorms. 'Can't we take the minutes as read? Can't we? Take the minutes as read? Can't we?'

Arthur, who was enjoying reading out the minutes to his captive audience, gave Eustace a drop-dead look, but the Chairman said, 'Well, yes, I see no reason why we should not. Does anyone object?'

'Yes. I do.'

They all turned to observe the tall, thin figure of Daniel Sykes who had entered the room very quietly without any of them hearing him.

'Well you Mafeking well would,' shouted Willie.

'I'll swing for you yet, that I will, Arkenthwaite. He shouted back in reply.'

'You probably will, with what I know.'

Before Daniel could reply again, the chairman intervened. 'Look here you two, sort out your differences outside the committee room, will you please. Now then Daniel, it has been carried by an overwhelming majority that we will take the minutes of the last meeting as read.'

'How do you know it's carried by an overwhelming majority when you haven't had a vote?'

'Because I am the chairman and I know the feeling of the meeting. Now can we get on? Sit down please, Daniel. I think we should start by asking Willie if everything is going well with the collection of the money.'

'Yes, Sarah Anne. No problem. We have it sorted out now and it doesn't take long of a Friday dinner time. Mind you, there's sometimes a long queue at the bank when I go, but I just have to be patient and wait my turn.'

'Do you manage to spend the Christmas club's money or your own when you call in here on your way to the bank?' asked Daniel Sykes with a smirk on his face.

'I'll swing for you, never mind you for me,' Willie bawled at him.

Once more the chairman intervened in the dispute.

'Item three, Arthur and Willie. What arrangements have you made for paying out the money?'

Willie looked at Arthur, who gratefully came to his rescue. 'Well we haven't yet finalised the plan hexcept to say harrangements are hin hand.'

'He's still talking posh gob,' Willie thought to himself.

'Madam Chairman, may I be permitted through the chair to ask Arthur Baxter if he is well enough to continue with the meeting, as he appears to have some form of speech impediment and I was wondering if he should be asked to go home and lie down,' said Daniel Sykes with an even broader smirk on his face.

'Don't take the bait Arthur. Ignore it,' commanded the Chairman. 'If however you don't mind me saying so, Arthur, I think you've just talked a lot and said nowt. Can you please be a bit more specific?'

Arthur stood up. 'Well madam chairman we know that the party's hon Friday twentieth of December and we know that the bank closes hat three thirty hon a Friday. So we, that is Willie and me, will have to be hat the bank just before hit closes to get hall hof hus money hout. Then we'll have to take it somewhere safe to look hafter hit huntil the party starts. Then we'll have to give hit hout hat the party.'

The proceedings were interrupted by Mr Anthony Murgatroyd coming into the committee room, a freshly pulled pint in his hand.

'Good evening, everyone.'

'Good evening, Mr Anthony.'

'Sorry I'm late. I hope you don't mind me interfering in your meeting. It's a good excuse for me to get out of the house for a drink. I don't go out often at night.'

'As usual, you are more than welcome,' said the Chairman, 'and might I add that any contribution you may wish to make to the proceedings will be much appreciated.'

There was a general grunt of approval from all but Daniel Sykes who made a noise a bit like a Bactrian camel with stomach trouble, the exact meaning of which, no one could decipher, but they all knew it was not a noise of agreement.

'Now can we get on please? Arthur you were telling us about the money.'

Arthur had already decided that, with the appearance of Mr Anthony, he had better revert back to his native tongue and give over trying to talk far back. 'Yes, the main problem is how to pay out.'

'Thank god that Mr Anthony's arrived and the posh gob's gone,' Willie thought to himself.

'If it were me, I'd count it before I paid it out.' Daniel Sykes sat smirking again.

Willie stood up and calmly said, with meaning, 'One more like that and you'll feel my fist.'

The chairman shouted, 'Willie. One more like that from you and you are banned. Treasurer or not.'

Anthony Murgatroyd intervened, 'At the last meeting, I offered you some wage envelopes to put the money into. Why don't you get them well in advance of the twentieth, and write each member's name on the outside ready for the big night. Put each member's payment in and pay them out at the beginning of the evening and you can all then sit back and relax and enjoy the party.'

'What a good idea,' said Arthur. That will mean that we can count it and put it in the envelopes as soon as we get it from the bank and, then lock them all into the club safe until party time. All we need to do is to write out the envelopes a few days in advance. Thanks, Mr Anthony.'

Dick's glass was empty so he said, 'Time for a refill. I think I'll just ring the bell for some service.'

'No, no, let me do it. I'm nearest to it.' Mr Anthony got up and pressed the bell push which stuck in and would not come out. 'Oh dear, what have I done now?'

'Don't worry; you've only upset Fat Harry,' said Willie laughing.

Sure enough there was soon the sound of a stampeded approaching and suddenly the door opened in all three directions at once.

'Who the bloody hell's gone and buggered the bloody bell?'

'Guilty,' said Mr Anthony.

'Oh,' said Fat Harry stopping short. 'Yes, it's inclined to be faulty at times. I'll just fix it.' He busied himself with the bell push whilst they all laughed silently at him behind his back.

'Can we have another round of drinks, Harry, please?' the chairman asked in her most seductive voice.

'Certainly, my love. Anything for you, you know that.' He turned around, having forgotten about his audience, turned crimson around the cheeks and rasped. 'Same again was it?'

When he had gone, they all had a jolly good laugh, but Sarah Anne made a mental note to remonstrate with him later. She then addressed the meeting again.

'Now the food situation for the party, does anyone know, has anyone done anything about it yet?'

'Dick gave a rather loud discreet cough. 'We've asked one or two of the committee wives and a few other women members if they would help, but we haven't got down to exactly what we're going to have or how much we're going to charge for it. However, Lewis and I thought it might be best if we could sort it out tonight so that we can say to the ladies that we'll have this and that, then our contribution would be to organise it.'

'That sounds to be a very good idea. Has anyone any suggestions for the actual refreshments?'

'Aye, Fat Harry's taking a long time with us drinks,' said Willie.

'I mean for the party refreshments,' said a very exasperated Sarah Anne.

'Pork pies, cold sausages and piccalilli.'

The chairman ignored him and said, 'Now I think we should have a good wholesome supper. Pork pies and cold sausages yes, sandwiches, potato crisps, cakes, trifle, tea and coffee. Does that sound alright?'

That sounds as right as rain,' said Dick.

'Oh, and I forgot some piccalilli for Willie.'

'I can get a list of who is going to do what,' continued Dick. 'Now the big question is, how much of what do we need, where shall we get it from and who is going to pay for it all before the big night?'

'Well to deal with the first question first of how much do we want, this depends on how many are coming to the do. How many members do we have, Willie?'

'Well, Sarah Anne, we've got in total one hundred and forty six members, so say about one hundred and twenty because they'll not all come. Then there's their husbands and wives, taking into account them what's not married and we've got about two hundred and fifty so that wants a bit of catering for.'

Eustace applauded Willie and Willie farted.

'A bit of a squash in the club room, never mind, they'll take a bit of catering for. Can we cope with so many?'

Mr Anthony intervened, 'Have you actually enquired who might be coming to the party?'

'Er, no, not exactly, we just assumed they would nearly all be coming except for a few as Willie has suggested,' said Arthur.

'Well I suggest you start tomorrow asking around and get a comprehensive list. I tend to believe that most of your members will be here but I do think you should check it out. Now then, about the catering. I could ask the works canteen staff to help out, in works time. There is one very important item you forgot from the food list, Sarah Anne, and that is mince pies, which I do think the canteen could help with. Dick, please do not think for one minute that I was trying any one-upmanship over your very good organisational abilities; I just thought you could do with the help.'

'Greasy Martha'll not help us out,' said Arthur.

'I'm sure she will if I ask her nicely. If you want, I could ask her to make a variety of small cakes and the trifles. She could even cook the sausages and it wouldn't cost you a penny. What you would have to do then, is to buy the pork pies, crisps, pickles and get every one of the ladies that are coming to make a round of sandwiches. The only thing I've left out is tea and coffee. If I provide the ingredients, can you organise the brewing and serving?'

'It shouldn't prove too difficult to persuade Porky Charrington to wait for his money from Friday until Monday for a large order of pork pies, crisps and pickles, particularly so if we buy the sausages from him as well. All that remains to be done, and it's a big task, is to organise an army of lady helpers for the night, cutlery, crockery and cruet. Finally, washing up. Have you considered that yet?'

'We'll sort out the helpers,' said Dick.

'Ask my wife Dick, will you please. Ask her please, my wife, please, ask her. Dick, will you Dick?'

'There's just one thing,' said Mr Anthony, 'You will remember that at an earlier meeting I suggested a faith supper. Well, I have been thinking that in view of the numbers coming to the party, it would result in total chaos, so please forgive me for suggesting it. I now think we should follow Dick's plans.'

'Cutlery and crockery won't be hay problem. There's hundreds of plates, cups, saucers, dishes knives, forks hand spoons from hay collection that has built up over many years from people who have bequeathed them and those that have been clearing hout their deceased relations houses. Hi have to say, however, that very few of them match.' Arthur sat back pleased with his new found accent.

'Posh gob again,' thought Willie.

The Chairman rose to her feet again and said, 'I think that before we go any further at all, we ought to thank Mr Anthony Murgatroyd for his more than generous offer and to say on behalf of all the members of the Christmas club, we accept. So we've no more problems left to deal with now, have we?'

'Just one.'

They all turned to look at Daniel Sykes, just as Fat Harry returned with the round of drinks, expertly balanced on a tray. Harry managed to rub his leg against Sarah Anne's arm as he walked past her, but she ignored him again making another mental note to have a word with him later.

'I think we had better elect a new bar steward,' said Arthur, posh gob forgotten, after Harry had left the room.

'Why?' enquired Lewis.

'Because he hasn't taken any money for the drinks, hasn't asked for it or anything. It's only just dawned on me.'

'Aye, you're right. Happen he's beginning to lose his marbles,' said Willie.

'I think I can possibly quell any false hope or rumour,' said Mr Anthony. 'I paid for the round before I came into the meeting or at least, to be more correct, I arranged to pay for it after the meeting.'

A chorus of thanks ensued, with a polite noise from the long dollop as Willie liked to call him.

'Now then, Daniel, you were saying?'

'All I was going to ask, was why we should have to have pickles just because of Willie Arkenthwaite?'

Willie belched, stood up at a gallop and began to leave his place at the table.

'Sit down now! Willie! This instant!' screamed the Chairman in a very commanding voice. 'For your information, Daniel, the pickles are for everyone. Willie was just implicated as a joke.'

Daniel stared at Sarah Anne, motionless and emotionless.

'Now, it just remains for me to thank Mr Anthony for his more than generous offer to help with the supper, for the drinks tonight and for all the help he has given us so far. Just a minute, we haven't mentioned the band. Is that all arranged Arthur?'

'Yes, Willie hand hi risked life and limb to go and book Sid Sidebottom and his Syncopating Sextet, mind you there are only five of them, but hall is arranged.'

'Are you alright Arthur? Are you? You're talking funny, are you? Arthur, are you? Talking funny, you are, aren't you?'

'Shut up Eustace,' said Dick.

'I ham talking very properly,' he replied.

'As I was saying, I think that all thanks are due to all of us, including myself for arranging this Christmas club and in particular to the two people who dreamed up the idea in the first place, Arthur and Willie. I think we should all look forward now to the party and to the return of our contributions with interest. Shall we now adjourn to the bar and close the meeting, or possibly the other way around.'

'There is just one matter that I would like to mention to Willie and Arthur before it gets too late,' said Anthony Murgatroyd, 'and that is, I do think you should warn the bank of your intention to draw out the money and give them a date and time so that they can be prepared in advance. It wouldn't do to surprise them, would it now?'

'Oh, we have to tell them we want us brass out do we? We can't just go and get it like?' asked Willie.

'Well, you could just go in and ask for it and they would be obliged to pay you, but it would be better for relations with them if you were to warn them in advance. When you go to pay in on Friday just tell them that you will want to withdraw all the money and close the account on Friday twentieth of December at three o'clock and they will have it prepared ready for you.'

'Come on, I've supped up, let's get to the bar,' said Dick.

'It's high time you concentrated your efforts on something other that the demon drink. It is the downfall of civilisation.'

'Just like a trip up Mafeking Street.'

Daniel Sykes jumped up and advanced on Willie who hurriedly removed himself to the bar, where he knew that Fat Harry would deal effectively with the long dollop.

Anthony Murgatroyd turned to Sarah Anne. 'Whatever possessed you to elect a man like Daniel Sykes to a committee such as this, that always meets on licensed premises?'

'As I remember it, he elected himself in order to see fair play for his fellow men and then tried his best to get us to meet in the Church hall. I'll tell you what though, if we do it again next year, we are not having him on the committee.'

'If you run into any more trouble with him, just let me know and I'll find a good excuse to sack him. He's as big a pain in the mill as he is here.'

When they ambled back into the bar, Fat Harry was very hurt to find Sarah Anne in the company of Mr Anthony, but she was soon on her own again and Harry was once again in attendance, flitting around her like a mother hen with her new born chicks.

'Now, what will you have to drink, my dear?'

'Nothing, thank-you Harry. Come into your storeroom with me.'

Harry thought that for the first time in his life, all his birthdays had come together and off he trotted to his storeroom behind the bar with Sarah Anne close on his heels.

'I wonder what those two are up to?' asked Arthur.

'I don't know, but just hang on a few minutes, we might find out.'

They hadn't long to wait for the two people returned very shortly, Sarah Anne with a big smile and Harry looking as if he'd lost a pound and found a penny.

'Now, I'll just have a whisky and dry before I go home,' said the chairman.

'Well now, that wasn't what you thought it was, was it?' Willie said to Arthur.

241

'No, just the opposite.'

'Are you ready for home?'

'Yes.'

'Let's just go round by Mafeking Street on the way, he disappeared a bit sharp after the meeting.'

'Don't forget, I've some curtains to hang for Jess yet tonight.'

'It won't take long.'

'No, I don't suppose it will. Sarah Anne, are you ready, we're going.'

'Not just yet. Dick'll walk me home, won't you?'

'Yes I will.'

'Okay. We're off. Goodnight.'

'What's up with them two?' enquired Harry after they had left. 'They're early for them.'

'Arthur has a bit of a domestic to do and Willie is up to no good and I bet I know where.'

'Where?'

'Mafeking Street.'

'That long dollop Sykes will belt him if he gets hold of him you know,' said Harry

'I don't think it will come to that,' said Sarah Anne.

'I think it might,' mused Harry wistfully.

Halfway along Mafeking Street, Willie looked at Arthur and asked, 'Well, what are we going to do now?'

'That's a very good question. I don't know either. We might as well go home. I'll have to go soon anyway to give Jess a hand with the curtains.'

They had walked along the full length of the street twice, not a soul was to be found anywhere, nothing stirred, not even the breeze, it was very frosty and cold.

'We'll just go up and down once more, then if nothing happens we'll go home.'

Willie's front room fire was beginning to have a magnetic effect on him.

Unknown to them they had been observed by two pairs of eyes and as they passed number nineteen on the way uphill again, they were not a little startled to hear the door open. They turned to look and found a somewhat buxom, ageing, trying to look young, lady in a long flowing chiffon dressing gown. It was gaping and concealed very little in certain places. She leaned on the door post, cigarette in one hand, glass of wine in the other.

'Hello boys,' she shouted.

'Er, er, good evening,' mumbled Arthur raising his cap.

'Er, yes,' said Willie.

'Are you coming in for a good time, then?'

'Er, well, er,' they stammered, both flummoxed. 'Er well, that is, not just…'

They were both rooted to the spot. Neither of them could take their eyes from the apparition in front of them and both were petrified.

'Come on in boys, it's a lot warmer in here than it is out there and we can soon be even warmer.'

Willie suddenly remembered his own front room fire. He grabbed Arthur's arm and began to run back downhill towards the village. Willie's grip was so tight that Arthur had little option but to follow him.

When they had turned the corner at the bottom of the street and both pairs of legs and knees had turned to jelly, Willie laughed and said, 'It's a good job I was there, Arthur Baxter, to rescue you from a fate worse than death.'

'Yes Willie, it is. Even the thought of going hanging curtains for Jess sounds not too bad after all.'

'Aye, we are both cowards when it comes to loose women. I think a nice hot mug of tea in front of a nice warm fire sounds all right as well.

At number nineteen Mafeking Street, Daniel Sykes gave the spare time love of his life a last farewell fondle and kiss for the night.

'Thanks a million. That was superb, just what those two needed, you couldn't have done it better if you had tried. I'll never forget the night you frightened off Arkenthwaite and Baxter, me and my shadow.'

With that he marched away into the night without a care.

*

The next day Thelma met Jess out shopping.

'Was your Arthur in a funny mood when he came home last night?'

'Not especially, mind you, he did help me put up the new lounge curtains that I've made, without so much as a grumble or argument now you come to mention it and it's not like him not to cause a fuss even if there's the smallest job to do. Why, was your Willie in a funny mood then?'

'He came into our house, gave me a hug and a kiss then made us both a pot of tea, following which he sat down in front of the fire with me and talked. I'll say he was quite normal but unusual.'

'I wonder what they were up to last night. I'll get it out of Arthur tonight.'

As the two ladies walked along the village deep in conversation, her from number nineteen Mafeking Street made a point of saying, 'Good morning ladies,' as she passed them by.

'What was all that about?' asked Thelma.

'I don't know, she's never spoken to me before. Funny that. I bet those two husbands of ours can answer that question.'

'Oh, I don't think they'll know anything about her.'

'Well I'm putting two and two together and coming out with an answer that's about twenty seven. I'll most certainly get it out of Arthur tonight.'

Down in the mill bottom at Murgatroyd's, Daniel Sykes made an unheard of appearance in the dyehouse. All he did was to walk straight through the room, in at one end and out at the other and shout 'good morning' to Willie and Arthur, with a knowing grin on his face. Arthur grabbed Willie around the neck to restrain him. Willie was rolling up his sleeves shouting, 'I'll kill the bastard. I will, I'll kill him.'

'Let him go. We've had our fun out of it and enough is enough.'

Willie gave up the struggle, stared after Daniel Sykes and mustering all his internal energy, he belched as loud as he could in the general direction of his enemy's disappearance.

'There, that's made me feel much better. It's as good as killing him.'

Arthur arrived home from the mill to find his tea not in its usual place on the table.

Jess was eating her tea, and his place was laid, but no food was in evidence.

'Where's my tea?' he enquired.

'Come sit down here.'

'Yes but where's my tea?'

'Sit!'

He sat.

'Now before you can have your tea, tell me what you and Willie know about that floozy that lives up Mafeking Street.'

Arthur's heart missed a couple of beats. 'What?'

'You know what I said as well as I do, and I want an answer before any tea's served up,' she continued to eat hers and Arthur sat in stony silence.

'I've got all night,' she said and continued to eat her tea.

Arthur was hungry. He wondered if Willie had got his tea or if he was being subjected to the same torture.

Willie was in fact enjoying neck of mutton stew with apple pie for afters because Thelma was waiting to see what Jess had found out before she started on Willie.

Arthur did not normally get fed as well as Willie and he watched Jess devour a slice of cold boiled ham with a tomato. He was hungry; Jess got up to take her dirty plate away and returned with a piece of currant pasty.

'Come on, let's have my tea.'

'You can have your tea when you've told me what you know about her up Mafeking Street.'

He still sat in silence, watching Jess finish her tea, then realising that he most definitely wasn't going to get his, he decided to spill the beans.

'Daniel Sykes is knocking her off.'

'I beg your pardon. Kindly do not use such language in this house.'

'Daniel Sykes is knocking her off.'

'Go and wash your mouth out.'

'No, no. It's true; he's been visiting her for months now. Can I have my tea please?'

'Not yet, carry on talking, but not in that foul and filthy manner.'

'Nobody knows but me and Willie. We found out by accident and last night after the committee meeting was over we went up Mafeking Street to see if we could catch him coming out, because the meeting finished early and we knew he'd have gone up there because he always does after a committee meeting and anyway, we got a bit of a surprise, me and Willie did, because as we were walking past for the second time she opened the front door and came out in her nightdress and said 'hello boys are you coming in for a good time?' and me and Willie ran home then and that's the truth and can I have my tea now?'

'You can get it yourself because I am going round to Thelma's to see if Willie's story is the same as yours.'

With that she put on her hat and coat and flounced out of the house, the front door coming to rest with an almighty crash behind her.

The Arkenthwaites had just finished a delicious tea and cleared away when the front door received a series of hammer type blows.

'Who on earth can that be?' asked Josie.

'Nay lass, go and see,' said Willie.

Josie opened the front door. 'Hello, Auntie Jess. Are you coming in?'

'Yes, I am that, is your mother in?'

Josie, realising that things were not quite as they should be, said, 'She's in the back washing up. I'll go and take over from her.'

Josie took over from her mother who came into the front to greet Jess. Other than the usual if not brusque, small talk, Willie had not got down to any serious discussion with Jess.

'Hello Jess. Are you taking you coat off?'

'Yes, I will. This might take a while to sort out.'

She always found it overpoweringly hot in their front room after her own lukewarm house.

'Now about what we were talking about this morning, I've got it out of him.'

'Have you now. Well this is interesting.'

Willie's ears pricked up.

'Have you mentioned it to your Willie yet?'

'No, not yet. I was waiting to see what you had to say first. I thought you might have waited until tomorrow.'

'I refused Arthur his tea until he spilt the beans.'

Willie's ears pricked up even further, his nose began to twitch and his bald head began to throb. He could sense a lot of trouble brewing. Bluntness was one of Jess's strong points and she didn't back off now.

'I think we should see what Willie has to say about it.'

Thelma had been prepared to mention the matter in her own good time, but not just yet, and not like this either, but she found it impossible to fight Jess when she was in roaring order.

'Well, so Willie, what about it then?'

'What about what?'

'Her that lives up Mafeking Street?'

'What, her what's having it away with long dollop Sykes?'

'So that's your tale as well is it?'

'It's no tale, it's true. It's been going on for months.'

'So what were you and Arthur doing at her house last night then?'

Thelma began to feel apprehensive.

'We weren't at her house, we were outside it. We thought long tall Sykes were in there, but she came out and invited us in for a bit of homely comfort. We decided to decline her offer because we love you two too much for that, and anyway we thought, that Sykes were in there all the time and had sent her out to annoy us and put us off the scent. Mind you, if we'd thought that Sykes wasn't there, we might have taken up her offer.'

'God only knows what you two would have done with a woman like her. Anyway at least you're both batting from the same hymn sheet, so I suppose I'd better believe you.'

'You speak for you own as you find them,' said Thelma.

The atmosphere returned to normal after that and Jess accepted the offer of a cup of tea, following which she returned home to an empty house. Arthur having gone to the club early.

Thelma looked at Willie. 'You wouldn't really have gone into that house up Mafeking Street would you?'

'Gone in! Gone in! You know full well that I would not. Apart from anything else I couldn't cope with a woman like her. I don't know how Daniel Sykes does. To tell you the truth, and don't let on to Jess, we ran all the way home after she invited us in, we were both scared stiff. I bet Daniel Sykes has had a right good laugh at our expense.'

'Never mind, love, at least I almost always know where you are.'

'We were just having a bit of fun at his expense and it backfired on us, but, by gum, I aren't half glad I'm not wed to Jess.'

He turned to Thelma and not for the first time in living memory he gave her a big hug and a loving kiss. She for the first time in living memory didn't ask why.

CHAPTER 17

Willie sat motionless, staring into space.

Arthur sat motionless, staring into space.

The pigeons moved their heads from side to side, staring at Willie and Arthur.

It was the next Wednesday evening following the committee meeting and the flame in the hurricane lamp began to flicker and die.

Willie continued to stare into space.

Arthur continued to stare into space.

The pigeons continued to stare at both of them and then the flame in the lamp died completely.

'Bugger,' said Willie.

'Hear hear,' said Arthur

'Well, that's it then.'

'What is?'

'Well, I'm not filling that lamp again tonight, so we'll now have to go to the band room and listen to Sid Sidebottom and his Syncopating Sextet practicing.'

'Coo, coo,' said the pigeons.

'Shut up,' said a couple of voices.

Grolsby Band Club was situated well outside of the village. In fact, for a man in Willie's condition, it was a long walk, particularly as it was up a long steep hill. Many years ago, in due deference to the wishes of the local community, on suggesting the building of a new band room, the people in charge of the project had built it in such a position as to not annoy the local populace on practice nights.

In its day, it had been a splendiferous building, constructed so that it could seat more than four hundred people to a band concert and a brass band as big as could be found could be seated on stage. Because of this, and because of its large bar areas downstairs, not to mention the changing, utility and committee rooms, it was still used for all major concerts and contests even if its general ambience was becoming a little dated. There was no doubt that it would have to go on with its present use for many years to come because it was the only such building in the area other than the Town Hall. No one in their right mind was going to propose the building of anything like it again and the acoustics in the concert hall were the best for miles around.

Willie stopped half way up the hill to get his breath back. 'Hang on, Arthur, till I get right again.'

'It's time you went to see Dr Mitchell to get yourself sorted out because you are going to be in one hell of a mess before long if you don't. You've got responsibilities with Thelma and the children and you could well do to go for a check up. It's free you know.'

Willie had by this time almost recovered. The breathing was easier and they set off walking again only more slowly this time.

'Aye, you're right; it is free now isn't it? I haven't been to see Doc Mitchell in years but now we've got this new fangled health service I might give it a try - after Christmas when all the excitement's over.'

'You should go see him now, before it's too late.'

'Nay, I'm only a bit overweight, that's all. Nowt that a bit of exercise and a lack of food won't cure.'

'But you never have exercise or lack of food.'

'True. So it might be difficult to cure me.'

By this time they had reached the ornate entrance to the band room and Willie was still upright, breathing fairly easily. Because of its popularity, the band room could support its own full time steward and stewardess. Unlike the Working Men's Club it had an accommodation unit for the incumbent steward, with wife to assist, (as advertised). It was in all aspects much more up market than the WMC, it was much better supported, but the drinks were more expensive. It held a dance almost every Saturday night, sometimes using Sid Sidebottom, sometimes using other bands or even gramophone records occasionally. To take an overall view, it was much too posh and expensive for Willie and Arthur to use on either a regular or irregular basis.

The building was much larger than the largest of the Methodist Chapels, with big thick, heavy, double oak front doors, sporting long, tubular brass highly polished handles which Willie now grasped and pulled open. The entrance hall that met them was brightly lit and warm with central heating radiators which had been installed recently for the comfort of guests. The bars, for there were three of them were situated along the left hand side of the corridor, accessed through another pair of big, heavy oak doors. The wide stairways to the concert room lead up to right and left from the entrance hall.

The terrible two went into the first bar on the left.

'Evening Stan. Evening Molly.'

'Well, I never did. Well you can take me to our house and bring me back again. The terrible two. I haven't seen the pair of you in years. How are you both?'

'I'm well thank-you, Stan, but Willie's a wee bit short of puff from walking up the hill and, as you can see, he hasn't quite found the wind to talk yet.'

'Comes to us all, it does. Would that my wind pipes were as good as they used to be. Mind, Willie, you're a might young for shortage of breath; still, you're several stones overweight and one goes with the other, of course,' continued Stan, 'it's when the shortage of breath becomes no breath at all that you've got to start worrying, haven't you Moll?'

Molly had just finished serving some other customers and she came over to them bearing a radiant smile.

'Pardon, love?'

'I was saying that Willie here is short of breath from walking up the hill, but as I tell him, it's when the shortage is permanent that he really needs to start worrying about it.'

'You mean when he's dead?' asked Arthur.

'Something like that.'

Molly laughed and said, 'Fools the lot of you.'

'Anyway, what can I get for you on this most surprising and welcome visit?'

'How much is it?' asked Willie, quickly.

'How much is what?'

'How much is best bitter?'

'Penny a pint more than it is at your usual drinking club.'

'How do you know how much we pay?'

'I keep my ear to the grindstone and my nose to the rail.'

'I don't think that was quite right.'

'Probably not, but it's near enough for you two.'

'Well, we'll have two pennyworth just short of two pints.'

Molly laughed again as Stan poured two pints. 'How's Thelma and the children and how's Jess, Arthur?'

'They're fine, just fine. We're getting ready for the Murgatroyd Christmas club, Christmas party,' answered Willie who was rudely interrupted by Stan.

'Is it at Christmas?'

'No, it's on Pancake Tuesday; anyway as I were saying, that's why we're here. We've come to listen to Sid Sidebottom and his Syncopating Sextet.'

'What on earth for?' asked Molly. 'And anyway, there's only five of them.'

'Because we've booked him and his band to play at the Christmas party.'

'At Christmas,' added Stan.

'And we know there's only five of them.'

'Well, you will not be disappointed for long, for they are due here in a few minutes; it's usually about nowish when they come puffing and wheezing in. You'll probably hear their van as it tries its best to come up the hill. There'll be much honking, rasping, scraping of gears, backfiring, cursing and verbal abuse before they fall into here. It's level odds as to who's in charge, Sid or the van.'

Stan brought two pints from the opposite end of the bar, one in each hand. He stood in front of Willie and Arthur, took a long slow sip from each glass, handed them over to the two friends and said, 'There you are, club prices. Your club that is, not mine.'

'Dirty bugger,' said Arthur.

'Sorry, you know the rules; we do not allow swearing on these premises. Now, how about paying for your drinks, and by the way, I might just let you have our club pints at your club prices next round, just for fun and just once.'

The two friends sat down in comfortably upholstered chairs at an oak table with an inlaid top, to await the arrival of Sid Sidebottom.

'Great pity the Club isn't as nice as this,' said Willie.

'Aye, we should bring Thelma and Jess up here one Saturday to the dance for a change.'

'Yes, we coulda' agreed Willie which he followed up with a big loud belch.

'Manners!' shouted Molly. 'You're here again are you, William Arkenthwaite?'

'Sorry.'

'That is one of the reasons that our Club is not as nice as this one,' said Arthur, 'anyway, whilst we are waiting, what have we got to sort out yet for the Christmas club and the party?'

'Well, we've got to sort out about getting t' money from t' bank, about keeping it until eight o'clock at night, about-'

Arthur stopped him whilst he found a minuscule piece of paper to write down the items. He also found a very short, grubby pencil stub. 'Now start again, and let me note it down.'

So as they talked, Arthur made notes, sometimes adding to the list himself. Finally the list read. One - get the money from the bank. Two - keep the money safe until eight o'clock at night. Three - count the money. Four - put the money into the envelopes. Five - give out the money. Six - discounts from shops. Seven - booze at party. Eight - band. Nine - food. Ten - room decorations. Eleven - arrangements at the Club.

'Well, I think you've made a very comprehensive coverage there, Willie.'

'Eh?'

'I think you've said everything. I've noted down eleven items and we'd best go through them all now, very slowly and carefully, one at a time.'

'Why?'

'Well, because it's time we were beginning to make sure we've nothing left to chance. We want everything to go just right don't we?'

'Oh yes, we do.'

'Right, let's start with item one. Drawing out the money from the bank. Have you made the necessary arrangements at the bank?'

'Well, er, not exactly.'

'Don't you think it's about time you were doing it? It was ordered by the committee, you know, and you'll be going on Friday to pay in.'

'So I will, yes, go on then, but what have I to do about it?'

253

Stephen Bailey

'No idea except you must tell the people who serve you that you will want to draw out the entire contents of the account on Friday the twentieth of December at exactly five to four. However, we do have a big problem with this money in the middle of all the other big problems.'

'We have?'

'We sure do, buddy. There's all the interest to work out, so this Friday you'd best ask the bank what the final figure will be. After that, we'd better work out what coinage denominations we want.'

'What's that for?'

'So that we can easily divide the money up amongst the members without us having to go seeking change.'

'So how are we going to do that?'

'Well now, let's see. It's easy, but it'll take a fair bit of working out. We'll have to list every member, and against their names, all the money that they have paid in then if we can get a total from the bank, we can subtract the principal amount and finally apportion the remainder to each member in the ratio of the amount paid in to the total of the fund.' Arthur beamed at Willie, proud of his analysis of the situation.

Willie was bored stiff, not understanding a word of it. He had done all his usual foul tricks and was beginning to have the sensation of certain pressures building up inside his body, when he was saved from further embarrassment by a commotion at the door. A set of drums, covered in leather cases, was barged in, closely followed by Jack France pushing and the other four members of the Sid Sidebottom's Syncopating Sextet carrying their various instruments and music. The instruments were dumped in a heap in the middle of the room whilst the members of the band attended the bar for liquid refreshments.

Sid Sidebottom, pint in hand, looked around and observed the terrible two sitting at a table, watching the proceedings. He walked over to them.

'Glad you two lads could make it up here to listen to us. We'll not be long, just have this one round then it's across the corridor into the dressing room where we normally practice. Mind you, if it was me I wouldn't rush. I'd enjoy my drinks for a few minutes until we get

254

warmed up. It's always a bit rough for the first few bars, it's Maud you know, she needs kick starting. She's getting on a bit now, as you can see if you're an observant sort of chap, but when she gets going, boy oh boy, does she get going. Anyway, give us ten minutes to get set up and started.'

He and the other members of his band sauntered away with their drinks, in the direction of the dressing room then reappeared a few seconds later to collect the pile of instruments and music.

'Right now,' said Arthur, 'point two, looking after the money. First of all it's obvious that once we collect it, we can't leave it alone for one second right up to paying out time at eight o'clock, so what are we going to do with it?'

'Take it to the Club,' said Willie brightly.

'No, I think not. Not until we've counted it and put it into the envelopes. Tell you what, we'll take it to our house, you and me, then we'll get Thelma to come around. Jess can make us a bite to eat, then we'll count it and sort it. It's a big job you know. It's bound to take us a couple of hours at least. Then when it's ready, we'll take it around to the Club and put it in the safe. If we do that, we can go home one at a time to get changed ready for the do whilst the other one and any others we can muster, can keep their eyes on the safe.'

'You'll have to make arrangements with Fat Harry to keep the club open for us.'

'No problem, the ladies will be there all the time preparing the supper and the room, so all we'll have to do is to make sure the safe is safe. Mind you, I'll be much happier with the money locked in the safe. Anyway, come on, I hear the tinkle of the ivories.'

They managed to get their second pint of the night at a cheaper price than before, after a little bit of argument as to whether or not Stan had been joking at the time of his offer.

'I don't think we'll get the next pint at that price,' said Willie.

'Oh yes, we will, but not here.'

They made their way out of the bar, across the corridor and into the somewhat cooler changing room suite, where Sid Sidebottom and his syncopating Sextet, minus one, were settling down into their practice routine, playing the music for the Gay Gordon to the tune of

Scotland the Brave. The terrible two sat down, facing the band, pint glasses in hand and surveyed the scene.

Sid himself on tenor saxophone and Dennis Shires on trumpet were both red in the face, both puffing merrily away and both concentrating on the manipulation of their shiny brass instruments. Jack France was banging happily away on his drums without a care in the world. Hubert Shaw was in another world strumming his double bass and Maud Lindley was tickling the ivories just like she had been sitting there for ever. After a short time had elapsed, both Willie and Arthur were tapping their feet on the floor in time to the beat of the band and were thoroughly enjoying what was an excellent performance.

Arthur turned to Willie and said, 'By gum lad, this is good stuff and it'll sound even better in evening dress. I'm fair glad we risked life and limb to go to his house and sort it out with him.'

'Yes, we should have a good party with this lot playing.'

They stayed to listen to another couple of items then took their leave of the band and the band room. Neither of them wanted to go back to the drabness of the Club and leave the luxury of the band room, but there again, neither of them wanted to stay and pay the elevated prices for the ale.

Before they left, Sid Sidebottom asked them if they would like a spot of carol singing at the party, but the subject was left open to be decided on the night. Sid promised to be prepared just in case.

'Let's call in on James Richard at the George on the way back,' said Arthur. 'The ale's cheaper than the band room and we haven't called for a long time.'

'You're right, it's ages since we heard his wit and wisdom, mind you it'll not be open yet.'

As they approached the George, Willie let out an exclamation. 'Miracle of miracles.'

'Pardon?'

'It's open.'

'What is?'

'The George, it's open and the Church clock's only just struck nine o'clock. It's early, but see, it's lit up.'

'Yes, you're right, come on let's get inside before it closes again.'

The drab interior of the hostelry well reflected its landlord's dowdy appearance. James Richard was leaning on the bar talking to a group of people who nodded to Arthur and Willie.

'How do lads,' shouted Willie. All right James Richard?'

'As usual.'

The group of people nodded and responded.

'Aye, you look bad. Two pints please.'

'Not like you to say please, Willie.'

Willie belched.

'I didn't think that'd be long arriving.'

'It wasn't long, more short and quick.'

A middle aged lady left the group and walked over to Willie.

'There's ladies here, you know,' she growled.

'Oh yes, I am so sorry,' he shouted. 'How do, lassies.'

'I wasn't referring to that,' she bellowed.

'What was you referring to then?'

'To that horrible noise you just made.'

'Oh that. That were nowt, nobbut a belch. Anybody could do that, even you.'

'But anybody would apologise.'

'Oh, all right then, if it makes you feel any better. Sorry.'

'Thank-you.' She turned and walked back to the group.

Willie snooked up as loudly as he could then, just for good measure, he farted as hard and loud as he could.

James Richard looked at Willie. 'If there's one more episode of that sort of behaviour, you're barred.'

'No problem, we can take our custom to the Club, where they make us very welcome.'

'Rumour has it you're not welcome, they just put up with you.'

Arthur decided that it was time to change the subject. 'Don't you think we should sit down and continue our discussion about the Christmas club party?'

'Go on then,' Willie agreed reluctantly as he was enjoying doing battle with James Richard.

257

The more serious side of Arthur prevailed and they found a table with comfortable padded seats, where it was quite warm. 'Let's go back to item four because we haven't discussed it yet.'

'What do you mean?

'Well we've got to get the envelopes from the wages office to start with, then mark them up with the recipient's names and amount due, then put the money in them, then we'll get a cardboard box of the correct size to fit in the safe and put the envelopes in it in alphabetical order. That way it will be easier to locate them to pay them out.'

'You're not stupid, are you Arthur?'

'No, no,' said Arthur, smiling contentedly. 'I pride myself on the fact that I can sort out this type of problem with mental agility.'

'Eh?' asked Willie with a typically blank expression.

'Mental agility. You know, active brain.'

'Oh aye.'

'Now then, item five, paying out the money.'

'We'll get them to queue up for it,' announced Willie.

'No, no, well yes and no.'

'What do you mean?'

'What I mean is, first of all, we want to get rid of the money as quick as possible after the start of the do, so whether or not we get them to queue up, or perhaps we should walk around with the box of envelopes and hand them out. Yes, that might be the better of the two ways and the easiest. You and me just walk around casually and pay it out.'

'Yes, okay. That's fine by me. Now what are we going to write on the outside of the envelopes, to go back to point four. We shall have to put the name of each member or else we shan't know whose envelope is whose. Then what?'

'Well, what we should put is the amount they have saved, then the interest they have earned, then finally the total. That should do it.'

The shadow of James Richard fell upon them. 'Up to your old tricks, I see. I though you might have sorted things out a bit by now.'

'Can't think what you mean,' said Willie.

'Existing all night on one pint each, that's what I mean. How you expect me to make a living with all this high speed drinking going on, I do not know. Are you having another round then?'

'You mean it's on the house? Are you inviting us?'

'Not bloody likely.'

'Nay, nay. I think we'd best be off, hadn't we Arthur?'

'Yes, best be off, that's right, goodnight.'

Arthur drained the very last dregs of his drink and got up from the table, slowly followed by Willie.

'Well that takes the biscuit that does,' shouted James Richard. 'Just what I expected from two such as you-' He was going to go on, going on and on and on, but what was the use when the two people at the receiving end of his tongue were no longer there.

Outside Arthur could not stop laughing and said, 'I was just going to have another when he came over.'

'Me as well, but never mind, it'll be nice and warm at the Club.'

'No, Willie, thanks. I think I'll go home and have an early night for a change. It's almost ten o'clock and I've had enough for one day.'

'Aye, go on then. I'll have a mug of cocoa in front of the fire. I haven't seen much of Thelma for a day or two.'

So for the first time in a long time, the two friends retired home early and both without too much comment from their respective wives.

The following morning Willie was up and about early. He spent more time than usual with the pigeons. He enjoyed an unusually leisurely breakfast and then waited on the canal towpath for Arthur.

'What's up with you?'

'Eh?'

'What are you doing waiting for me, stood standing here? You never, never, ever are early, so why break the habit of a lifetime?'

'I were up early.'

'Why, did you wet the bed or something?'

'Nay, come off it, I were early to bed last night so I were up early this morning and so I'm here early. Don't worry; it won't happen again in a great hurry.'

'I should hope not, it's more than I can take at any one time. It's a wonder I didn't have a seizure.'

They walked quickly to the mill in the late autumn morning; it was just coming light.

During the course of the morning, Arthur attempted to discuss the party arrangements as and when he could in the midst of the busy schedule in the dyehouse.

When he finally cornered Willie he asked, 'Well what about item six?'

'I'd rather talk about item seven, my favourite subject, drink.'

'Yes, but we really should talk them through in numerical order.'

'I know, but I really don't fancy talking about boring old discounts this morning. Let's talk about drink.'

'Very well. You know I suggested that we could, as a committee, help Fat Harry behind the bar, but if we do we can't enjoy the party, can we?'

'No we can't, although it would be nice to get around the other side of the bar for a change. It would be free beer all night and that has never happened before, has it?'

'No, I don't think it has, except possibly for VE night and I wasn't there then. Were you?'

'You know I was in North Africa enjoying the sunshine. In fact, when I look around here, I wish I was there right now.'

'Anyway, don't you think we should ask Harry if he can muster his own troop of assistants, to save us the trouble? I know it will cost the Club more to employ temporary staff than it will to use us, but I do think they will sell more drink and therefore the club can afford it.'

'Well yes, I do agree with you. But I was looking forward to pint after pint of free ale.'

'Willie, it's supposed to be a party for husbands and wives, no drunkenness, just plain, clean, wholesome fun.'

'Alright have it your own way,' said the, by now, very bored Willie.

'Well, we'd best call and see the fat one tonight to make arrangements.'

Willie arrived early to the canteen at dinnertime, just as Greasy Martha was blowing her nose into the bottom of her apron. She took a long drag from a cigarette that was very carefully hidden behind a wooden partition in the kitchen, and then turned to face the servery, exhaling the smoke. She gave a start as she saw Willie watching her.

'Don't worry Martha, I won't let on.' Although they all cursed her behind her back, most of them had a lot of affection for her.

'How's the arrangements for the mince pies and so on coming along? Oh yes, and what's for dinner?'

'Thanks. Alright. Stew.'

'Eh?'

'You're bloody thick William Arkenthwaite. What I said was thanks for not telling, the arrangements for the party is alright and dinner today is sheep stew with spring cabbage and boiled potatoes.'

'Spring cabbage at this time of year?'

'Well, it's dark coloured.'

'Come on, get a move on,' came a voice from the back of the queue.

Martha stuck her head out of the servery hatch and looked in the general direction of the back of the queue. 'Percy Kettlewell, if I hear one more squeak from you, you can go without dinner today. I were just having a quiet and confidential word with my friend Willie, so you can either piss off without dinner or enjoy waiting until you get served. Got it?'

'What was the confidential word about Martha?' came back the reply to howls of derision from the rest of the queue.

'That's it, no dinner for you,' she retracted her head into the servery. 'Here Willie, you'd best take your dinner before there's a riot.'

Over dinner, Arthur tried his best to talk about item nine, but to no avail. The others were having none of it. Firstly they wanted to eat their dinners in peace, then they wanted to play cards without interruption and then it was time for back to work.

On the way back to the dyehouse, Dick asked, 'What is item nine?'

'Don't you know?' asked Arthur with well acted incredulity.

'Why should I know?'

'It's the item for your department.'

'What is?'

'Catering.'

'Catering?'

'Yes, catering. You volunteered to oversee the catering department.'

'Yes indeed I did, but that were a few weeks ago now.'

'So is all in hand?'

Dick swallowed, opened his mouth, closed it, farted, swallowed again and said, 'Well I've been a bit busy lately, what with the decorating and other things. Well you know, don't you? So I haven't just got it sorted out yet but I shall do by the time that party night comes around.'

'This will not do. In fact it will not do at all. We had better get it sorted out tonight. Everything else is shipshape and Bristol fashion. Club tonight, eight o'clock sharp, all of you.'

'Yes,' agreed Dick, very pleased that someone else was taking an interest in what had to be done, because he hadn't.

'Everyone else?' asked Arthur.

'Me,' said Willie.

'Me said Lewis.'

'Is Eustace coming?'

'No idea.'

'Best bring him along if you see him.'

'I'll get him,' said Willie. 'Arthur, I've something else to do tonight so I'll meet you at the club.'

'That's all right, so have I.'

Willie had had his tea, tended to the pigeons, washed, shaved, and was spruced up by the time half past seven arrived. Early for him.

'What's the big rush?' Thelma asked him.

'I'm just going to call at Greasy Martha's before I meet Arthur at the Club.'

'What on earth are you going to Martha Sykes' for?'

'To see exactly what it is she's baking for the Christmas club party.'

'Why you?'

'Because I'm the only one that dare ask her other than Mr Anthony and I think we'll give him a miss on this occasion. He's told her to sort it out and all I need to do is to find out what she's sorting out. She'll tell me, seeing that I'm her favourite dinner time customer, and then I'm calling for Eustace on the way to the club.'

'Why?'

'Because we're meeting Dick, as he's supposed to have sorted catering out and he hasn't, so we're going to.'

'So what use is Eustace at such a gathering?'

'None.'

'So why take him along?'

'The exercise will do him good and anyway it's not safe to leave him with the dragon for too long. She might burn him to death with her fiery breath.'

'Is she helping with the party?'

'We're not sure, but not if we can help it.'

'Well if she is, keep her as far away as possible from me and Jess. Anyway get gone if you're going. Josie's staying in tonight so I might wander round to see Jess for a while.'

Willie decided to do things the other way around. He waited a few seconds outside Eustace's front gate, then, plucking up courage he walked up the short front path and after a further few seconds, followed closely by one very deep breath, he grabbed the brass knocker in his hand and crashed it against the plate.

She opened the door.

She stared at Willie.

'Good evening, Mrs Ollerenshaw, is Eustace ready?' He got his spoke in first.

'Ready for what?' she rasped.

Willie decided that it was no good messing about with this nasty woman.

'To go to the Club, he should have been ready and waiting for me.' He looked her straight in the eye. 'Why, isn't he?'

She was a bit taken aback by this onslaught.

'I don't know anything about it. He hasn't informed me of his intended movements.'

She turned around and bellowed down the hall. 'Willie Arkenthwaite's here to collect you. Are you ready?'

Eustace came out of the back kitchen. 'Yes, er, no, er are you going to the Club Willie? Are you? Going to the Club?'

His dear wife interrupted, saying, 'Get you coat on and go with Willie. See if I care whether or not you stay in to look after me.'

'It's a very important meeting we're having about the Christmas club party.'

263

'Which Christmas club party?' she demanded.

'Hasn't Eustace asked you to help with the catering, as the wife of a prominent committee member?'

'The first time he's prominent will be the last. Are you still wanting helpers?' She turned on Eustace. 'Why haven't you mentioned it to me before?'

'I did ask you, my love. I did, I did. I asked you, I did.'

'You didn't.'

'I did.'

'Never. You never asked me. Not at all. You daren't. You're too scared. You're a coward.'

Willie decided that he could very easily be a coward under the circumstances. However he decided that this was not the time for cowardice, so he said, 'We need to know if you're helping or not. We've got this meeting tonight to sort out the catering and we have to have an answer. So what's it to be?'

She wasn't used to being talked to like this by anyone and it threw her a little bit sideways. 'I don't know. I don't think so. If I change my mind, I'll let you know, you'll always be able to find me a job won't you? Anyway when is this party?'

'Friday twentieth of December, at the Club. Eustace'll have to help and that's why we asked you to help along with all the other committee wives and husbands.'

'Who says Eustace'll have to help?'

'We do, the committee, he's a member, so he's got to help.'

'Well I'll see, I might come, there again I might not, I'll let you know. Have you got your coat on yet, Eustace, come on, Willie's waiting for you.'

She took hold of Eustace who was struggling to get his second arm into the sleeve of his mackintosh and forcibly assisted him through the front door. 'And don't wake me if I'm in bed when you come home.'

By the time they were halfway to the Club, Willie had recovered his composure and Eustace had managed to get his mac on properly.'

No conversation had passed between the two of them, but then Eustace spoke. 'I hope she doesn't come to the party. I hope she doesn't. Can't stand her at the do, annoying everybody, I can't, I can't, can't stand her at the party. Can't stand everybody and their cousins being there, with her bawling and shouting at them as if she owns the place. It's not fair on the others, Willie, it's not, Willie, it isn't, it's just not bloody well fair. I haven't asked her to help Willie, I haven't. I know I said I have, but I haven't. Can't stand the woman, I can't, no more, can't stand her. I used to be able to, but not now, can't stand her. I hope she doesn't come, she'll cause nothing but trouble if she does, nothing but trouble.'

The two mates ambled slowly along to Greasy Martha's house. Willie said nothing; he couldn't for he could not stop Eustace moaning about his dearly beloved.

'Hang on, Eustace, shut up a bit; we've got to call at Greasy Martha's house.

'Oh, why, where are we, Willie? What have we come this way for? I hadn't noticed we'd come around by Ashbourne Road. What have we to call at Martha's for, Willie? What for?'

'Because I want to have a word with her.'

Willie knocked, or more like hammered, on the front door. There were shouts from within of, 'Alright, don't knock the house down, I'm coming.'

The door was opened by Hector Sykes, otherwise know as Horrible Hector.

'Hey up, Willie and Eustace. What can I do for you two at this time on an early December evening?'

'Now then Hector, is your Martha in? We've just called to have a few words with her about the Christmas club party.'

'Have we, Willie? Have we? Called to have a few words about the party, have we, Willie?'

'Well at least it proves he's listening if nowt else,' Willie whispered to Hector.

'Aye, it does, but it's a great pity when you come to think about it, isn't it?'

'What is?' enquired Willie.

'Why him and her what he's married to as well. You'd not like her for a daily companion and a nightly comfort would you?'

'Not likely, I'd run a mile.'

'So would most men, but not him, anyway, come along in, Martha's in the back.'

So they followed Horrible Hector into the cosy back room where there was a hot fire blazing away and Martha was sitting in a rocking chair by the fireside, knitting.

'Hello, hello, what's all this then?' she asked.

'Well, I thought it best if I called in to see you and get to know properly about the Christmas club party, seeing that it's impossible at dinner time, even if I am your favourite customer. You see, we have a committee meeting at the Club in about half an hour and that is only to talk about party catering arrangements.'

'You've left it a bit late to start making arrangements, haven't you?'

'Well, Dick Jordan was supposed to be sorting it out, but it seems he hasn't.'

'Never could sort anything out on his own that lad. I've known him all his life, he never could, never has, and he never will. He will be a good help to you, mind you, if you tell him what to do. Why don't you both sit down?'

Willie had been standing with his cap in his hand, rolling it around and around. Eustace had been standing, just vacantly. They both sat down on the same settee and Hector resumed his fireside chair opposite Martha.

'Now,' began Martha, 'to start with I don't want it broadcasting to all and sundry that I am helping you out of the goodness of my heart, only that Mr Anthony has made me bake some mince pies, with the emphasis on made. The fact that I'm going to bake whatever you want for the supper, using the mill canteen and its ingredients, is another matter between you and me and the gatepost. It'll be no problem because Mr Anthony has asked me to help you and to do whatever I think necessary for you to have a blooming good party and on the other hand I have my rotten reputation to maintain in the canteen. All you need to tell your committee is that Mr Anthony has made me do it and you all know there's nothing I won't do for the Murgatroyd family.'

'That's alright, absolutely smashing, thank-you. You can rely on me to spread the word as to how you've been forced to do it.'

'How about you Eustace?'

Eustace was in another world, dreaming of ways to legally dispose of his wife. The problem was that he couldn't manage to live with her any more and he certainly couldn't manage to live without her.

'Eh? What? Oh, yes, what was it you wanted to know? Sorry I was thinking about something else. What-'

Martha continued talking, 'No problem there then, is there Willie?'

'It doesn't look like it. Mind you it never does.'

'Right. Now then, as far as I know you want sausage rolls, mince pies and trifles for the party, all of which I can make fresh in the canteen on Thursday and Friday, ready for Friday night, if that is alright with you. I shall want some help. Will your Thelma come along and give me a hand? I suppose she thinks the same things of me as everyone else around here, but if you explain that it's all a big act and that I'm a pussy cat really, and she's to keep quiet about that, do you think she'll help me?'

'I'm sure she will. I think she knows you're alright anyway without me having to tell her. Don't worry; I'll make sure she helps you.'

'So that's alright then. How many am I catering for?'

'Well we're not right sure and that's something we have to settle yet, but we think between one hundred and eighty and two hundred.'

'Good, good. So if Thelma comes to the canteen on Thursday afternoon, I'll stay back and by the time you lot finish work we'll be all about done, leaving happen just a bit to do on Friday afternoon. What are you going to do about the rest of the food?'

'We're going to finalise that at the club tonight, now, when I leave here, so I can't tell you just yet, but I'll let you know as soon as I do. Anyway, thanks Martha.'

'Still messing about with the pigeons, Willie?' Hector enquired.

'Oh yes, always will. Nice and steady is pigeons.'

'Hey, what's up with him then?' Hector turned to look at Eustace who was whimpering to himself.

'Oh, nowt. It's just the dragon, she's been having another go at him and he's wondering what to do about her. Not that short of either divorcing her or putting her in an early grave, there's much he can do. Mind you, if it were me, I'd kill her till she were dead, then murder her, following which I'd take her life from her. But then she'd come back to life again, she's that sort of woman.'

'Mmmm, it's a mess for him, a real mess.'

'Come on, Eustace.'

'Eh? What? Where are we going Willie?'

'To the club. Come on.'

They both got up and Hector came with them to the front door.

'Don't forget, Willie, mum's the word,' shouted Martha from the back room. 'And Willie, I think you're wrong, it's not her that wants attending to.'

Willie walked down the street laughing. Eustace followed, still whimpering.

Arthur had also left home early that evening but he had headed straight for the Club. When he arrived it was deserted except for its cheerful and grossly overweight steward. Who, as Arthur entered, chimed up with, 'Hail the conquering hero comes, sound the trumpets, beat hell out of the drums and him as well.'

'Shut up.'

'Thank-you, music lovers, it's nice to know that my happy thoughts are much appreciated. Why are you here so early?'

'I came specifically-'

'Is it catching?'

'-to have a word with you about the bar for the Christmas club party.'

'All arranged squire, no problem. You and the little engine and others appointed by you two are doing it.'

'Little engine? Who's the little engine?'

'Little, fat, not much hair, belches, farts and throws snot a lot.'

'Oh, that little engine. Yes we were, but we've come to the conclusion that our help and expertise will be needed elsewhere and therefore I've come to ask you if you can get hold of an outside crew to help.'

'That's a bit gross, isn't it? Dropping a bombshell like that on a bloke after all this time and all those committee meetings that you've had. There was me thinking I was going to have the pleasure of your company behind the bar that evening.'

'Sorry, but we've only just realised.'

'Alright.'

'What?'

'Alright, alright, you know, it's OK.'

'Eh, What?'

'Well, I decided weeks ago that it would be bloody hard work for me, towing with a bunch of amateurs like you lot. I've done it before for other functions and there's no pleasure in it, I can tell you. Where's this Harry? What's that Harry? How much is this Harry? This won't work, how do you do that? It's just not on. I was going to have a word with you to see if it was alright if I used my usual crew and seeing that it is, I'll get them organised. Well actually, I already have, in anticipation.'

'I know it will cost more to get hired staff, but the club will sell more ale to make up for it if customers aren't queuing all night waiting for us.'

'True, true and anyway, my crew don't cost a lot. Free ale all night and ten bob out of the till before they go home. No problem.'

'Is the meeting room free?'

'When?'

'Now.'

'Yes, why?'

'The committee are coming just to finalise a few details about the party.'

'Is Sarah Anne coming?'

'Yes or even maybe.'

'Go put the heating on will you, please?' Harry asked him. 'Hey up, it smells as if one of them might be here now.' A far distant belch was heard followed by the door opening to reveal Eustace and Willie. 'I was just saying to Arthur that we smelt you coming - you can't creep up and surprise us like that you know. What the hell is that that you've fetched with you, Willie? Quick Arthur, pull up a chair and let me pull a quick pint before he expires. My goodness, you've one committee member here in body but not in spirit tonight.' Arthur carried a chair to the bar and Fat Harry downed the pint in one quick swallow. 'That's better.

'I thought you wee pulling that pint for Eustace,' observed Arthur

'No, not likely, it were to help me get over the shock. Anyway, what on earth's up with him?'

'He's had a bit of trouble with the wife,' Willie explained.

'Only a bit, it looks like a maximum sentence job to me,' Harry laughed out loudly.

They ushered Eustace into the chair. Harry pulled another pint which they gave him which he also downed in one long swallow, immediately handing them back the glass.

'Another please.'

They stared aghast at his expressionless face. Harry poured yet another pint which they gave to Eustace and which he drained straight down again. This time as he lowered the glass a faint flicker of a smile crossed his face.

'I think I'll just have one more please. Yes, just one more, just one, yes-'

'Who's paying?' ventured the steward.

'I am.'

'I think it's time I had one,' said Willie, 'I can't stand all this excitement.'

By the time the remainder of the committee arrived, Eustace was well into his fifth, if somewhat slower, pint but he was beginning to giggle and talk a lot. Sarah Anne was enjoying flirting with Fat Harry who was more that enjoying it.

Having given Josie her instructions about the younger children, Thelma went round to visit Jess.

'Here, throw your coat over that chair. Have you brought your embroidery? Good, I'll just get my knitting. Those two are gone for the night. Arthur went off early to talk to fat Harry; I don't know his proper name, about staffing the bar at the party.'

'Yes, Willie went off early too, to collect Eustace, then to visit Martha Sykes to find out what Anthony Murgatroyd had asked her to bake for the party.'

'Do you want a rum and blackcurrant?'

'Oh, yes please.'

'Well I don't see why we shouldn't. They do. Now, what about Eustace and his dragon as they know her?'

'Well I don't know. I can't say that I like the woman though.'

The evening passed with the pulling to bits of Fat Harry, Greasy Martha and Eustace.

Thelma was home and in bed, long before Willie appeared.

Meanwhile, down at the Club, after a bit of slap and tickle between Sarah Anne and Fat Harry, which he was loving, and she was also enjoying just a little bit, Arthur, once again, managed to assemble the committee in the meeting room.

'Now there is just one item to discuss and that will not take up much of your time. Almost everything is under maximum control except for the catering and that I think, and hope, we have under control also.'

Arthur stopped as a loud snoring came from Eustace. 'Someone thump him, please.'

'Madam Chairman, may I interject?'

'Pardon?' She looked at Daniel Sykes.

'Who the hell invited him?' asked Willie.

'To continue without interruption, if I may.'

'You may.'

'Madam Chairman, it is farcical that we have one member of this committee fast asleep at a vital meeting. I appreciate that his entire contribution to this whole affair have been less that zero, but I do think that he could refrain from sleeping at a meeting, and I do think that we should immediately give him the sack.'

'I think you will find that you are in a minority of one on that issue. I agree that the situation is very far from ideal, but for the moment it is as good as it can be.'

'Well I think it's ridiculous.'

'Please now carry on Arthur and ignore the snoring if you can.'

'Yes, thank-you. Willie and I realised that although we had covered most aspects of the arrangements for the party, the catering was not coming along just as it should be. The reason for this, I will not divulge, but suffice to say that tonight we have already addressed one or two of the problems. Firstly the bar. As you know it had been arranged that we would all lend a hand behind the bar on a rota system so that Harry did not get overloaded and to save the Club the expense of hiring extra staff. However on reflection we came to the conclusion that it would probably be better all round if Harry engaged a crew of helpers and then we could all spend our time with other aspects of the party. Harry would not then be frustrated teaching a lot of raw recruits at a very busy time, and as well as that, we could all enjoy the party much more than if we were behind the bar all night. So I came along earlier to have a chat with Harry and it's all agreed. The club will run its own bar without interference from us.'

'Excuse me. I'm sorry I'm late again.' They all turned to welcome Anthony Murgatroyd who had entered the room quietly and unseen. 'Why is Eustace asleep?'

'Well, Mr Anthony, he's had a bit of a stand up fight with his wife so now he's blind drunk and sleeping it off. Best place for him at the moment, I think,' said Arthur.

'Yes, probably you're right. Please ignore me and continue.'

Arthur resumed. 'So now to food catering. We were aware that Greasy Martha was baking mince pies and possibly something else, but just exactly what we did not know, so Willie and Eustace called at her house earlier this evening to ask her and I will now ask Willie to explain, rather than Eustace.'

'Yes, well, me and Eustace went on to Greasy Martha's house. Mind you, Eustace didn't listen to her because he was in a tizz over the dragon.'

'Excuse me interrupting again, but who's the dragon?' Mr Anthony enquired.

'Eustace's wife, and the word is a bloody good description of her. Anyway, Martha says she's making sausage rolls, trifles and mince pies, but she's only making them because Mr Anthony's told her to and not she's not doing it to help us lot out.'

'Well, first of all, a very big thank-you to you Mr Anthony. Now what else do we want?'

Dick took the floor. 'Pork pies, crisps, sandwiches, cakes, tea and coffee. I have ordered the pork pies from Porky Charrington's butchers and the crisps from Fat Harry to give the Club a bit of trade. Harry's promised us a bit of discount off the crisps, but I bet it will be a little bit knowing Harry.'

'Excuse me yet again, but I would like it to be put on record that I did not force Martha Sykes into baking various items. I asked her to. I also thought that I'd asked her to bake some cakes. I will check that out first thing tomorrow morning and if she isn't intending to bake them, I'll make sure she does.'

Willie made a mental note to add cakes to the list. He was going to tell Thelma about the list and also that Martha wanted her help.

'So that just leaves tea, coffee and sandwiches,' said Sarah Anne. 'The tea and coffee presents no problem whatsoever. We have facilities for brewing up, plus a more than ample supply of crockery and cutlery, even if it isn't an exactly matching set. All we need is milk and sugar. Dick, can you please attend to the list if I work out the quantities that we need?'

'Yes miss. No problem.

'Sarah Anne put her tongue out at him.'

'We can order the milk through the Club steward, then all I have to do is to buy the other items from Freddy Nevershut's.'

'Well now, that only leaves the sandwiches. Plates again are no problem, there's a mountain of them in the kitchen. If we ask Mr Bun the Baker-'

'Mr who?' Willie enquired.

'You know, old Traps the baker, to make us some bridge rolls, one for each person cut into halves should be adequate, then when we get this party of ladies organised, and I intend to organise them next week, half a dozen of us can get the sandwiches put together on Friday teatime whilst the rest of them dress out the club.'

'Now that just leaves us with costs, we have all the food we have discussed tonight, then there's the band, the Club room and any other incidental expenses that we might encounter before the night. We will have to reckon up how much a head that's going to come to.' Arthur posed to draw a fresh breath. 'So, all in all, we've a lot of reckoning to do yet. Mind you, I've one suggestion that might just answer the problem. We banked all the money in a deposit account, but up to now, we've no idea just how much interest we've earned. The members don't know it's on deposit, or that they are going to get back more than they put in, so why don't we use that interest to pay for the party? I believe I did suggest this course of action at a committee meeting a few months ago.'

Daniel Sykes rose to address the meeting. 'I do not often lavish praise on members of this committee, but I must say that this idea put forward by Arthur is a most excellent suggestion and one that is to be thoroughly recommended.'

'If you are short at the end of the night, I'll make up the difference,' said Anthony Murgatroyd. 'But what happens if you have some left over?'

'A weeks holiday for me and the wife,' shouted Willie before he belched and farted with over excitement.

'Who is? To the Channel Islands? When Arthur? Willie? When? Who is?'

'For heaven's sake go back to sleep,' barked Daniel Sykes.

'Might I suggest you wait and see what happens on the night?' said Mr Anthony.

'Right, that's it. It's downhill with a following breeze all the way to the party. Said the Chairman. 'Sixteen days to go. Good luck everybody. If we need to meet again before the party we will have to do it on an as required basis. Thanks for all your help all of you. Please enjoy the party and we'll have a debriefing meeting on the first Wednesday after Christmas here at half past seven. Thank-you all and good night.'

'Just one thing,' said Arthur. 'Don't you think that we should put the matter of spending the interest on the party to the vote?'

'Yes, you are right. Any objections?' She looked around. 'Motion carried.'

With the exception of Daniel Sykes they strayed back into the bar to share a convivial pint or two and by the time that Fat Harry called time, Eustace was too alcoholically paralysed to support his own weight. He therefore fell down, before he got up, to fall down again, to go home.

Arthur looked at Willie, who reluctantly agreed. 'Go on then.'

Anthony Murgatroyd had a better suggestion. 'Let's bundle him into the back of my car and we'll run him home, though I doubt very much that he wants to go. But he'll have to.'

'Are you sure you don't mind? He's not very good you know and could easily be very sick.'

'It's not far. I'll drive steadily.'

When they arrived safely at Eustace's house, the debate began.

'What are we going to do with him now?'

'Well the last time we brought him home in a state like this, we hung him on the door handle, hammered the knocker and ran like hell,' said Willie. 'So let's do the same again. As soon as we get him out of the car, you get gone Mr Anthony and me and Arthur'll deal with him.'

But the best laid plans of mice and men and so on.. Eustace refused to get out of the car and amongst the four of them they made more than a substantial amount of noise trying to move him. So much so, that they disturbed she that they were trying not to. None of them had seen the dragon approaching down the front steps, dressing gown, curlers, harsh slippers, hairnet and face like a badgers bum.

She startled them all by rasping, 'What state is he in?'

'Not good, Mrs Ollerenshaw, not good and at this precise moment he is refusing to leave my car.'

'Don't worry, I'll get him out. Come out of my way man.'

She then realised that, although she didn't now who the driver of the car was, perhaps it might be prudent to be a little more polite to him in the future. Eustace, left ear first was soon in a heap on the pavement, but still required the combined resources of all four of them to get him into the house and slump him into an armchair in the back room. Joan Ollerenshaw thanked them all profusely.

Anthony Murgatroyd waited for Willie and Arthur, to give them a lift home.

'I'm not surprised he's in that state, I've only met her briefly just now, but if I was married to her, I'd be quite prepared to murder the woman on a continuous basis.'

'Yes, he is as he is, but she makes him much worse,' said Willie. 'I hope she doesn't come to help at the party. Anyway, he isn't the only one that doesn't want to go home tonight. I've something to tackle Thelma about.'

'What's that?'

'Oh it's nowt really, nowt at all.'

'Thelma, love,' he said as they were getting into bed. 'I've got a favour to ask you. Will you go and help Greasy Martha do the baking for the Christmas party?'

'Will I what?' She sat up and looked at him.

It was late that night before Willie finally secured an agreement and went happily to sleep.

CHAPTER 18

It was party day minus one and Thelma as requested made her way to the mill canteen at half past one to help Greasy Martha bake for the party. She hadn't been to the mill before and Margaret Murgatroyd had allowed her time off from her cleaning job to help Martha. Mr Anthony, being the benevolent man that he was had told his wife to pay Thelma for the time she put in at the mill canteen, as she was on mill business as it almost was.

Thelma walked into the penny hoil to find George Schofield beaming at her.

'You've come to help Greasy Martha with the baking.'

'How do you know?'

'It's my job to know everything. All movements in and out of the mill, I have to know them all. It's strategic planning you see, the most important job in the mill I have, top responsibility.'

'Where is the canteen please?' said a very unimpressed Thelma.

'Seeing that it's you, I'll take you over there. I wouldn't do this for just anyone you know, but come along with me and we'll walk over there. It's on the top floor of the low building yonder, next to the office block.'

They ambled over, chatting away and climbed the stairs to the first floor. George opened the door of the servery to let Thelma in to be greeted by, 'What the hell do you want?'

'I've brought Thelma over.'

'Show her in, then bugger off out of it.'

Thelma began to wonder why she had let Willie talk her into helping and George Schofield began to wonder just what sort of afternoon Thelma was going to have helping Martha.

But Thelma was very soon put at ease, for as soon as George was out of earshot, Martha said, 'Come on in, Thelma, and make yourself at home. You can hang your coat up over there on one of those hooks.'

Martha pointed to a row of hooks on the wall by the sinks and whilst Thelma was putting her pinafore on, Martha continued talking.

'Now, I know you'll have heard nothing but bad about me, and you've just seen a good example of what they're talking about, but it's all a big act really that over the years I've developed into a fine art, especially for his lot here. I don't remember how it began, but I'll tell you what, I don't half enjoy it. The fouler, dirtier and nastier I become, the better it is. But away from here I'm a different character, and you'll see the different side whilst you're here working with me. But if anyone comes through that door, the other side will come back out in a hurry, so just be warned and don't be alarmed.'

'Yes, Willie has told me many times about how you carry on in here.'

'I've no doubt you've both had a good laugh about it. I treat Willie just the same as the rest, but much better if no-one's looking.'

'Yes, I know that as well.'

'You'll also have heard the Anthony Murgatroyd has ordered me to bake for the party.'

'Yes.'

'Well don't believe that either. He asked me if I would help and there's nothing I wouldn't do for the Murgatroyd family. You work up at the house for Margaret, don't you? How do you like it up there?'

'Oh, I like it very much, I love my job, she's a super lady to clean for and she looks after me very well. She often helps me a bit with the cleaning when none of her golfing friends are there.'

'It sounds to me as if you and I are going to get on very well together and I'll tell you this, I don't usually allow anyone other than the Murgatroyds in here, but you are very welcome. Well, we'd best get on, we've almost a thousand items to prepare, but I'm well on with it already. The list is sausage rolls, mince pies, trifles and cakes. I've already baked six hundred mince pies, made big squares of robin cake so they'll cut up, ice and decorate and we'll put a layer of jam into some of them. The pastry's made for the sausage rolls but they're to fill and bake yet and we've got to start on the trifles. So where do you want to start? I don't mind.'

'Well I don't mind either. You say.'

'Sausage rolls, I think. They can be baking whilst we decorate the cakes and start the trifles.'

So they set to work with a vengeance and by the middle of the afternoon the sausage rolls were baking, the trifle bottoms were in place, the custard was boiling and footsteps were heard climbing the stairs.

'Right Thelma. I don't know who it is but watch this.'

The door began to open.

'What the bloody hell do you-' she stopped abruptly.

Margaret Murgatroyd looked at Martha with a wide grin and said, 'Hello Martha. I see you've not improved with keeping!'

'No, and I don't intend to. Please come in won't you.'

'Hello Thelma, I've just popped in with a couple of bottles of sherry for you to put into the trifles.'

'You're almost too late but I think we'll manage to shove it in somehow. Thanks,' said Martha.

'Do you want a hand with anything whilst I'm here?'

'I don't think so, unless you want to cut those big squares of robin cake into fairy cake size pieces. But no, let's ice them first. There are four big squares so we can have vanilla, orange, lemon and strawberry. The icing sugar's in there as are the little bottles of colouring.' She pointed to a cupboard. 'You can mix it in that basin that's in front of the cupboard.'

So whilst Thelma kept her eye on the boiling custard, and Martha more than liberally laced the trifles with sherry, Margaret mixed and spread the icing. By the time the mill hooter blew for the end of the day's work, there was only the synthetic cream to mix for the top of the trifles, plus the big squares of cake to cut up and decorate with nuts, cherries, hundreds and thousands and anything else that could be found.

'How are you going to get all this food to the Club tomorrow?' asked Margaret Murgatroyd.

'The one thing the brains of Britain haven't thought about,' laughed Martha. 'Just like a committee of men. Still, it's best kept here until late tomorrow afternoon, out of harm's way.'

'I'll ask Anthony if he can arrange a van to take it round.'

'It'll smell of nothing to do with catering,' Martha observed.

'Yes, but it's only a short journey. It should be alright, there won't be time to get it contaminated. What time will you be here till tomorrow Martha?'

'Till the van comes. No problem.'

Later that same evening, Sarah Anne did a walk around the houses of the various lady helpers, just to check that they were still alright for making the sandwiches for the big do on Friday evening. She called at Cutside Cottages and got Thelma's yes, the same from Jess Baxter, Kathleen Jordan, Norah Armitage and Brenda Sykes. She had asked Thelma's advice as to how many helpers she thought they needed and it was agreed that they could manage without asking old dragon Ollerenshaw. Mind you, if she did turn up they'd have to find her something to do. So it was agreed, four o'clock at the club tomorrow, armed with pinafores and of course, best hats.

Meanwhile down at the club, the menfolk including a very yonderly Eustace were engaged in a heavy bout of drinking. Even Daniel Sykes was breaking the habit of a lifetime, standing at the bar, glass of orange juice in his hand and in good humour with everyone. The ambience of the gathering was shattered by Fat Harry.

'Don't you think that you collection of gormless, idle lumps should at least be starting to look for the decorations and bunting before closing time arrives?'

'Aye, happen you're right,' said Willie.

They all made their way, as best they could considering their alcoholic state, down the stone steps into the cellar to search for the string of flags, bunting, streamers, and Christmas decorations that had not seen the light of day for years and years.

'I know where they are,' exclaimed Arthur, 'they're in that cupboard over by the far wall. Mind you, I don't know what else there is in there, so let's get it opened up and have a look.'

They pulled out all the trimmings they could see and began to carry them upstairs.

Willie said, 'Hang on a minute, it's a bit dark in this corner, there might be summat else in this cupboard yet. Has anyone got a flash light?'

Dick, being the nearest to the top of the stairs was despatched to the bar to locate one. When he returned, they shone its meagre light into the back of the cupboard.

'Well I'll go to our house and back again,' Willie exclaimed. 'Just look here, there's this old set of fairy lights what we had before the war, you know what fit over the King's picture at the end of the Clubroom. Let's take them upstairs and find out if they work.'

'We shall have to change the plug by the look of things,' observed Arthur. 'They've changed the wiring in here from two pin to three pin since this lot were last plugged in. Do we have a three pin plug?'

'Go and ask Fat Harry,' said Daniel Sykes.

'You go and ask him yourself,' Willie replied.

Daniel retained his composure and said, 'It's no good me going and asking him. He'll do nothing for me.'

So Arthur approached Harry to see about a plug.

'A plug? A plug? What do you think this is? Woolworth's? Yes of course I have a three pin plug, here you are. Can you fit it or are you all completely incapable and need my expertise?'

'No, it's alright thanks, I'm sure we can manage.'

'So you'll be wanting the loan of a screwdriver now then?'

'Yes please.'

'I just knew you would. I did. I knew you would. Here.' He put the screwdriver into Arthur's hand.

Arthur arrived back in the Club room to find everyone gasping for breath and about to evacuate the room as Willie had played a tune on the anal flute yet again. He stayed out in the corridor until the dust had settled then he went back in, changed the plug and connected the lamp to the electricity.

'Absolutely amazing,' said Lewis as the lights came on. 'It's unbelievable.'

Arthur agreed saying, 'Yes it's far more than could be hoped for. Anyway let's hang them around the King's picture like we used to. Now Eustace, we need an extension lead for up here. There should be one with that jumble that came out of the cupboard. Can you go and find one please.'

Willie returned with it a few minutes later. 'It's no good asking Eustace to do something like that, and anyway it's nobbut a two pinner you know.'

'No, I didn't know, but I should have done. Best go and ask the steward for both another three pin plug and a three pin socket.'

'We haven't a cat in hell's chance of getting that.'

'Oh, give it here; I'll sort it out myself.'

So Arthur went again to see Fat Harry who agreed, after a little persuasion to get a new extension the next morning to test out the lights in good time for the party.

The remainder of the evening was taken up with drinking, putting up the streamers, drinking, putting up more streamers, drinking, getting the room ready for the party and drinking. They got all the card tables and trestle tables they could find and arranged them around the perimeter of the room, along with the chairs, which left a very nice area in the middle for dancing. The low stage for the band was in one corner next to the King's picture. Fortunately the Club's one and only honky-tonk piano was on the stage already so that wasn't to move.

'Willie, do you think we should have the piano tuned?' asked Arthur.

'Nay, it's only an old honky-tonker, do you think it's worth tuning?'

'Well I expect that it's a matter for debate, but let's go and have a pint and ask our fat friend.'

'Well you lads, you are in luck and make no mistake. It was tuned about three months ago for Susie Stomachache's dancing class and furthermore, and this will amaze you, it was tuned by none other than that master of the musical ear and beer belly who is also a pianoforte virtuoso, Ivan Ivory.'

'Well to start with, who on earth is Susie Stomachache?'

'Her what runs the dancing class. Always moaning about her guts of which she has more than her fair share and everything else. You know her, her father works in Murgatroyd's carding department. Just to give you another clue, she never eats one fish when two will do.'

'Oh, I know who you mean. Eats a bit like a starving cannibal, a bit of a pain,' said Willie.

'Has one and is one.'

'What?'

'A pain. You will of course be acquainted with Ivan Ivory?'

'Oh yes, he's been tuning pianos around here since the early seventeenth century. I don't know his real name except it's Ivan. Does he work for himself or somebody?'

'Yes.' said Harry.

'Well,' said Arthur. 'We are as ready as we're going to be so I reckon, we'll go and get an early night, ready fro the big day ahead. What say you, Willie?'

'Yes okay, but we'd better take Eustace home on the way.'

'Your missus coming to help tomorrow Eustace?' Arthur enquired.

'I hope not. I do. I hope not. She'll make a good do into a bad one if she does. She will Willie, she will, she'll make a right good do into a right bad one.'

He became very quiet and retreated into his own little world.

'What shall we do with him now?' asked Willie.

'Oh, let's lean him over his front gate and leave him there. We don't want another confrontation with the dragon.'

CHAPTER 19

'That's it, they've got me. I'm going fast. Help. Help.'

Thelma sat up in bed with a start. It was pitch black.

'Whatever's the matter? What's happened?' She was half asleep, coming more awake by the second. She fumbled for the light switch and in so doing she hit Willie who was sitting up in bed, waving his arms about and jabbering wildly.

'What'd you hit me for?'

'It was an accident. I was trying to find the light switch and still am for that matter.'

Eventually she grabbed the swinging pendant that Willie had already hit several times and switched on the light. Willie was sitting up, calm now, with sweat pouring out of him.

'Now, whatever is the matter?'

'I must have been having a nightmare. It was those pound notes, they had me, they were wrapping themselves all around me and starting to suffocate me.'

Thelma laughed out loud.

'It's not funny; it's nowt to laugh about.'

'It is and it isn't. Never mind, this time tomorrow it will all be over and you'll be able to relax. Anyway you've nothing to worry about, you've only got to get the money from the bank and pay it out.'

'Aye, but, it's a big responsibility.'

'Well here's another responsibility, go and make me a mug of tea seeing that you've wakened me up.'

Willie put on his dressing gown and slippers before going downstairs to make Thelma and himself a mug of tea, following which they both fell into a deep sleep.

'I'd a nightmare last night, all about pound notes that were strangling m,.' Willie told his mates at morning break time, 'and what were more horrible, were that Thelma made me get up and brew us a mug of tea for waking her up.'

'Happen it's an omen,' said Lewis.

'What's one of them?' asked Willie.

'It's like a warning of bad times to come.'

'Nay, I think it's more like a bad worrying dream about what we have to come later today,' observed Arthur. 'We've a big job on this afternoon. Yes, we have that.'

'What time are you going to the bank?' Dick asked.

'Two o'clock from here, three o'clock at the bank.'

'Does Mr Anthony know that you're both skiving off work?'

'Oh yes, he does that,' said Willie. 'He's been very helpful and supportive as we all know. Have these women got the supper sorted out?'

'Yes they have that, and I'll make sure that it's all ready on time,' said Dick.

'Sarah Anne will, you mean,' said Arthur.

'I don't know what she thinks she's doing interfering like that in what I was doing.'

'But you weren't, were you! Or else she wouldn't have.'

Further argument was forestalled as it was time to start work again.

On his morning tour of the mill, Mr Anthony stopped with Willie, just to reassure himself that everything was in hand and that both Willie and Arthur were all prepared for going to the bank.

Although Willie was early at the canteen, Sarah Anne had beaten him to it and she saw him coming.

'Change of staff today, Willie.'

'Eh?'

'Your Thelma's in charge.'

'No I'm not, I'm only helping Martha.'

'Have you finished tonight's food?'

'Almost Willie, love. Martha's just putting the cream on the trifles and we've then just got a bit of final decorating to do after dinner, then we're all ready for off to the club.'

'Is it real cream?' Willie asked, his mouth watering at the thought.

'You know better. It's synthetic, but it tastes good. It's that sweet powder you mix with milk and get cream.'

'I wish it were real cream straight from the cow, it used to be lovely did real cream. I wonder if we'll ever be able to get it again, ever.'

'Oh I'm sure we will, sometime before long now. They're beginning to relax some of the final wartime rules about food and I don't think it'll be long before we can get such luxuries again,' said Sarah Anne.

'What's for dinner, I'm starving?'

'That sounds more like my Willie.'

'Fish,' said Martha. 'You know full well it's always fish on a Friday. It's been fish every Friday sine Mafeking was relieved.'

'Don't mention Mafeking.'

'Why?'

'It's a long story,' said Thelma.

'So why ask the same question every Friday when you know the answer?'

'Nay, well, I only wanted to check. You might have changed it, and then I might have to think about it before I could eat it.'

'The day you have to think about anything before you eat it will be your last. I don't know how you put up with him and his table manners, Thelma.'

'Oh, and what pray is wrong with his table manners?'

They turned to look at Thelma then at Martha.

'Well he does grunt and squeal a bit you know.'

'I suppose he does. But that's my Willie.'

'Rather yours than mine,' Martha mumbled to herself.

The conversation was ended abruptly by the growing murmur of complaint, from further back in the queue, about the speed of service.

Despite the unknown experiences that lay ahead, Willie dined like a king as usual, whilst Arthur picked and poked at his food in a more sombre mood, his mind on the task ahead.

At two o'clock, Willie and Arthur placed their time cards in the time clock on the penny hoil wall and clocked out.

'Big day today,' said George Schofield from his warm seat inside the penny hoil. 'Taking your assistant with you today are you, Willie?

Going to help Willie are you Arthur? Yes, well, you both need help so if you help each other along the way; it will be almost as good.'

'Almost as good as what?' demanded Willie, his hackles beginning to rise.

'Almost as good as if I come and help the pair of you.'

'I think we can manage, thank-you,' said Arthur.

'You probably can of a fashion.'

Willie was about to launch into another tirade when Arthur said, 'Come on, we've got to get to the bank. We haven't time to stand here talking with the lower echelons of society.'

'Lower what?' asked George.

'Echelons.'

'Yes, that's what I thought it sounded like.'

They left him thinking and both went home to get changed.

They met up again at Arthur's house on the way to the bank.

'Where's Jess?' Willie enquired.

'She'd better be at the Club, helping to get it set up for tonight, or helping Thelma with the sandwiches or something.'

'Hey, I hope Mr Anthony's managed to get a van for our Thelma and Martha.'

'I think he will have, they were going to sort it out this morning. I had a word at the mill garage and all was merry and bright.'

In front of the Grolsby branch of the Northern Counties Bank, Willie, as was his weekly custom, emptied the contents of his nasal passages into the gutter at the side of the road.

'You filthy bugger,' said Arthur.

'Well that was the last time. I've done it every week until now so I wasn't going to miss doing it today. One windy day it floated away, all over a passing car.'

'Good job it wasn't the Co-op horse.'

'Aye, you're right there. Old Dodson the drover would have got off his cart and killed me. Now then, Arthur, are you ready?'

'Yes, lead the way; let's get on with it, troops to the fore, onward Christian soldiers.'

Willie gave him a withering look.

They entered the magnificently appointed hall of the bank and joined a queue at one of the counters.

'Mr Arkenthwaite, sir, good afternoon. You'll not be paying in today,' said the young spotty faced individual that Willie had got to know quite well over the last twelve months and who, after a time, had realised that beneath the noise and the smell there was a warm hearted human being, and had quite taken to him eventually.

'You've actually remembered then?' Willie questioned him with a smile.

'How could we forget, sir, when the entire bank staff has been up all night, counting and guarding your money?'

'Give over, you've not been.' Then he laughed. 'One up to you, young'un, still it is your turn. Now give us t' brass and we'll get out of your hair. This is Arthur by the way. Arthur Baxter, my chief assistant.'

This time it was Arthur who gave Willie a withering look.

'Good afternoon, Mr Baxter, it's a pleasure to meet you sir. However I am afraid gentlemen that I am unable to give you your money.'

'Can't give it us! What do you mean?' screamed Willie in a violent mood swing.

'Mr Sharples our dear manager wishes to have a word with you.'

'Is there a problem?'

Both Willie and Arthur were beginning to get to little panic stations.

'Yes, sir. I would imagine so. However, probably only a large one. I'll just let Mr Sharples know that you have arrived.'

Little panic stations were rapidly turning into big panic stations.

'Please come this way Gentlemen. Mr Sharples will see you now.'

They walked into the oak panelled office. Horatio Sharples stood there a smile on his face, his arm outstretched in welcome.

'Come in, Mr Arkenthwaite, come along in. Oh, there are two of you. Fetch another glass Brushwood, there's a good chappie. Well, it's taking out day and I thought you might like to have a glass of sherry with me to celebrate your success and as a thank-you from the bank for your business. I would also like to add that if you are going to run

the scheme again, next year, and as I understand it there's no way that
you can't. The bank will be very happy to accommodate you.'

Brushwood returned with two more glasses which he put down on
the desk.

'Only one glass thank-you, Brushwood. I only asked for one glass.'

'Yes Mr Sharples. Sorry.'

Brushwood picked up the glass and looked longingly at the sherry
decanter.

'Well Brushwood?'

'Yes, sorry Mr Sharples,' and he went out of the room.

Following an awkward bout of small talk, they thanked Mr
Sharples for his generous hospitality and told him they'd best get
back to the counter and get the money.

'Oh there's no need, it's all here. All counted and bagged, all the
money you've paid in plus the interest. Do you know what you're
going to do with the interest?'

'Well we thought we'd pay for the food for the members
Christmas party out of it,' said Arthur.

'What about the tax on it?' Willie enquired. 'Some one told us we
had to pay tax on the interest.'

'Well, strictly speaking, it's unearned income and therefore subject
to income tax, but we at the bank do not deduct basic rate tax at
source like they do at the building society. You will have no means of
deducting it so I am of the opinion that as it is to be used for a social
gathering and to be spread between so many of you, I would risk a
non-event and ignore the matter, if you get my drift.'

'Yes, I think I do,' said Arthur

Willie replied otherwise, 'I don't.'

'Anyway isn't it time we were away Willie?'

'Aye, give us t' brass and we'll get gone.'

They thanked Mr Sharples again for his help and hospitality, and
then walked quickly to Arthur's house with the money in a big blue
canvas bag that had to be returned to the bank later.

Jess was home when they arrived and made them both a steaming
hot pint of tea before they counted the money. She gave them an up to
the minute report on the fact that everything was in order at the club,
that Thelma had arrived with Martha and the food in the works van

and with a very handsome young driver, that the club was now cleared, cleaned and decorated for the occasion and that the whole of the club and the arrangements were in first class working order.

'Good. Has Fat Harry been helping you?' asked Willie.

'Yes, he's spent most of the time flitting about, flirting with all of us, but yes, actually he has been a great help to us.'

They laid out the money on Arthur's dining room table to count it.

'Exactly right, not a penny to the good. Where are the envelopes, Willie?'

'They're round at our house,' he said with a grin. 'I'd best go and fetch them.'

Over the past few nights, the friends had met at Willie's house, carefully naming the envelopes and inserting into each a slip of paper telling the amount due.

Willie soon returned and the correct amount of money was put into each envelope. The envelopes were sealed and put into Arthur's box in alphabetical order. By the time they had finished it was five o'clock and Thelma had arrived to help Jess with the tea.

'What's for tea? I'm starving.'

'Is that the only question you ever ask?' enquired Jess.

'It's usually the only question worth asking.'

'Well the answer is, wait and see.'

The table was soon laid and in Willie's eyes, a light snack of sausage with baked beans, bread with thinly spread butter and fruit cake for afters appeared.

'How's supper looking?' Willie asked without a thought for anyone's feelings. Thelma looked at him, Jess looked at him, Arthur looked at him. Willie observed the three staring faces and realised he might just have put his foot in it regarding the size of the tea, so he decided that a diplomatic comment might be in order.

'No, like I was just running through the arrangements in my head for tonight and we've heard about everything except supper. So how's supper looking?'

'Alright.' snapped Jess, wishing that she hadn't asked them to stop for tea and certainly deciding that she wasn't asking Willie ever again.

'Fine, just fine,' said Thelma.

'Good, excellent,' replied Willie, who continued to eat his tea carefully so as to avoid making any rude noises because he knew he had upset Jess already and he didn't want to make the situation any worse.

Tea being over, the two friends set off for the Club with their box of envelopes. Arthur had already changed into his best, grey, three-piece suit and the plan was for Willie to go home and get changed as soon as the money was safely stowed in the safe. They were very pleasantly surprised by the decorations in the Club. The ladies had put up miles and miles of streamers whilst the Christmas tree was in its place of honour with its lights lit.

'See it's right champion,' said Willie.

'Yes, it's a credit to the ladies is this. Now come on let's stash all this money into the safe before anything happens to it.'

Arthur produced the safe key from his pocket and unlocked it with a little difficulty. They put the money on the top shelf and Arthur was about to lock it again when he decided that it might be a good idea to oil the lock .So he went off in search of the mythical oil can, rumoured to be kept by Fat Harry, but never before seen.

'Harry, can we have use of the oil can please, just to oil the safe lock, it's a bit stiff after all these years of no use. The hinges wouldn't say no to a drop either.'

'Yes it's here.' He looked under the bar. 'No it isn't, its...it's er, nowhere to be seen. Let me see now, last time I had it was, let me see now. I haven't had it since, nay, I don't know the day when. Sorry can't help.'

'Have you got an oil can at home, Willie?' Arthur asked on his return to the office.

'Oh yes, a couple.'

'Bring one with you, will you, when you've got changed, and in the meantime, we'll just push the door to, turn the handle and I'll sit guard until you return.'

'Haven't we got time for a quick pint before I go home?'

'Under the circumstances, I have, but you haven't. You'd better get off home, straight home, do not pass go, do not collect two hundred pounds and on you way out, please call in on the fat one and ask him to deliver a firkin of his best ale to the office. Under the circumstances.'

Willie addressed Harry from a safe distance, 'Hoi you.'

'Yer what?'

'My good and kind friend Mr Baxter, wishes it to be known that he would welcome a firkin of your best bitter served by your own fair hand in the office, now, immediately if not sooner.'

With that he made a double acceleration out of the bar.

Fat Harry walked around to the office and stared at Arthur sitting primly in the chair at the side of the safe.

'For what it the reason, Mr Baxter, sir, for why you find it impossible to get off your fat idle backside and enter the noble portals of my bar in order to get your own pint of ale, without me wearing out my body and soles carrying one round here for you?'

'Because we've got all this money in the safe and we daren't lock it until my little friend returns with the lubricating machine. Seeing that I dare not leave it, I asked Willie to ask you if you would mind bringing me a pint whilst I sit here.'

'Okay.'

Harry was no sooner gone for it than he returned with it.'

'Thanks.'

'No problem for you, it's Arkenthwaite that gets at me.'

'Oh, he's alright, it's all noise. Take no notice of him.'

'I don't.'

Willie arrived home to find Thelma dressed and ready for the party.

'By gum you look superb, just like a millionairess. Remind me to take the oil can back to the club with me, we daren't lock the safe, because the lock's stiff and we can't find the Club oil can. By jove, I wouldn't want to live at Baxter's regularly. I aren't half hungry. Supper looks good, club looks good. I'd best go and get changed. Arthur wouldn't let me have a drink until I get the oil can there because he's having to sit and guard the money.'

Thelma was laughing at him.

'What's up?'

'You are. You haven't stopped talking since you walked through the door. Now go and get changed and I'll come back to the club with you. I'll get the oil can out of the kitchen and put it in a bag.'

'Thanks, love. I'll go and get changed.'

So arm in arm, Willie and Thelma walked slowly back to the Club in their best Sunday outfits, looking every bit as if they were in charge of the evening to come and as if they were very much in love with one another.

'Where on earth have you been?' Arthur demanded of Willie.

'Been home to - you know full well where I've been and by the way, here's the oil can.'

He took the can out of the bag he was carrying. Thelma had gone to inspect the final layout of the food.

'Well, go on then, oil the lock seeing that you have brought the can.'

'Right, yes, okay.'

Willie proceeded to squirt the oil into the keyhole. 'There, that'll do.'

Arthur opened the door of the safe then tried the lock half a dozen times, found it to be working well, shut the door again and locked it. As a last precautionary check he tried the handle several times to make sure it was locked, then he put the key in his waistcoat pocket and in a jovial mood, went off to get a drink and join the rest of the party. Willie went to get Thelma and Jess so that they could all have a starting drink together to get the evening away well.

'Won't be long now,' said Arthur. 'All the happy and smiling punters will be here, starting in about half an hour. It's about time – oh, I spoke too soon.'

A very smart Sid Sidebottom arrived, accompanied by his sextet minus one. He was decked out in full morning dress, complete with striped trousers and tails.

'Evening folks. Thought I'd put the best clobber on seeing that it's a special occasion. In the Club room are we? Good, we'll just go and get set up. By the way is Eustace Ollerenshaw coming here tonight?'

'Yes, why?'

293

'Well I've just passed him a couple of hundred yards back, looking very smartly turned out, but being tried to look even smarter by the ugliest woman you've ever set your eyes on.'

'Oh, the dragon's coming then, is she?' asked Willie.

'If that's her, and no doubt it will be, the yes, the dragon's coming. Have you prepared a special fire dish for her supper?'

'Bugger,' said Willie and farted.

'Willie!' screamed Thelma.

'Sorry, love, it was directed at her.'

'At who?'

'The dragon.'

'You've no need to do that to her.'

'Yes I have, for Eustace's sake.'

'Yes, well for him. We all feel very sorry for him.'

'I'd best go and get the band set up.'

'Oh aye, Sid, you go and get on with it, don't let us hold you up with our idle gossip.'

The Chairman and her husband Bill were the next to arrive. She played up to Fat Harry, but he didn't take the bait, although he hoped he might be able to later.

'Eustace and his wife will be here shortly, I think,' she said.

'What do you mean you think? What has happened to him now? Let's have the next news bulletin.'

'Well the dragon is just giving him a lecture outside the front door about staying sober. Anyway you can ask him yourself, here he is now.'

A very smart Eustace walked towards them in his best black trilby hat, best grey woollen overcoat, and best grey worsted three-piece suit, accompanied by his dear wife. He greeted them with a warm smile; she greeted them with a face like a quarry bottom.

'Hello Willie, hello Arthur, hello Harry, hello Jess, hello Thelma, hello Sarah Anne, hello Bill, hello everybody. How are you all? Are you? It's cold outside isn't it? Very cold, outside, isn't it? Do you all know my wife Joan?'

The smile left his face at this point.

'Pint Eustace?' asked Arthur. 'And how about you Joan?'

Joan was just about to say that Eustace would have lemonade, when he said for himself 'Yes please, and Joan would like a dry sherry please. A dry sherry, please Arthur, thanks. I'll just go and take my coat off, I will, my coat, can I take yours Joan?'

She removed her coat, hat pin and hat which he took away to the hooks in the corridor.

Arthur ordered their drinks, but the conversation was a little bit sparse and awkward.

'Now what can I do to help?' Joan asked.

The other seven were dumbstruck. Willie wanted to belch but daren't. Harry turned and escaped into his little back room for a laugh. Sarah Anne was the first to recover enough to speak.

'Well actually Joan, it's all done. The only thing we've overlooked, and a job that does want doing, is that we want someone to sit at the door to act as a welcoming hostess, along with my husband who is going to act as host. The object is to welcome all our guests, to make them feel at home and to show them where the cloakrooms and bar are. Also you have to look out for gatecrashers.'

'Fine, that suits me just fine. Just make sure, all of you, that Eustace doesn't drink too much. Come on then let's get to our post, the visitors will be arriving soon.'

'Bit of good quick thinking, but why didn't you put her on car park duty?' asked Willie.

'Now, now, Willie.'

'Thanks, thanks a million, thanks again, Sarah Anne.' Eustace had by this time rejoined the group. 'I'd buy you all a drink if she'd let me have any money. I didn't think she'd go with Bill like that, I didn't. I thought there'd be a big argument, I did, a big argument.'

'Method in my madness,' said Sarah Anne to herself as she quietly went behind the bar into Harry's back room where she closed the door, then hugged and kissed him for quite some time.

'By gum I enjoyed that, but I thought you hated my guts.'

'Let's just say it's party night and I'm here to party. If I can think of some good excuse to get rid of Bill later I'll come back for more. But beware this is only party night, so make the most of it.'

As it was getting near the arrival time of the bar staff, Sarah Anne came back into the bar and bought Eustace, who was on his own, a pint, the others having dispersed in different directions to see to other pressing matters.

CHAPTER 20

The band was tuning up, the bar staff were in position, the host and hostess were at their posts, Willie and Arthur were parading backwards and forwards keeping their eyes on this, that and nothing in particular. The three ladies, Thelma, Jess and Sarah Anne were making sure that supper was fully prepared and Eustace was drinking and drinking as people bought him yet more pints.

The time was twenty five past seven. Joan walked over and, as well as harsh words, gave Eustace a sharp smack around the head.

The first guests started to arrive at the party, the band struck up with a quickstep and by the time a quarter to eight arrived, the function was in full swing. The atmosphere in the club was warm and friendly, the bar was doing a brisk trade and the event was going like clockwork.

At a quarter past eight Arthur, followed by Willie, entered the Club office to retrieve the money. Arthur produced the safe key from his waistcoat pocket, put it in the lock.

But it would not turn.

They tried turning it, forcing it, removing it and putting it back in again. They tried it in different positions, gently moving it in and out at the same time as trying to turn it, all to no avail.

'Problem,' said Arthur.

'Willie belched and asked, 'What are we going to do now?'

'Panic.'

'Then what?'

'Panic again.'

'We'd best fetch Harry.'

'Aye, go and get him, but quietly.'

So Willie walked behind the bar and tugged Harry's sleeve. 'Hey, come here a minute with me, will you?'

'Shut up and go away, can't you see I'm busy.'

'Come on, now, please. It's a matter of life and death.'

'What on earth's the matter?' asked Harry.

'Please, Harry, just come into the office, now.'

So Harry reluctantly followed Willie into the office. 'This had better be good. So what's up?'

'We can't open the safe.'

'Try unlocking it.'

'We can't.'

'You locked it. So what's the problem?'

'The so and so key won't turn.'

'It did turn a couple of hours ago.'

'We all know that, but it won't turn now.'

'Here, let me have a go.' Harry knelt down in front of the safe, took the key from Arthur, inserted it into the lock and tried to turn it. Once again it would not turn. 'Well now, there's a problem and no mistake.'

'So what do you reckon we should do?' Arthur asked him.

Willie also asked, 'Have you any suggestions, Harry?'

'Police job, I think. They'll know where there's a locksmith.'

'Can I go and ring nine, nine, nine,' enquired Willie eagerly.

'Fat lot of good that'll do. Just go down to the phone box and ring the police station. Better still, run around there, you'll nearly be a quick as telephoning.'

So Willie ran out of the Club and around the corner, as fast as his little legs would carry him, to the headquarters of the Grolsby constabulary, the nerve centre of local crime, manned by one solitary sergeant on night duty with a back up of two constables out on foot patrol. They also had at their disposal, for emergencies, two bicycles and a squad car at head office, eight miles away. It was into this hive of activity that Willie burst at half past eight to find Sergeant Crabtree sitting in the constabulary chair, in front of the fire, fast asleep. The very act of Willie banging on the doors as he entered and of knocking on the desk top woke Sergeant Crabtree from his slumbers.

'Now, now, what's going on? What's all this noise about? Oh, it's you, Willie. A very rare honour to have you in here. What's the matter?'

Willie explained the predicament.

'Well now, there's a turn up for the books. What are we going to do? I can't leave the station unmanned, now can I? Hey up, I know, the other two will be back shortly for their suppers, then I'll come with you if you'll just hang on. In the meantime, come around here and stand with your back to the fire, so that you can warm your brains.'

Willie stood there enjoying the warmth on the bottom of his back and the backs of his legs, chatting to Sergeant Crabtree about this and that whilst the Sergeant assembled his tools and paraphernalia for the job.

'It's a little known fact that I'm an expert safe breaker, so I'll bring the tool bag along and see what I can do.'

Laurel and Hardy, as the two constables were well known throughout the village because of their build, soon arrived back at the station. They were instructed to stay there until the sergeant returned and he and Willie then set out for the club.

Arthur and Harry were both beginning to worry about the length of time that Willie had been away. They were about to send out a search party consisting of Thelma and Jess so as not to alarm the revellers, when they heard a commotion in the bar. Sergeant Crabtree appeared, followed by Willie, followed by a crowd.

The crowd was trying to get into the office, making it impossible for anything to happen in any way whatsoever. The sergeant, having been highly trained to take command of situations, took control of this one. 'Now then, ladies and gentlemen, there is no panic, just a small problem that I have to deal with so please go back to your party.' With one almighty push he shoved the party goers out of the office, leaving just himself and the three others to sort out the door lock.

'Keep watch on that door, Harry. No-one's to enter under any circumstances. Now, let the dog see the rabbit.'

He knelt down I front of the safe, tried the key, withdrew it, got a bunch of skeleton keys from his pocket, selected one from the bunch and inserted it into the lock. He slowly turned it backwards and forwards at the same time moving it sideways, carefully moving the levers of the lock out of the engaged position. He tried to turn the door handle several times, when suddenly it moved one eighth of a turn, allowing him to bring it to the open position after another bout of slow key manoeuvring.

'There you are. Fetch me a pint, Harry, please.'

'With the greatest of pleasure. However no drinking on duty you know.'

'Shut up, shove off and get me a pint.'

'Yes Sergeant.'

'By the way, Harry, don't lock this door again until you've had the lock repaired. The handle's locked in against the lock. Have you had it locked and opened recently?'

Arthur looked at him and said, 'Well, yes and no actually. We oiled the lock because we knew it hadn't been locked for many years, tried the lock with the door open and it worked fine, put the money in and locked it.'

Sarah Anne opened the office door and peered in.

'I said nobody in here,' said the sergeant.

'Hang on Sarge, she's in charge,' said Willie.

'What do you mean she's in charge?'

'Sarah Anne is the committee Chairman and therefore she is technically in charge of the money,' Arthur pointed out.'

You'd best come in then, lass. You've had a near do with that safe. You almost didn't get to pay the money out tonight.'

'Why, what happened?'

Willie related the story in a few choice words and Fat Harry came back with the sergeant's pint plus three more.

'Where's mine?' asked Sarah Anne.

'I'll go and get you one in a minute,' he said with a twinkle in his eye. 'But first of all, I must say that years ago, and I mean years, before the start of the war when I was a drinking member here and not the steward, I remember that they had a lot of bother with this safe. They locked some important documents in it and couldn't get them out again. There was all hell to pay at the time I seem to remember, something to do with the Club deeds. They couldn't get them out of the safe, they were locked in, just the same as tonight. They had to get a locksmith to unlock it. It's all coming back now. The locksmith told them never to lock it again until they had had it repaired, but it looks like it never did and I bet It's never been locked since then until today.'

Anthony Murgatroyd popped his head around the door.

'Good evening, Mr Murgatroyd, sir,' said Sergeant Crabtree.

'Good evening, Sergeant Crabtree, is everything alright?'

'It is now, sir, it is now. However I suggest that the Club gets it's safe mended as soon a possible.'

'By the way,' said Fat Harry. 'Has anyone seen the club deeds in recent times?'

'Not tonight, Harry, not tonight. We'll sort out that matter after Christmas. Let's get back to the party now and pay out all this money,' said Arthur.

Harry looked at Sarah Anne, 'If you want that pint you'd better come and get it.'

Willie and Arthur entered the Club room clutching the box of envelopes and there were loud cheers. The band stopped playing and the revellers crowded up to the terrible two in order to retrieve their money.

'Right, queue up in orderly fashion. We've got them in alphabetical order so it won't be any trouble to fine your particular envelope.'

Willie handed them out as Arthur sorted them. The operation lasted all of five minutes before it was completed. Willie and Arthur went to find their respective wives to take them for a drink. Arthur ordered four whisky and waters.

'We don't want whisky,' said Jess.

'Shut up woman and get it into you. Willie and me have just had a very traumatic experience and we are ready for a relaxing drink. So you two can enjoy it with us.'

They had just taken their glasses in hand when they heard cries of 'speech, speech. We want Willie. We want Arthur' coming floating into the bar from the Club room next door. Dick came through to the bar and escorted them to the small stage where the band was situated. The band struck up with 'For he's a jolly good fellow' whilst the crowd sang and cheered.

'What are we going to do?' Willie cried.

'I don't rightly know. You go first.'

'Nay, I'm no good at this sort of thing, you're much better at it than me.'

'Well go on then,' said Arthur with a superior look on his face. 'I had actually prepared a few words in anticipation of this happening.'

Arthur mounted the stage and managed to squeeze himself in between the piano and the big drum. 'Ladies and gentlemen, friends, members of Murgatroyd's Christmas club,' he paused for effect. 'Well, we've done it.'

Loud and prolonged cheers came from the audience.

'This has been a first class team effort right through the twelve months, and it has worked out as planned. I would like to point out that we have gained a small amount of interest over the year on the money that we banked and we decided to use it to pay for tonight's party, rather than charge you for it. There was not enough to pay for the whole of the party, but through the generosity of the ladies of the committee, that is committee members wives, the club committee itself and more importantly Anthony and Margaret Murgatroyd, we have managed to give you a free do.'

Even louder and longer cheers came from the crowd.

Arthur continued, saying, 'I would especially like to thank Mr Anthony Murgatroyd for his major financial contribution and also for his physical help, particularly with the supper. Two members of the committee deserve special mention, Sarah Anne Green for her tireless devotion and total impartiality to the job of Chairman and finally our little friend with the big heart, enormous appetite, gargantuan thirst and double, triple, even quadruple indigestion, who has worked his clogs off on your behalf, Willie Arkenthwaite.'

Cheers and shouts of 'we want Willie, we want Willie' resounded around the room.

Willie tried to hide, but could find nowhere to go and was picked up by the crowd to be carried shoulder high around the room. Sid Sidebottom had a minor problem, what sort of music to play to accompany the revelry. He had no time to reach a decision as events were overtaking him so he shouted, 'See the conquering hero comes.' He raised his hand to conduct and they played as well as they could with a long since played piece. Willie was carried around and around for a long time until they put him down again.

When the noise finally subsided, Anthony Murgatroyd mounted the stage and found a tiny space between Sid Sidebottom and the big drum. He called for order. 'Ladies and Gentlemen. I think we should all be very grateful to the whole of the committee who have worked so hard of your behalf. I also think we should thank the ladies of the committee and the wives of committee members for their hard work in preparing for us such a magnificent supper. For those of you that haven't seen it yet, it's a feast fit for a king. So I ask you all to join me in three cheers for the committee and their wives. Hip hip-'

The Grolsby Working Men's Club and not heard such uproar and cheering in many a long year and it was several minutes before Arthur could attract the attention of the crowd again.

'Now, for one or two serious bits. Is everyone familiar with the discount scheme operated on our behalf by various shops in the village? Has everyone ordered their various items from these shops, ready for collection on Christmas Eve? If, by any chance, any of you have yet to order, it is not too late and you all know which shops have joined in the scheme.

Secondly, and more importantly, supper is now ready, so before you all rush into the supper room, thank-you all for joining the club, we have enjoyed running it and a very Merry Christmas to you all. Just one thing, we will be open for business, the first Friday in January if any of you want to join again.'

He got down from the stage to tumultuous applause and a tidal wave heading towards the supper, then he struggled to get back onto the stage again as he met the band getting off. He banged the big drum and shouted for quiet. 'I was just thinking, so that we do not break with tradition, we should allow Willie to be first in the supper queue. I know that he is treasurer and that at any function, family holds back, but he is always first in the dinner queue at the mill so I think we should let him and Thelma head up the queue tonight. Any objections?'

There was once again a lot of noise which Arthur took to mean no objections and at the same time both Willie and Thelma were propelled into supper at the head of the crowd with all their friends following except for Eustace and Joan. A heavy hand was being applied to Eustace's shoulder preventing him from standing up.

'What's all this about a discount scheme?' she shouted in his ear.

Eustace screwed up his eyes and gave her a sheepish smile. 'Hello my love. Shall we have another drink?'

'A drink? A drink?' she shrieked. 'When you've had more than enough for every one at the party. Now, what's all this about a discount scheme?'

Eustace looked at her, tried to focus his eyes, then slurred his words, 'Why don't you sit down and let me get you a drink?' He indicated a non-existent chair somewhere near him with an unsteady wave of an uncontrollable arm.

'What about the discount scheme?' she persisted.

'Which discount scheme, my love?'

Supper was becoming of secondary interest to many of the party goers who were gathering around listening to Joan and Eustace.

'What do you mean which discount scheme? Don't you know anything about it?'

'No. Can I have another pint please, Harry. What will you have Joan?'

'Nothing, and neither are you. Get up off that chair right now; I'm taking you for your supper.' She gave poor old Eustace a smack with her clenched fist across his back, knocking him off the chair and onto the floor. He picked himself up, dusted himself down and very meekly followed Joan into the supper room.

Willie and Thelma were receiving right royal treatment at the hands of the supper room staff. With their being first in the queue, there was no worry as to what might have been eaten by those that had gone before and at the end of the table. Willie, with a groaning plate, had only one complaint which was that the plates were not big enough.

Willie, Thelma, Arthur and Jess sat at a table near to the food laden buffet and began to enjoy eating their supper. They had just nicely started eating when they were disturbed by the noise coming from Joan Ollerenshaw as she dragged Eustace towards the supper buffet.

'Why didn't you tell me about the discount scheme? I bet you didn't know anything about it. I reckon you never heard them talking about it. You were probably asleep at the meetings you went to. I don't know why you bother going to these meetings. I can't understand how you ever got yourself elected to the committee. Were you absent the day they gave brains out? I think...' The whole of the supper room stopped eating to listen in, as the tirade continued.

Thelma nudged Jess. 'Come with me a minute, it's time we sorted this mess out.'

They got up and Jess followed Thelma over to Eustace and Joan. As they got near, Thelma whispered, 'You grab her left arm, I'll take the right one. We'll have to grip tight to her.'

They carried out their plan, much to Joan's surprise as they gripped hard on her arms.

'Now then,' said Thelma.

'Let me go,' shouted a very shocked Joan, struggling.

'Oh no, not yet, not for a while. Now you are disturbing the party that we've all, including Eustace, put a lot of time into to make it into a success and you are making a laughing stock out of yourself and Eustace as well.'

Thelma turned to Eustace. 'Go and sit down with Willie and Arthur.'

Joan was still struggling, but the two ladies held onto her with grim determination in order to finish what they set out to do, whatever that might have been.

Thelma continued, 'I'm not in the least surprised that Eustace didn't tell you about the discount scheme. For a start, he probably didn't understand it properly, and secondly, he wouldn't dare tell you about it because you'd probably go off at the deep end at him about it.'

Joan remained silent, fuming and wriggling. Jess took a turn.

'We heard you say you didn't know why he got elected to the committee. Well I'll tell you why. He wasn't elected because of his ability, he was asked to attend by Arthur and Willie so that they could look after him of an evening like they do as best they can during the day at work. They both think a lot about him, as do Thelma and me. In fact a damned sight more than you do.'

Joan said nothing. She had given over struggling and held her head bent, just staring at the floor. Thelma took the lead again.

'You've been causing a disturbance at the party, upsetting all the guests and ruining what was a very nice evening, so if there's any more of it we're going to throw you out.'

'You've no need to worry on that score. I'm not stopping here where I'm not wanted. Are you coming?' She looked at Eustace.

Before he had time to answer, Thelma answered for him. 'No he most certainly is not, he's staying here with us to enjoy himself. At least he'll enjoy it as much as he can now that you've ruined it for him. We'll drop him off on the way home. No doubt he'll be well and truly drunk out of his mind by that time and I don't blame him. In fact, we'll probably help him get there and if I hear one word about you having taken it out of him later, me and Jess'll be round at you house to sort you out once and for all.'

Joan removed herself from the party, quietly with head bowed. The throng in the supper room applauded Thelma and Jess as they returned to their table. They walked back arm in arm.

'I'm shaking all over,' said Thelma.

'I'm sweating, shivering and shaking,' replied Jess.

Eustace stood up and began to walk away.

'Where do you think you're going?' asked Arthur.

'Going? Me? Going? Going to the bar, to the bar, that's where I'm going. to the bar.'

'No, you are not. Sit down and I'll get you some supper,' Arthur grabbed Eustace, making him sit down.

'I'll get you two girls a brandy each,' said Willie. 'I reckon you deserve it.

'I reckon we need it,' murmured Jess.

Eustace began to talk to all of them at the same time. 'Thank-you. Thank-you. I don't know what I'm going to do, now, I don't, but thank-you anyway. I don't know what for, but thank-you.' He belched, screwed up his eyes stared at nothing in particular whilst trying to focus properly, then started to talk again. 'I'm sorry for belching, I'm also very sorry for putting you to all this trouble. I am, very sorry, but I don't know what I'm going to do now I don't.'

'Well I do,' said Thelma who was fed up with listening to him 'First of all you are going to have a good, big supper, as much as we can force into you, then you're going to drink as many cups of coffee as you can drink, then you're going to go to the bar and getting drunk, then we're all going to take you home again when the party's over.'

'But I don't want to go home, not to her, no, not to her. I don't want to go home.'

'But you'll have to go home eventually, later.'

'Yes I know, but I shan't want to, I shan't.'

When Willie went to the bar, Anthony Murgatroyd followed him. 'Your girls did a sterling job on Joan Ollerenshaw, as far as I know, she's been asking for it for more years than I care to remember. What are you going to do with Eustace now?'

'We think the best thing we can do right now is to get him paralytic.'

'I don't disagree.'

'There's just one problem, she never let's him have much money, right now he has nowt, he's skint and I can't afford to get him drunk.'

Anthony Murgatroyd caught Fat Harry's eye and gave him a big white five pound note. 'Now then, Harry, that is specifically for use by Eustace Ollerenshaw. Let him get drunk on it to drown his sorrows. Let Willie and Arthur and their wives have one each and one for yourself, but mainly it's for Eustace. May he be happy in drink.'

'What's all that about?' Harry asked Willie after Anthony Murgatroyd had left.

'Have you not heard about the big row in the supper room between Eustace and Mrs Eustace, or the other way around? She nearly killed him with her mouth; it was like the start of the third world war. Anyway, she's gone home, he's having his supper and that brass is for him to drown his sorrows. I'll bring the others back later for their free drink and don't tell him where the brass is coming from for his bout of heavy drinking.'

Eustace thanked Willie yet again when he returned to the supper table. Most people had by this time finished eating and were slowly drifting back to the dance floor. The band had eaten enough for themselves and several others, the bar staff had taken the opportunity of the lull to have a bite to eat, but the poor old steward had been left looking after the bar, without food.

'Good supper, Harry,' Dick said when he went to replenish their glasses.

'How the hell should I know?'

'Not had yours yet then?'

'Call yourselves mates. You come in here year in, year out. You reckon to be my pals, but when it comes down to it, I can get lost, I can. Poor old Harry, let him starve, feed everyone else but ignore the steward. No recognition at all for all the help I've given.'

'Oh for havens sake, shut your gob and go and get you supper. I'll look after the bar.'

'Thanks, I will.'

He ambled off to the supper room, leaving the temporary, temporary staff in charge of the bar. On the way he had a thought. He changed direction towards the music and searched for Sarah Anne Green. He innocently asked Daniel Sykes, 'Have you seen Sarah Anne anywhere?'

'Why? Are you going to have your wicked way with her this party night?'

'No and furthermore, I will not smack you in the gob this party night because I'm in a good mood. How's your lemonade?'

'Have you met my wife, Harry?' asked Daniel 'My dear, this is Harry the Club steward, whose charm and effervescent wit I have often told you about after our committee meetings.'

Harry was somewhat taken aback at the sight of a most beautiful, well groomed and very presentable lady who gave him a radiant and very genuine smile as she shook his hand.

Harry stuttered, 'How, how do you do, pleased, yes pleased I am to make your acquaintance.'

He espied Sarah Anne in the distance, made his excuses and escaped to her. She was dancing with her husband Bill when she saw Harry standing on the edge of the dance floor beckoning to her. She left Bill and came over.

'What is it Harry?'

'I haven't had my supper. Everyone else has but me. I've been left out in the cold. Your oldest mate and you've all ignored me.'

Sarah Anne told Bill to go dance with Thelma as she had a small problem to attend to, then she took Harry by the arm and walked him to the supper room. As it happened there was plenty of food left and they filled two plates which were then taken discreetly into Harry's little back room. Behind a locked door, she fed him a giant supper, and then amused him in several other ways.

Eustace was enjoying, or enjoying as much as he could because of the state in which he found himself, an excellent supper under the gaze of four pairs of watchful eyes. Willie brought him another pint at the same time as he brought their drinks.

When Eustace had eaten the last crumb and the pattern from the plate, Arthur asked him. 'Do you want some more Eustace? Or some coffee?'

'Yes, please, Arthur, some more. Yes please and some coffee, please yes, some coffee, please and some more supper please. Where's Joan gone?'

Thelma answered him, 'Home I hope. Anyway, give over worrying about her tonight and enjoy yourself instead.'

'Yes, but what is she going to do when I get home? What is she? I didn't understand about the discount scheme. I didn't Thelma, Jess, I didn't. She'll kill me, she will, it'll be horrible, it will, horrible, I don't want to go home, I don't, not tonight, no, not tonight, not ever , I don't want to go home.'

Fortunately Arthur arrived back with a huge plate of food and Jess fetched him some coffee. He tucked into the food with gusto.

Thelma said, 'Don't worry Eustace, we've already had words with Joan about treating you properly.'

'That'll only make it worse that will, worse, much worse.'

'Now you've finished your supper, let's take you for a drink,' said Arthur.

So they all five returned to the bar. They put Eustace on a bar stool and had their free drink after some argument with the temporary, temporary bar staff in the absence of Harry.

They then left Eustace to the tender mercy of Harry when he emerged from the back room very indiscreetly bearing a broad grin, accompanied by a very guilty looking Sarah Anne, who tried to creep very quietly, with a smile on her face, back to the dance floor without being noticed by the crowds around the bar. The remainder of the evening passed with everyone enjoying the festivities, the dancing and the party.

At a quarter to midnight, everyone who was left at the party gathered around in a big circle to sing 'Auld Lang Syne.' Arthur went to get Eustace but left him when he saw the state he was in.

'Has he drunk all of that brass?' he enquired of Fat Harry.

'Every last drop and some more of mine.'

'Ah well, never mind, leave him there and come and enjoy the festivities on the dance floor.'

So Harry joined the big circle. Sarah Anne, Bill, Willie, Thelma, Arthur and Jess were pushed into a smaller inner circle. The band struck up and the crowds whilst singing surged back and forth, squeezing the small party in the inner circle at every rush forward. Fat Harry positioned himself so that he could squeeze Sarah Anne discreetly at every opportunity. When the music had finally stopped and the crowd had settled down a little, eagerly awaiting the next happening. Anthony Murgatroyd walked into the middle of the three couples and waved his arms in the air calling for silence.

'Well ladies and gentlemen, that is, I am sorry to say the end of the proceedings. I know from looking around that you have all thoroughly enjoyed yourselves as have Margaret and I.' He shook the hands of the six people round him in the inner circle. 'I just want to thank-you all for a most excellent evening. You have done more than you'll ever know for friendship and comradeship at the mill and I have thoroughly enjoyed being a part of it even if I did foist myself upon you. Are we going again next year?'

'Yes,' came a chorus of three voices.

'Good. Then it only leaves me to bid you all good night. A very merry Christmas and a Happy New Year to you all.'

The cheering started and went on and on. Then the band started to play a selection of Christmas carols to round off the evening. The whole of the party stood and sung for as long as they could. When the band finally stopped, the revellers shouted for more and more and it was only the steward's insistence that they should all go home that eventually persuaded them to do so.

Thelma went to get Eustace's coat and hat whilst Willie tried to stand him upright. With Arthur's help they eventually succeeded, then with Thelma's help they managed to get him dressed for the outdoors. It took all four of them to get him to the door, then, as everyone was shouting their goodnights to their friends, actually leaving the Club took some little time.

Walking Eustace home took a lot longer than it should have done. It took all four of them to get him there, some pulling, some pushing, at times picking him up, and at times stopping him from his tuneless singing. When they finally arrived, a hurried conference took place as to who was going to knock on the door.

Eustace, having recognised his own front door was protesting that he didn't want to go inside. The conference came to an abrupt end as the door opened and Joan stepped out.

'Bring him in will you please?'

'But we usually leave him out here,' protested Willie.

'Please, just bring him inside, and come in yourselves, all of you. Please.'

They looked at each other, then with telepathic agreement, they ushered Eustace inside, still protesting that he never wanted to go into that house again and that he would go home with them for the night.

Joan motioned them into the back living cum kitchen cum dining room where there was a meagre fire burning. Willie was later heard to remark that it was the first time he had seen a cold fire. They sat down on the hard chairs and surveyed the cold unwelcoming atmosphere.

Joan carefully removed Eustace's outdoor garments, hung them up and escorted him to a chair.

'Why haven't you hit me? You haven't. Hit me, you haven't. Why not?'

Joan looked at the four silent people then began to speak. 'Now look. I don't know how to say this, but I came home from the club, boiling mad as you can imagine, but then sat down here and began to think about things. You two ladies stood up for my Eustace tonight.'

'That's more than you've ever done,' Jess got a quick one in.

'Yes I know. Anyway as I was saying you two stood up for him and it's made me realise just what good friends he's got and just how bad I've been with him.' A tear began to roll down her face and Eustace stared at her disbelievingly. 'So I want to thank you ladies for what you did to me tonight, from the bottom of my heart. I want to thank you two gentlemen for being such good friends to him for all these years when I haven't been and finally I want to tell you that you've no need to worry about Eustace coming to any harm by me ever again.

Now that I have said all that, and believe me it has taken some saying, I would like you all to go please, as it has been a very different night for me which hasn't turned out quite as I expected it to do. In fact, I think it will have eventually turned out much much better. I would also like to think that perhaps next year you will have Eustace on your committee again and I hope that I will be able to play my full part by helping you ladies with the party.'

An uncomfortable silence followed. Arthur was lost for words. Jess was getting ready to tell Joan to get lost and Willie wished they could go as he wished to release some inner gas, daren't, and was having extreme difficulty containing himself.

Thelma was the one who spoke first, 'Yes, we'd love to have you help us. In fact we'd love to see much more of you during the year, providing of course that you are alright with Eustace.'

'You've no need to worry any further on that account. I know they call me the dragon, but that will be at thing of the past, although I assume the name will stick. They usually do.'

The four friends got up to go and made their way to the front door.

'Goodnight and thank-you very much,' said Joan.

'Yes, thank-you, thank-you, Arthur, Willie, thank you. Thank-you for everything and I mean everything. Especially thank-you Thelma and Jess. Thank-you, yes, thank-you all.'

Because of his state Eustace would have gone on talking all night, but as his guests disappeared, he gave over talking and turned with trepidation to face Joan who smiled at him for the first time in years, helped him inside, made him a pot of tea and took him to bed.

'Well I'll go to our house,' Willie was the first to speak.

Jess was second, 'Nay you'll not. You'll go to ours and have a pot of tea. You've nothing to rush home for.'

So they sat in the Baxter household until well into the night, talking and drinking tea.

Willie summed it all up. 'Been a bloody good do all around it has.'

'Yes, you're dead right,' agreed Arthur, 'except there's just one thing. Is everything in apple pie order with the discount scheme?'

'Well as far as I know, it is, but I were thinking of going around the shops tomorrow morning just to make sure that they are behaving as well as we expect them to do.'

'So here's to next year,' said Jess and Thelma nodded.

Willie felt yet another overwhelming urge to fart. He got up to go to the bathroom but could contain it no longer.

'Willie!' screamed Thelma.

'Take him home,' said Jess.

CHAPTER 21

Willie was up and about fairly early the following morning. He could not sleep any longer and was eager to go into the village and retrieve his free goodies from the participating shops. Thelma stayed in bed all snug and warm, the younger children were up and playing and Josie had long since gone on her paper round.

As soon as he had made up the fire and finished his pint of tea, he put his cap and coat on and set off walking to the village.

His first port of call was at the emporium of Freddy Ogley the grocer, better known in the village as Freddy Nevershut.

'Now what made me think late last night, as I was putting the cat out, that one of the first faces I would see this morning to welcome the day as it were, would be yours, Willie Arkenthwaite? It was probably looking at the cat's backside as it disappeared across the yard and jumped the wall. Did you have a good party last night at the Club?'

'Aye, Freddy, we had a right good do at the club last night. Everything went off very well. The dragon nearly killed Eustace but we got her off him just in time.'

'So what was that all about then? Or to put it another way, what had he done?'

'Well you see, it was more like what he hadn't except get very drunk and not telling her about the available discounts from people like yourself...and talking about discounts.'

'They've only just spent enough for you to get your box of groceries. I reckon it will be about twenty pounds. I'll go and get a box and we can fill it with whatever you want.'

'No, Freddy. If it's all the same to you, I'd like to bring Thelma to do the choosing because it will be wrong if I pick it.'

'When will she come?'

'This afternoon with a bit of luck.'

The conversation carried on for a while when football became the main topic. Eventually Willie said he would have to go, but as no other customers came into the shop, Freddy was loathe to let him and kept on talking. It was only when another customer arrived that Willie managed to make his escape.

Len Charrington the butcher, well known as Porky, had his shop next to Nevershut's so it was only a few strides and Willie was sitting on a conveniently placed orange box in a corner, leaning on the wall, waiting for Porky's customers to finish their business and depart.

'Well now, Len, have you managed to get some extra trade from our Christmas club members?'

'Yes Willie, I've done very well really. Was it the party last night?'

'Yes it was and we had a right good do.'

'You had Sid Sidebottom, didn't you?'

'Aye, we did, and I'll tell you what, he turned out real smart. Proper formal evening dress and his music were super. He really did us proud.'

'I've had one or two in here already this morning that were at your party and they really had a right good time, they fair enjoyed it. Anyway I thought you'd be coming this morning so there's a little something for you in this envelope.'

He reached into his trouser pocket, and then stopped as a customer entered.

'Hello Willie, hello Len, are you shopping Willie? Shopping, are you? Joan's here with me somewhere, I think she might be in Nevershut's, yes, I think she might, in Nevershut's. She'll be here in a minute.'

'Good Morning, Eustace,' said Len, 'and how are you this bright and merry morning?'

'Good, yes, very good, yes very, very good. Thank you for asking.'

'Did you enjoy the party Eustace?'

'Oh yes I did, did, I really enjoyed it, I did. Why are you sitting in that corner Willie?'

Len got in first, 'Because that's the naughty corner and Willie's been very naughty and I've made him sit there.'

'Have you Willie? Been naughty? Have you-'

'No he hasn't,' Joan had entered the shop quietly, unseen by the others. 'Good morning, Willie, Good morning, Len. Don't take any notice of these two Eustace, they're having you on.'

'Are you Willie? Len? Having me on? Are you?'

'Afraid so,' said Willie. 'I was just sitting here talking to Len about last night's party.'

'I did enjoy the band,' said Joan, 'in fact I really did enjoy the whole affair, it was very well organised. Now Willie, are you being served or can I get my meat?'

'No, you can get your meat, I'm only here for the beer and seeing there isn't any I'll just have to sit here and cogitate.'

Joan gave him a peculiar look and went about getting her meat.

They all exchanged the usual pleasantries and then the Ollerenshaws went.

'Well I never did,' said Len, 'what's up with her?'

'Can't think what you mean,' said Willie laughing.

'No, but I mean she's usually like a bear with a sore arse. I dread her coming in here. She only speaks the minimum words necessary, she never looks up and she treats Eustace like a piece of dirt. But this morning she was pleasant, and she treated Eustace like a human being. So what's up with her?'

'Ah well, you see, I know,' and Willie tapped his nose.

'Well come on then, let's be knowing, the suspense's killing me.'

'Now as it happens, and I don't want you to have a fit or anything when I tell you, that last night at the party, in front of everybody, Eustace got very drunk.'

'So what's new?'

'Well if you'll let me finish, the dragon, Mrs Dragon Ollerenshaw, smote Eustace a great smite in front of the whole crowd.'

'She did what?'

'By gum, you are ignorant. She fetched him a crack around the head such that she nearly knocked him out.'

'Did it do him any good; he seemed a bit chirpier than usual just now, but not a lot different.'

'Well, no. He fell off the buffet onto the floor. Now my Thelma and Jess Baxter saw red at this carry on, so in front of everybody, except them what weren't there, they marched up as smartly as a parade of WACS and threatened to knock seven bells out of the dragon if she ever touched Eustace again, because they said to her that they were fed up of me and Arthur always going on about what a dog's life he leads and we are mates of his and we stick up for him and he doesn't.

Anyway, she went home and left him with us and we, including Anthony Murgatroyd got him drunker and drunker. Then me and Thelma and Arthur and Jess took him home and we daren't go in, but the dragon invited us in and she were very nice and said she'd look after him proper like from now on and that's why they're both alright this morning. Here Len, give us that envelope, I've a lot to do yet this morning.'

Len, dumbfounded, gave Willie the envelope who then left to walk around the corner to Mouncy's the greengrocers.

'Good morning, William Arkenthwaite, champion of the Christmas club party and dragon slayer. News travels faster than the speed of light in this village. I hear that you and Arthur and your families are the heroes of the hour.'

'No it was the girls, not me and Arthur. It was our two super lasses who got up and gave the dragon what for.'

'So what happens now?'

'You give me some money or some fruit and veg or something.'

'No, not that, I mean with Eustace?'

'Oh that. Well, nothing really. Mrs Dragon's being nice to Eustace this morning, I've just seen them around at Porky Charrington's and she was looking after him like a new woman.'

'So he'll be alright, will he? I know he is as he is, but I've always felt a bit sorry for him living with her.'

'Well, it should be a case of all's well that ends well, but it remains to be seen. Anyway, talking about all's well that ends well...'

'Yes. I've had a good lot of extra orders this Christmas, a lot of them from your Christmas club so I'm going to give you a big box of mixed fruit and veg and some cash. Just wait here one minute.'

He left Willie in the shop and went into the back, emerging a couple of minutes later with a huge cardboard box and an envelope. He gave both items to Willie.

'Help yourself to whatever you want to fill that box and take the envelope home with you.'

'Will you mind if I don't fill the box just yet, but bring Thelma down after dinner so she can pick her own?'

'No, go ahead bring her along s that you can carry the box for her. We wouldn't want your Thelma to get a double strangulated one carrying your box, now would we?'

Willie had to admit that they should not. So he put the envelope in his pocket and left the greengrocers.

Next, he then called at the electrical shop where he was given the poor tale. 'Bad trade this Christmas, not much extra trade, can't afford a lot.'

They gave him a thin envelope and on the basis that owt's better than nowt, Willie left the shop.

He was going to go home for his dinner but decided to pop into the toy shop and see Herbert and Agatha Chew. He didn't expect to get anything, but thought it might be fun to hear another shouting match between the two shopkeepers.

'Good morning, Willie, and how are you this glorious cold morning?'

'I'm very well thank-you, Agatha, and how are you?' Willie was on his guard. This was not what he expected from the wizened oldish lady.

'I, that is, we, are very well indeed, thanks to you and your Christmas club.'

'Oh, have you done well with it then? Has it brought you some extra trade?'

'What do you want Willie Arkenthwaite?' Herbert Chew appeared from the back room.

'I was just about to tell Willie what a good-'

'Tell him nothing. Keep your gob shut woman. We've had an awful Christmas trade. It's been terrible.'

'So I'll not recommend you next Christmas then.'

'Eh? What's that you say? Speak up; I'm a bit deaf you know.'

'A bloody hell of a lot,' Willie said quietly.

'What?'

'Willie said shut your noise you stupid old idiot and sod off into the back again.'

Herbert grunted turned his back on them and stomped off to where he came from.

'Now then, Willie, take no notice of him. Your Christmas club and your recommendation have contributed to a right good Christmas and we would like you to select a good quality toy for each of your children.'

'There's three of them, you know?'

'Yes, we know. So, what would you like?'

'I think I'd like to bring Thelma along after dinner and let her choose.'

'I think that's a right good suggestion.'

'Yes, she'll have far more idea than me what they want. So we'll see you this afternoon.'

Willie went straight home from the shops making only a very short detour just to see how Fat Harry was the morning after the night before.

'Well, well, well. I really didn't think she'd let you out this morning. I thought she'd be threatening you with violence after her war like performance last night. St George killing the dragon, that's what it was. Marvellous, fantastic, best night we've had in ages and the party wasn't bad either.'

'You given Sarah Anne back to her husband yet? Give us a pint.'

'Once again, sir, may I venture to enquire if, sir, is intending to pay for his liquid refreshment before I go through the rigours of operating the pump and dirtying a glass, which I might hasten to add has been very carefully washed by one of my very attractive handmaidens.'

'You've never had a handmaiden, at least not an attractive one. Who's washed it?'

'Me.'

'In that case, I think I'll just stick my head under the pump. Will it be cheaper that way?'

'No, sir. Dearer.'

'Come on, get on with it, my dinner will be ready.'

'So what are you doing out and about on a Saturday morning?'

Willie thought carefully before answering. 'I'm out doing a few errands for Thelma.'

'So how is the gibbering idiot this morning or don't you know?'

'Yes, I do know. He's out shopping with his wife and looking very happy.'

319

'I'm talking about Eustace you know.'

'Yes, I know. I think things will be very different for him from now on. I do hope it cures his speech impediment as well. He never used to be like that before he was married.'

'Hence the reason why I never got married,' said Harry.

'No, you just use other fellow's wives.'

Willie drank up and went home laughing.

When Willie arrived home he found the children playing upstairs and Josie out with her pals. 'Thelma I want you to come back to the village with me after dinner.' Then he explained just what he wanted her to do.

She readily agreed then said, 'What about the children?'

'What about the children?' Willie asked.

'If we are going looking for toys for Christmas, we can't take them with us.'

'I never thought about that.'

'We'll have to ask Arthur and Jess to look after them.'

'Yes we could,' said Willie. 'Shall I nip round and ask them?'

'Yes please and don't forget where we live.'

'What do you mean?'

'No going to the club or the pub.'

Willie smiled. 'No my dear.'

Willie hit the big brass knocker on the Baxter's front door hard, but there was no response. He tried again but still nothing happened. Feeling very despondent he retraced his steps then he began to wonder if Arthur might actually be at the club, but he fought the idea and continued towards home. As he rounded the corner to enter the canal towpath he came across Eustace and Joan linking arms and walking along the side of the canal.

'Hello, Willie, have you been for a walk? Have you? We have, haven't we Joan? We have, for a walk.'

Joan said nothing but smiled at Willie.

'No, Eustace, and yes, Eustace. I've been to Arthur's to see if they can look after the two young ones for a couple of hours whilst Thelma and me go do a bit of Christmas shopping, but there's no one in, so I don't know what we're going to do.'

Joan looked at Willie. 'Eustace and I could help out, if you would let us.'

'You mean you could look after the children for us?'

'Yes. It's a long time since we looked after any children but we'd love to give it a try. Wouldn't we Eustace?'

'Yes we would, we would, we most certainly would. I'd love to look after your children, Willie.'

Willie took but a few seconds to make up his mind. 'Well then, thank you very much. You'd best come home with me it's only just there.' Willie pointed to his cottage.

'I didn't know you lived on the side of the canal towpath, Willie,' said Joan.

'Yes, he does, my love, he does, lives on the towpath, he does, I know he does.'

Willie went into the cottage ahead of Joan and Eustace and he called out for Thelma, who came out of the back kitchen. 'Arthur and Jess are out, but I bumped into Eustace and Joan who said they'd love to look after the kids.'

Thelma looked quizzically at them.

'Yes, hello Thelma,' said Joan. 'We'd love to be given the chance to look after the children for you for a couple of hours. That is, if you will let us? Wouldn't we Eustace?' But before he had time to reply, she continued, 'I know we don't know them, and they don't know us, but I really would appreciate being given the chance to help and make amends for years of-'

'We'd love you to have them, wouldn't we Willie.'

'Yes, absolutely no problem.'

'What would you like to do with them?' Thelma asked. 'Peter's ten and Margaret's seven, I'll just fetch them in.' She went into the back kitchen and called them in from the garden where they were playing.

In the meantime, Joan took the opportunity to look around the living room of the cottage. 'My words it is lovely and warm and cosy in here, Willie, not like ours that is cold and miserable.'

Willie didn't know what to reply to this and was delighted when the children appeared.

'Now,' said Thelma, 'this is Mr and Mrs Ollerenshaw and they are going to look after you two this afternoon because your daddy and I have something we must go and do.'

Margaret closed ranks with Peter and hid behind him, looking around him at Eustace and Joan.

'Have you got a football, young Peter?' Eustace enquired.

'Yes, I've got a big one.'

'Well shall we take it to the wreck and play with it?

'Oh, yes please.'

'You are very welcome to stay here if you want whilst we go, but it might be better if you are not here when we get back.'

Joan said, 'I understand perfectly. What time shall we bring them back?'

'Well, we should be done by four o'clock at the latest. Are you sure that's alright?'

'Perfectly,' said Joan and so the small party made its way to play and do whatever the afternoon decided.

Willie and Thelma hurried along to the village as soon as the children were out of sight and it finally took two trips to get all the freebies back home.

'We should really let Arthur and Jess have some of these goodies,' said Thelma, 'after all Arthur did just as much, if not more, than you towards the Christmas club, Willie.'

'Yes, you are right. We should divide it up a bit. We'll have words with them tomorrow.'

By the time they had hidden the toys and put the food away, it was almost four o'clock. 'I'll go and put the kettle on; they're bound to want a drink when they get back,' said Thelma and sure enough, dead on the stroke of four, the children walked in.

'Now, you two, have you been good for Mr and Mrs Ollerenshaw?'

'Yes daddy, we've been very good,' said Peter.

'They've both been as good as gold,' said Joan. 'I don't know where the afternoon's gone. I haven't enjoyed myself as much as I have this afternoon in many a long year.'

'What about you Eustace have you enjoyed it?' Willie asked

'I can't tell you how good it's been. Young Peter's run me out of puff with his football, he has, he's run me out of puff, but I've fair enjoyed myself. We went to our house and got some bread, we did, some bread, and Joan and Margaret have been feeding the ducks in the park whilst we played football. Then we went for some ice cream to the park café. We did, we went to the park café for an ice cream. It's been real this afternoon, real, really real.'

Willie could not believe the change in Eustace's speaking.

Thelma came back into the front room with a tray containing a big chocolate cake, a teapot and cups. 'Now the take your coats off and sit down, there's a cup of tea ready.'

So they all sat down in front of the fire and chatted whilst devouring big slices of chocolate cake.

'We want to thank you for this afternoon,' said Thelma. 'Without you, we could not have done what we did.'

'No. I want to thank you from the bottom of my heart for last night and for this afternoon,' replied Joan. 'There's another world out there that I had forgotten existed, much to the detriment of both of our lives. I really have enjoyed looking after Margaret although we didn't really do much, it was just right nice to be able to help and Eustace has enjoyed it as well.'

So they sat and chatted, beginning to get to know one another and finding that they got on really well together. Just when the Ollerenshaws were taking their leave, Thelma asked, 'What do you do on Christmas day, then?'

Joan looked very crestfallen. 'Nothing. Nothing at all. We've no one to share it with and nowhere to go, we just sit at home and listen to the wireless.'

'Well you must come here for Christmas dinner. We have it about three. Please say you will come, we'd love to have you here.'

'Yes we would,' said Willie.

Joan made pretence of 'well we couldn't' and 'you've enough on without us' but she really didn't take much persuading to accept.

So the Ollerenshaws departed and as soon as they had gone, Willie asked the children if they had been alright this afternoon. Peter said they had had a nice afternoon and enjoyed it, but Mr Ollerenshaw doesn't half talk funny.

Later that night Willie took a box of meat and vegetables round to Arthur's house. The freebies were well received, but it took Willie quite a time to explain just how he had come by them.

When he got home again, Thelma asked, 'Where are those envelopes with the money in from the shops?'

'Here,' said Willie as he fumbled in his pocket. 'Hey there's quite some money here.'

'Yes,' said Thelma, 'we'll be able to go to Scarborough for our holidays next year.

Christmas Day at number six Cutside cottages was the best there had ever been. The children had super presents that they just had not dreamed about and so did Thelma. Willie got his present from seeing the happy looks on the others faces. Later in the day, the Baxters and the Ollerenshaws came for Christmas dinner and a feast such as had not been seen in many a long year was laid before them. The men drank beer, the ladies Sherry and the children lemonade. They all ate their fill. Willie made his usual share of rude noises and the day went off without a hitch. Even Eustace and Joan began to relax and really enjoy themselves.

When the day was over and the Baxters along with the Ollerenshaws began their walk home in the frost night air, the cry could still be heard along the canal bank. 'Willie!'

Thank-you for buying and reading

We hope you enjoyed it.

If so,

We would be honoured if you leave a review on the

Facebook page

www.facebook.com/Murgatroyds

Or at

www.amazon.co.uk

www.smashwords.com

Have you written a book?
Would you like to see it on this screen?

Fishcake Publications is looking for writers to publish
onto eBooks right now.
We are especially keen to hear from new, unpublished
writers who are trying to get their work out there.
If you've taken the time to write it, it deserves to be read.
For further information, visit our website at
www.fishcakepublications.com

The Independent Publisher with the Author in Mind

Other Books are available from Fishcake Publications
See our website and our webstore at
www.fishcakepublications.com
for information on where to find them.

Stephen Bailey

Tall, thin and handsome, well educated and extremely suave...well actually this is pure fantasy, just like his writing. In fact he's short, fat, ugly and an educational failure (in his own words).
Having spent his entire working life as an engineer to the textile trade, he decided to write about some of the characters he had met and their problems. Actually, the personal bit is fantasy again; in fact, it's all somewhere in between.
Any reference to any person dead or not living is purely coincidental.
Stephen is an entertaining fellow and a popular member of the Holmfirth Writers' Group where he often has the other members in hysterics with his funny stories and has one such piece in the Group's second anthology *Pennine Reflections*. He was also a member of the Huddersfield Author's Circle and his short stories can be heard on Two Valleys Radio.